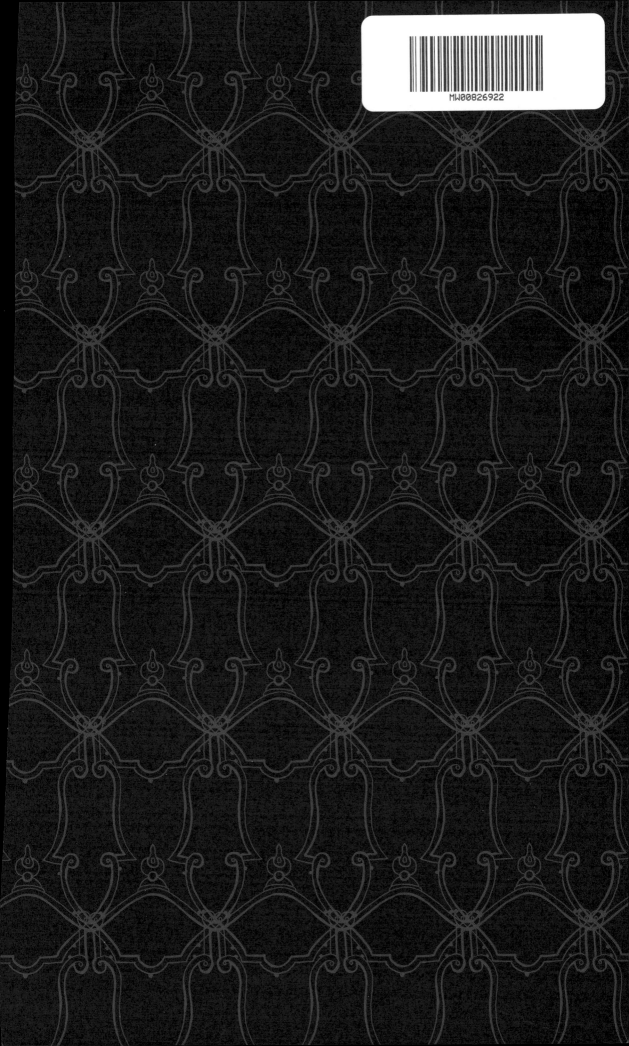

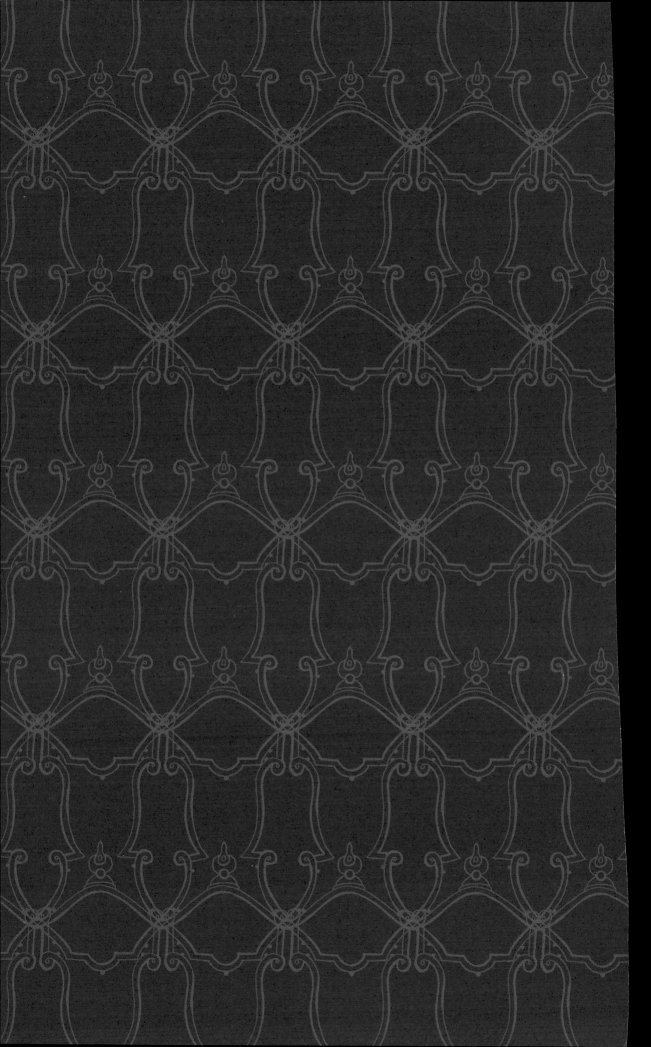

Image Comics

presents

DRACULA
A Storybook Portfolio

by

J H Williams III

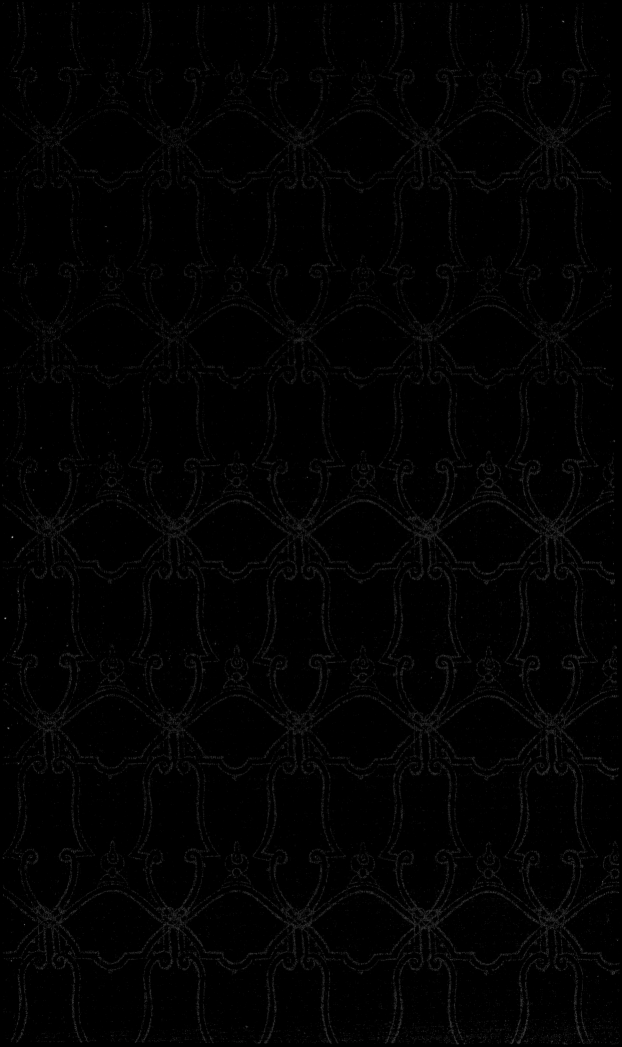

IMAGE COMICS, INC.

Robert Kirkman – Chief Operating Officer
Erik Larsen – Chief Financial Officer
Todd McFarlane – President
Marc Silvestri – Chief Executive Officer
Jim Valentino – Executive Vice President

Eric Stephenson – Publisher / Chief Creative Officer

Nicole Lapalme – Vice President of Finance
Leanna Caunter – Accounting Analyst
Sue Korpela – Accounting & HR Manager
Alex Cox – Vice President of Direct Market Sales
Margot Wood – Vice President of Book Market Sales
Chloe Ramos – Book Market & Library Sales Manager
Kat Salazar – Vice President of PR & Marketing
Deanna Phelps – Marketing Design Manager
Jim Viscardi – Vice President of Business Development
Lorelei Bunjes – Vice President of Digital Strategy
Emilio Bautista – Digital Sales Coordinator
Dirk Wood – Vice President of International Sales & Licensing
Ryan Brewer – International Sales & Licensing Manager
Drew Gill – Art Director
Heather Doornink – Vice President of Production
Jan Baldessari – Print Manager
Melissa Gifford – Content Manager
Drew Fitzgerald – Content Manager
Erika Schnatz – Senior Production Artist
Wesley Griffith – Production Artist
Rich Fowlks – Production Artist
Jon Schlaffman – Production Artist

IMAGECOMICS.COM

DRACULA: A STORYBOOK PORTFOLIO

First printing. October 2024. Published by Image Comics, Inc.

Office of publication: PO BOX 14457, Portland, OR 97293. Copyright
© 2024 J. H. Williams III. All rights reserved. "Dracula: A Storybook
Portfolio," its logos, and the likenesses of all characters herein are
trademarks of J. H. Williams III, unless otherwise noted. Image Comics
logo designed by Rob Liefeld. "Image" and the Image Comics logos are
registered trademarks of Image Comics, Inc. No part of this publication
may be reproduced or transmitted, in any form or by any means (except
for short excerpts for journalistic or review purposes), without the
express written permission of J. H. Williams III, or Image Comics, Inc.
All names, characters, events, and locales in this publication are entirely
fictional. Any resemblance to actual persons (living or dead), events, or
places, without satirical intent, is coincidental.

Printed in China. For international rights, contact:
foreignlicensing@imagecomics.com.

ISBN: 978-1-5343-7156-9

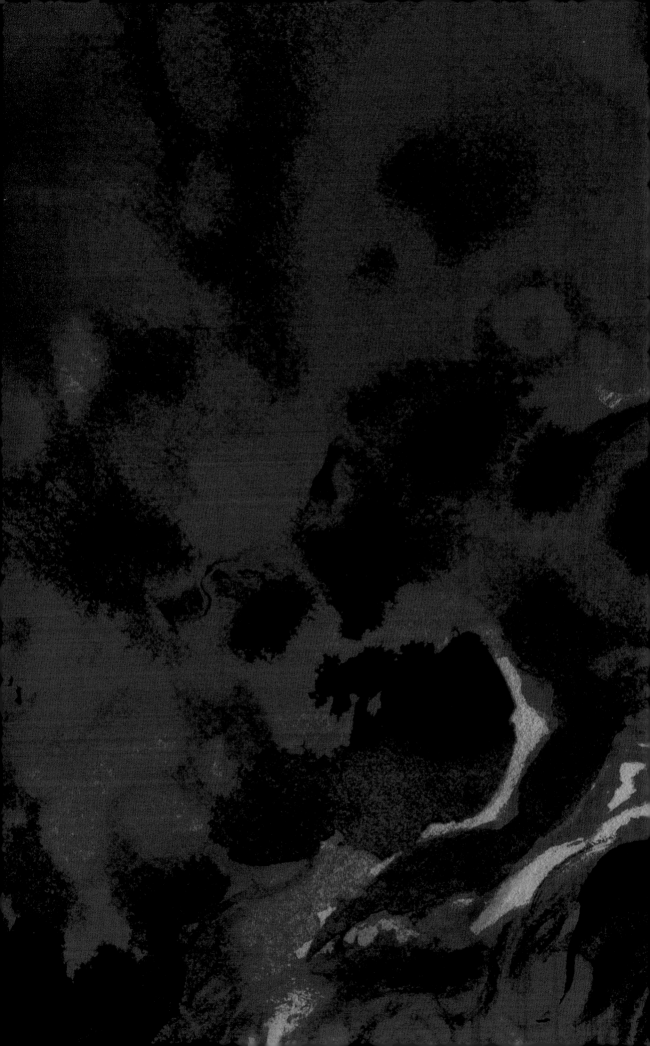

SEARCHING FOR MY VOICE ON A BELOVED OLD WORK: DRACULA

THIS COLLECTION IS A NEW PRESENTATION OF WORK THAT IS FROM SEVERAL YEARS AGO, BUT HASN'T BEEN AVAILABLE IN THIS FORM BEFORE. IT WAS DONE WHILE RECOVERING FROM SEPSIS. AND ALTHOUGH I WAS EXHAUSTED FROM A DEADLY ILLNESS, I TRIED TO TACKLE THIS WORK WITH A SENSE OF TRIAL-AND-ERROR FERVOR, MOVING THROUGH IMAGES AS QUICKLY AS I COULD. THE RESULT IS FASCINATING IN SOME OF THE MORE LOOSE, VISCERAL ASPECTS OF THE TECHNIQUES I APPLIED. ALL OF IT EXPLORING TERRITORY STYLISTICALLY THAT WAS SOMEWHAT NEW FOR ME AT THE TIME.

BRAM STOKER'S DRACULA IS PROBABLY THE MOST FAMOUS WORK OF GOTHIC HORROR FICTION OF ALL TIME. AND VARIOUS INTERPRETATIONS LIVE IN SO MANY OF OUR MINDS, EACH DISTINCT IN THEIR VISUAL APPEAL. EVEN FOR ME, VARIOUS IMAGERY FROM THE PROSE, COMICS, AND CINEMATIC WORKS LIVE IN THE RECESSES OF MY SUBCONSCIOUS. UPON READING THE NOVEL AGAIN, IT REVEALED SOME SURPRISING CONTRASTS COMPARED TO WHAT WE THINK WE KNOW OF THE CHARACTER AND STORY. THE VARIETY OF FILM VERSIONS FOCUS SO MUCH ON A ROMANTICISM, BUT THAT IS BARELY RECOGNIZABLE IN THE ORIGINAL WRITING. IN THE BOOK, DRACULA IS TRULY A MONSTER. A MONSTER THAT NEVER APPEARS THE SAME WAY TWICE, HE IS EVER TRANSFORMING. THIS IS THE DIRECTION I TOOK. AND THAT INFORMED SOME OF MY CREATIVE DECISIONS WHEN IT CAME TO VISUAL STYLE THROUGHOUT THIS WORK. MY GOAL WAS TO BE PLAYFUL WITH IT, LET IT FLOW AND CHANGE, WHILE ATTEMPTING TO MAINTAIN A SENSE OF CONSISTENCY. I ALSO WANTED FOR IT TO FEEL CLASSIC, LIKE ILLUSTRATIONS YOU MIGHT COME ACROSS IN AN OLD NOVEL. I THINK IT'S THIS SLIGHTLY NOSTALGIC VIEW THAT LED TO THERE STILL BEING A HINT OF ROMANTICISM, AS IF THE VARIOUS FAMOUS ENCOUNTERS THROUGH FILM, COMICS, AND LITERATURE WERE CREEPING INTO THE VISUAL NARRATIVE.

THE OTHER THING I WANTED TO DO FOR THIS ART BOOK WAS TO PRESENT IT IN AN UNUSUAL WAY. SINCE ALL OF THE WORK IS BASED ON A SINGULAR SUBJECT, I THOUGHT IT MIGHT BE ENTERTAINING TO CREATE SIMPLE WRITTEN PASSAGES LOOSELY SOLIDIFYING THE VISUAL NARRATIVE INTO A STORY-DRIVEN WORK. WHILE KEEPING THE PASSAGES BRIEF, IT CAME TO REMIND ME OF OLD CHILDREN'S STORY BOOKS, BUT CLEARLY THIS ISN'T FOR CHILDREN. REGARDLESS OF THE INTENDED AUDIENCE, I DECIDED TO PURSUE THAT TYPE OF STRUCTURE. AND THAT'S HOW THE IDEA OF USING "A STORYBOOK PORTFOLIO" AS PART OF THE TITLE CAME TO BE. I HOPE THAT YOU FIND THE WORK ENJOYABLE AND WORTHWHILE.

J H WILLIAMS III

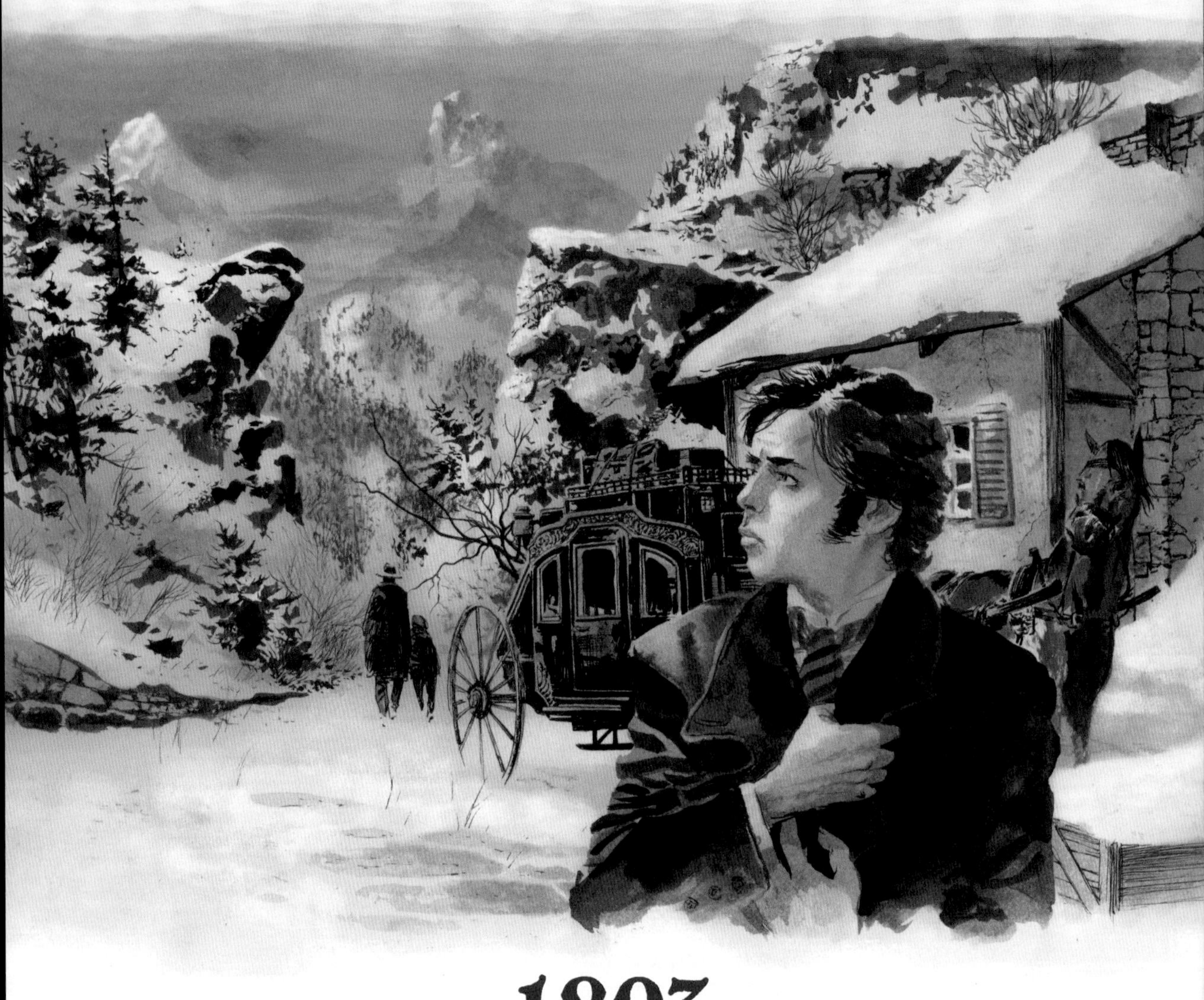

1893

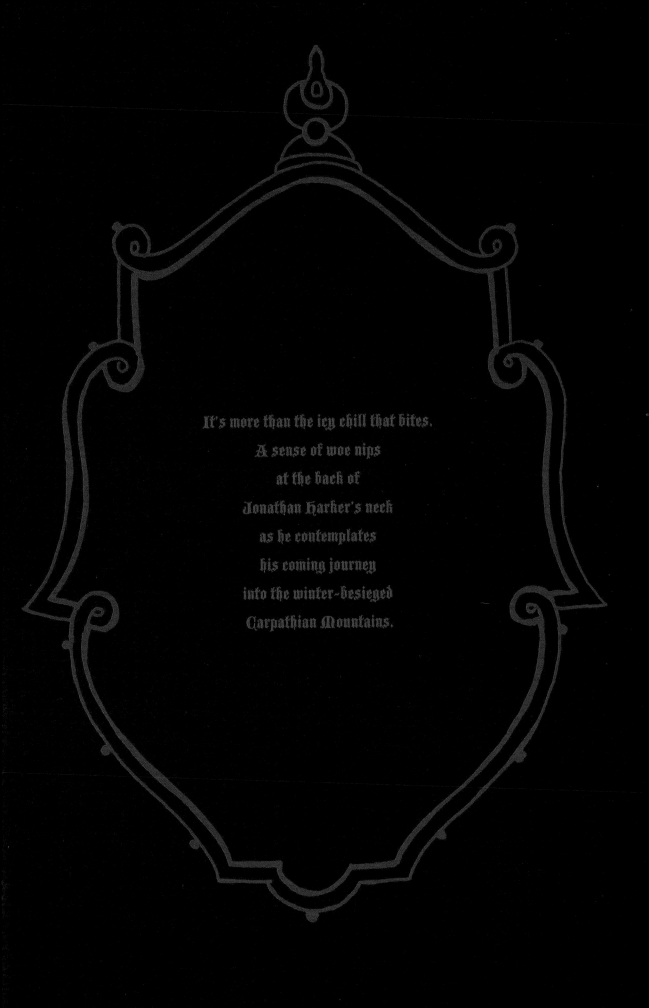

It's more than the icy chill that bites.
A sense of woe nips
at the back of
Jonathan Harker's neck
as he contemplates
his coming journey
into the winter-besieged
Carpathian Mountains.

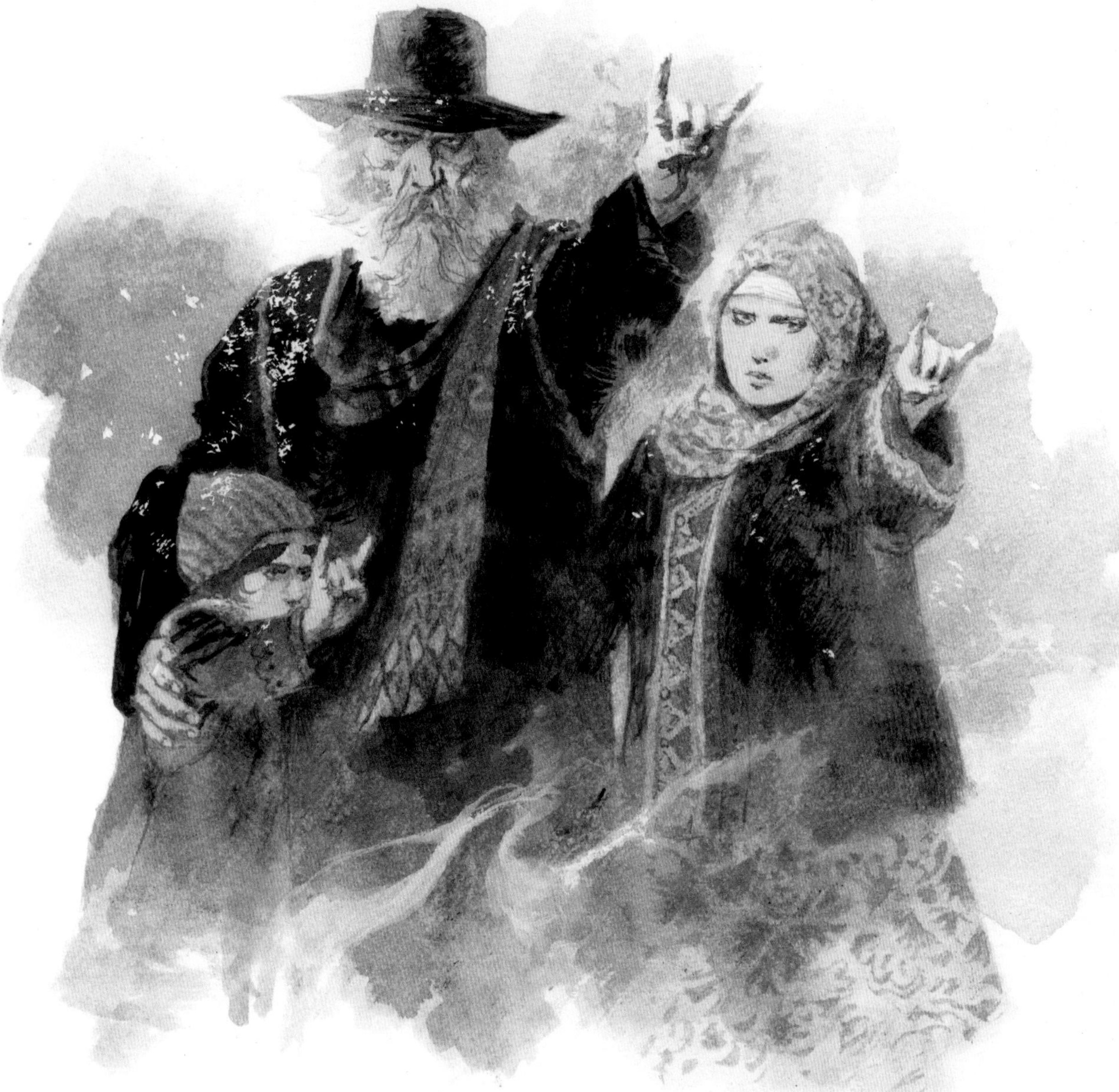

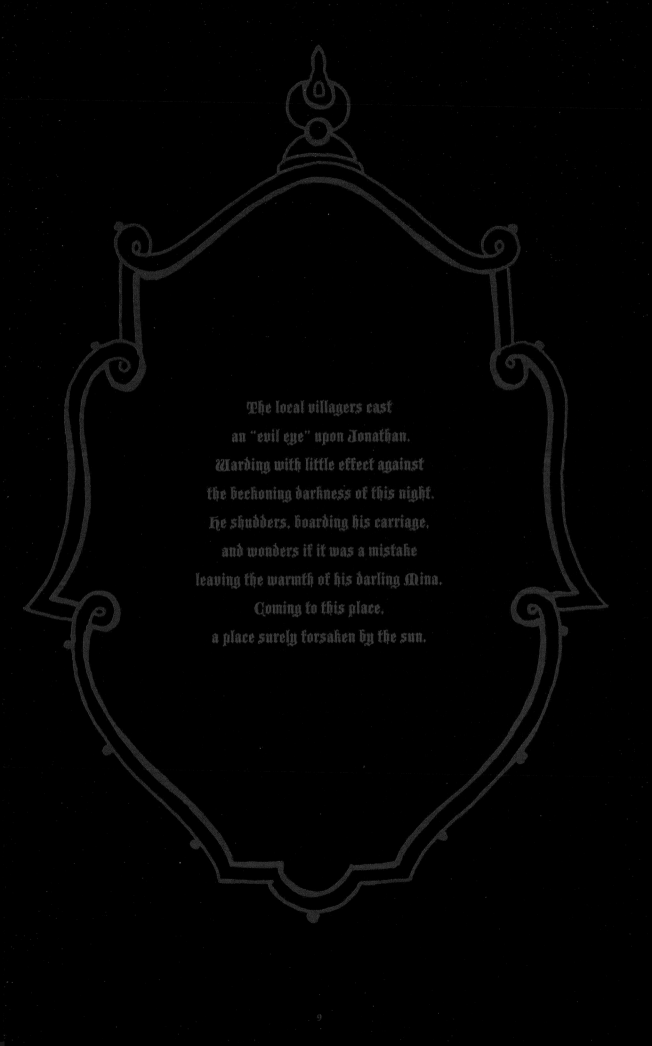

The local villagers cast
an "evil eye" upon Jonathan.
Warding with little effect against
the beckoning darkness of this night.
He shudders, boarding his carriage,
and wonders if it was a mistake
leaving the warmth of his darling Mina.
Coming to this place,
a place surely forsaken by the sun.

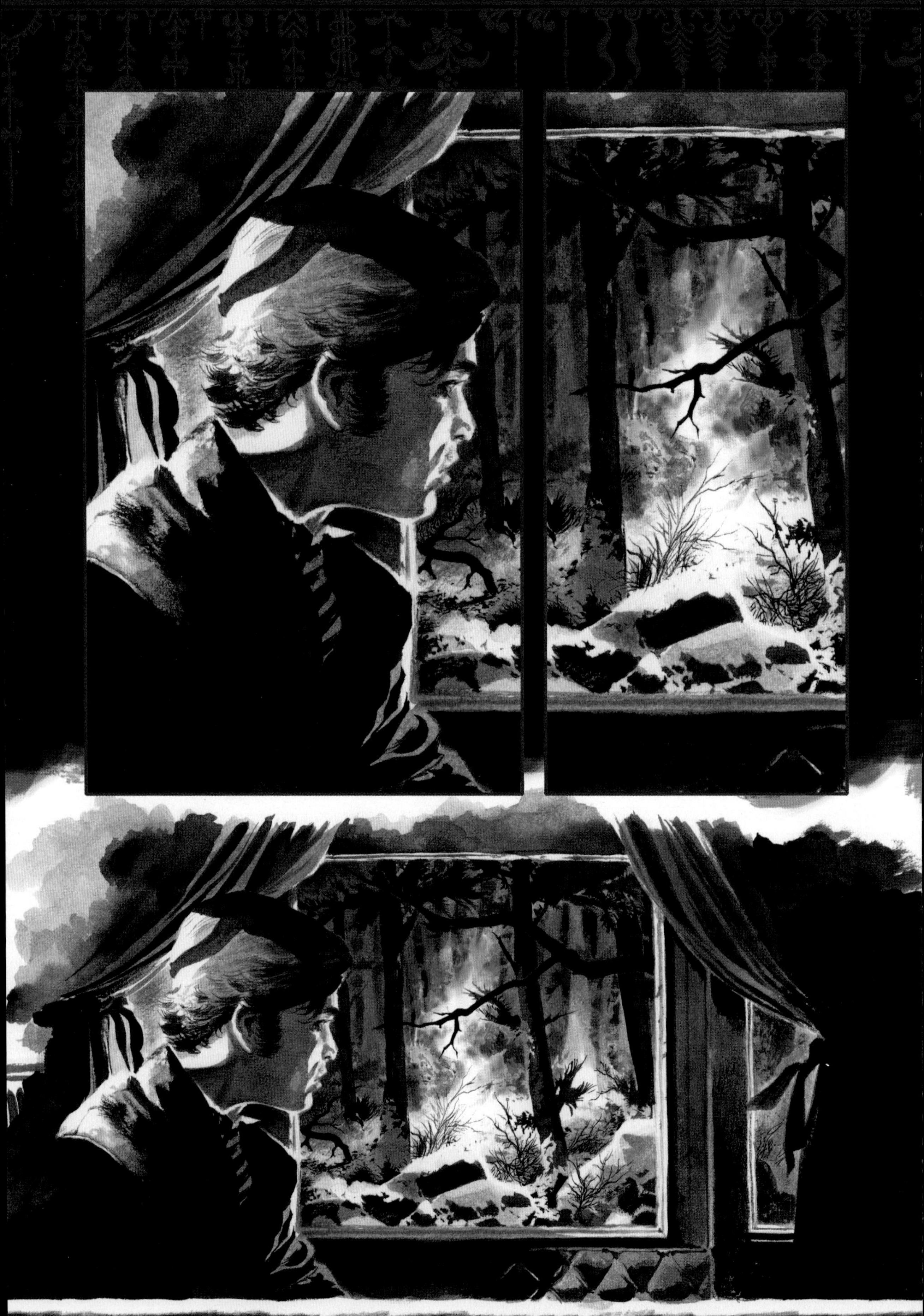

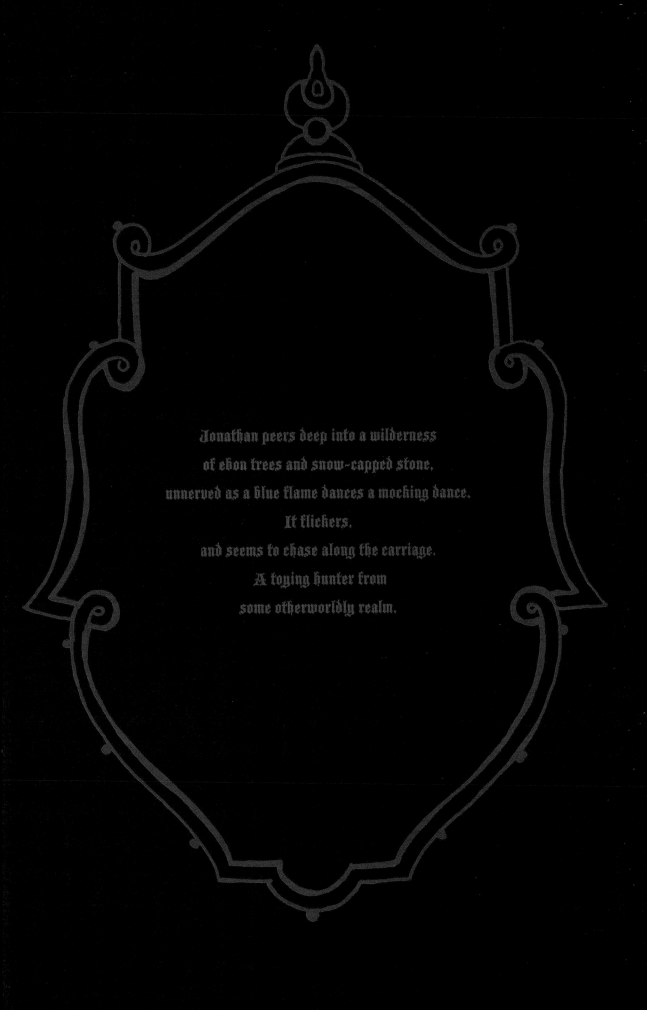

Jonathan peers deep into a wilderness
of ebon trees and snow-capped stone,
unnerved as a blue flame dances a mocking dance.
It flickers,
and seems to chase along the carriage.
A toying hunter from
some otherworldly realm.

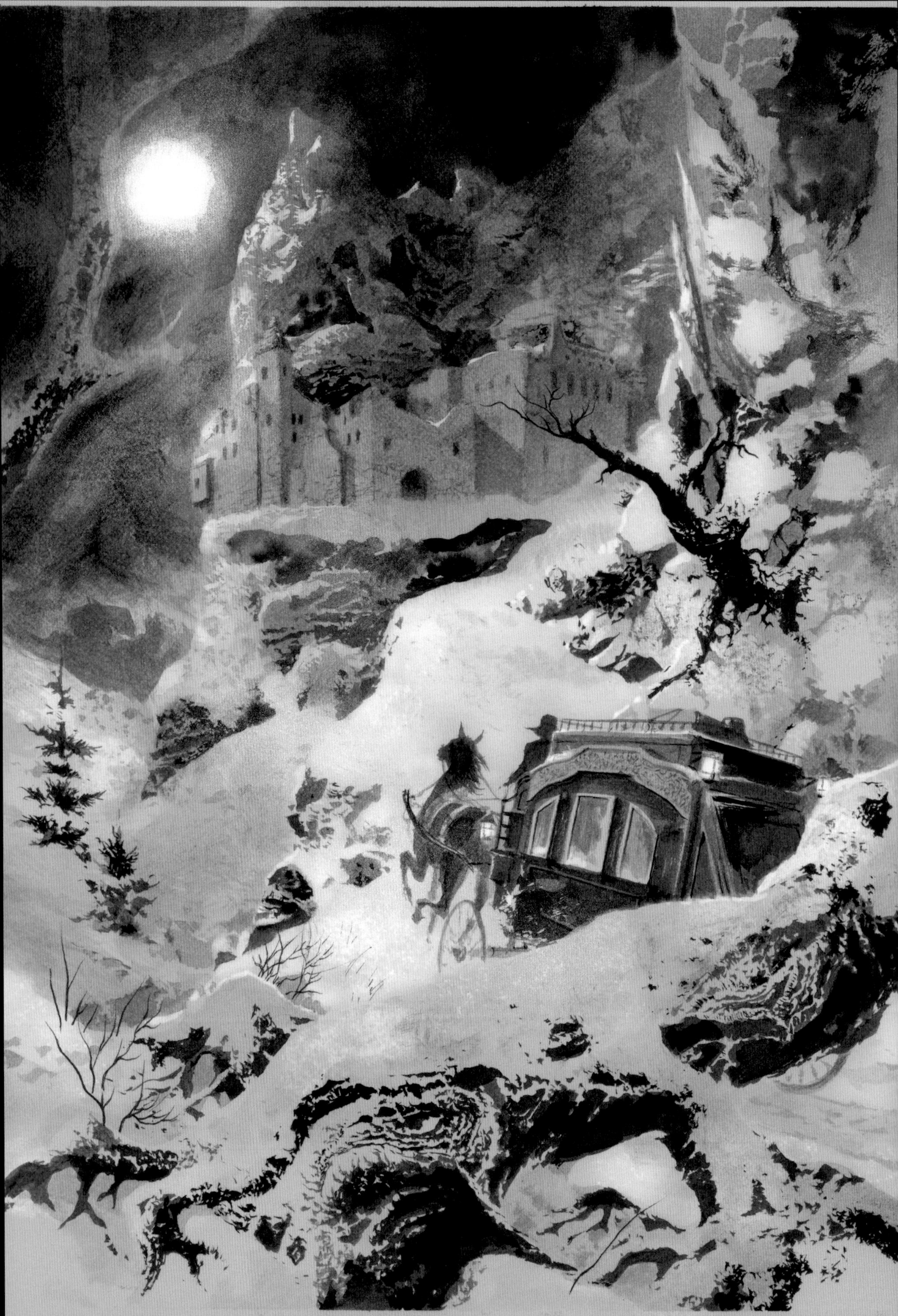

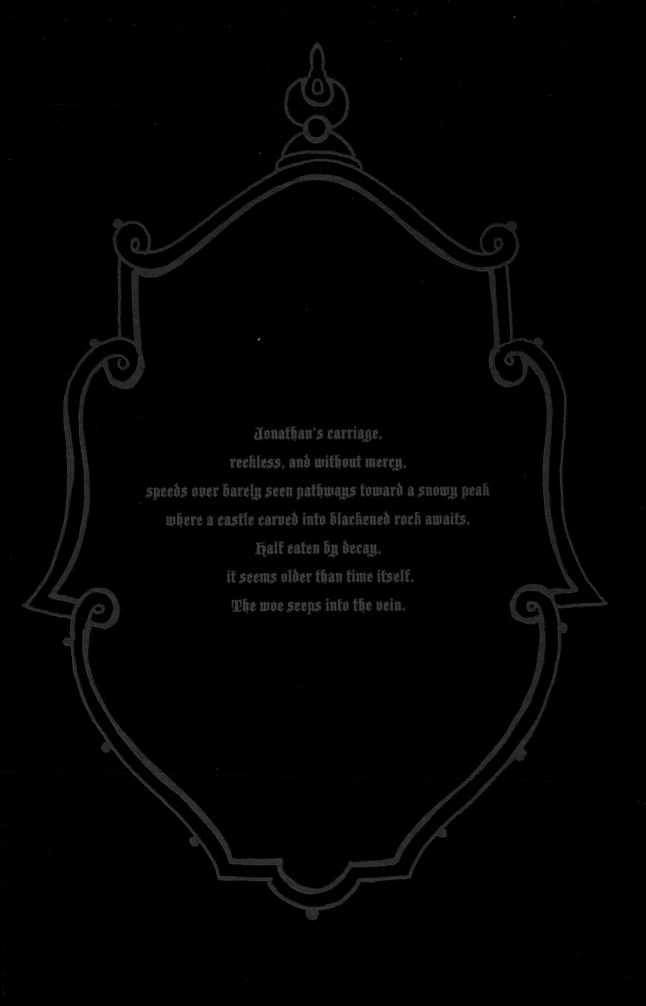

Jonathan's carriage,
reckless, and without mercy,
speeds over barely seen pathways toward a snowy peak
where a castle carved into blackened rock awaits.
Half eaten by decay,
it seems older than time itself.
The woe seeps into the vein.

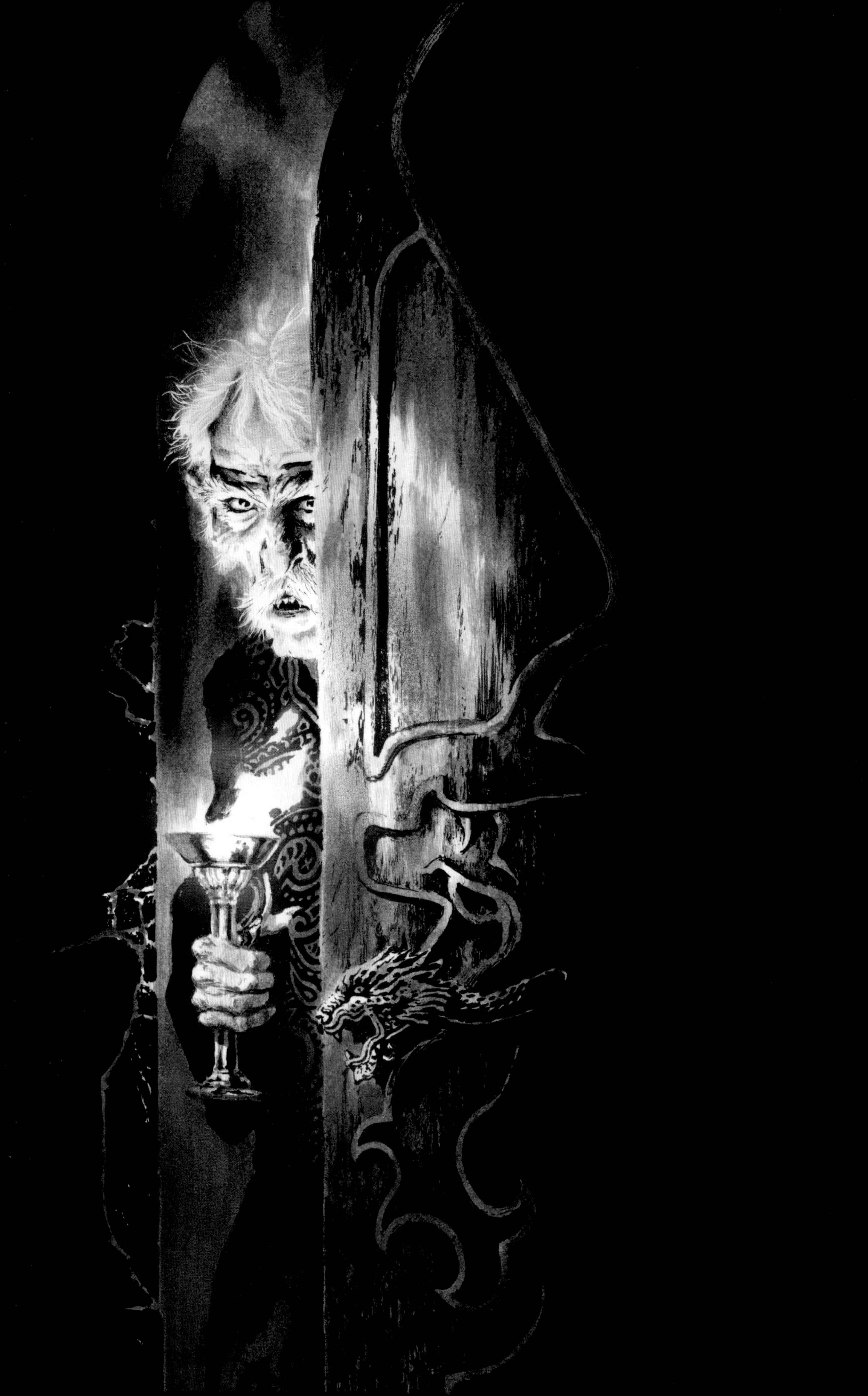

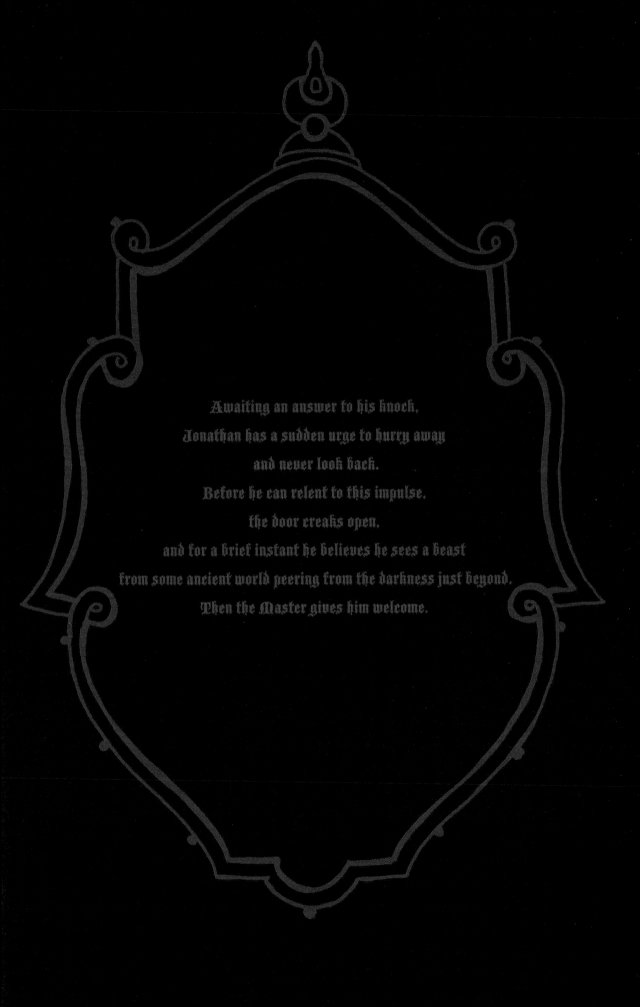

Awaiting an answer to his knock,
Jonathan has a sudden urge to hurry away
and never look back.
Before he can relent to this impulse,
the door creaks open,
and for a brief instant he believes he sees a beast
from some ancient world peering from the darkness just beyond.
Then the Master gives him welcome.

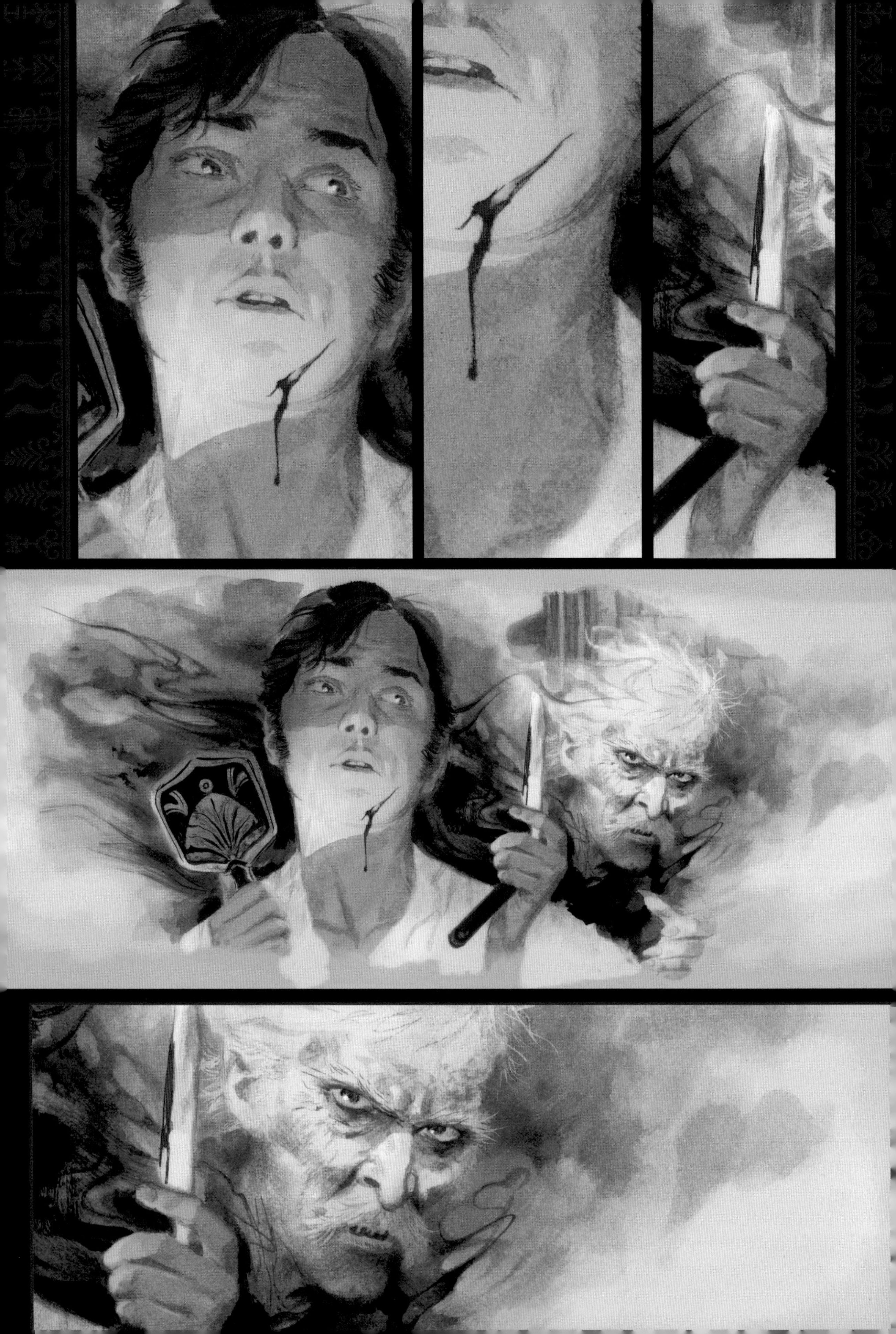

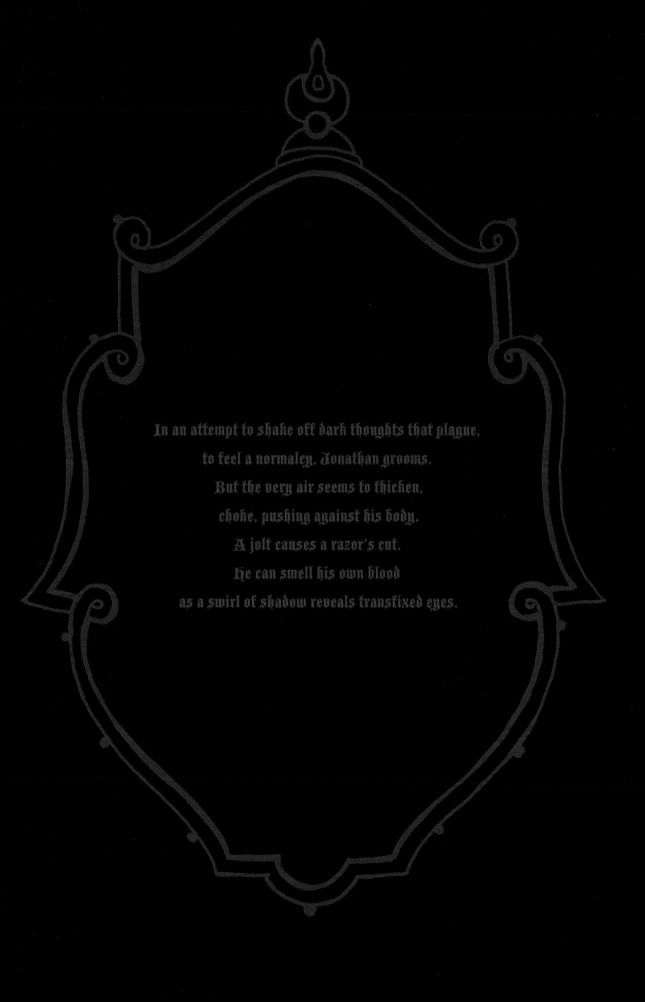

In an attempt to shake off dark thoughts that plague,

to feel a normalcy, Jonathan grooms.

But the very air seems to thicken,

choke, pushing against his body.

A jolt causes a razor's cut.

He can smell his own blood

as a swirl of shadow reveals transfixed eyes.

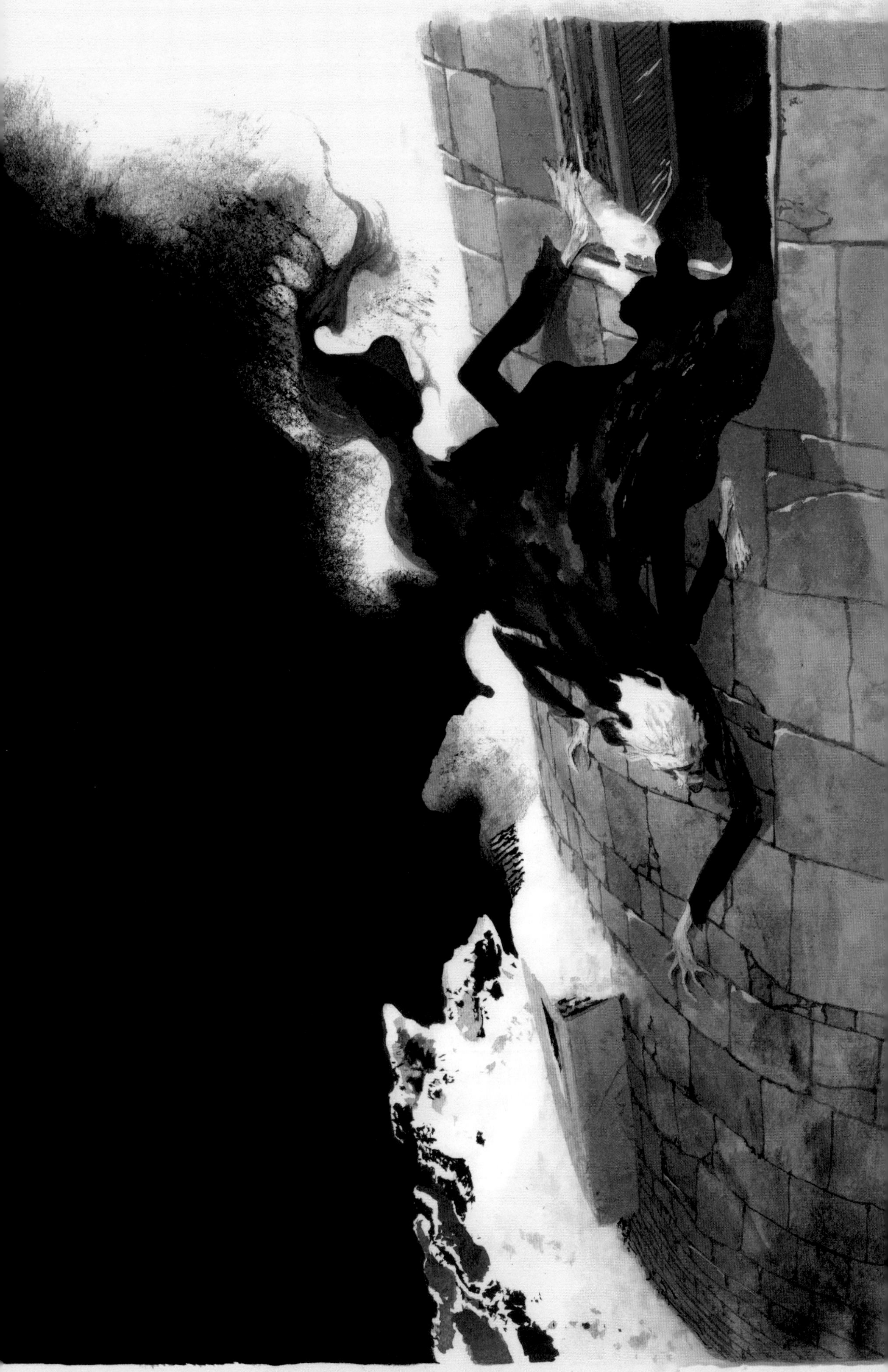

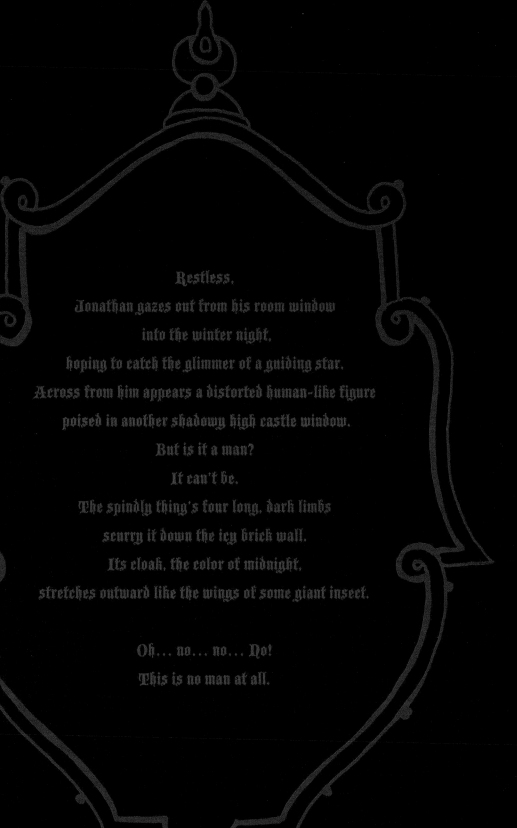

Restless,
Jonathan gazes out from his room window
into the winter night,
hoping to catch the glimmer of a guiding star.
Across from him appears a distorted human-like figure
poised in another shadowy high castle window.
But is it a man?
It can't be.
The spindly thing's four long, dark limbs
scurry it down the icy brick wall.
Its cloak, the color of midnight,
stretches outward like the wings of some giant insect.

Oh… no… no… No!
This is no man at all.

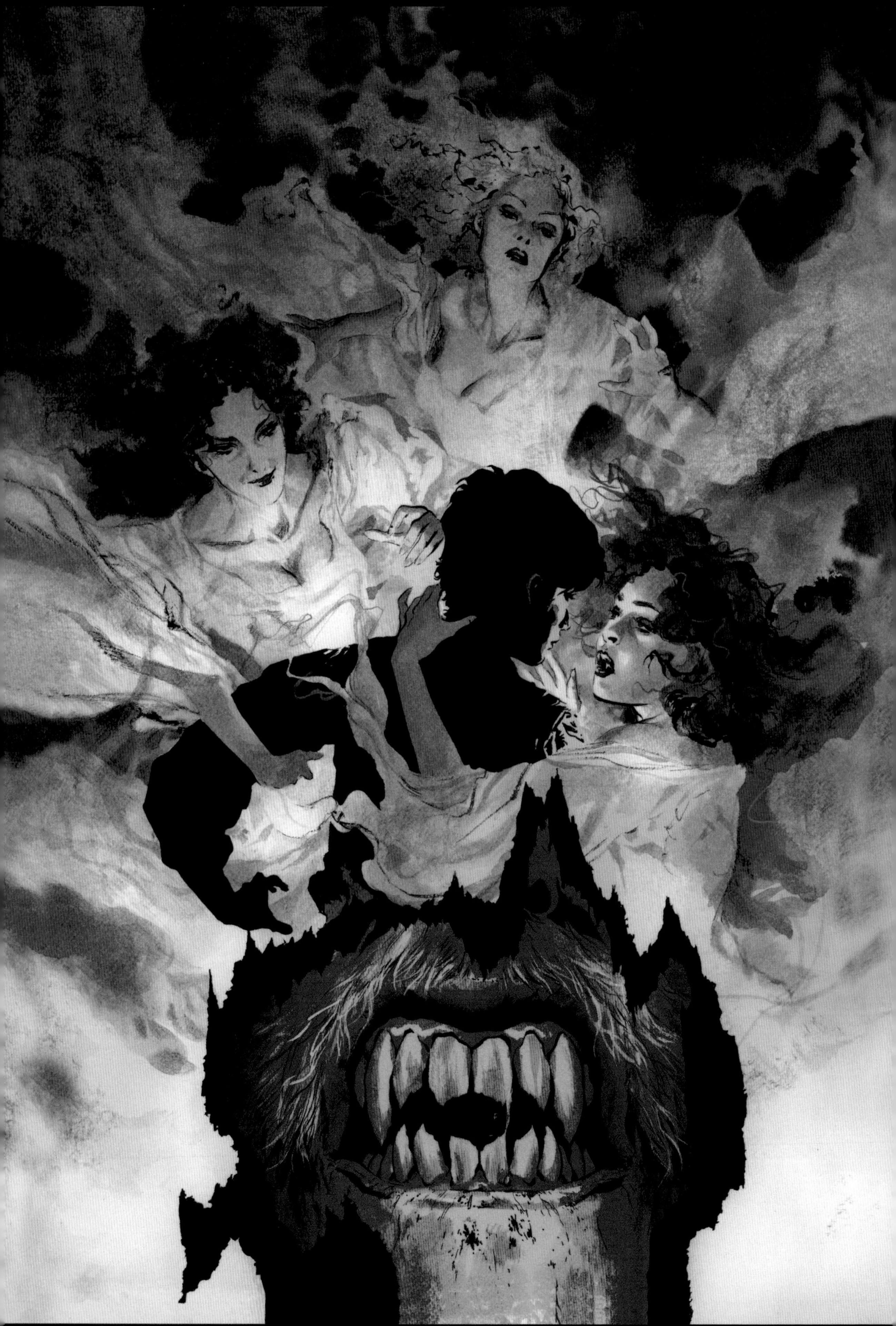

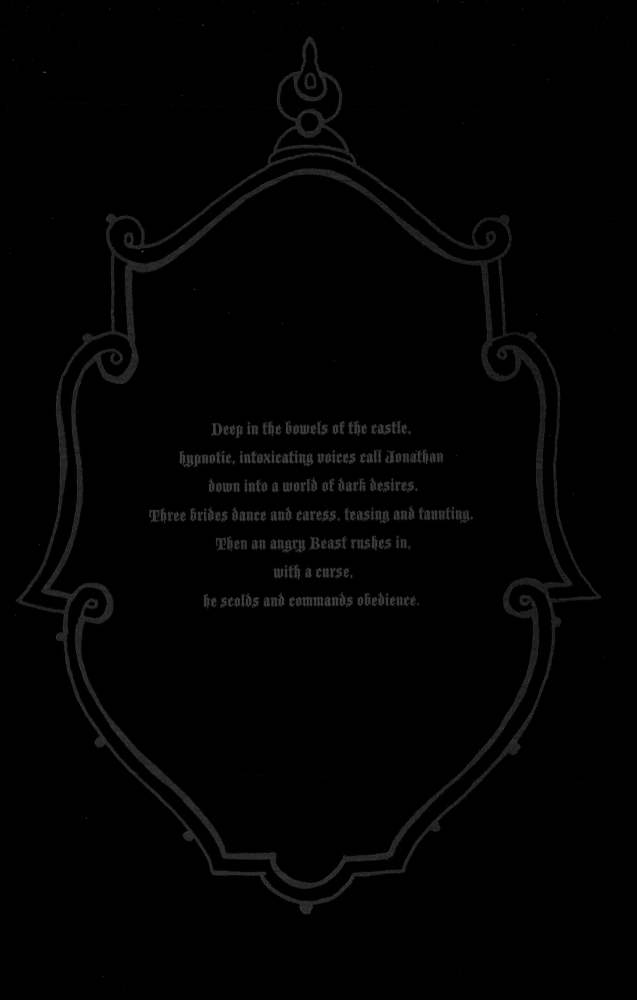

Deep in the bowels of the castle,
hypnotic, intoxicating voices call Jonathan
down into a world of dark desires.
Three brides dance and caress, teasing and taunting.
Then an angry Beast rushes in,
with a curse,
he scolds and commands obedience.

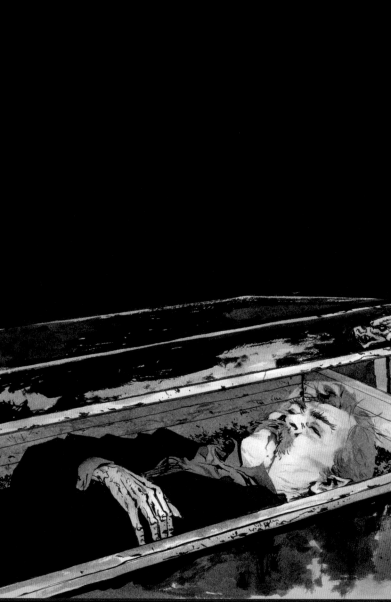

The Lord of Hell sleeps
a dreamless black sleep.
His visage softens,
his age retreats,
as if death itself has been chased away
by a defiant ritual of a resting day
on a bed of grave-dirt filling a burial coffin.

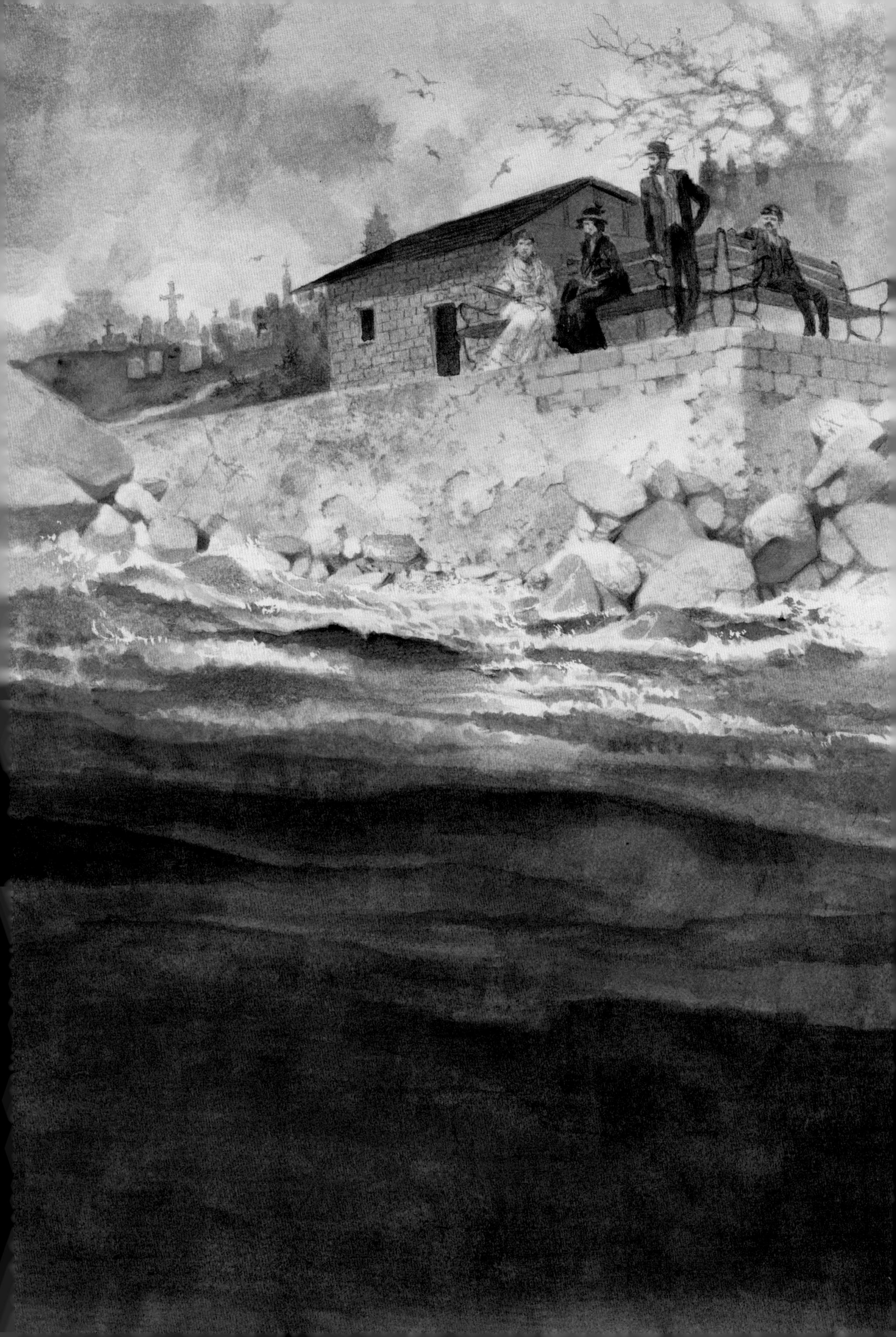

The world is bright with spring.
Mina, mesmerized by Lucy's beauty, blushes
as courting men dote.
A sudden chill wisps from the sea,
and she can't help but feel like this day
will be her last.

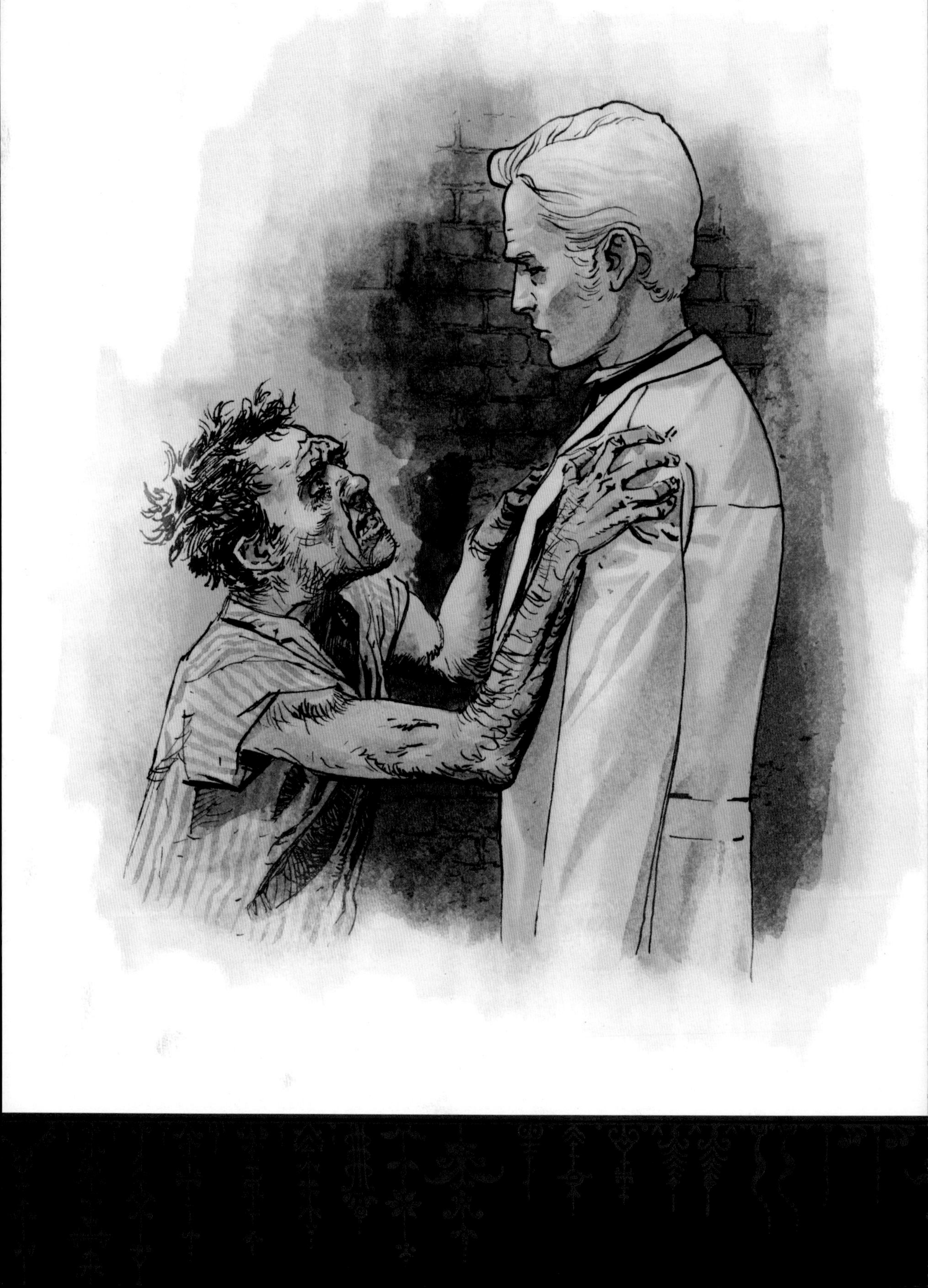

Doctor Seward attempts to help Renfield,
now more a creature of delusion than a man.
But as he begs for his freedom,
Renfield, in secret, covets the bidding of his Master,
the Beast that has stolen his sanity.

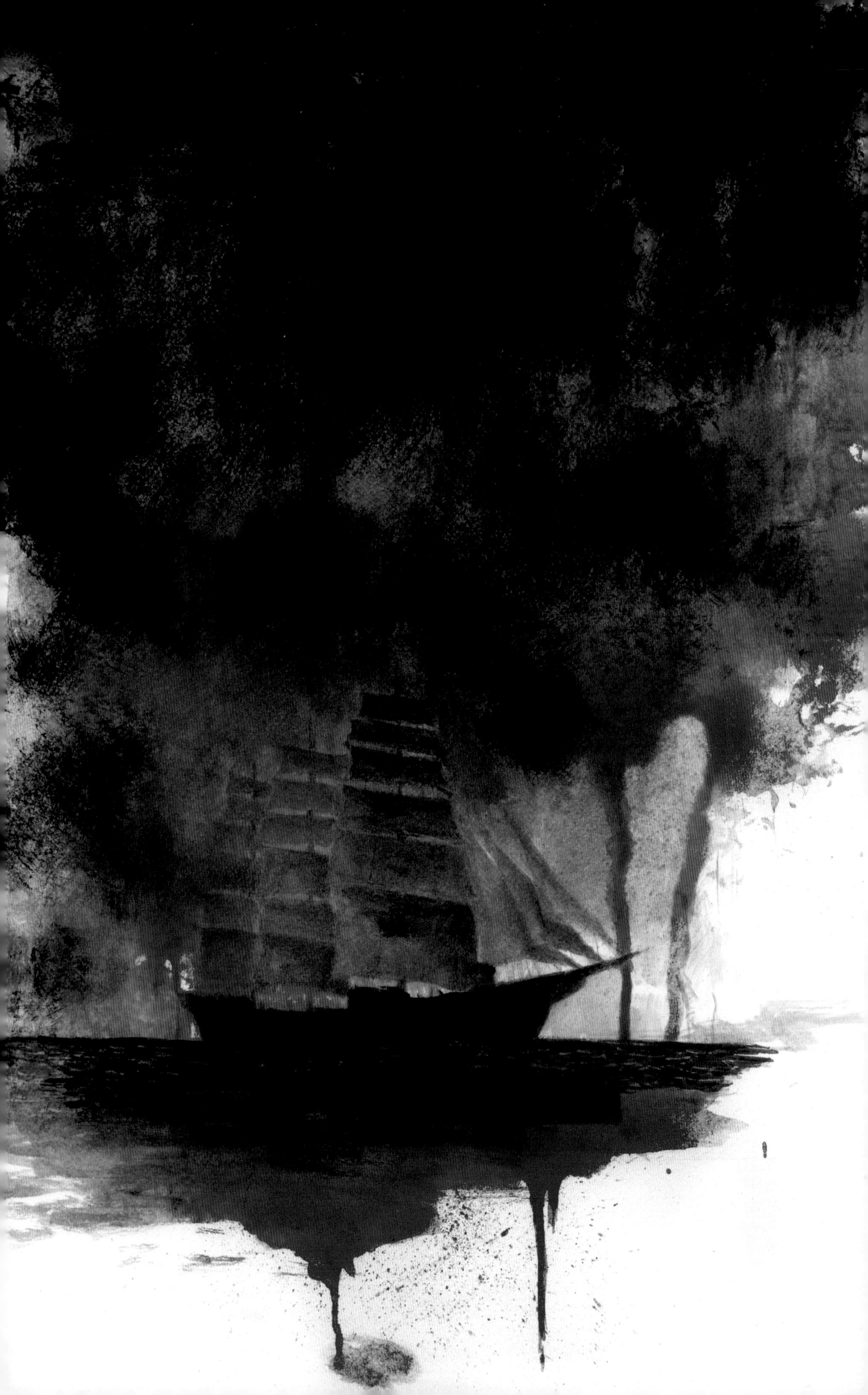

The Demeter,

now a vessel sailing only maggots and rot.

Death drifts into port.

Demonic lapping dark tides

carry a cargo born from the pits of Hell.

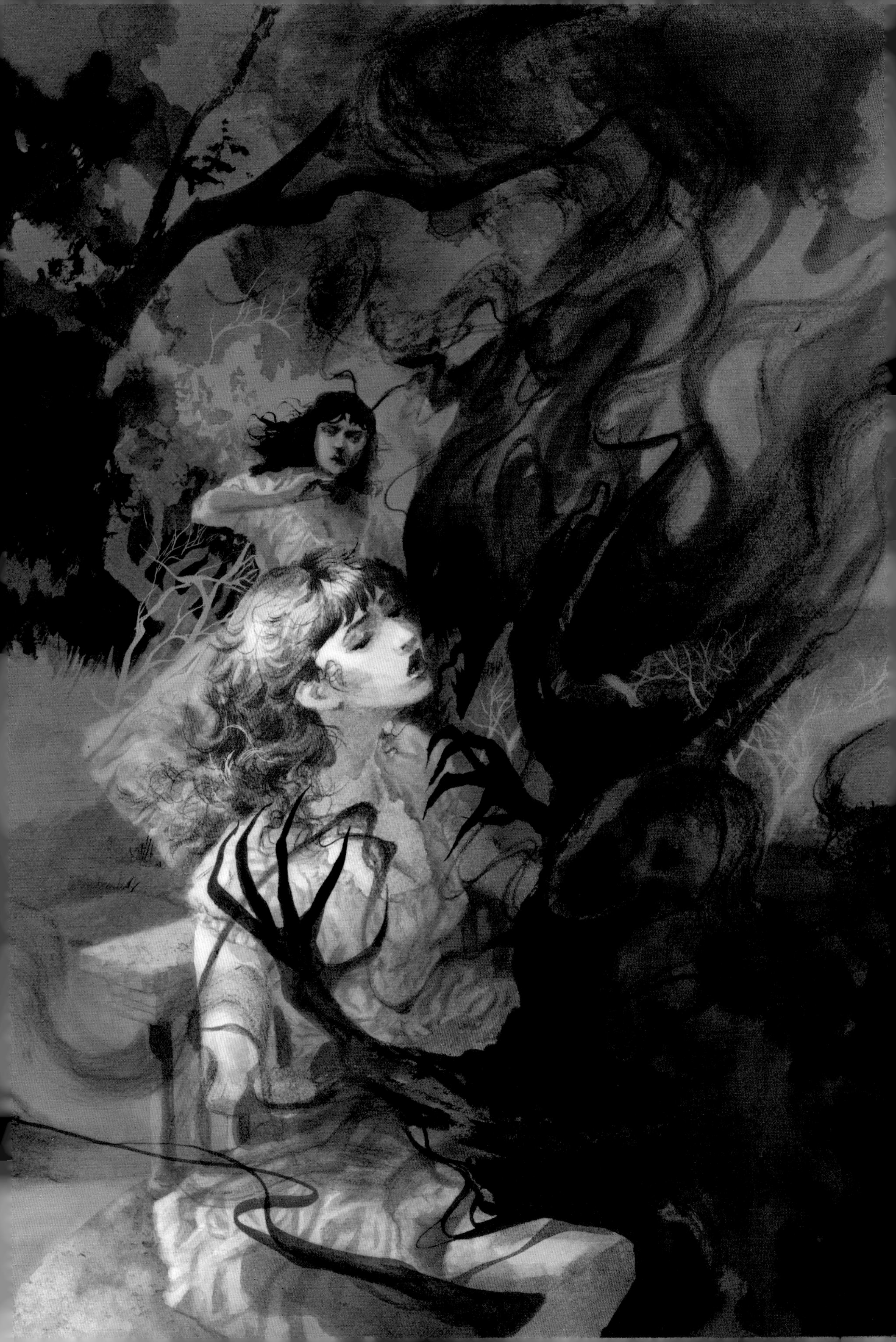

Mina's sleep is disturbed,
broken by haunting sounds in the night,
coming from the gardens.
She discovers Lucy,
enthralled by a ghastly thing.
A shadow thick as blood and smoke.
It corrupts her.

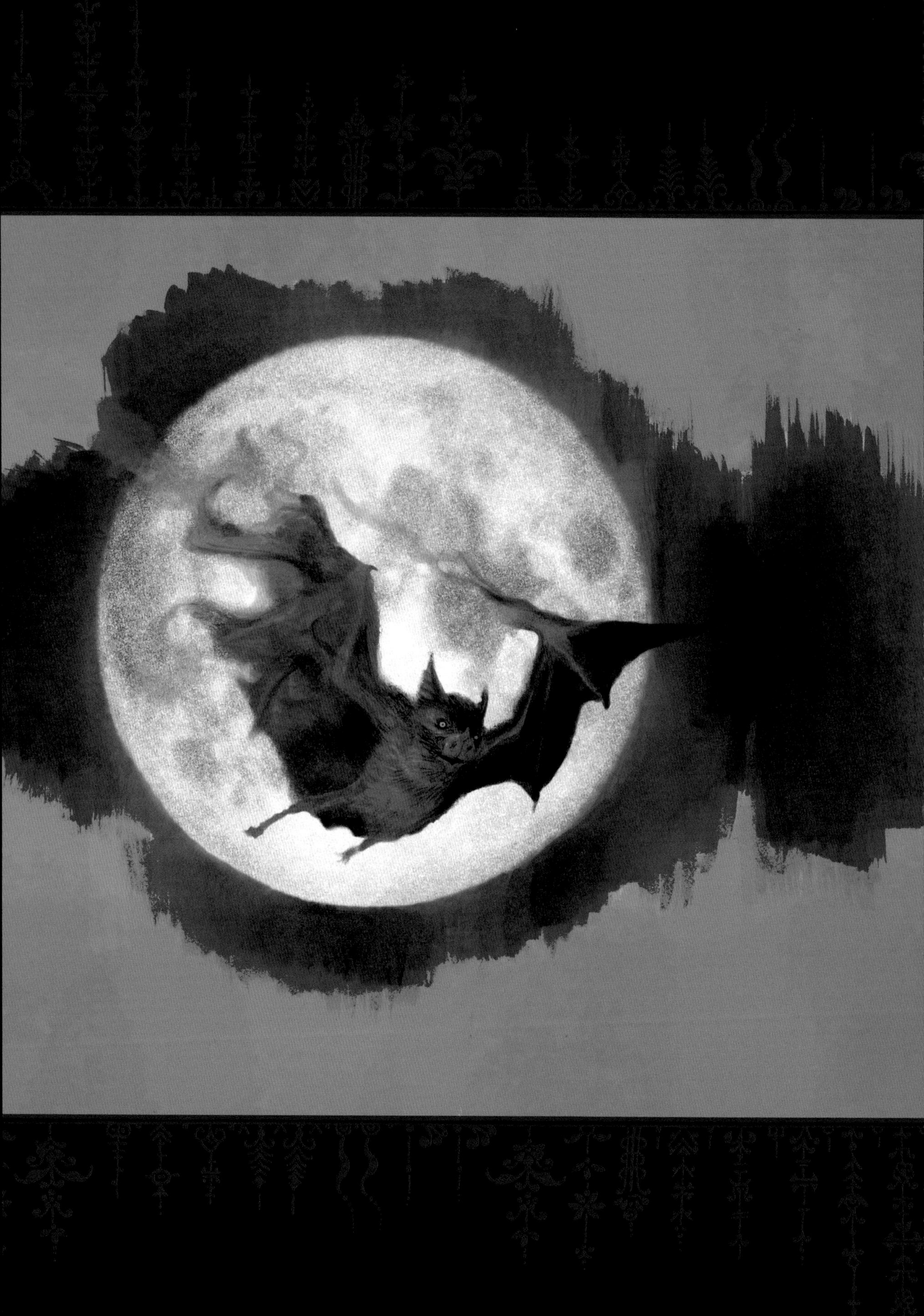

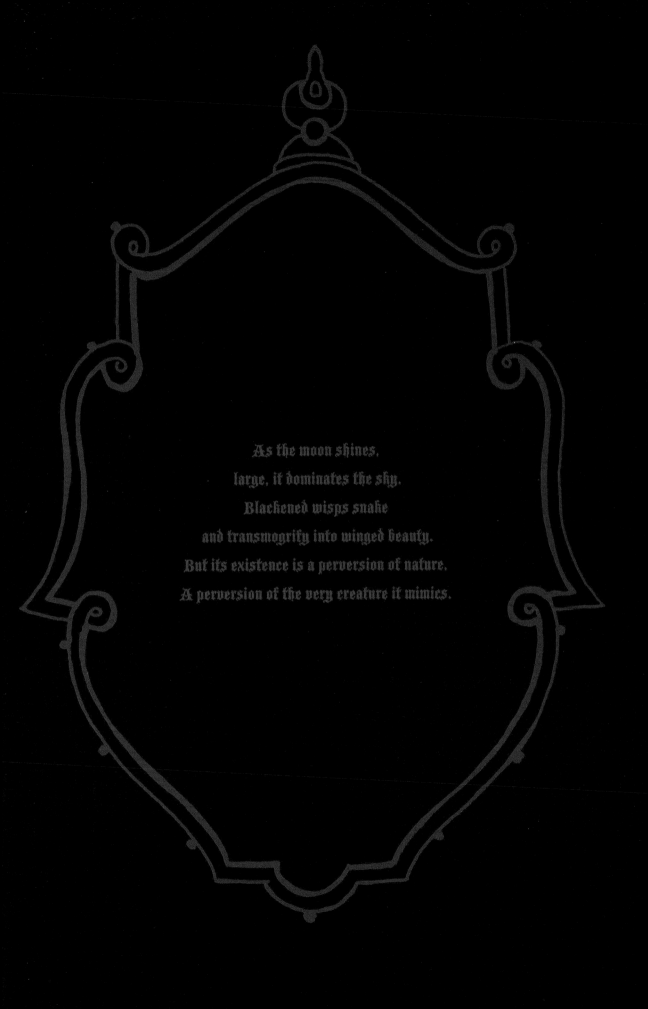

As the moon shines,
large, it dominates the sky.
Blackened wisps snake
and transmogrify into winged beauty.
But its existence is a perversion of nature.
A perversion of the very creature it mimics.

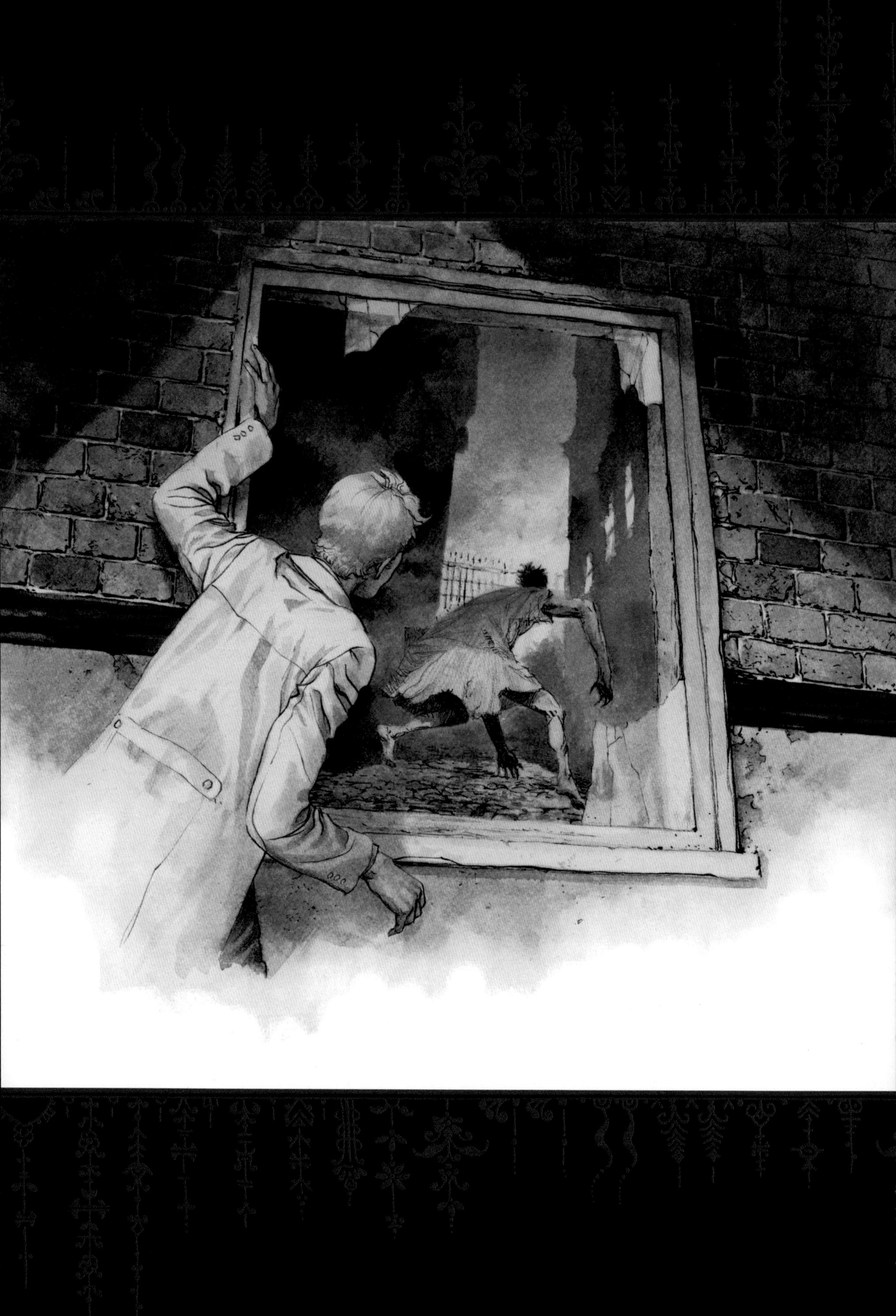

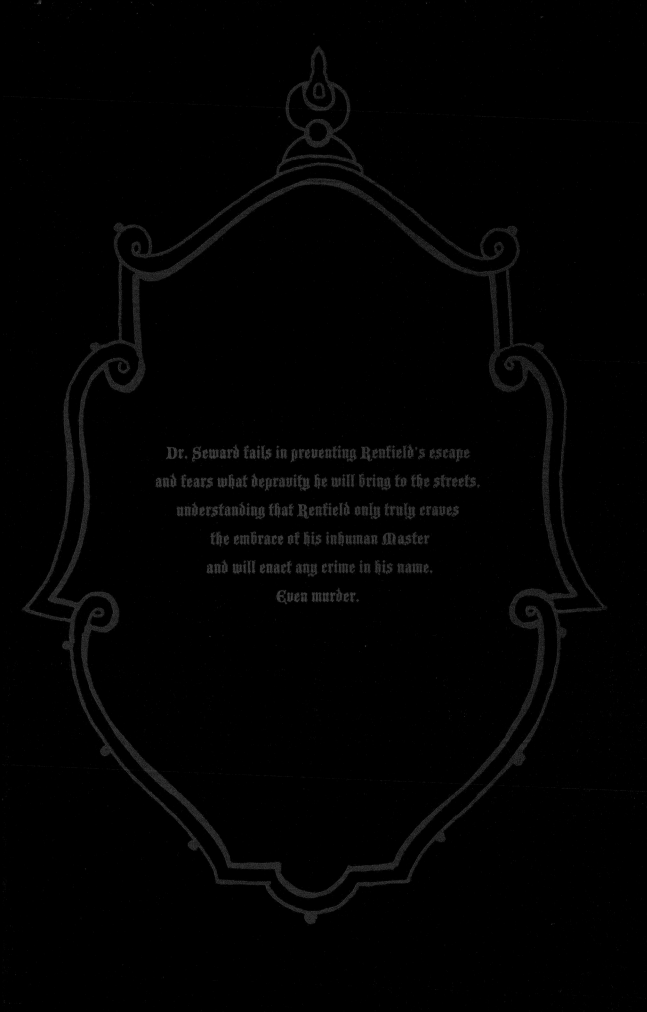

Dr. Seward fails in preventing Renfield's escape
and fears what depravity he will bring to the streets,
understanding that Renfield only truly craves
the embrace of his inhuman Master
and will enact any crime in his name.
Even murder.

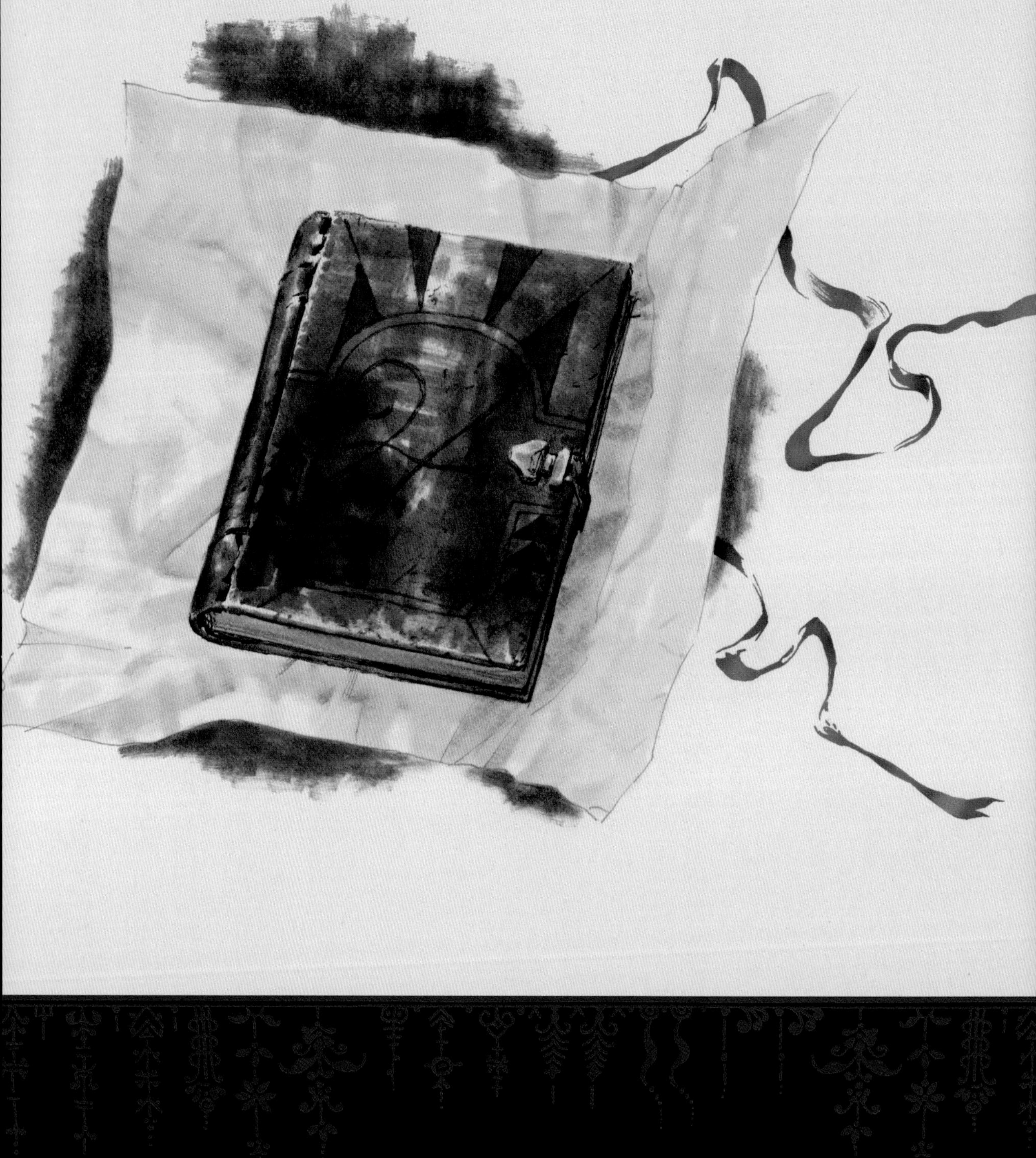

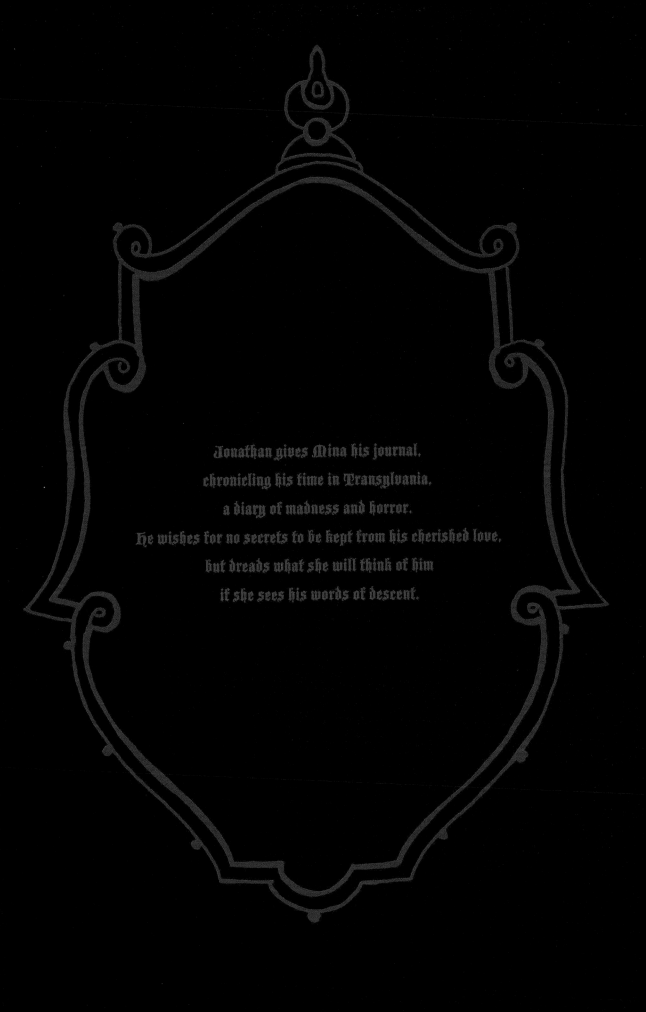

Jonathan gives Mina his journal,
chronicling his time in Transylvania,
a diary of madness and horror.
He wishes for no secrets to be kept from his cherished love,
but dreads what she will think of him
if she sees his words of descent.

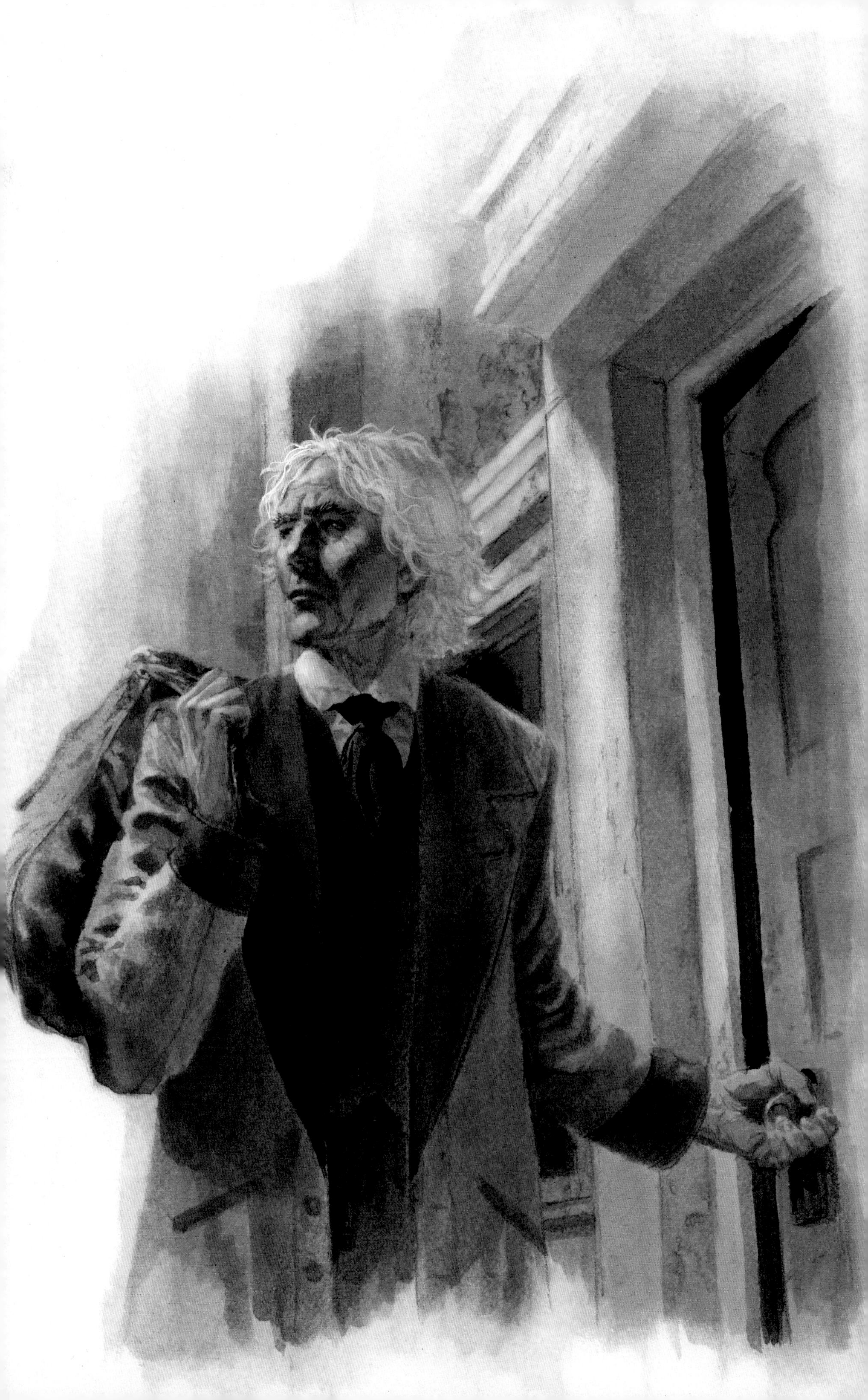

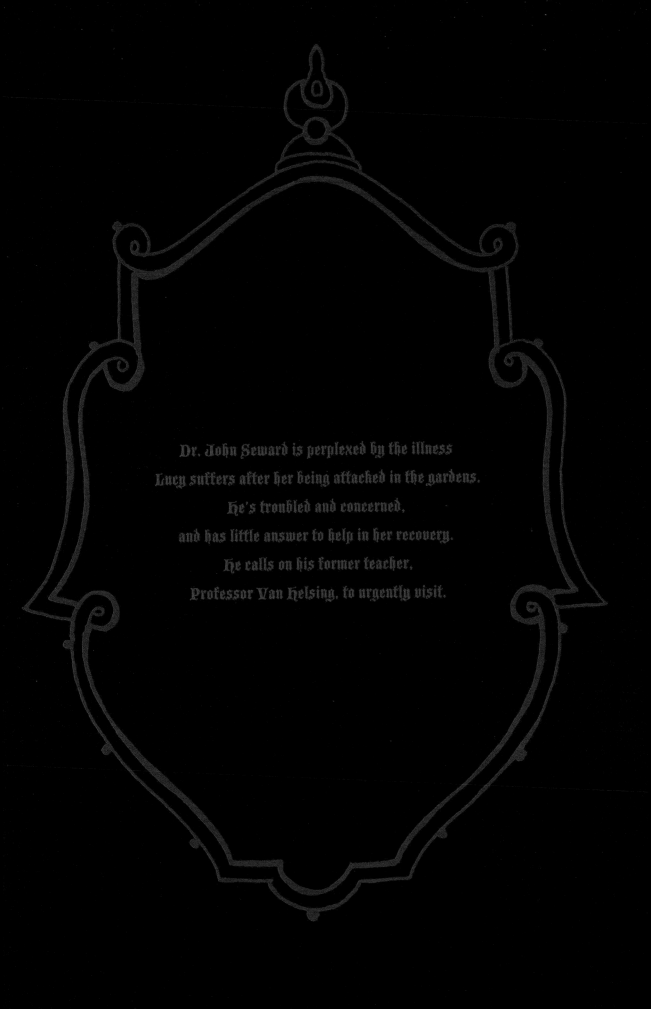

Dr. John Seward is perplexed by the illness
Lucy suffers after her being attacked in the gardens.
He's troubled and concerned,
and has little answer to help in her recovery.
He calls on his former teacher,
Professor Van Helsing, to urgently visit.

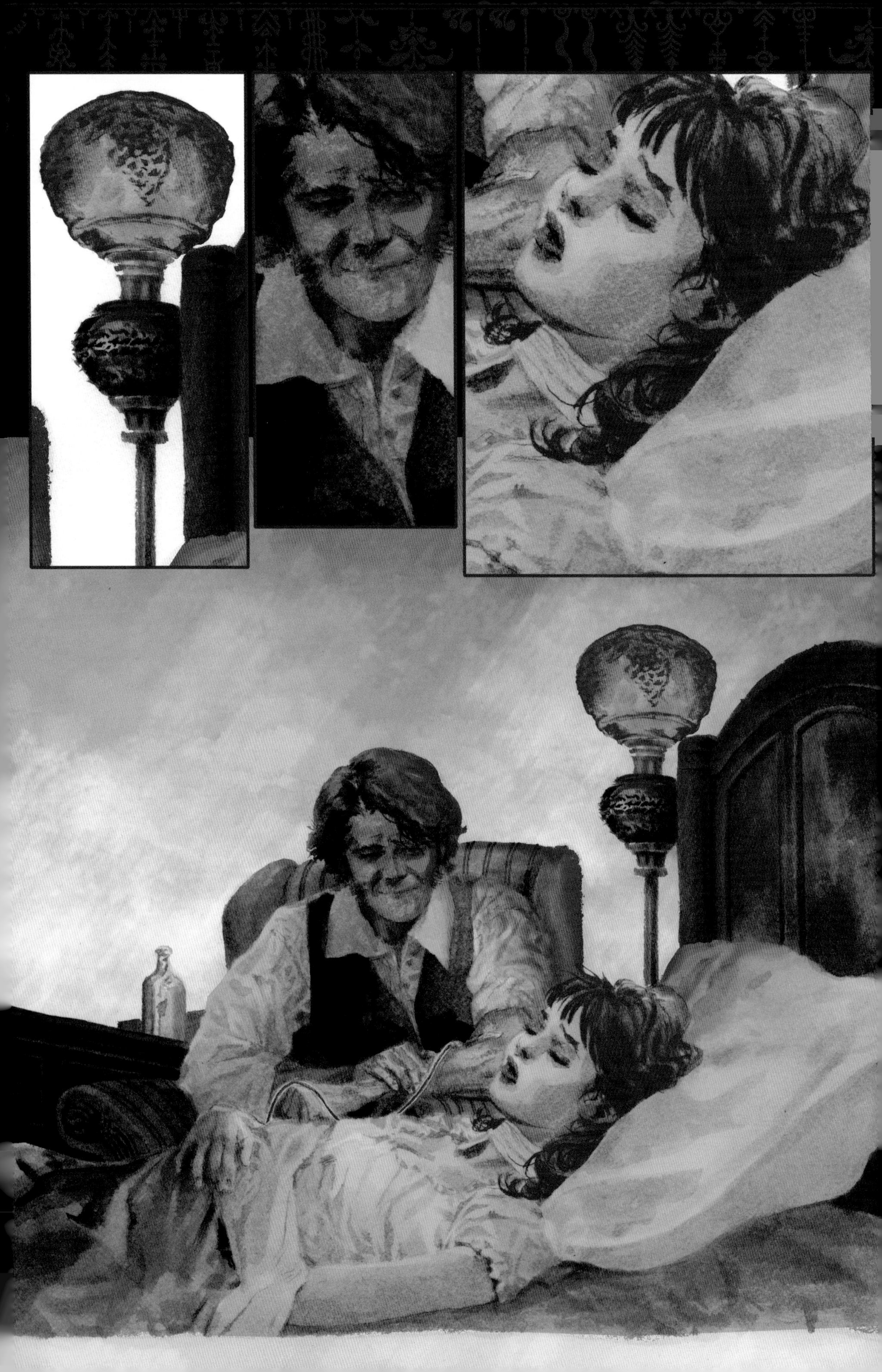

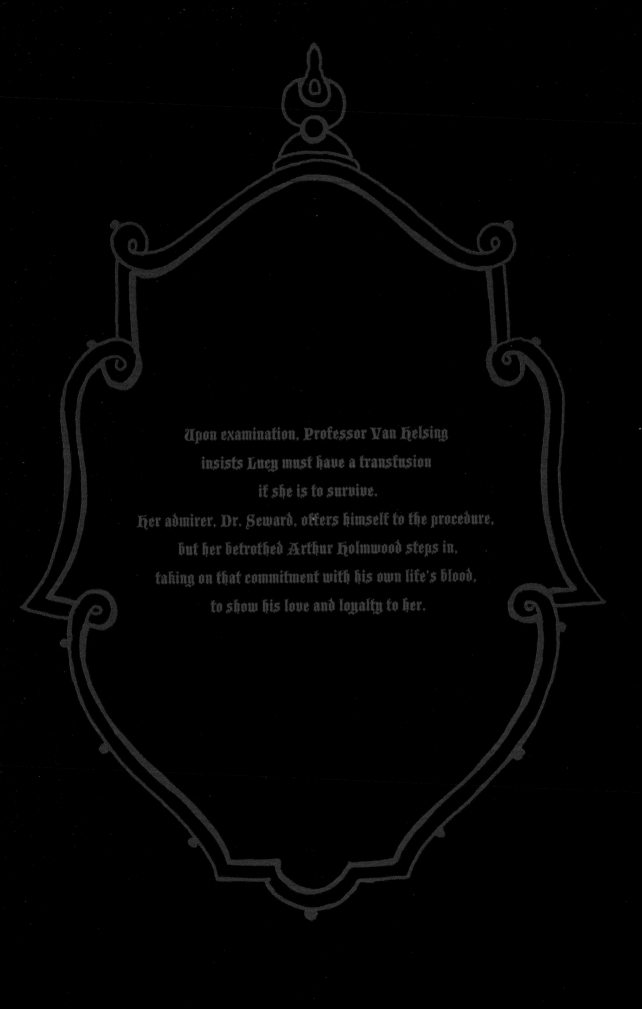

Upon examination, Professor Van Helsing
insists Lucy must have a transfusion
if she is to survive.
Her admirer, Dr. Seward, offers himself to the procedure,
but her betrothed Arthur Holmwood steps in,
taking on that commitment with his own life's blood,
to show his love and loyalty to her.

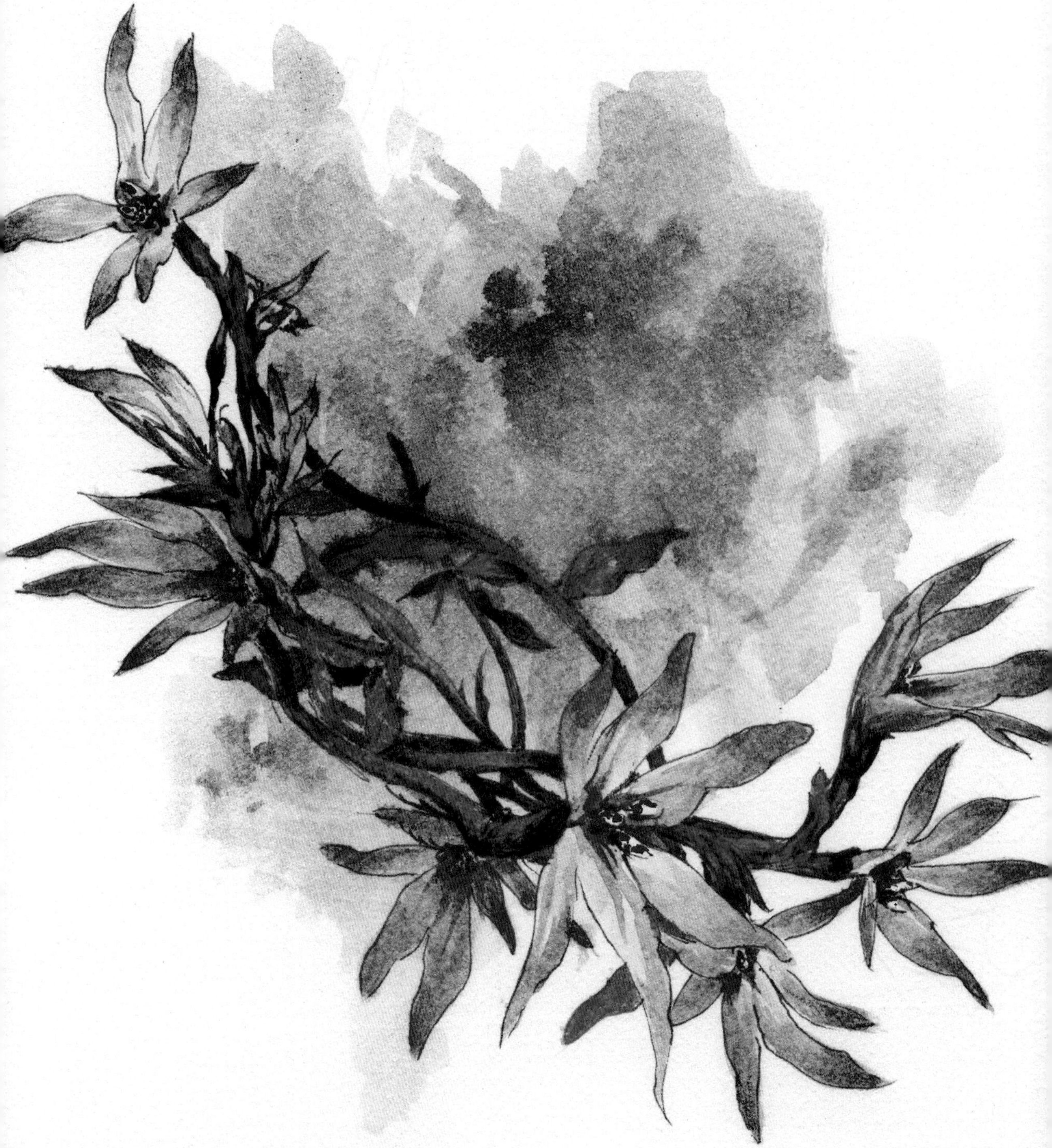

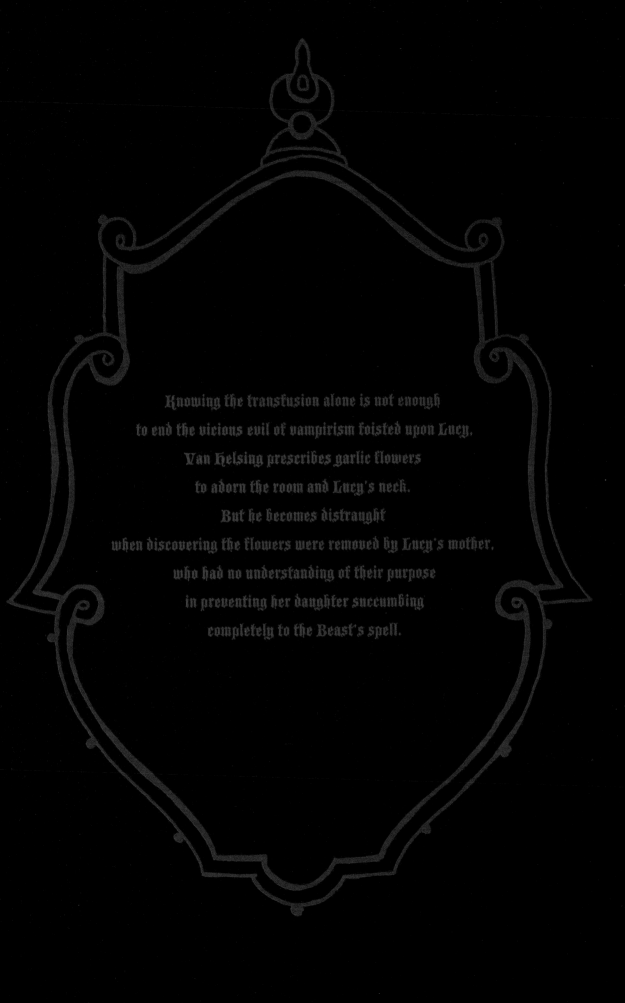

Knowing the transfusion alone is not enough
to end the vicious evil of vampirism foisted upon Lucy,
Van Helsing prescribes garlic flowers
to adorn the room and Lucy's neck.
But he becomes distraught
when discovering the flowers were removed by Lucy's mother,
who had no understanding of their purpose
in preventing her daughter succumbing
completely to the Beast's spell.

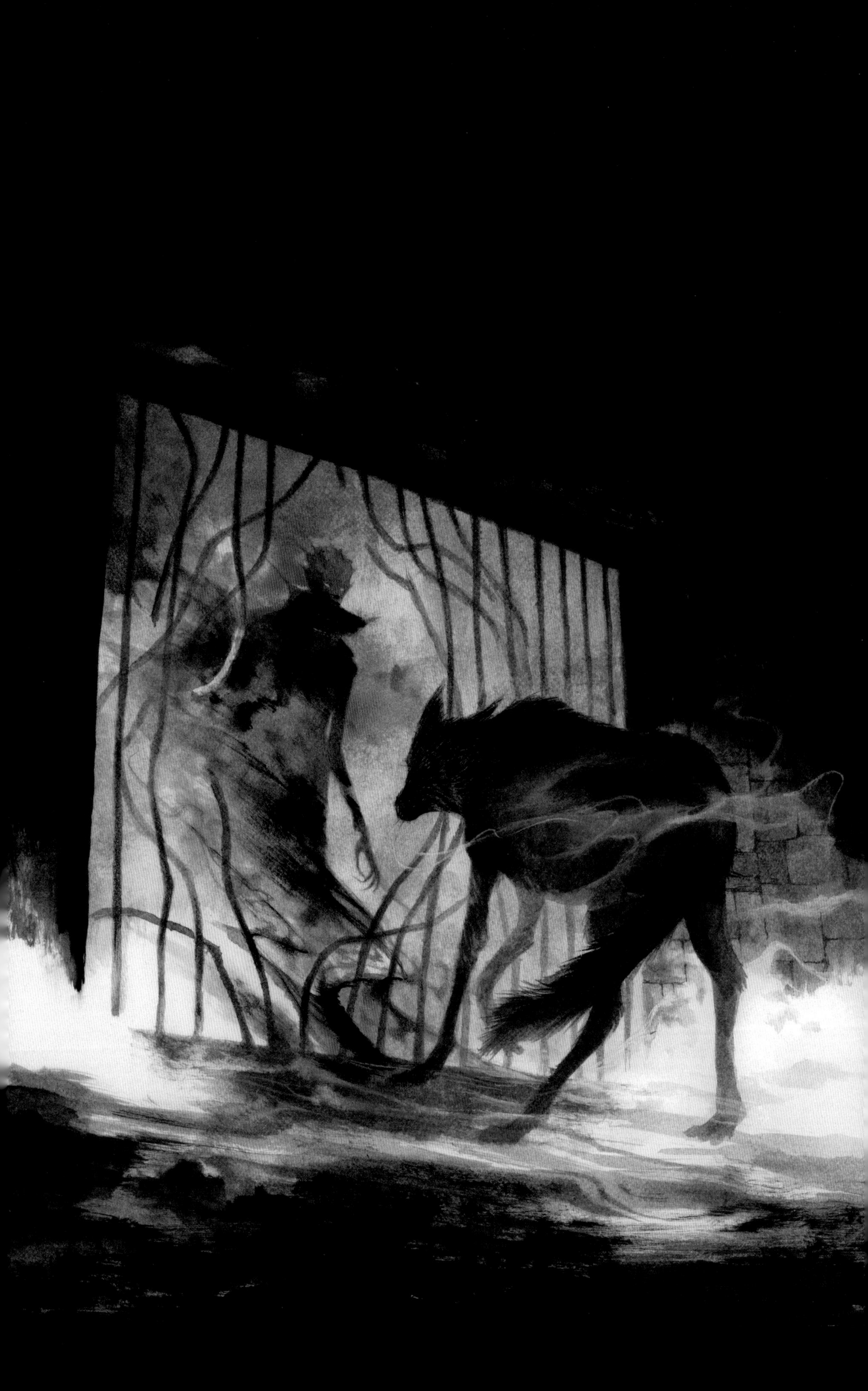

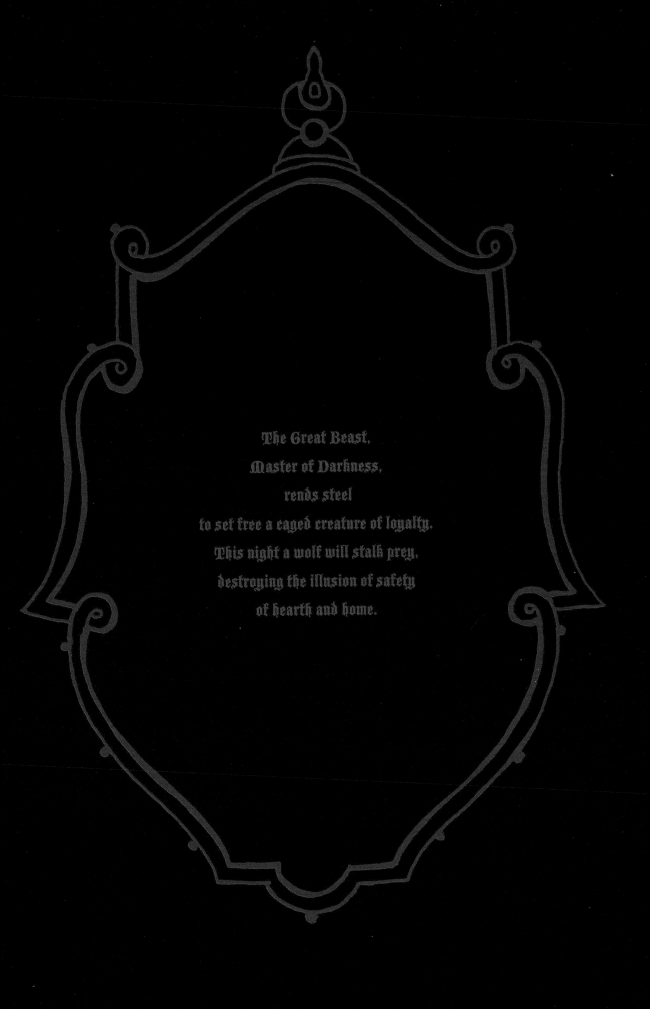

The Great Beast,
Master of Darkness,
rends steel
to set free a caged creature of loyalty.
This night a wolf will stalk prey,
destroying the illusion of safety
of hearth and home.

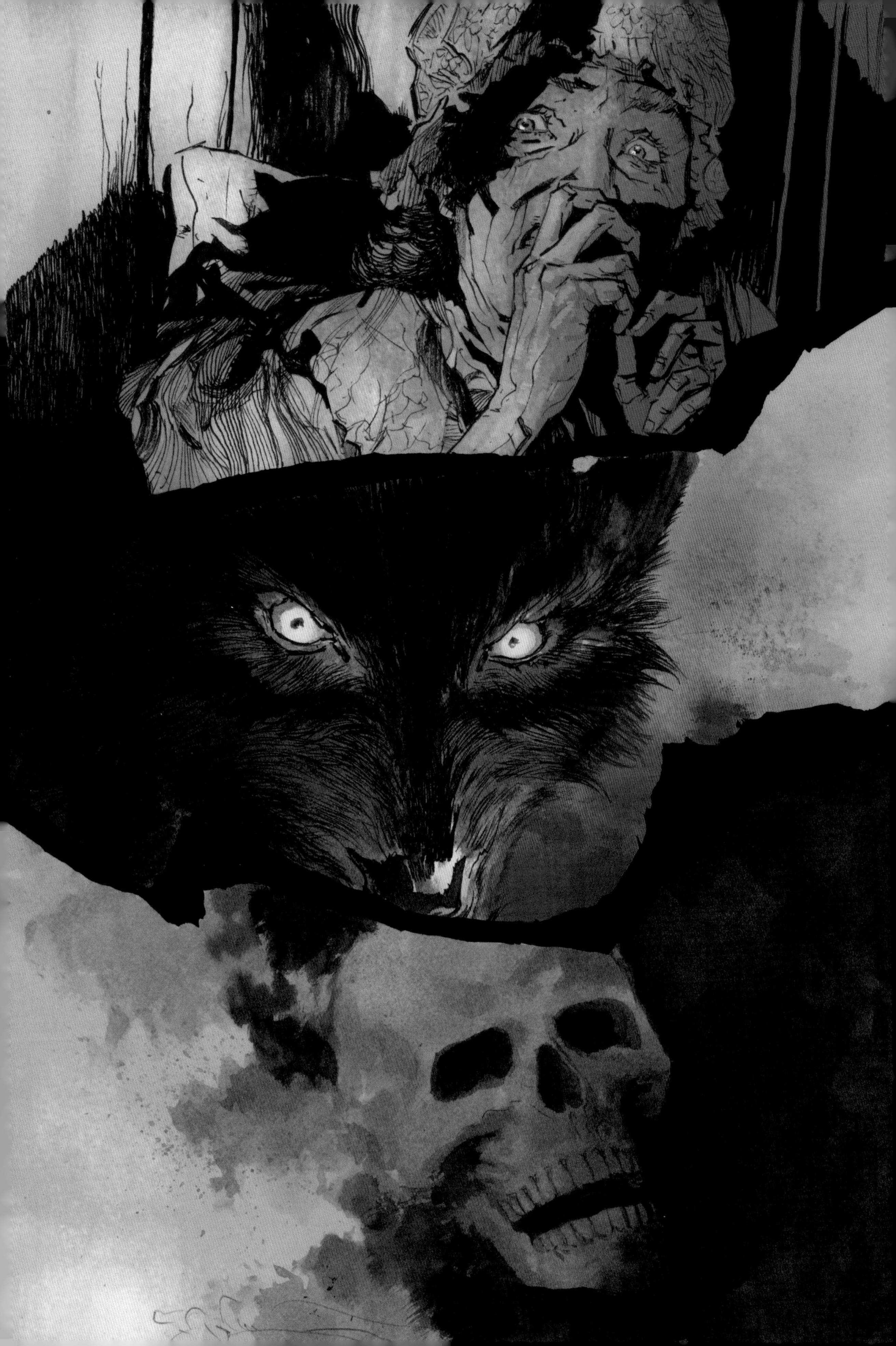

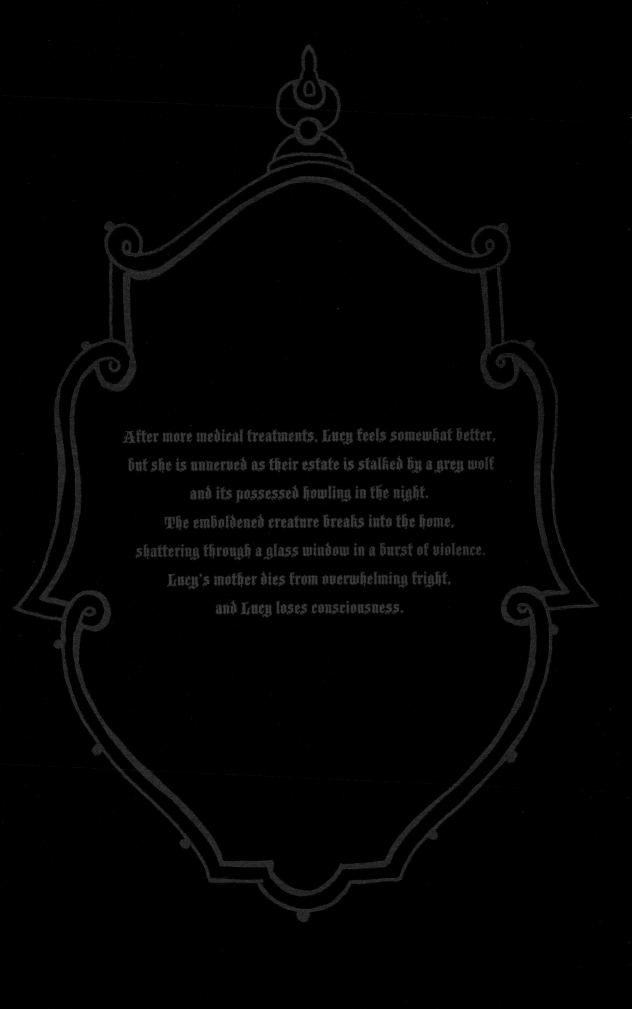

After more medical treatments, Lucy feels somewhat better,
but she is unnerved as their estate is stalked by a grey wolf
and its possessed howling in the night.
The emboldened creature breaks into the home,
shattering through a glass window in a burst of violence.
Lucy's mother dies from overwhelming fright,
and Lucy loses consciousness.

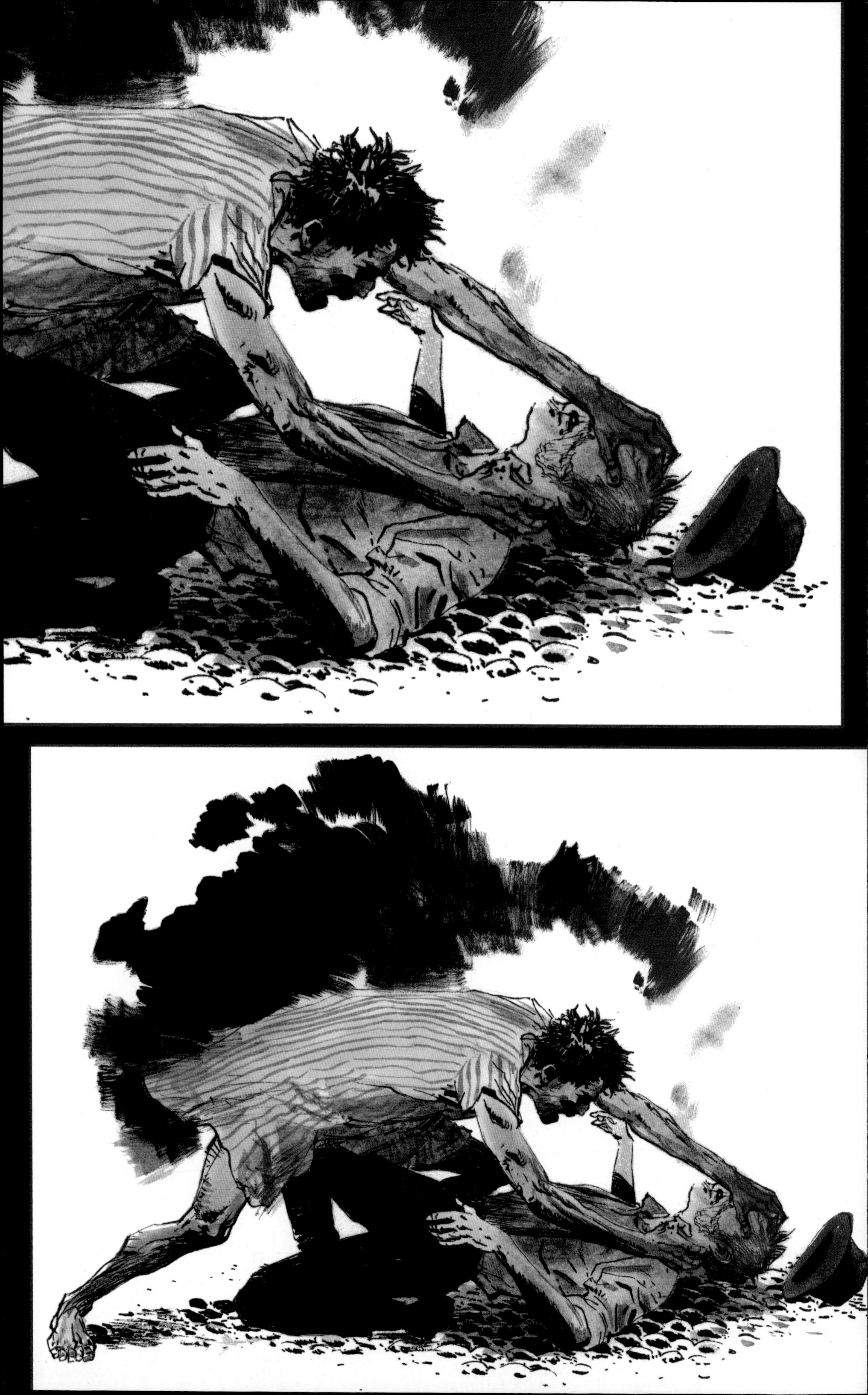

Having been wounded by a knife
during a prior attack from Renfield,
Dr. Seward's worry
over what this twisted man might do to innocent citizens
is proven founded
as Renfield's brutality becomes unleashed.

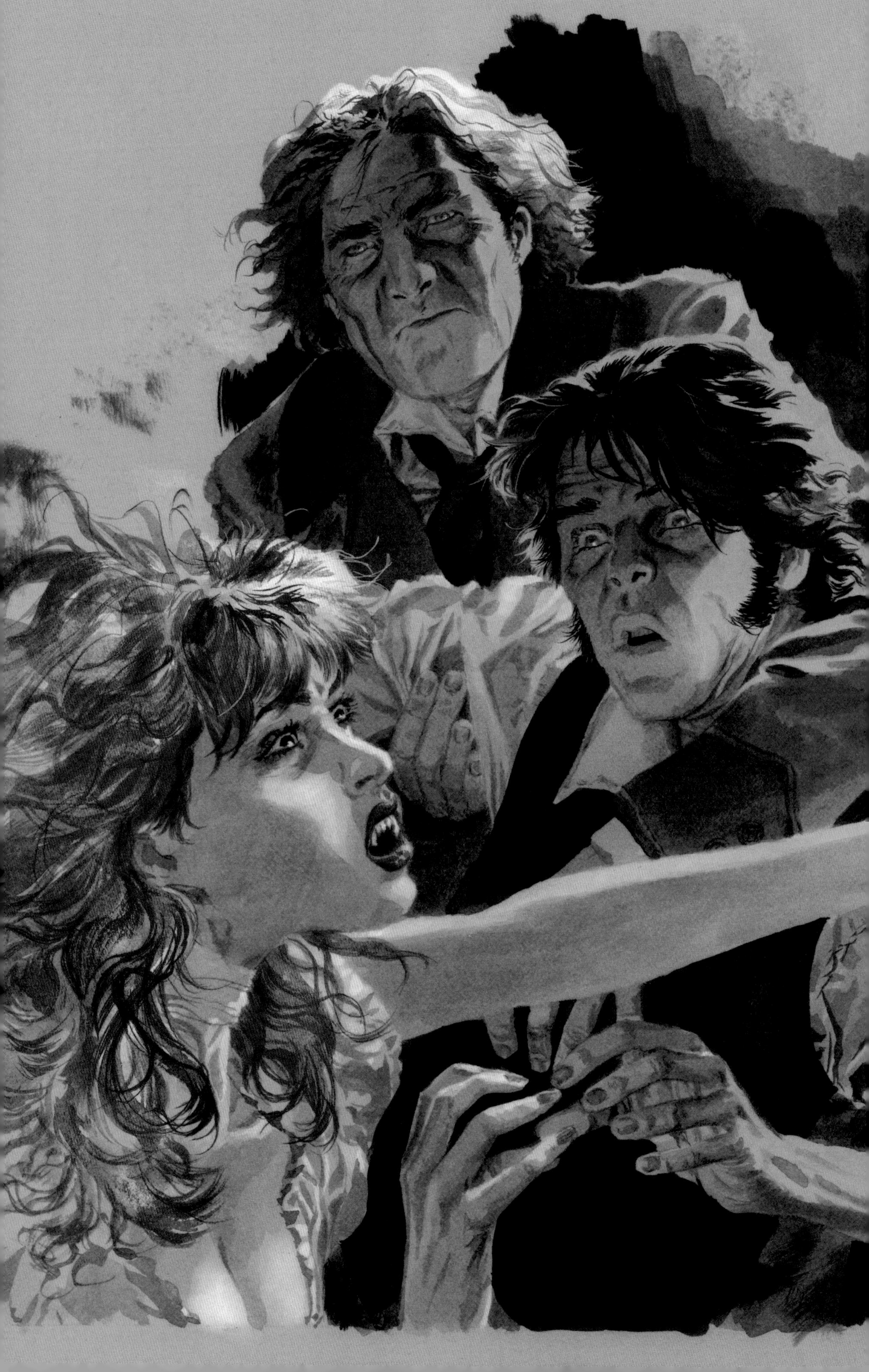

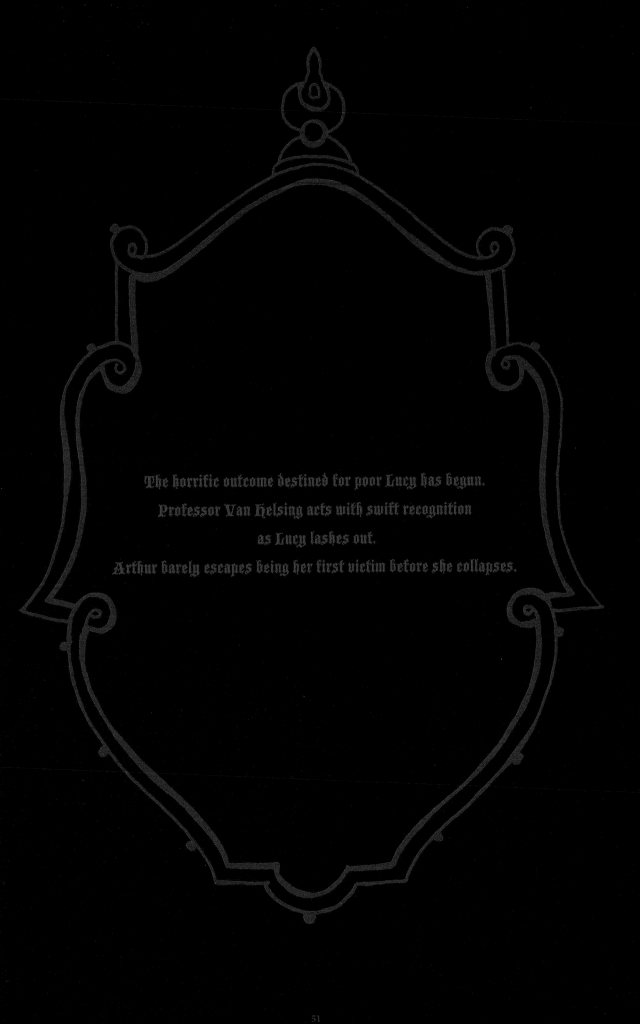

The horrific outcome destined for poor Lucy has begun.
Professor Van Helsing acts with swift recognition
as Lucy lashes out.
Arthur barely escapes being her first victim before she collapses.

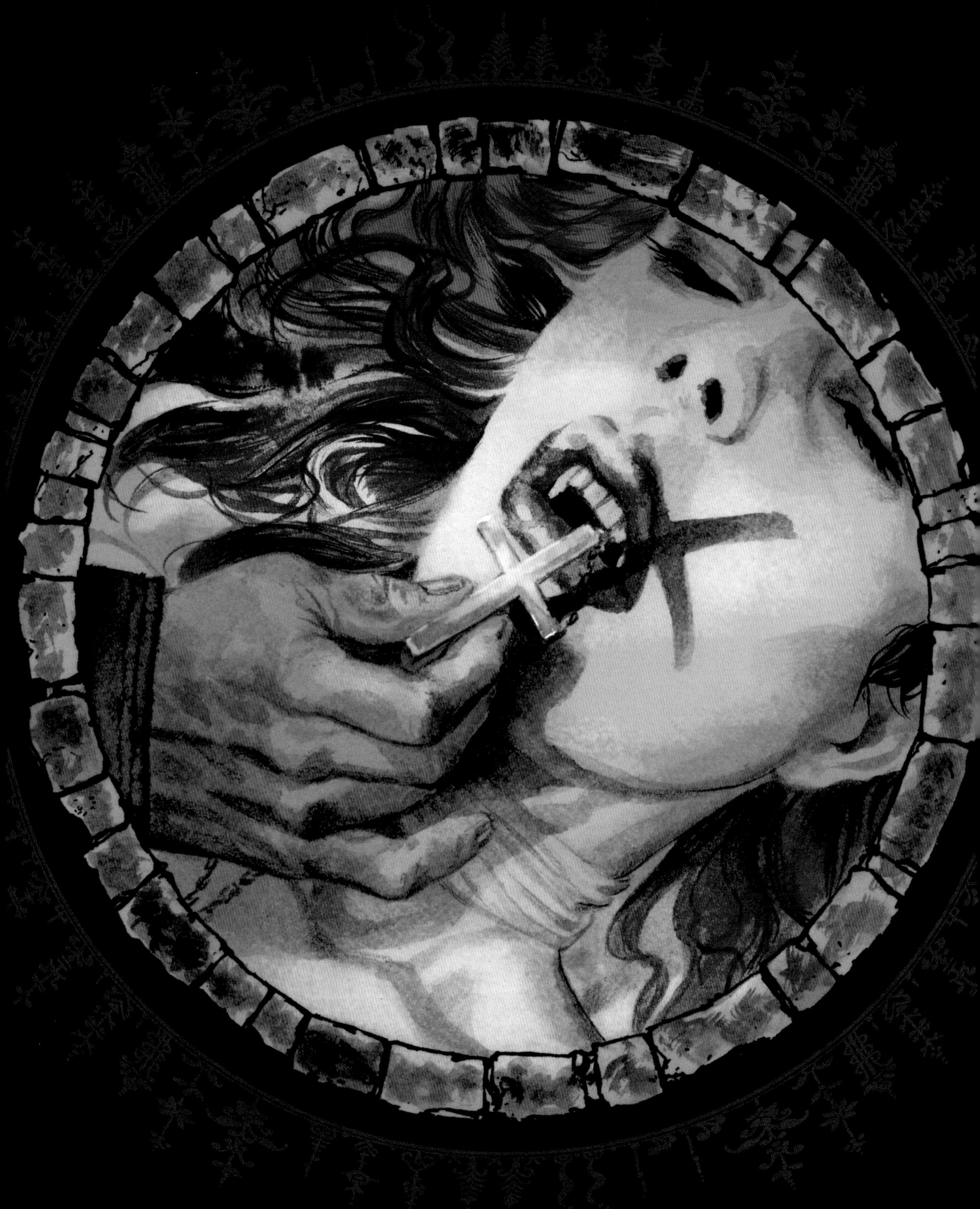

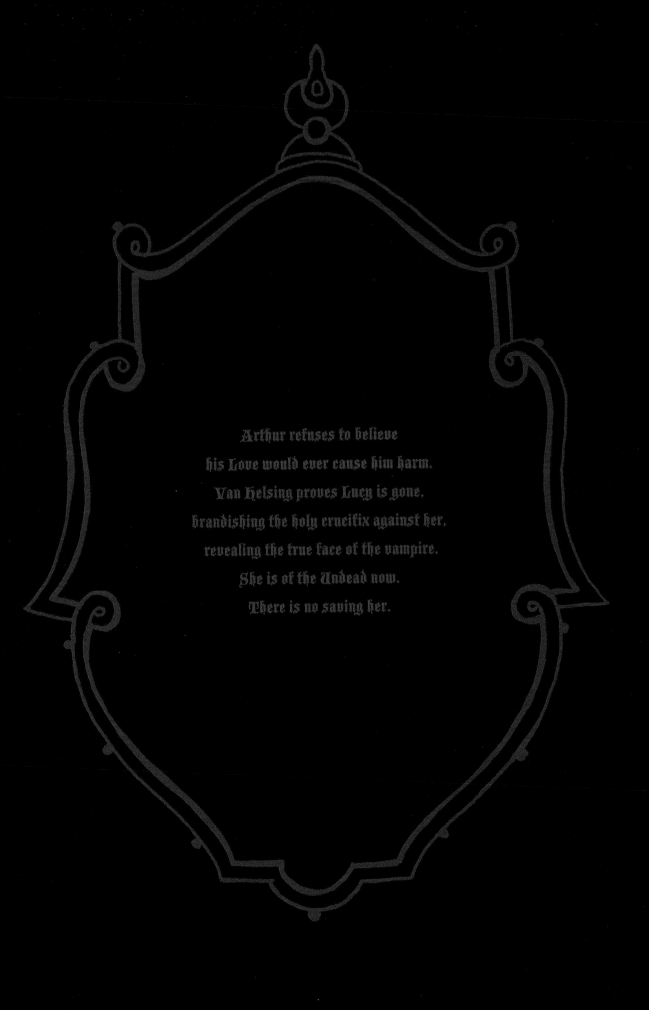

Arthur refuses to believe
his Love would ever cause him harm.
Van Helsing proves Lucy is gone,
brandishing the holy crucifix against her,
revealing the true face of the vampire.
She is of the Undead now.
There is no saving her.

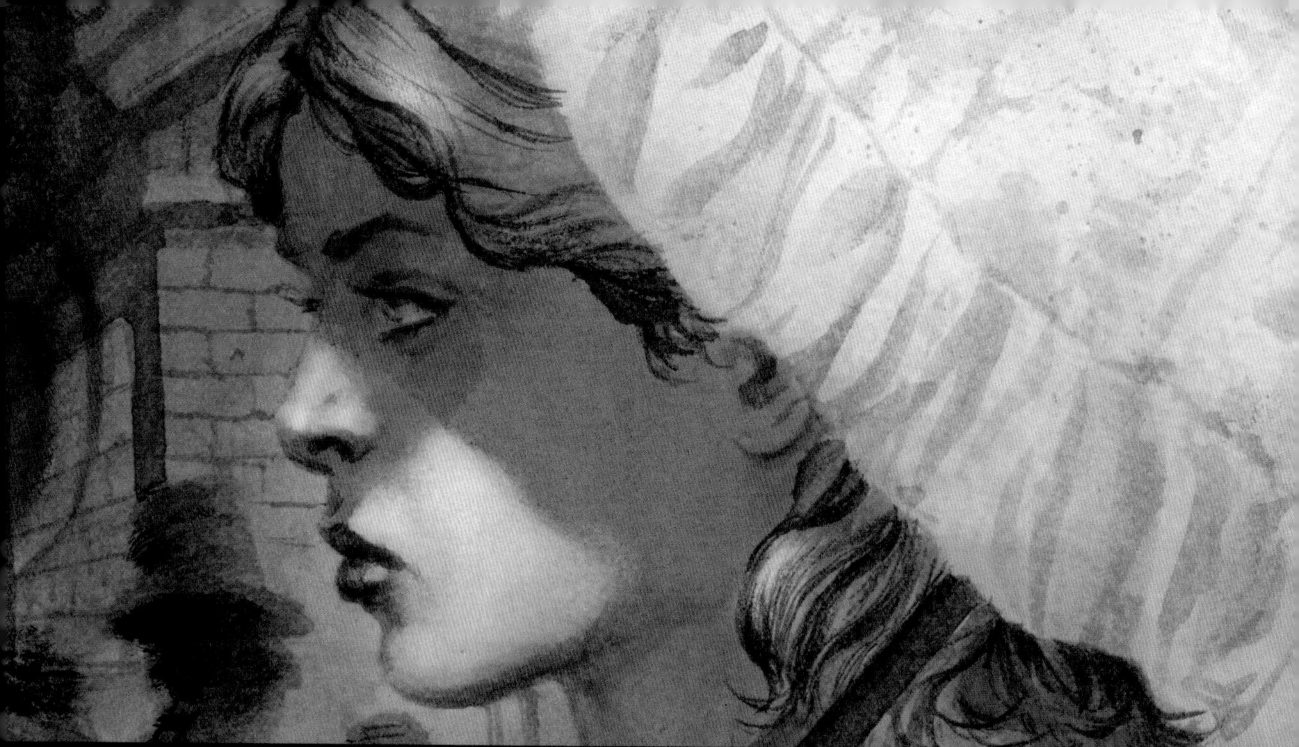

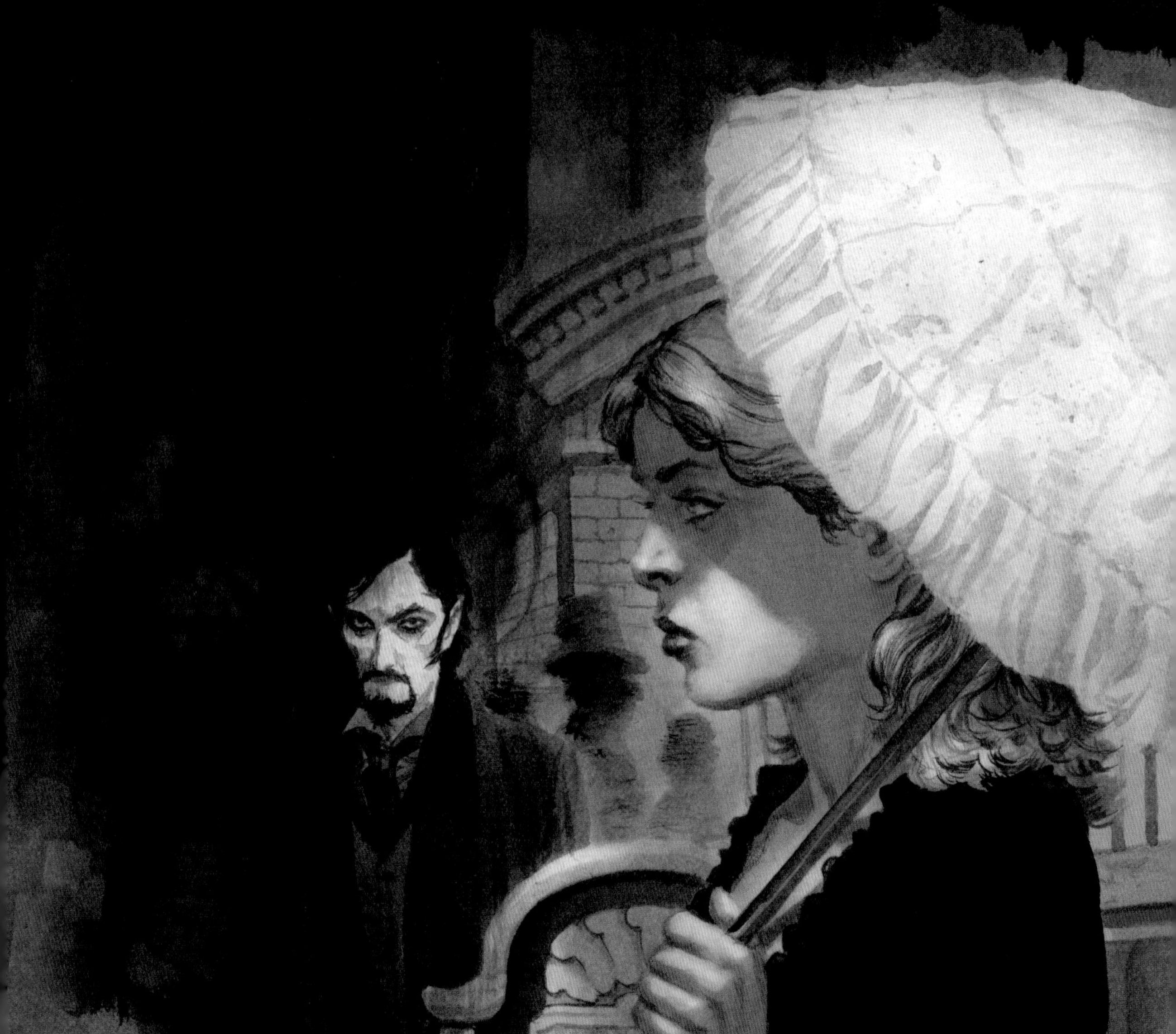

The good townsfolk,

oblivious

in their routines of social etiquette,

would flee in terror if they truly knew

that the Devil himself

hunts among them,

seeking new flesh to conquer.

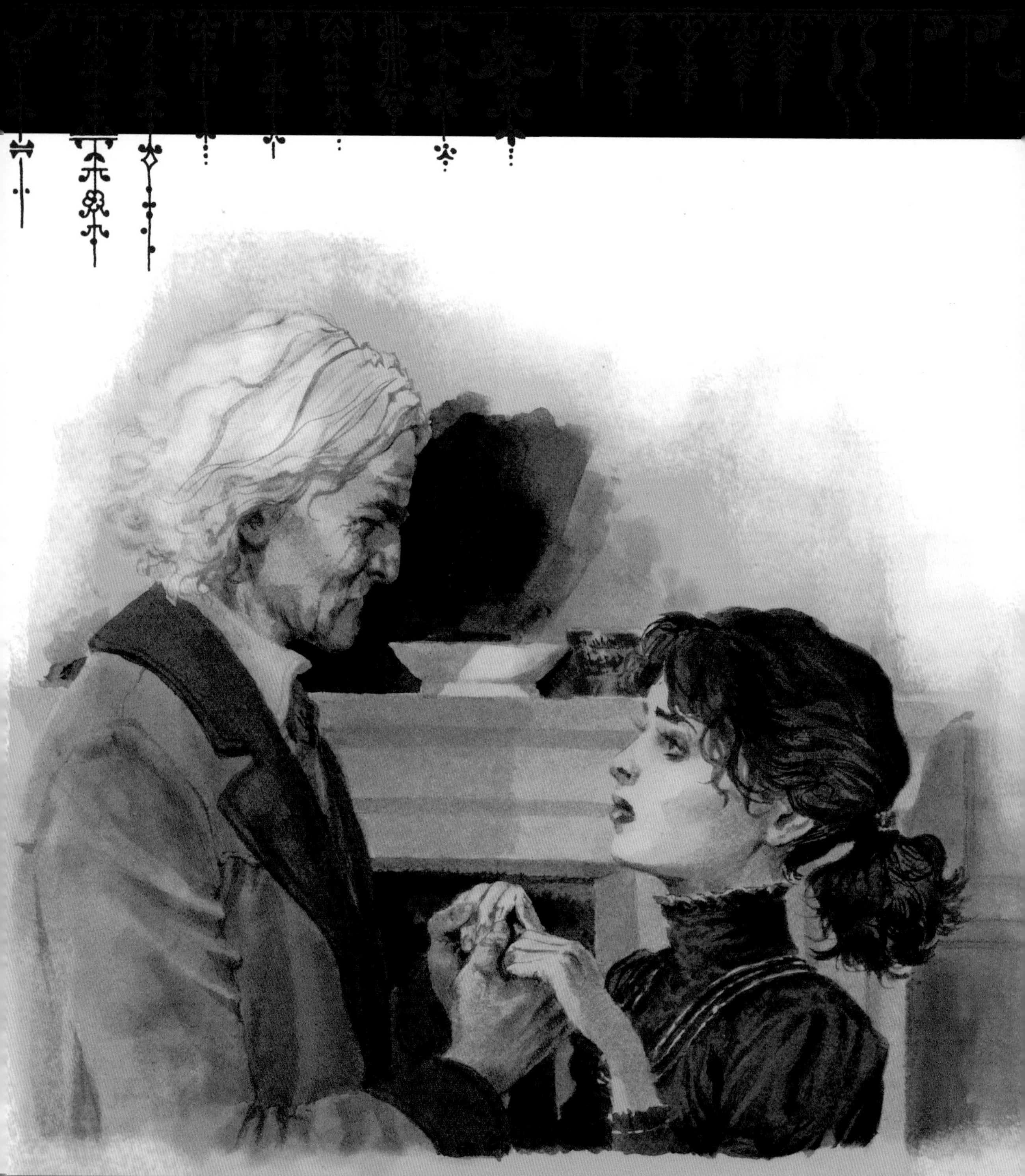

After Professor Van Helsing writes a letter to Mina,
he comes to meet with her about Lucy's "illness"
and what it means for them all.
Mina feels she can trust him and gives him Jonathan's journal,
in hope that somehow,
it can help end this nightmare that engulfs them.

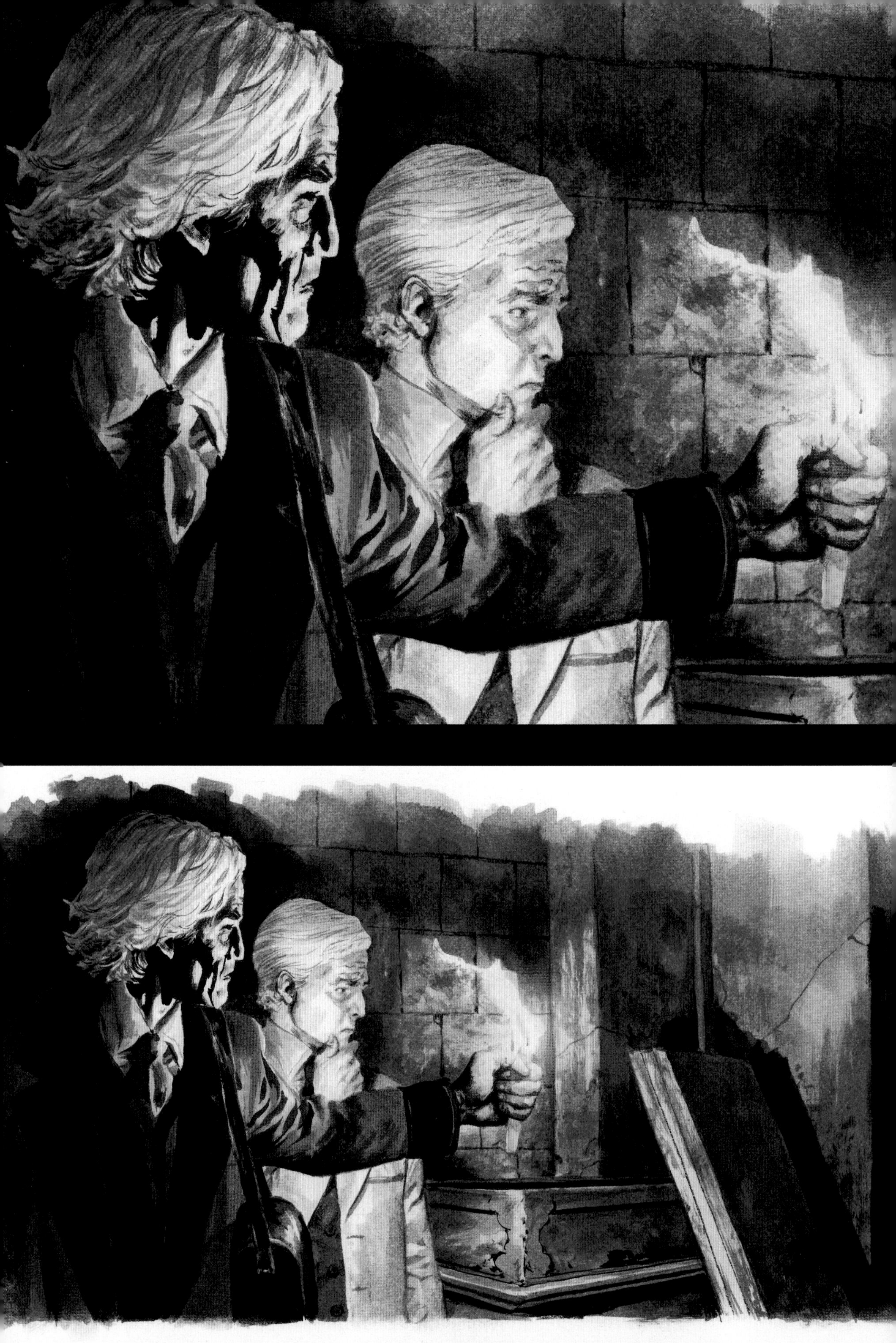

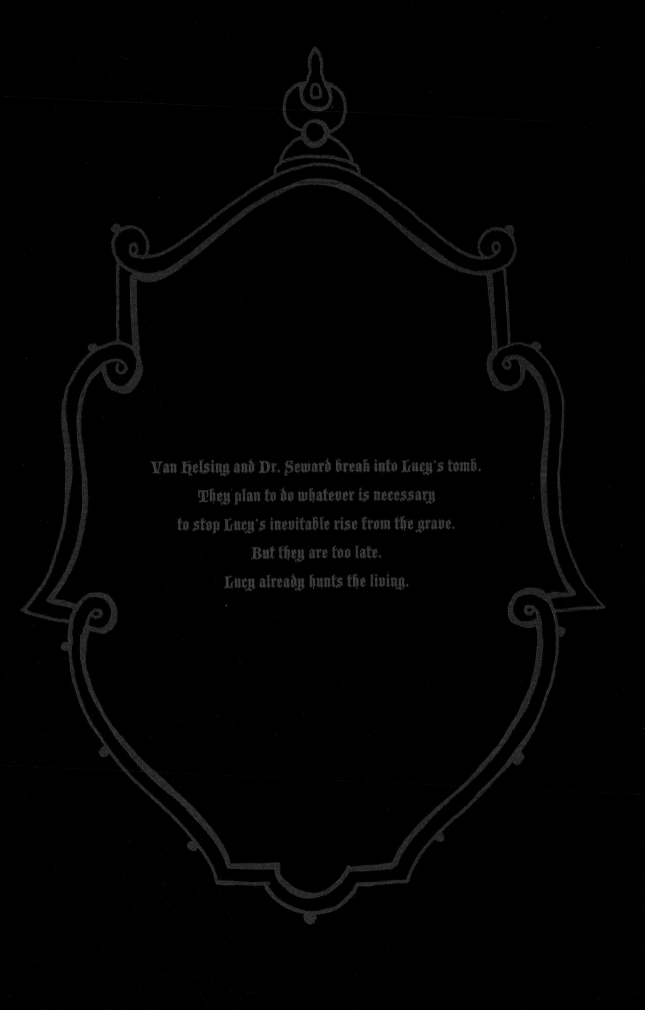

Van Helsing and Dr. Seward break into Lucy's tomb.
They plan to do whatever is necessary
to stop Lucy's inevitable rise from the grave.
But they are too late.
Lucy already hunts the living.

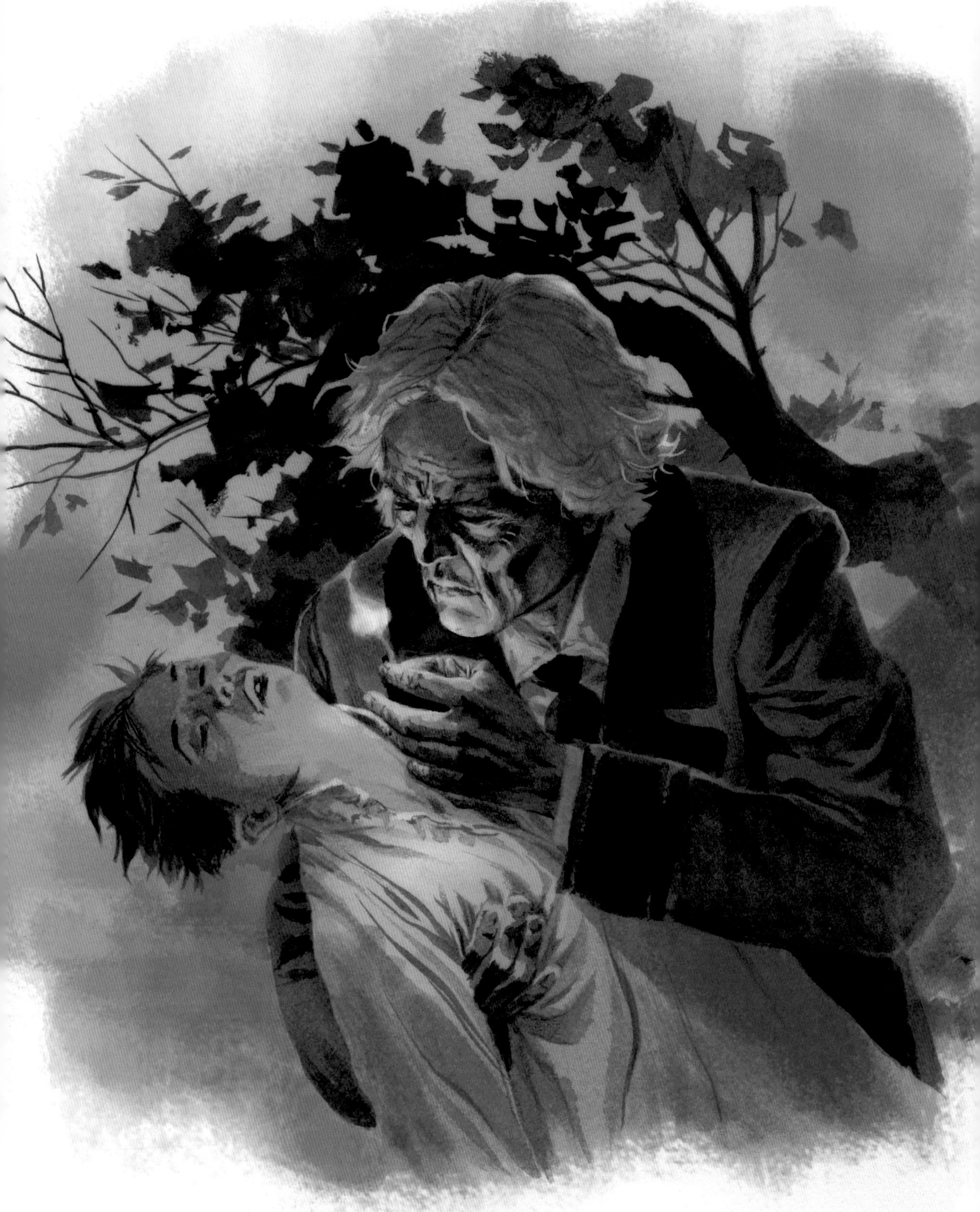

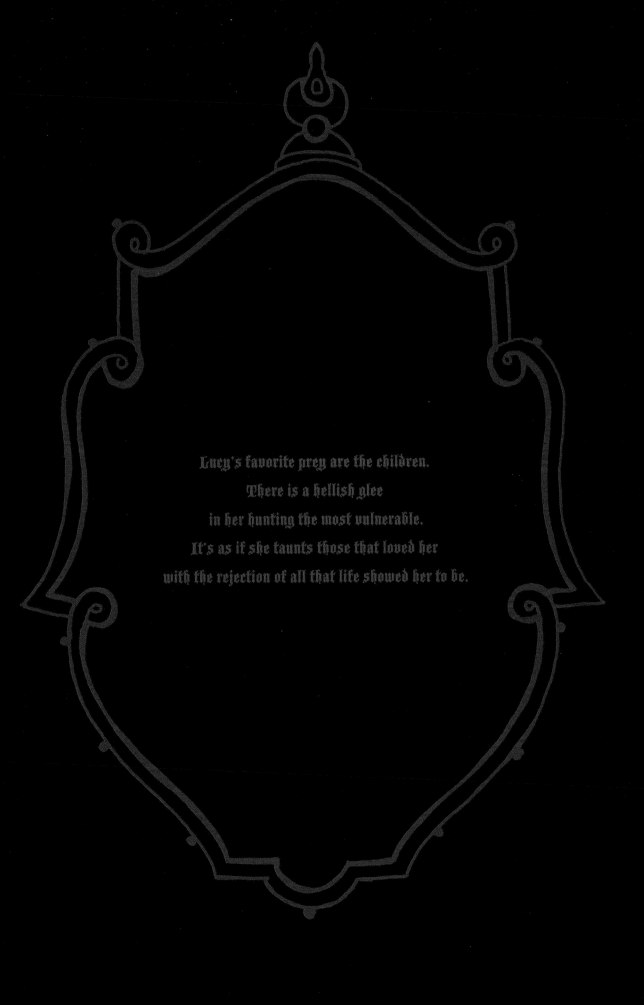

Lucy's favorite prey are the children.
There is a hellish glee
in her hunting the most vulnerable.
It's as if she taunts those that loved her
with the rejection of all that life showed her to be.

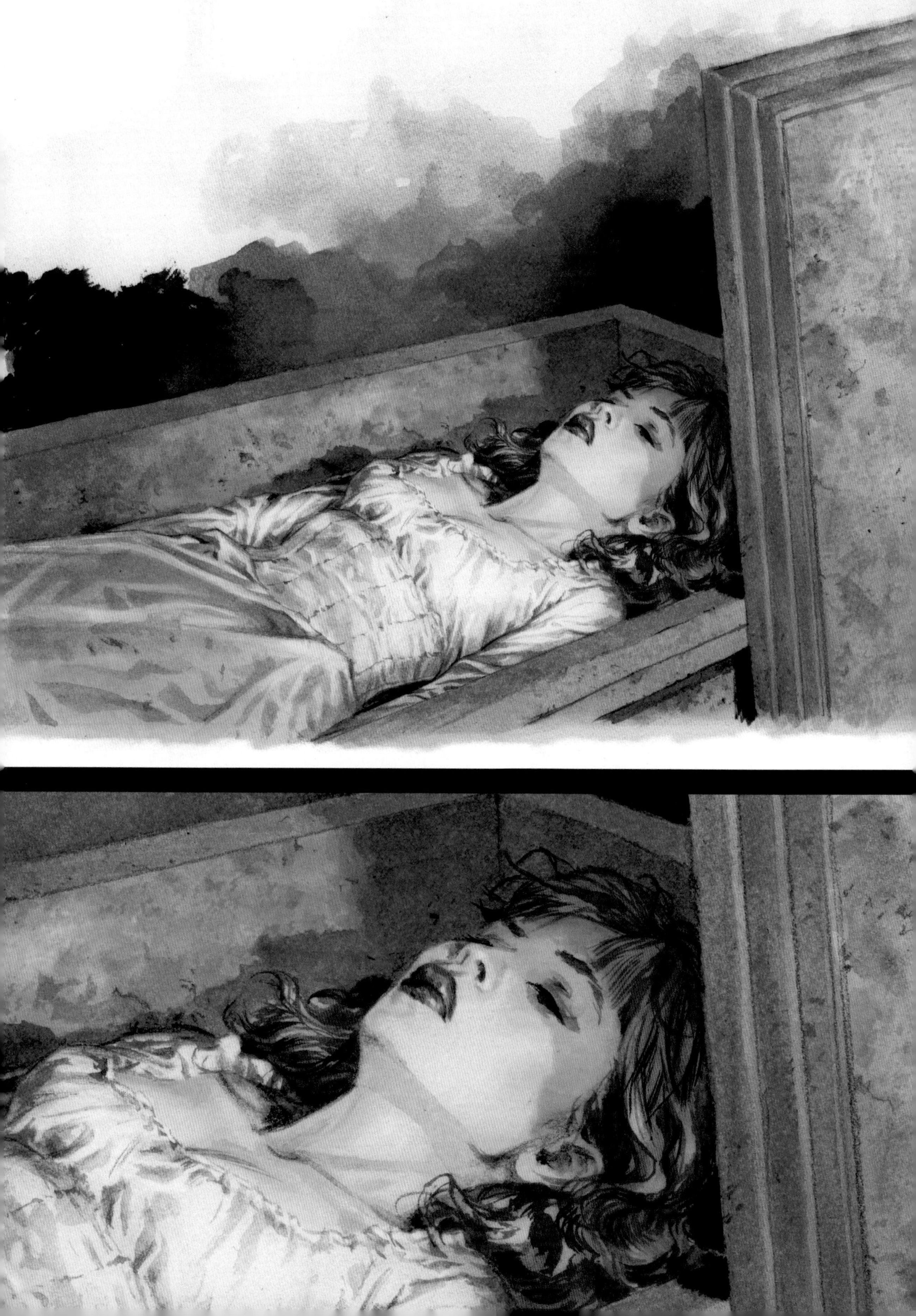

By day,
Lucy does just as her maker has done
for untold years.
She sleeps a dreamless black sleep.
But in the corruption of her soul,
her beauty,
in some strange way,
is more enamoring in death than in life.

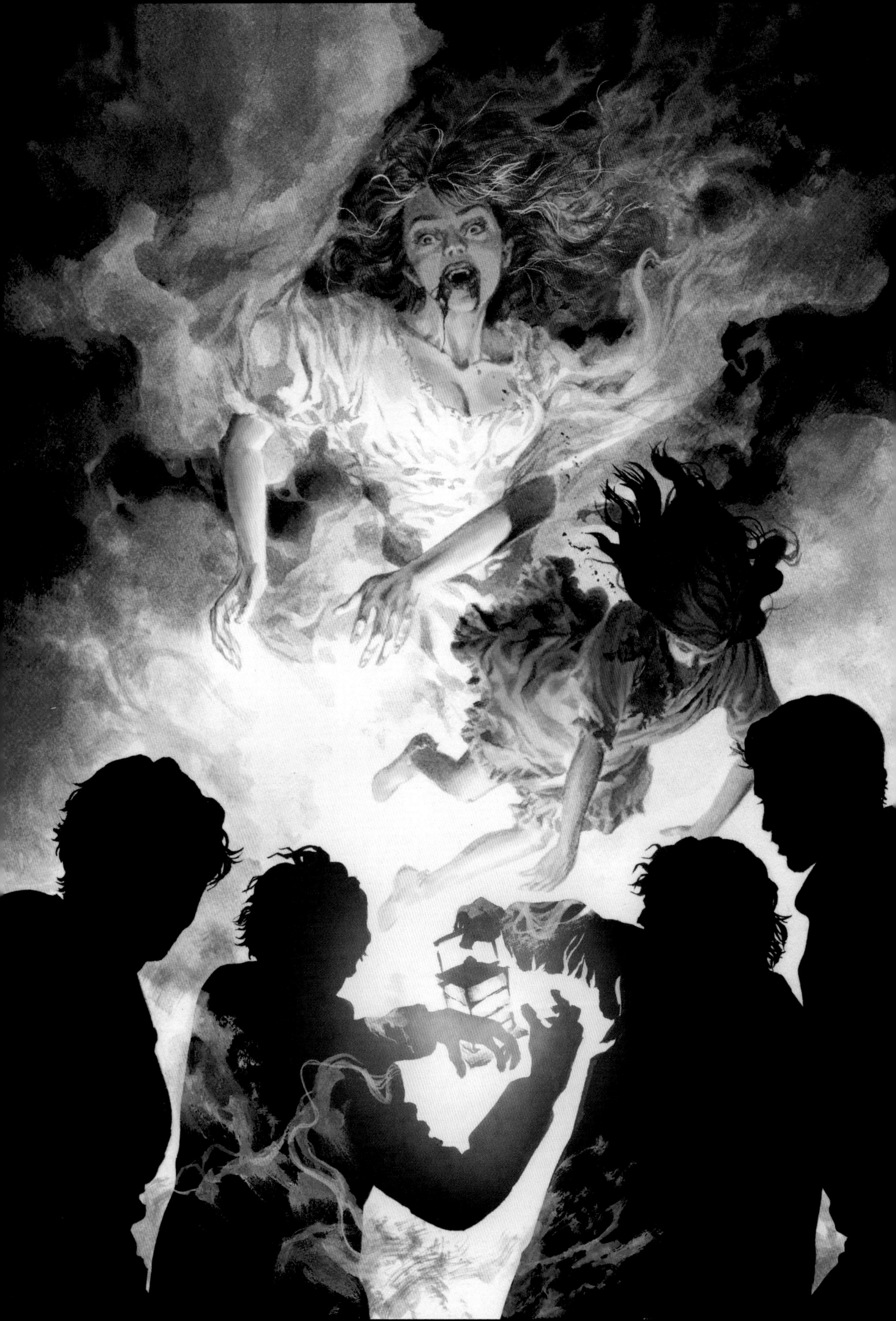

Lucy inflicts horror upon horror among the children.
She feeds upon them,
becoming the ghastly monster
Van Helsing knew she would be.
Now she is the one hunted this night.

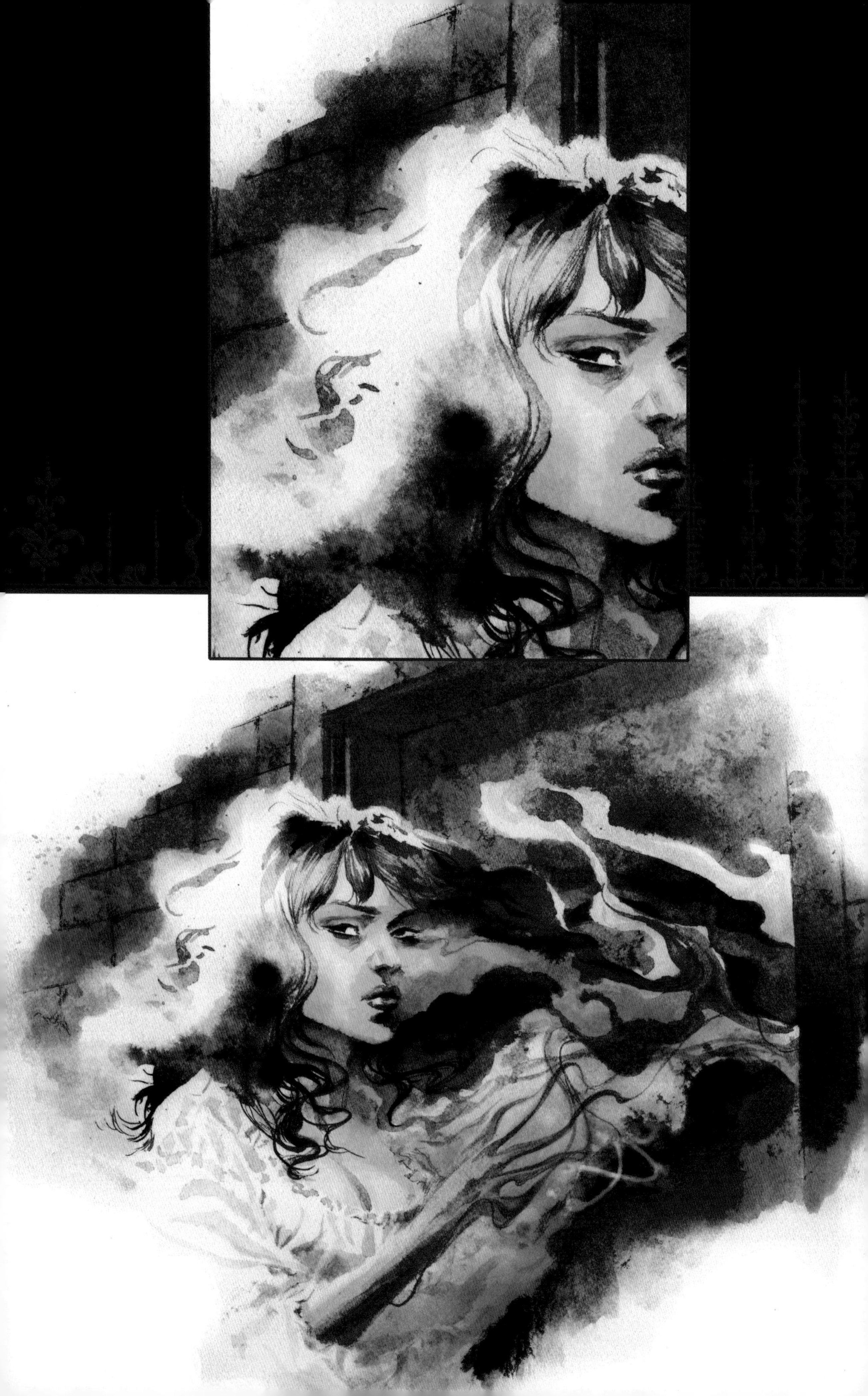

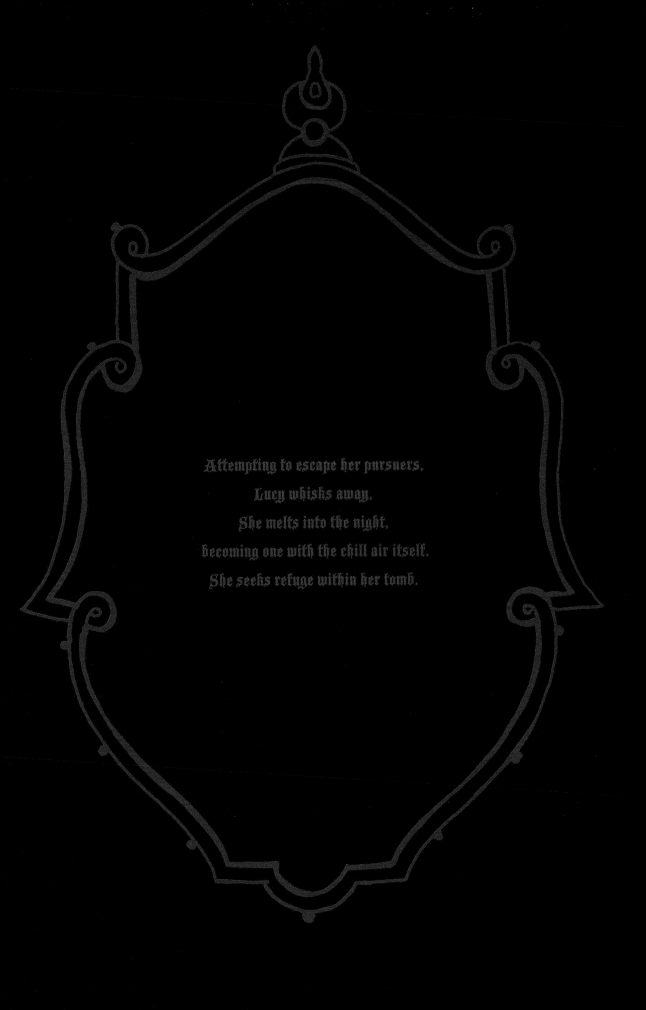

Attempting to escape her pursuers,
Lucy whisks away,
She melts into the night,
becoming one with the chill air itself.
She seeks refuge within her tomb.

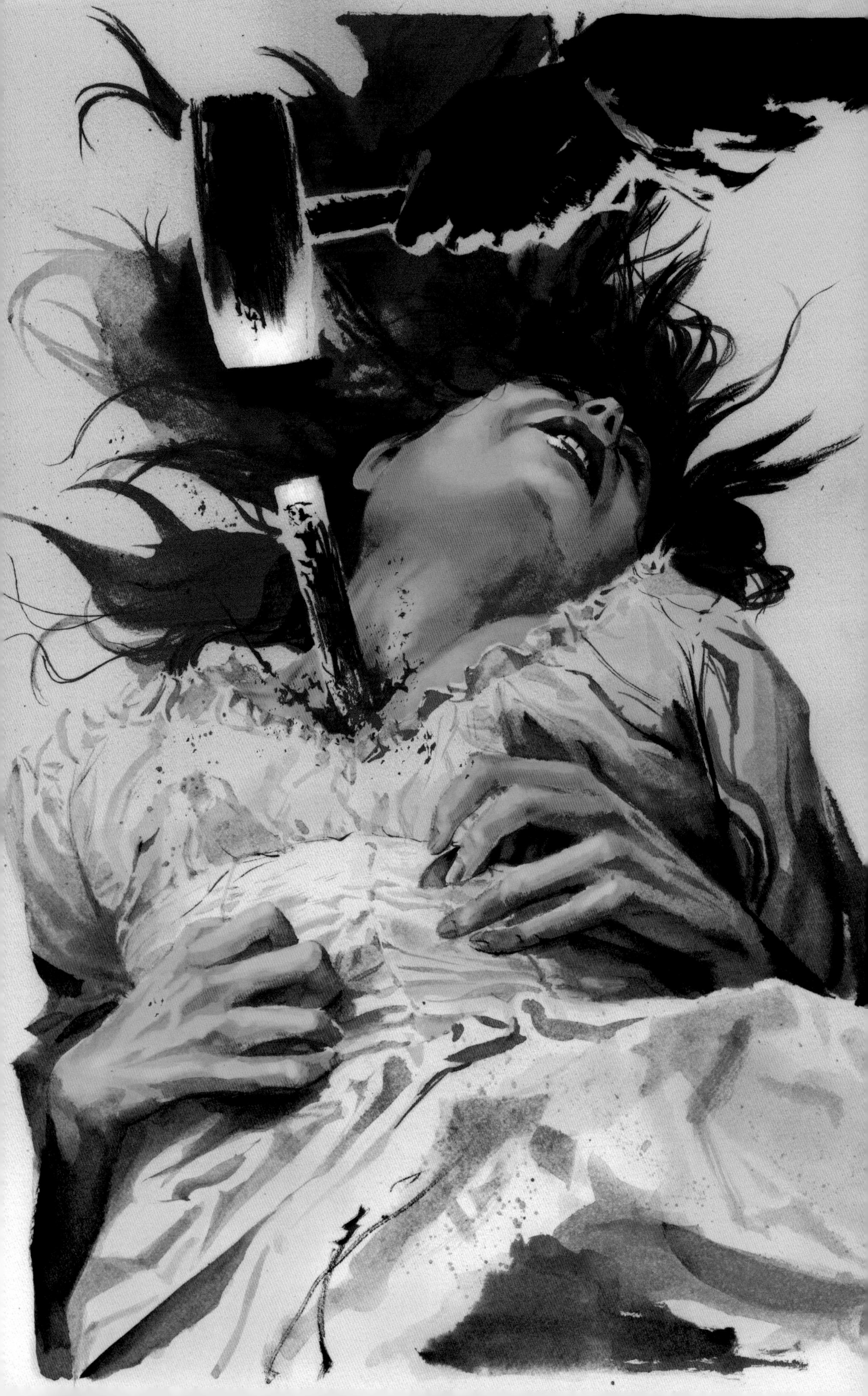

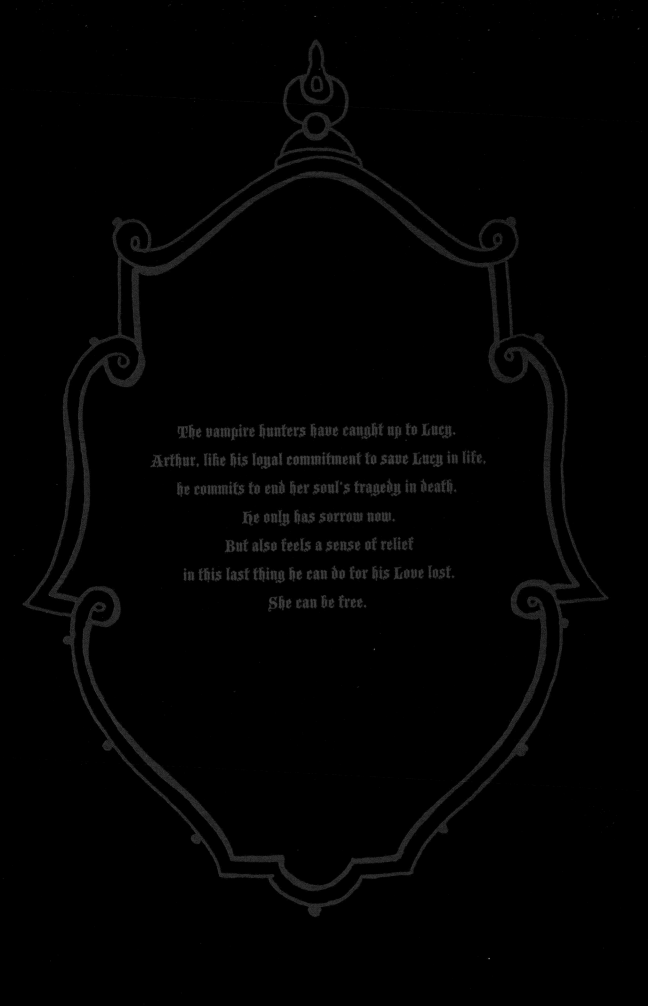

The vampire hunters have caught up to Lucy.

Arthur, like his loyal commitment to save Lucy in life,

he commits to end her soul's tragedy in death.

He only has sorrow now.

But also feels a sense of relief

in this last thing he can do for his Love lost.

She can be free.

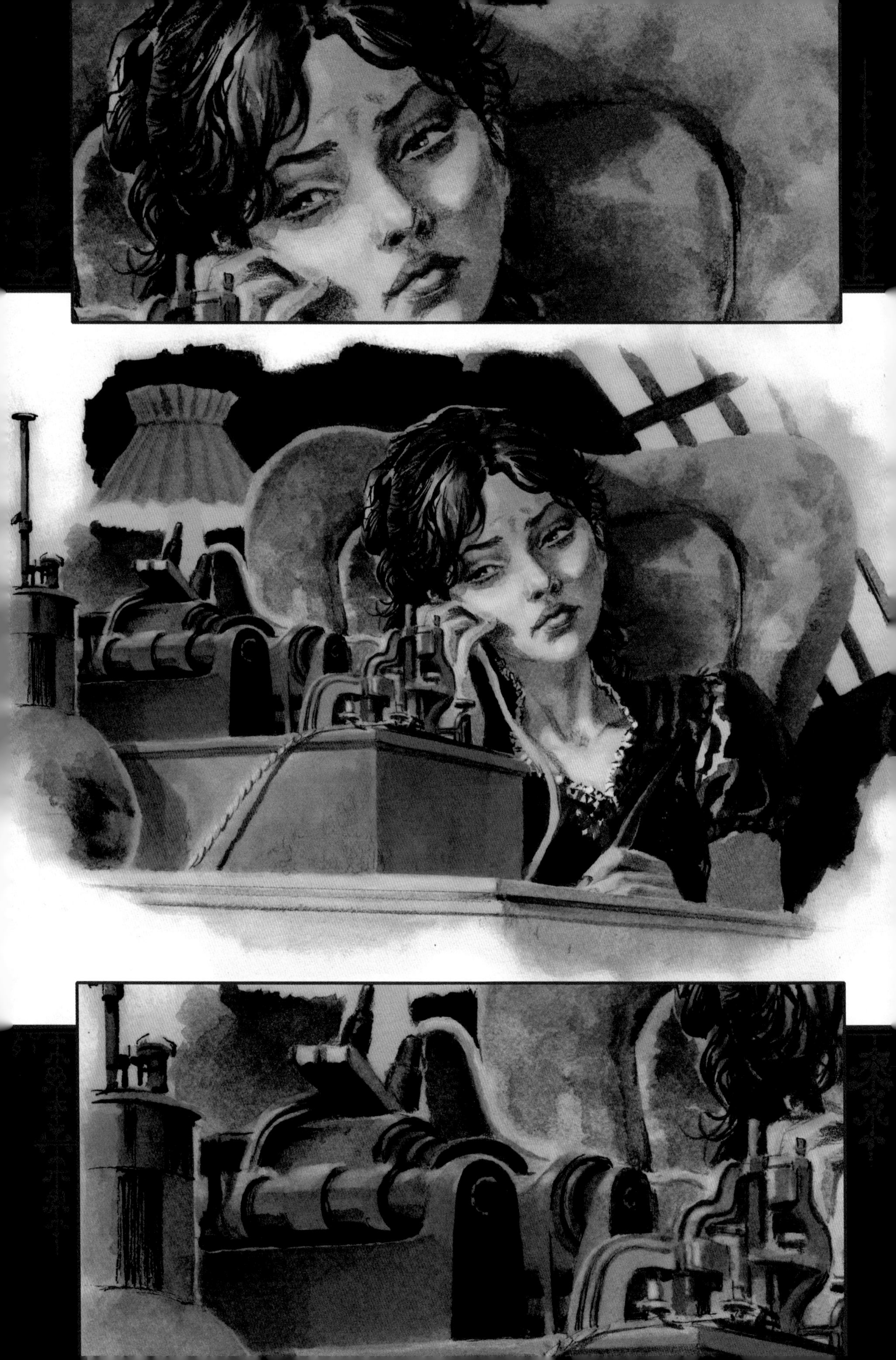

Mina, in pursuit of documenting Dr. Seward's clinical findings,

transcribes his recordings into a diary.

But in truth,

she wishes to discover

what has happened to her beloved Lucy.

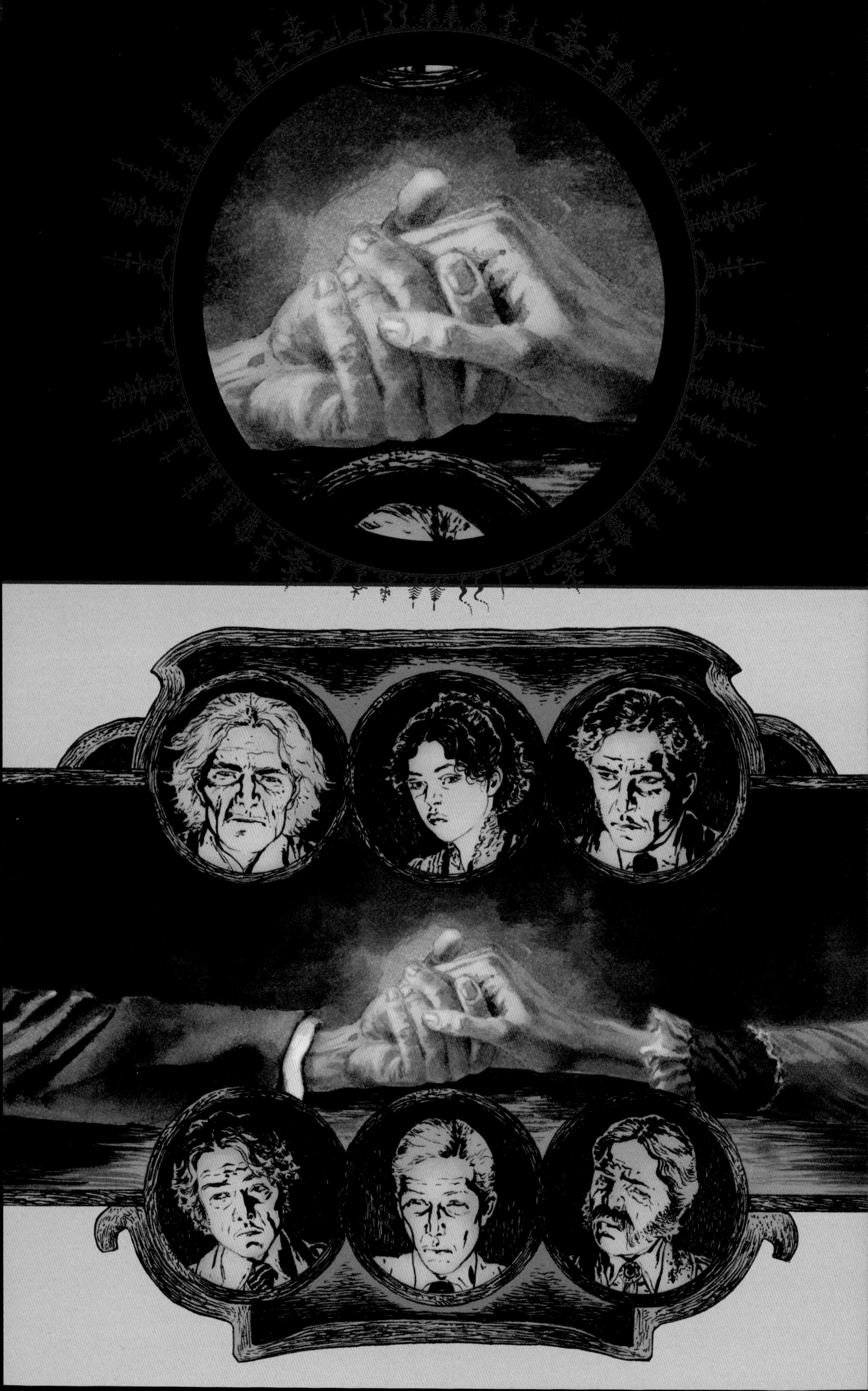

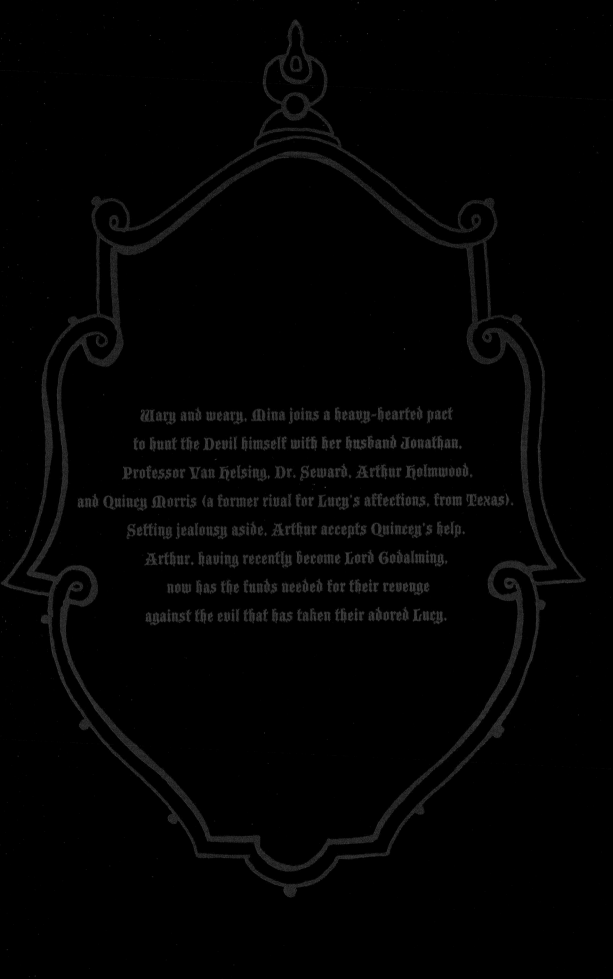

Wary and weary, Mina joins a heavy-hearted pact
to hunt the Devil himself with her husband Jonathan,
Professor Van Helsing, Dr. Seward, Arthur Holmwood,
and Quincy Morris (a former rival for Lucy's affections, from Texas).
Setting jealousy aside, Arthur accepts Quincey's help.
Arthur, having recently become Lord Godalming,
now has the funds needed for their revenge
against the evil that has taken their adored Lucy.

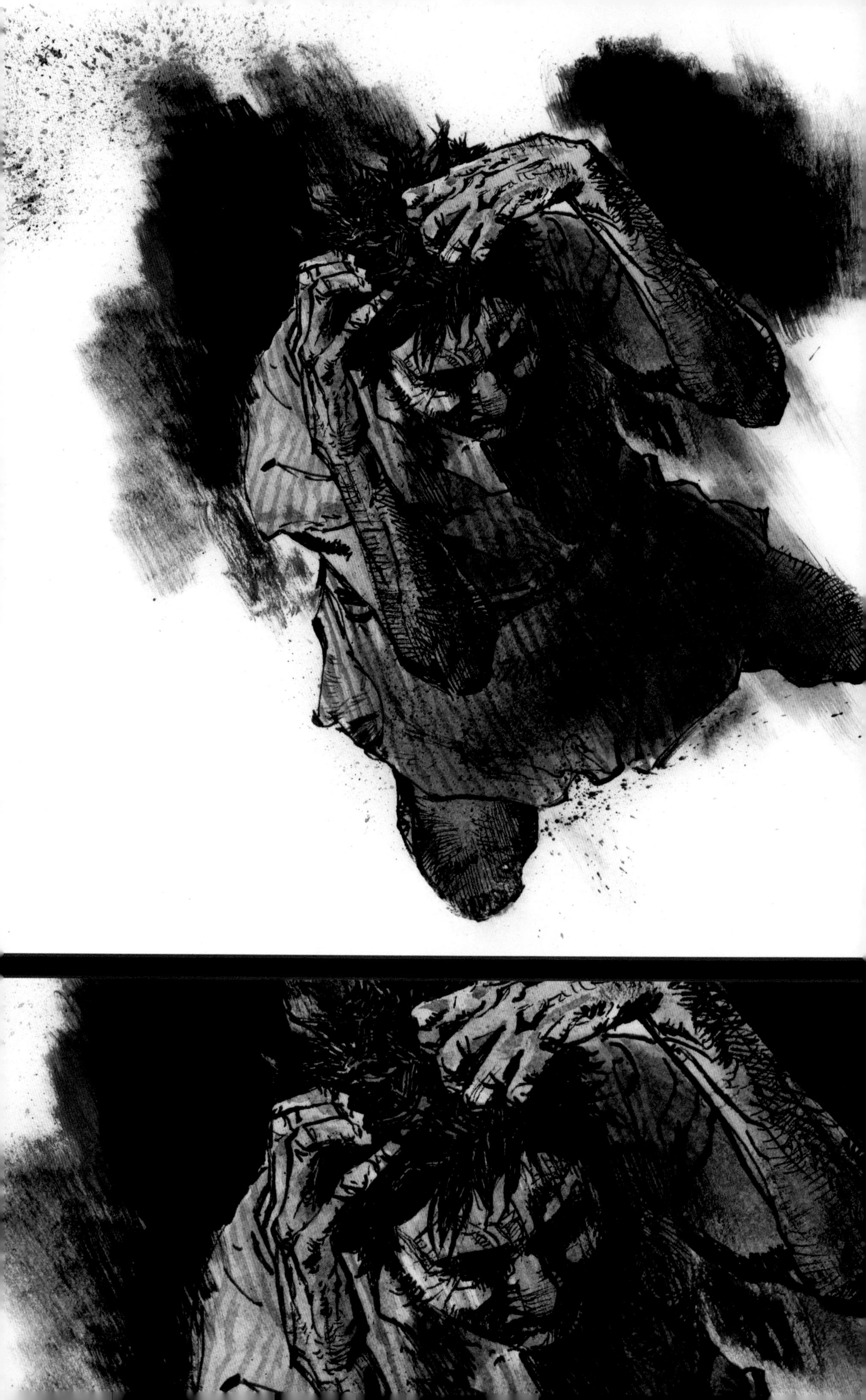

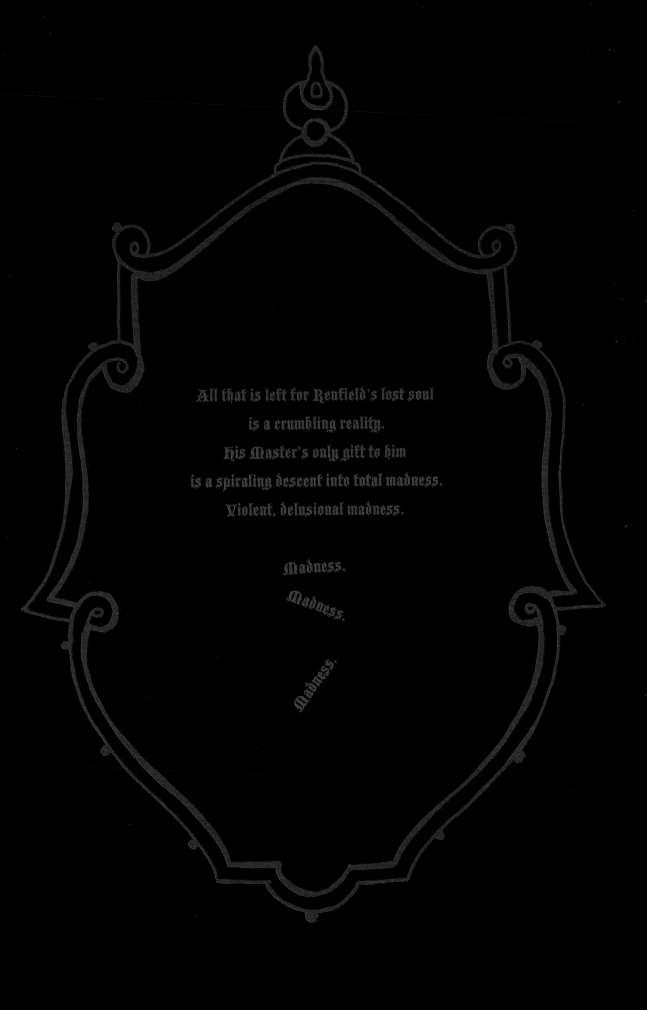

All that is left for Renfield's lost soul
is a crumbling reality.
His Master's only gift to him
is a spiraling descent into total madness.
Violent, delusional madness.

Madness.

Madness.

Madness.

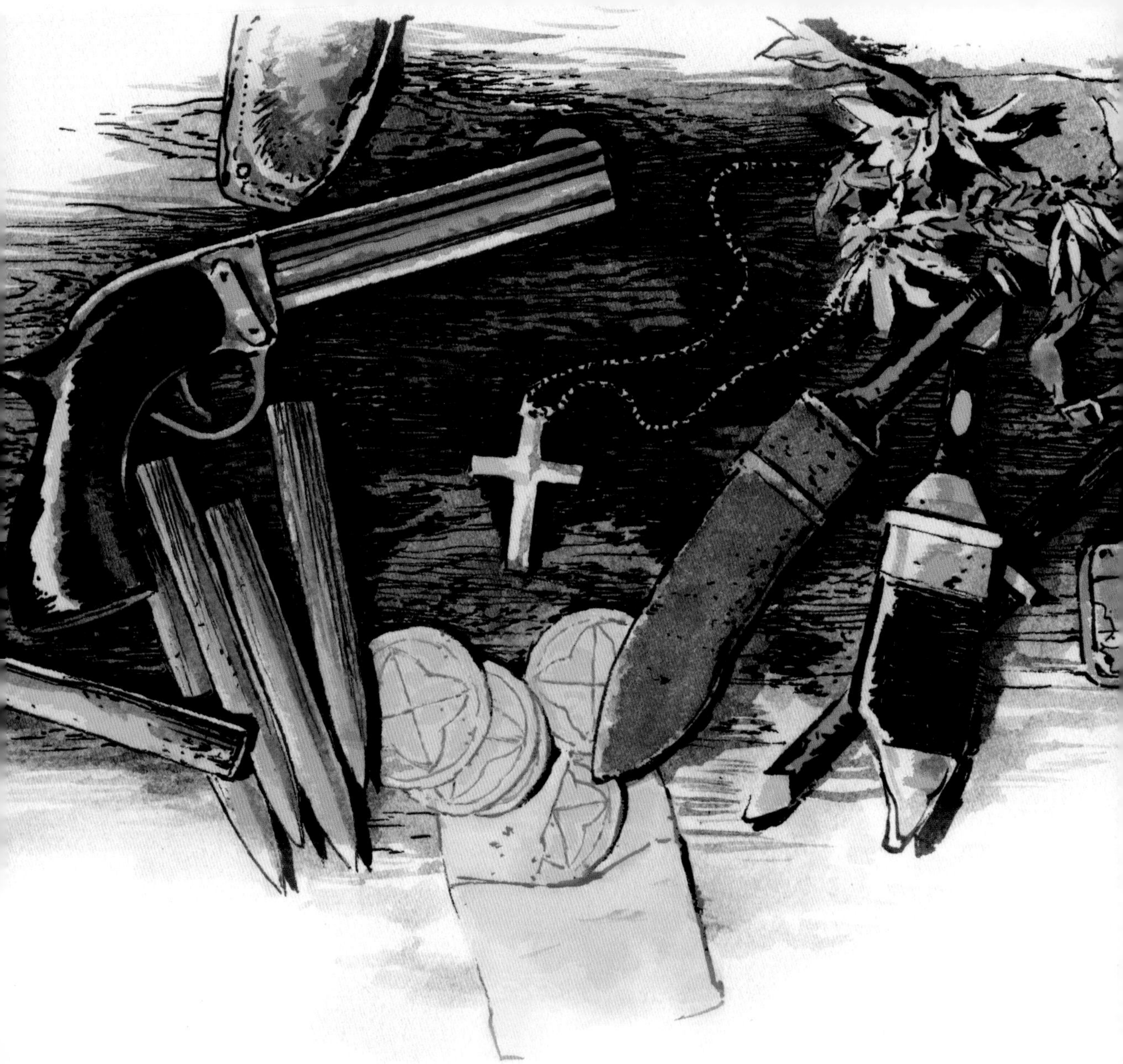

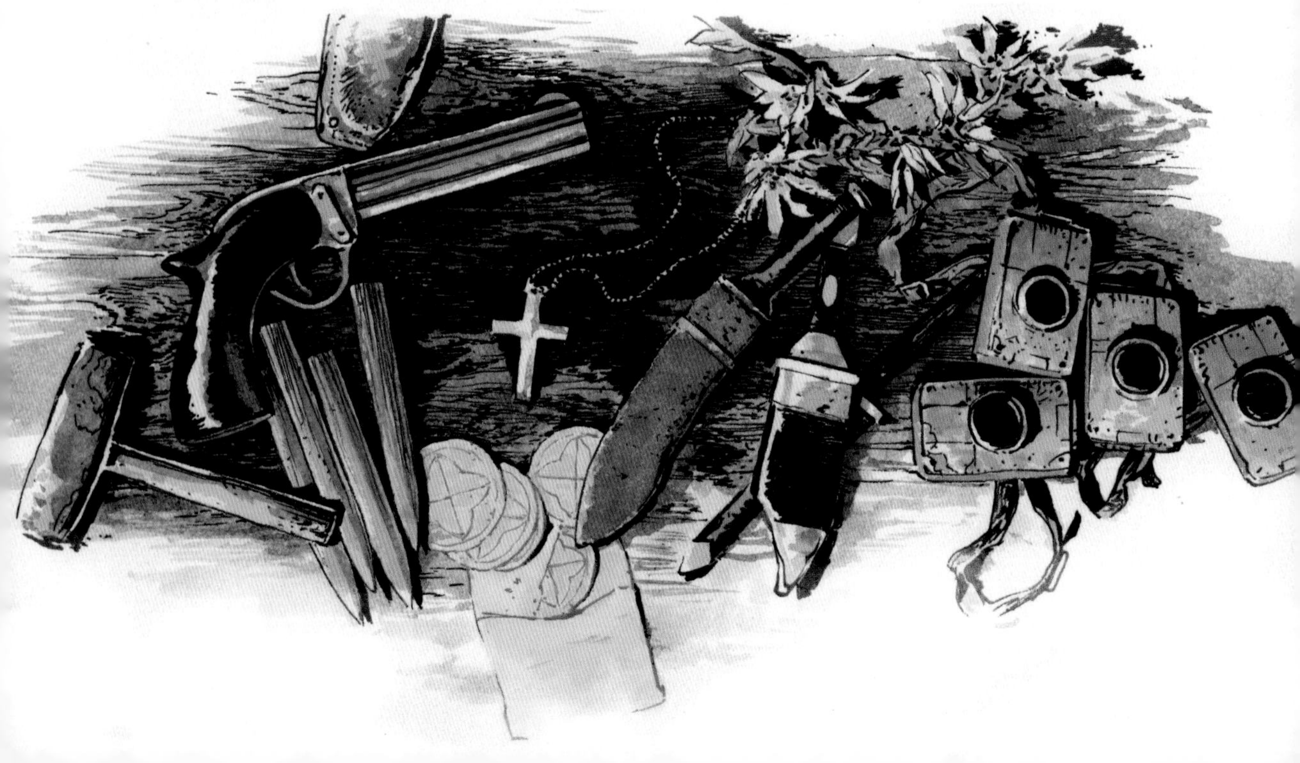

The vampire hunters gather,
reviewing tools and weapons they need
to hunt down and destroy the Beast:
pistols and blades, electric lamps,
hammers and wooden stakes, garlic flowers,
and objects blessed with the Holy Power of Heaven.
But the most potent weapon they share
is their grim resolve in the face of death.

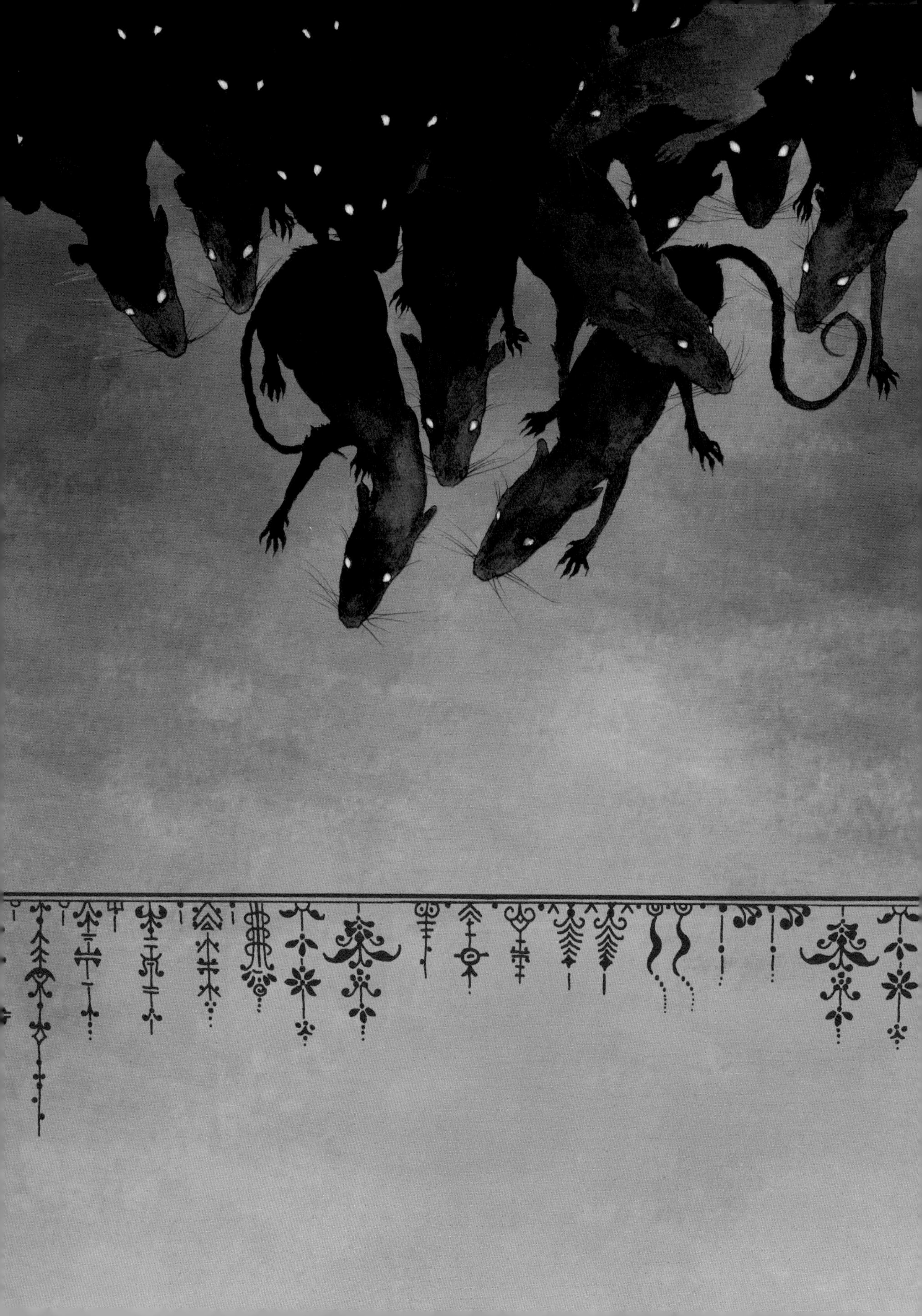

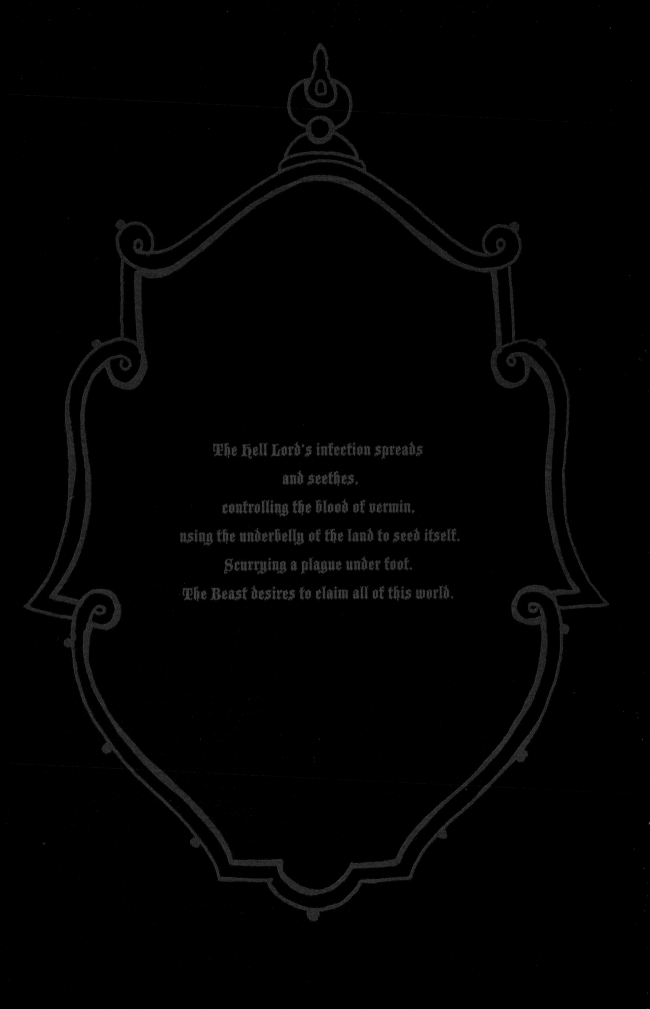

The Hell Lord's infection spreads
and seethes,
controlling the blood of vermin,
using the underbelly of the land to seed itself.
Scurrying a plague under foot.
The Beast desires to claim all of this world.

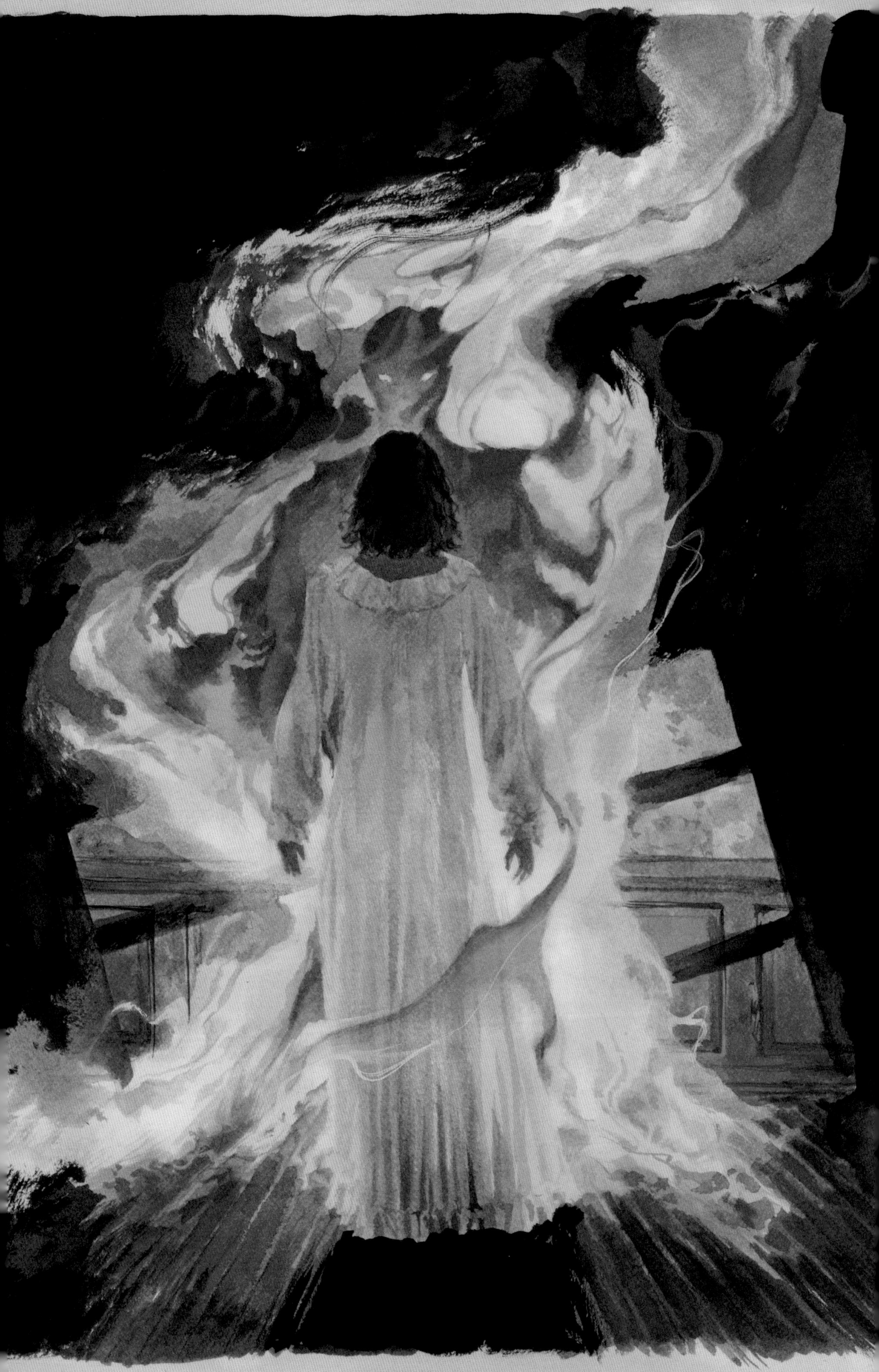

A putrid mist
oozes upward
through the cracks in floorboards.
The air chokes.
It thickens.
It mesmerizes
with a poisonous, transfixed, inhuman gaze.
The Beast has come for Mina.

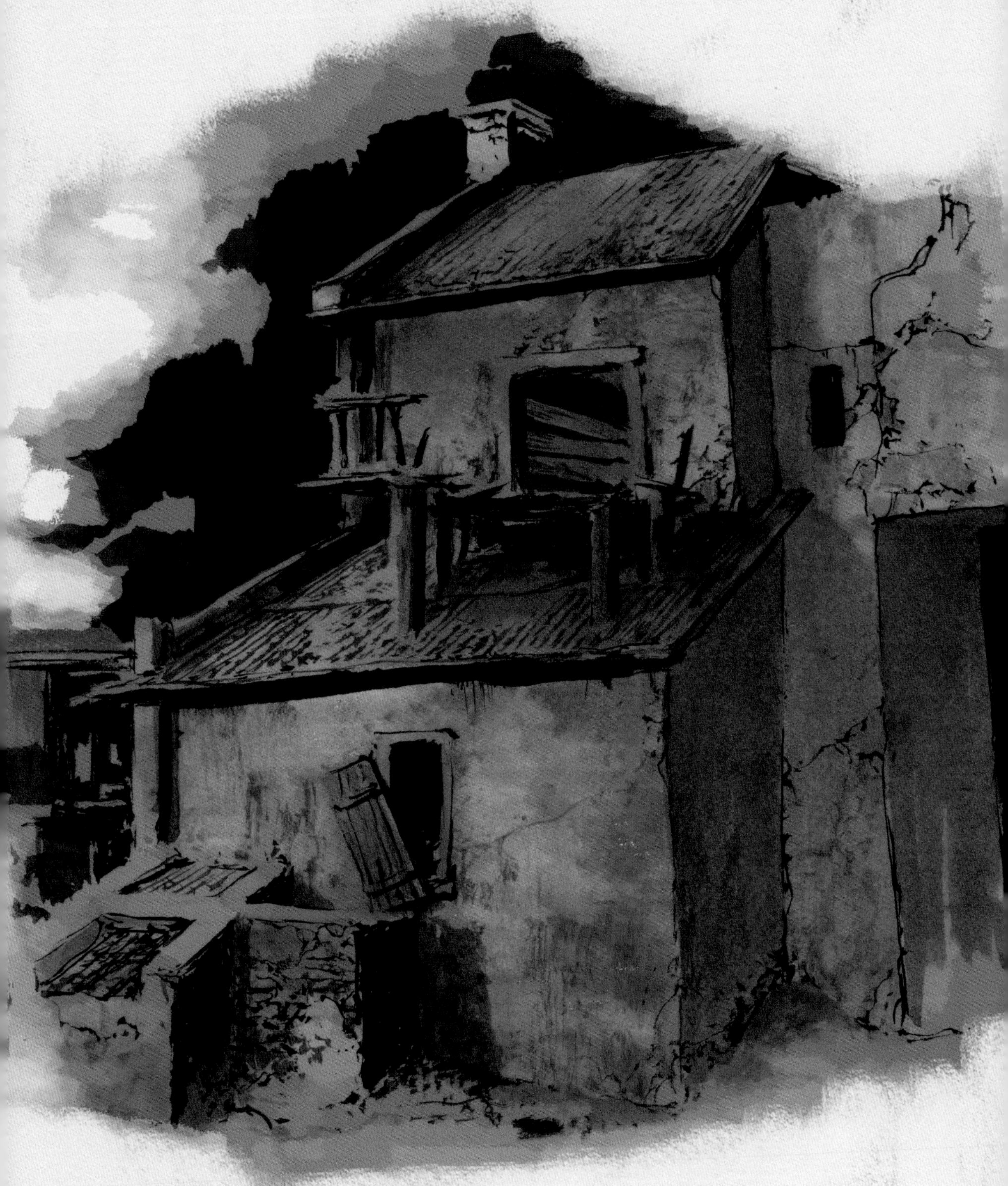

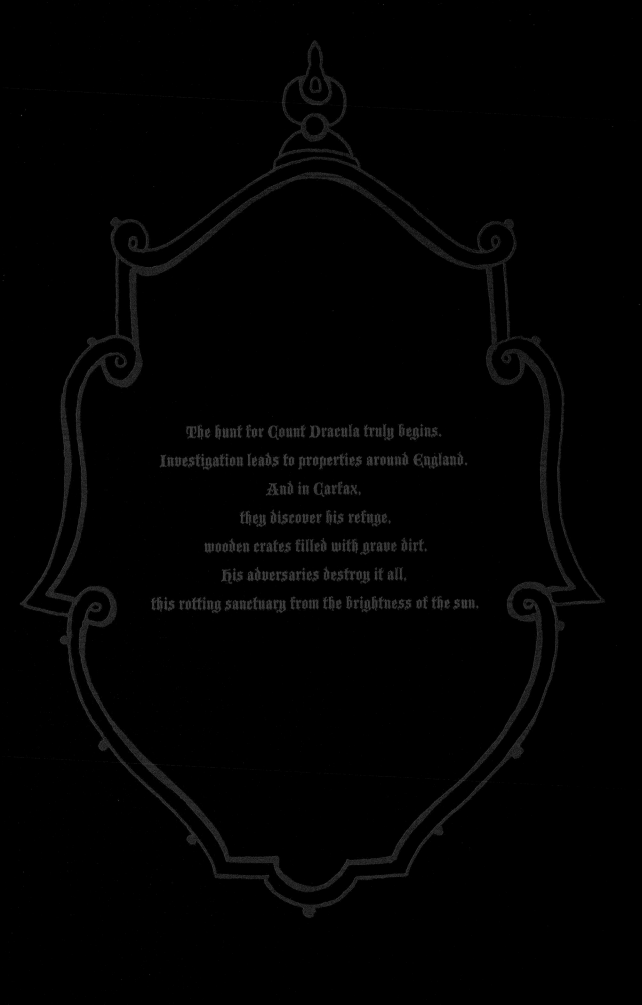

The hunt for Count Dracula truly begins.
Investigation leads to properties around England.
And in Carfax,
they discover his refuge,
wooden crates filled with grave dirt.
His adversaries destroy it all,
this rotting sanctuary from the brightness of the sun.

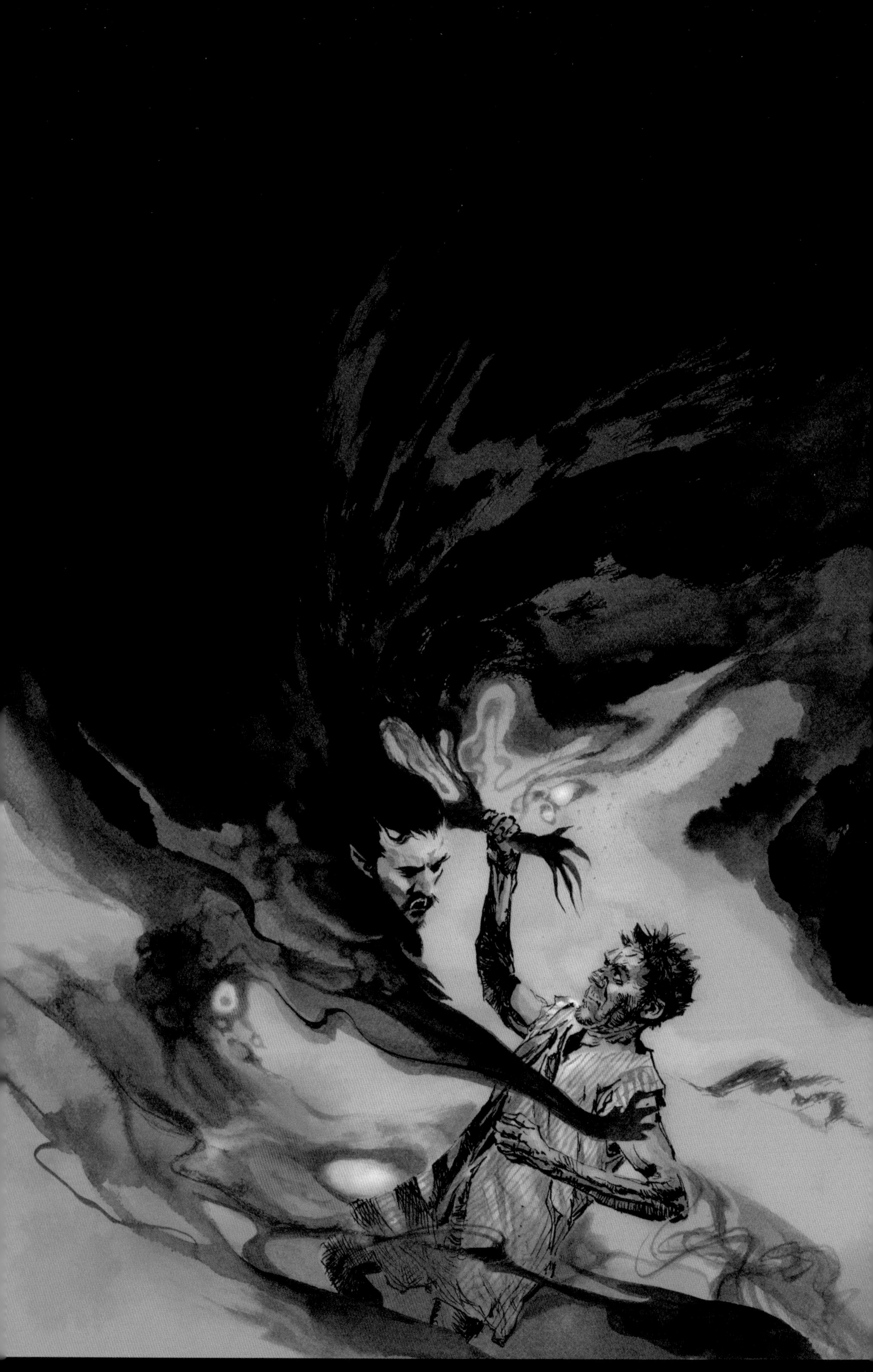

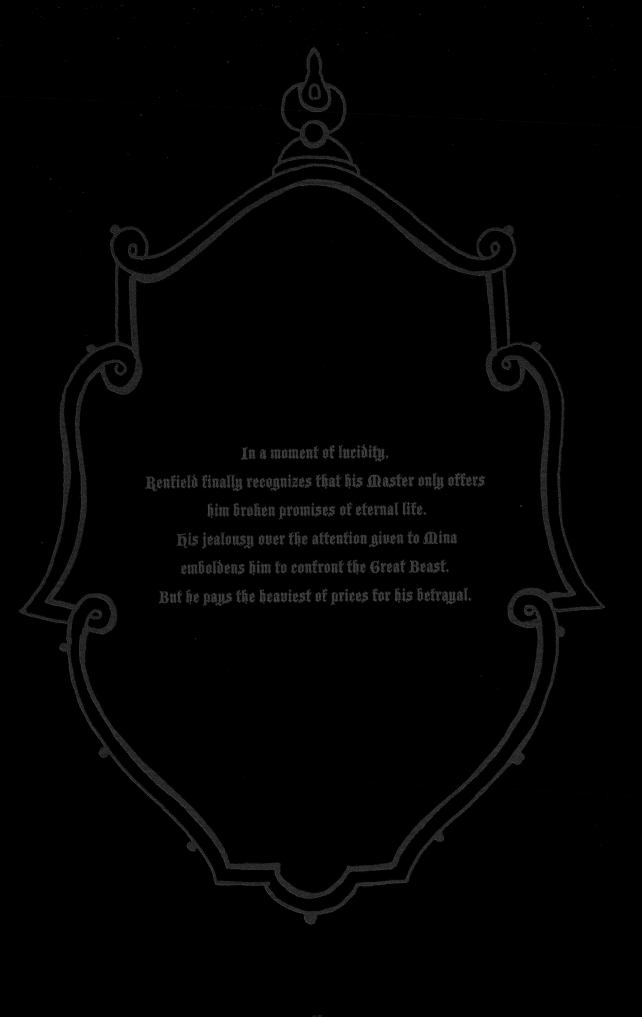

In a moment of lucidity,
Renfield finally recognizes that his Master only offers
him broken promises of eternal life.
His jealousy over the attention given to Mina
emboldens him to confront the Great Beast.
But he pays the heaviest of prices for his betrayal.

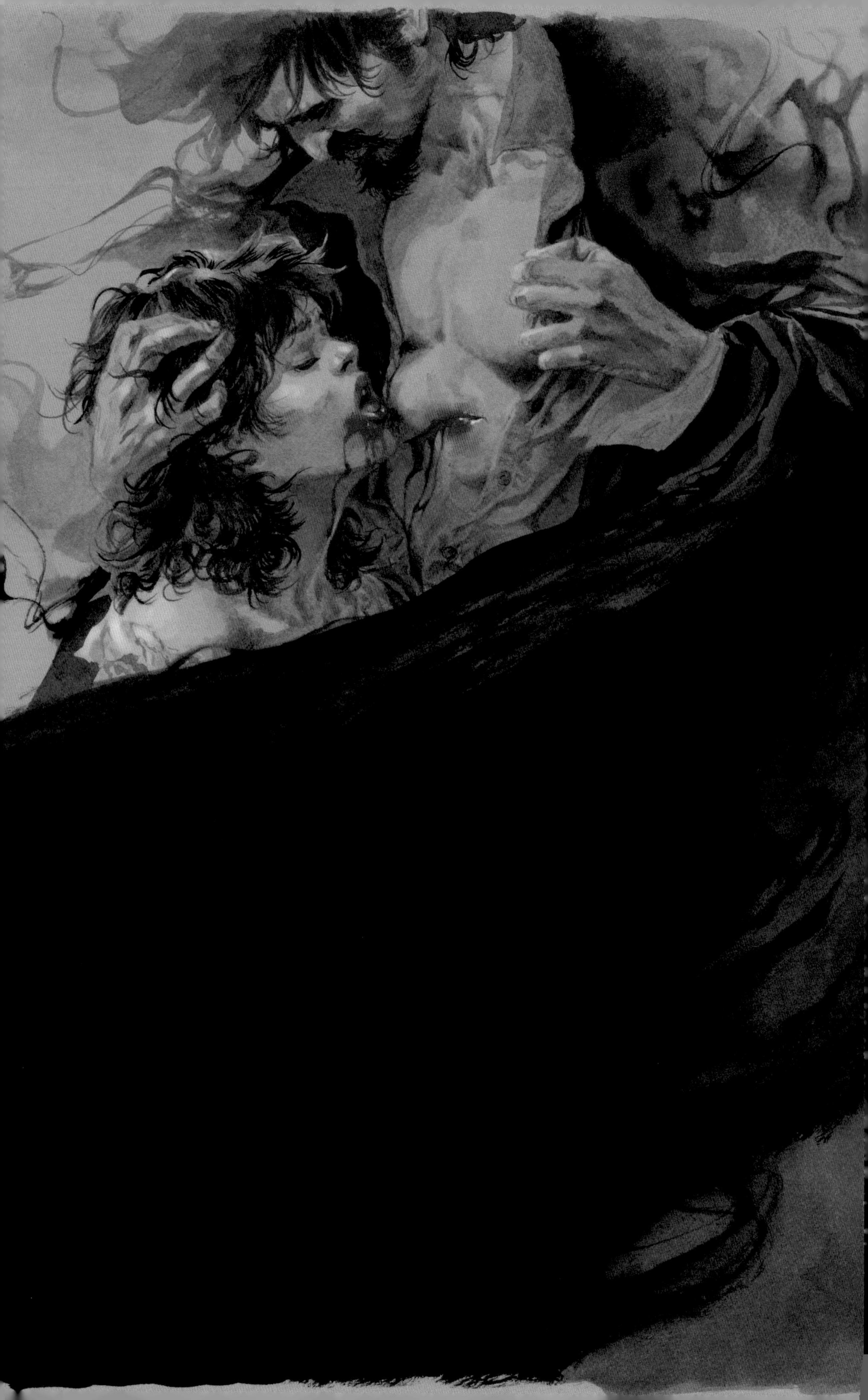

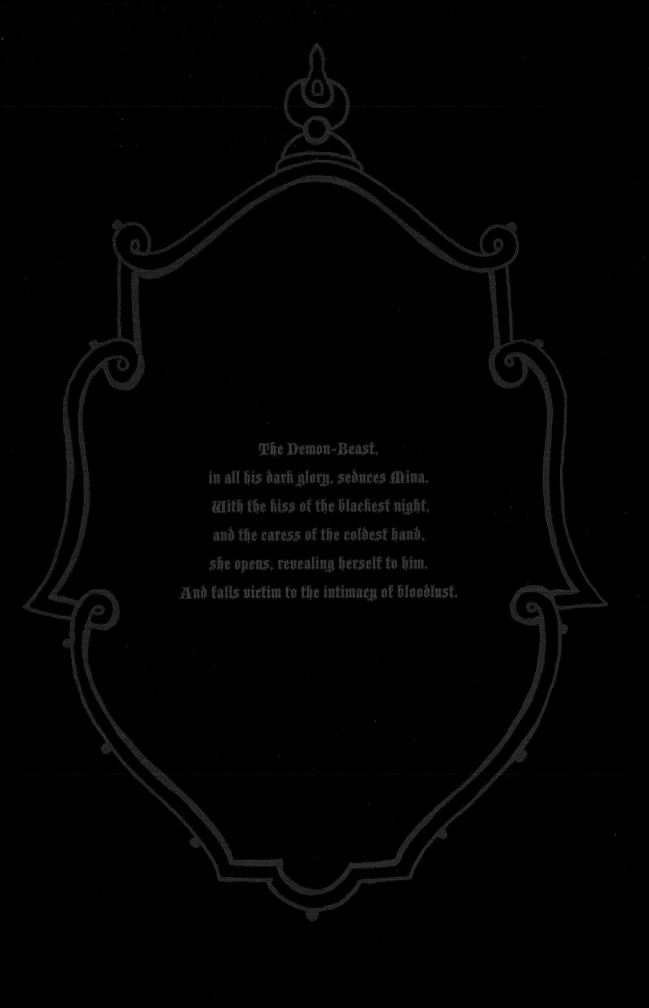

The Demon-Beast,

in all his dark glory, seduces Mina.

With the kiss of the blackest night,

and the caress of the coldest hand,

she opens, revealing herself to him.

And falls victim to the intimacy of bloodlust.

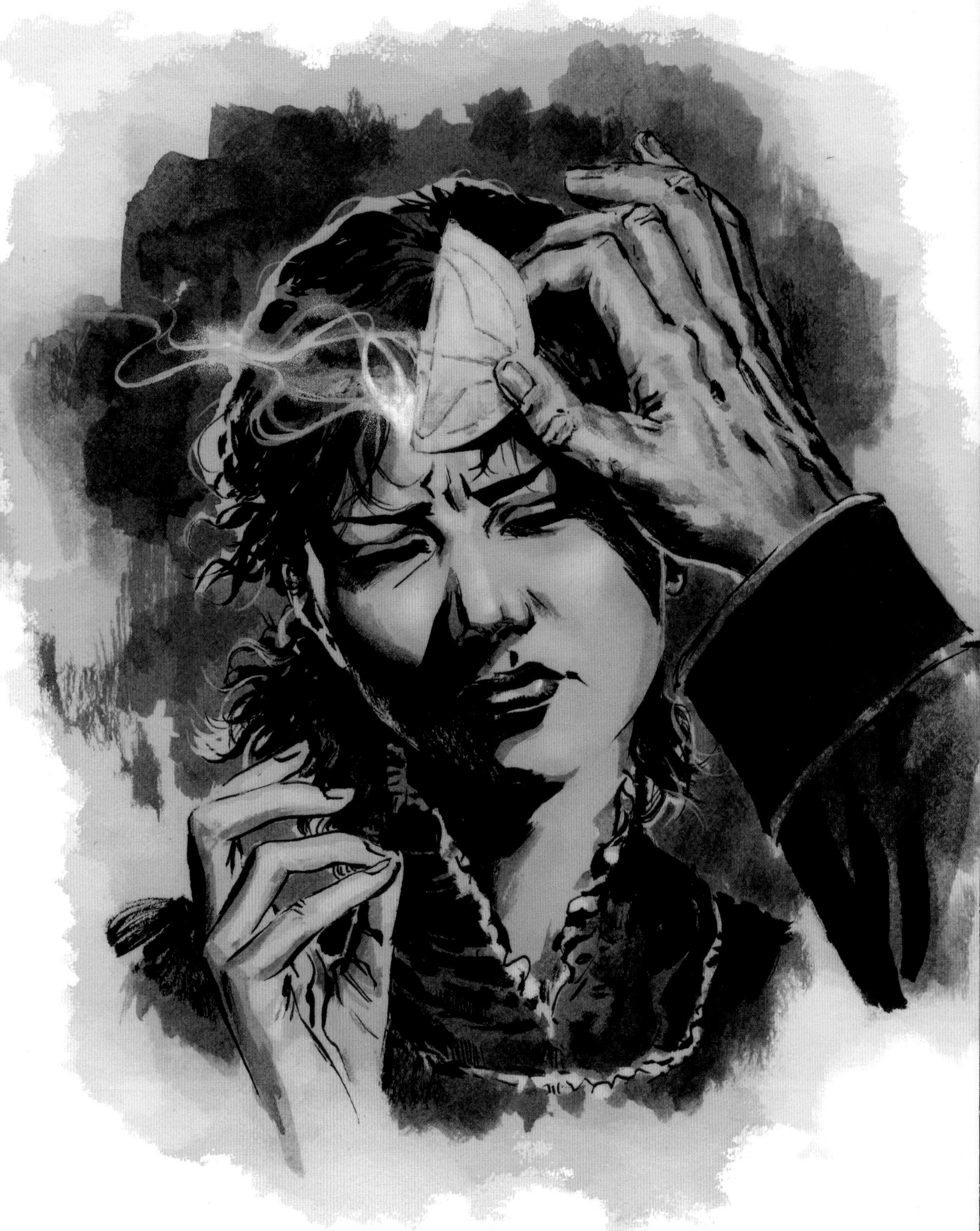

In an attempt to protect Mina's darkening soul,
Van Helsing crumbles Holy Wafer against her forehead.
It marks.
It burns.
The hunters all know the only path
to her true salvation
demands the complete destruction
of the alien creature that lays grasp upon her.

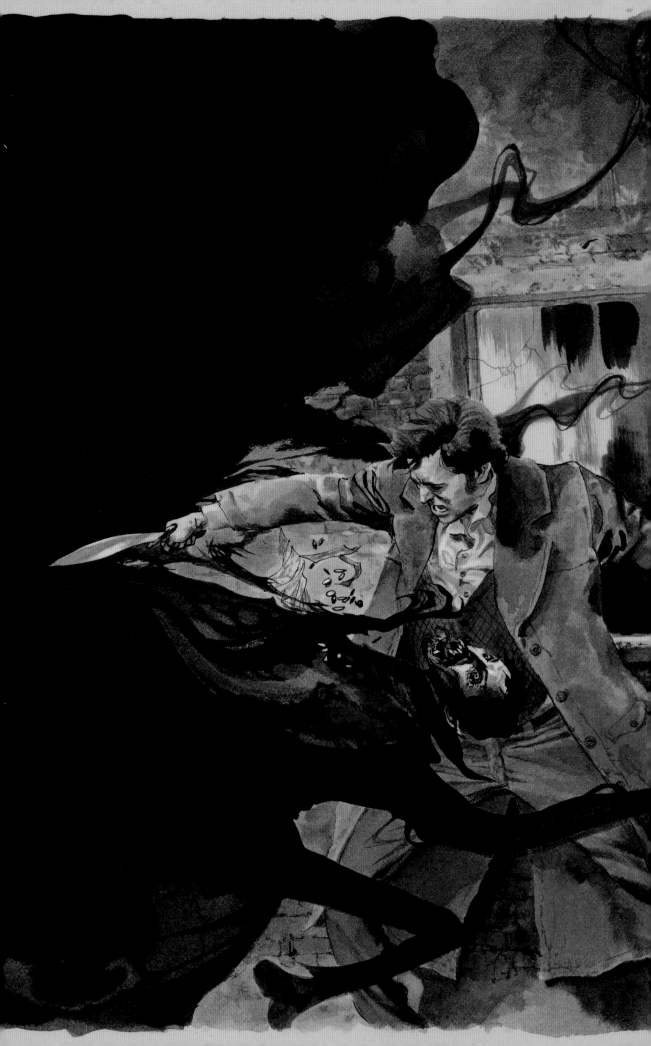

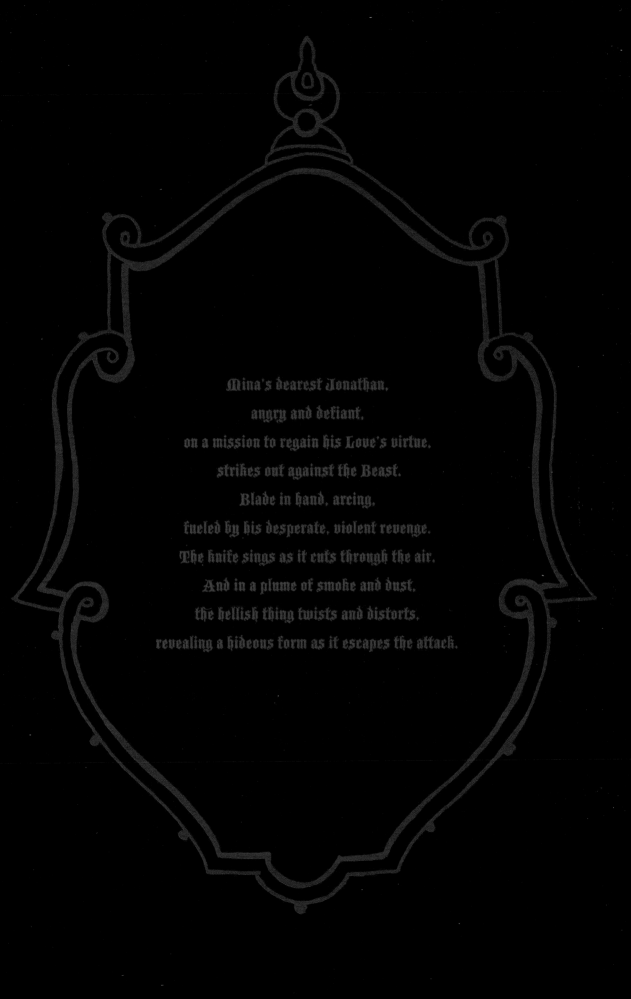

Mina's dearest Jonathan,

angry and defiant,

on a mission to regain his Love's virtue,

strikes out against the Beast.

Blade in hand, arcing,

fueled by his desperate, violent revenge.

The knife sings as it cuts through the air.

And in a plume of smoke and dust,

the hellish thing twists and distorts,

revealing a hideous form as it escapes the attack.

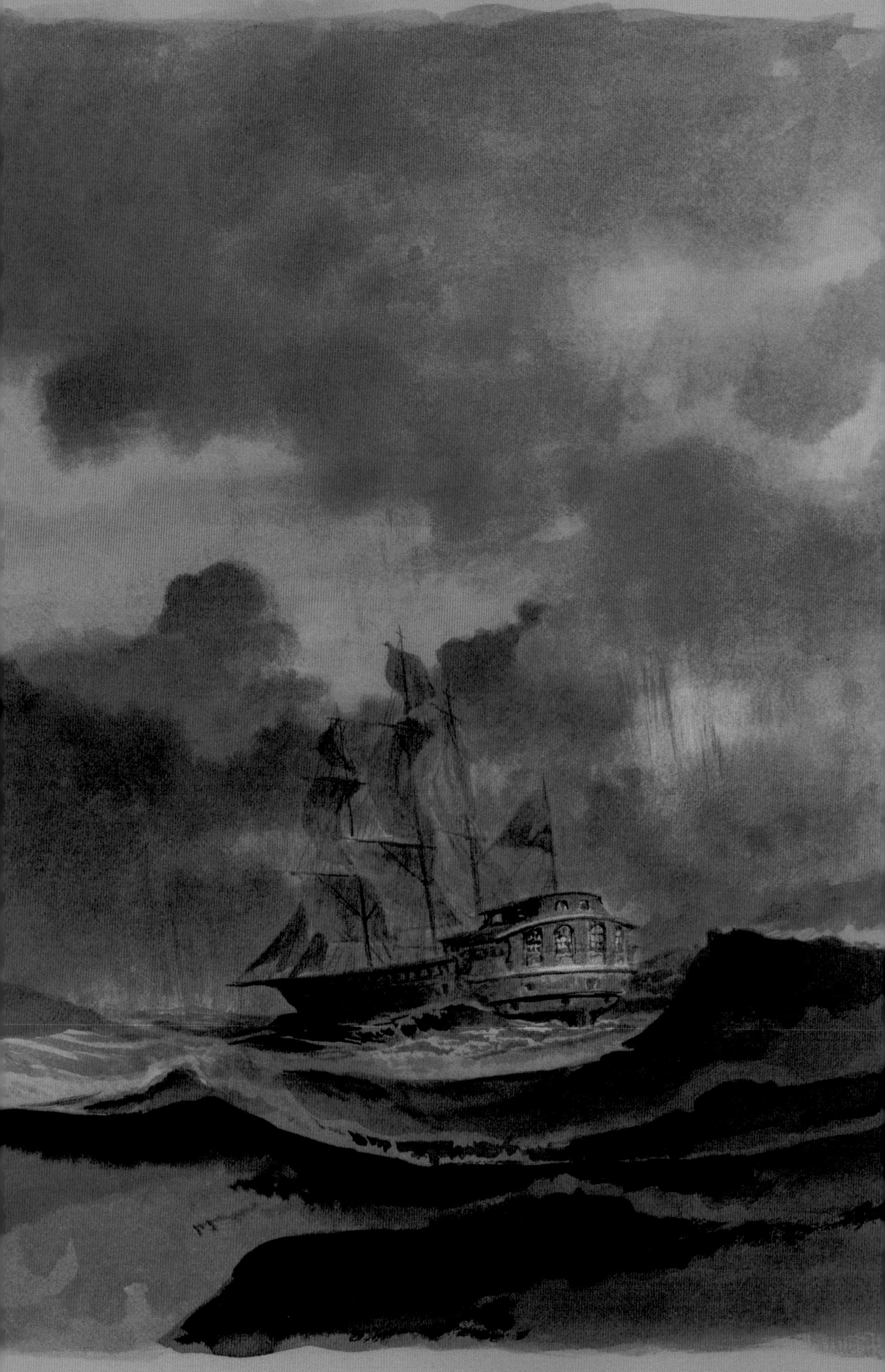

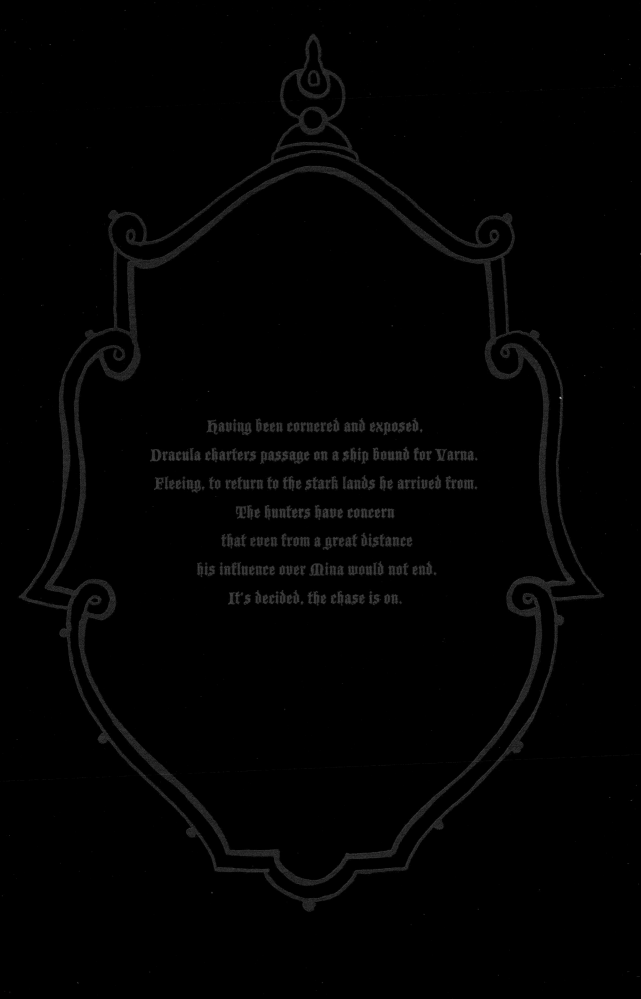

Having been cornered and exposed,

Dracula charters passage on a ship bound for Varna.

Fleeing, to return to the stark lands he arrived from.

The hunters have concern

that even from a great distance

his influence over Mina would not end.

It's decided, the chase is on.

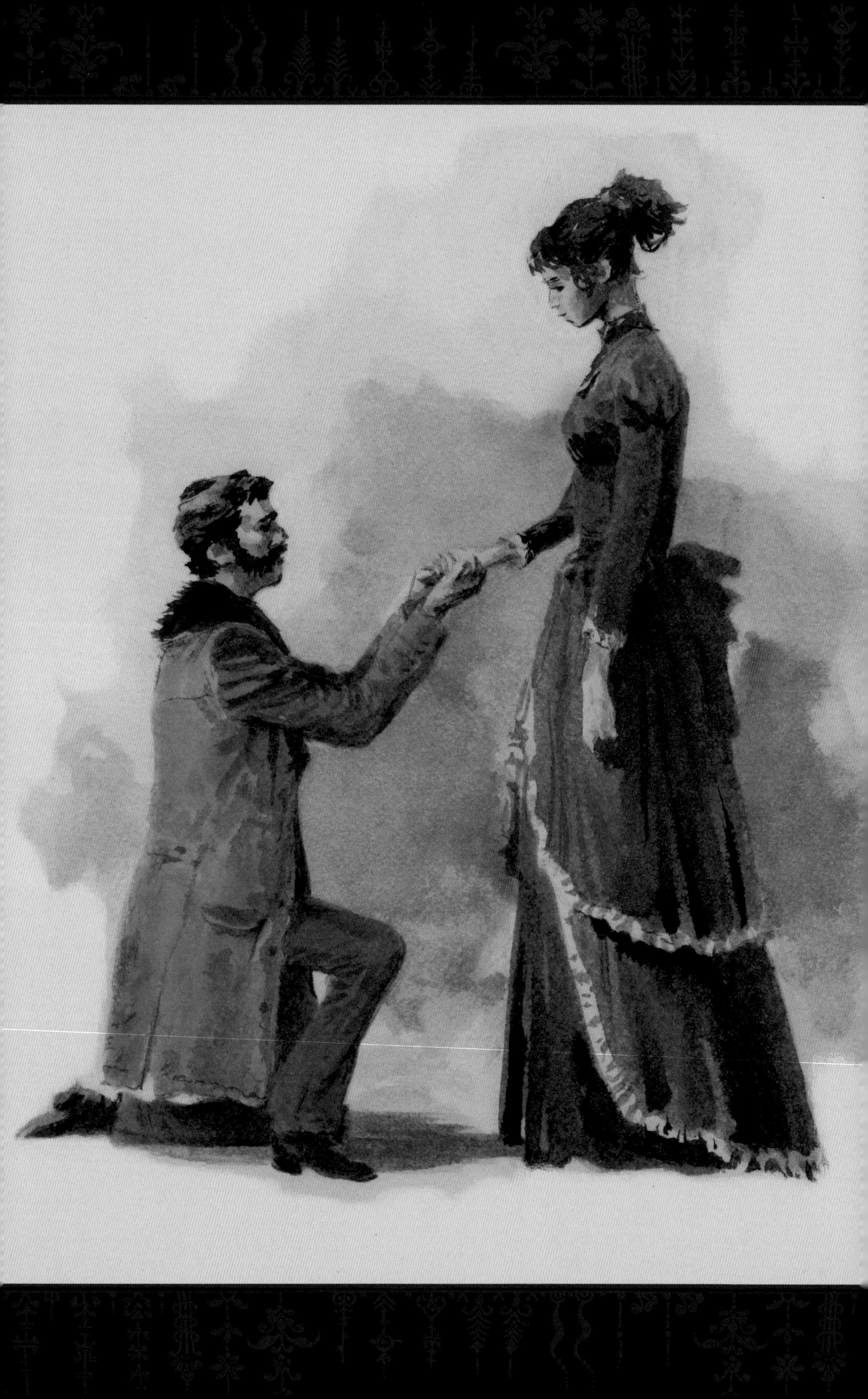

Mina has no illusions of what is happening to her.
She sees the horror in the eyes of her loved ones
as they witness the vampire's infection spreading in her veins.
She makes them all promise
to kill her if they cannot prevent the consuming of her soul.

The hunters strategize
about what is the best course of action to safeguard Mina.
Even if they must hide their plan from her,
in fear the Dark Lord can see through Mina's sight.
Quincey Morris vows to her with a soft assurance
that they will all do whatever is necessary
to break the Demon's curse upon her.
Mina insists she must accompany them
on their perilous journey.

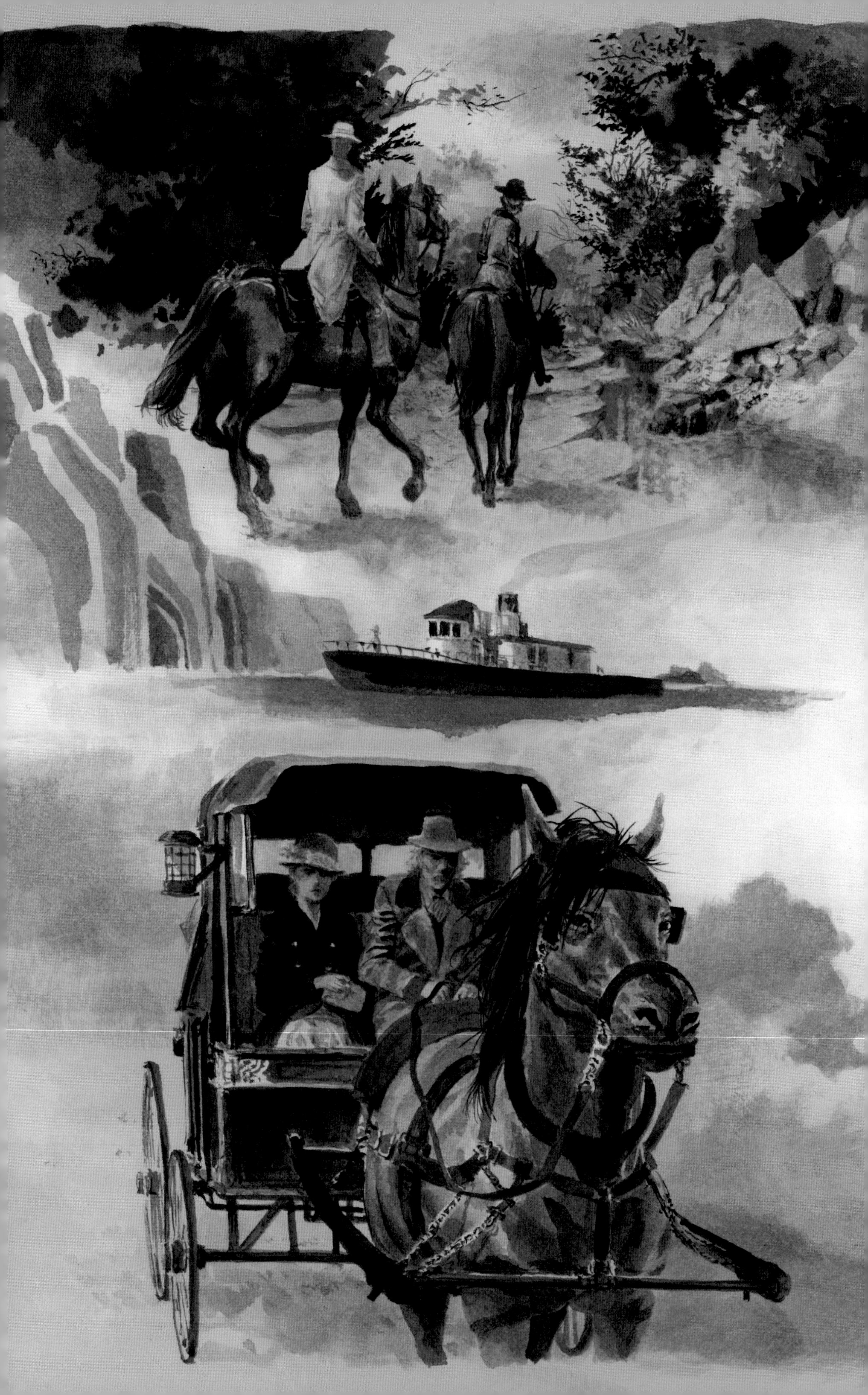

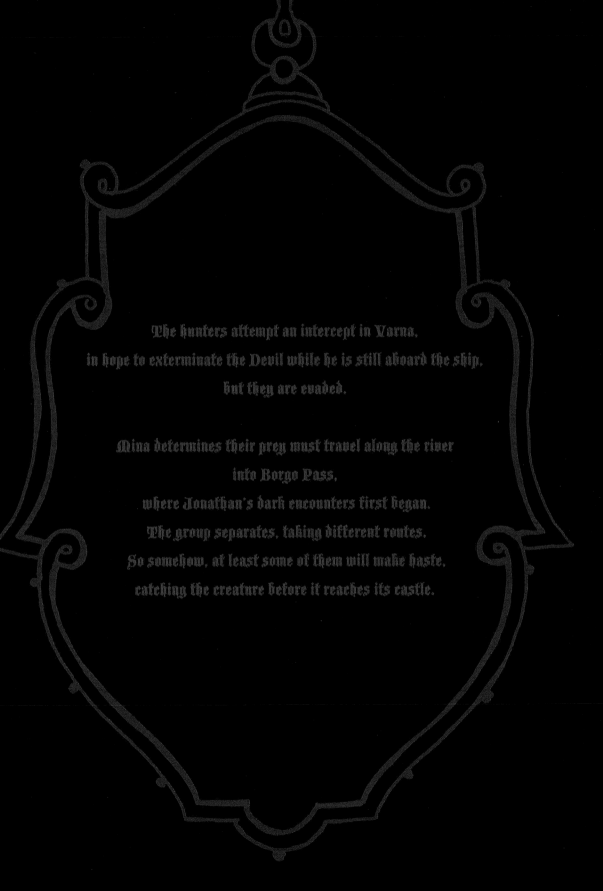

The hunters attempt an intercept in Varna,
in hope to exterminate the Devil while he is still aboard the ship,
but they are evaded.

Mina determines their prey must travel along the river
into Borgo Pass,
where Jonathan's dark encounters first began.
The group separates, taking different routes,
So somehow, at least some of them will make haste,
catching the creature before it reaches its castle.

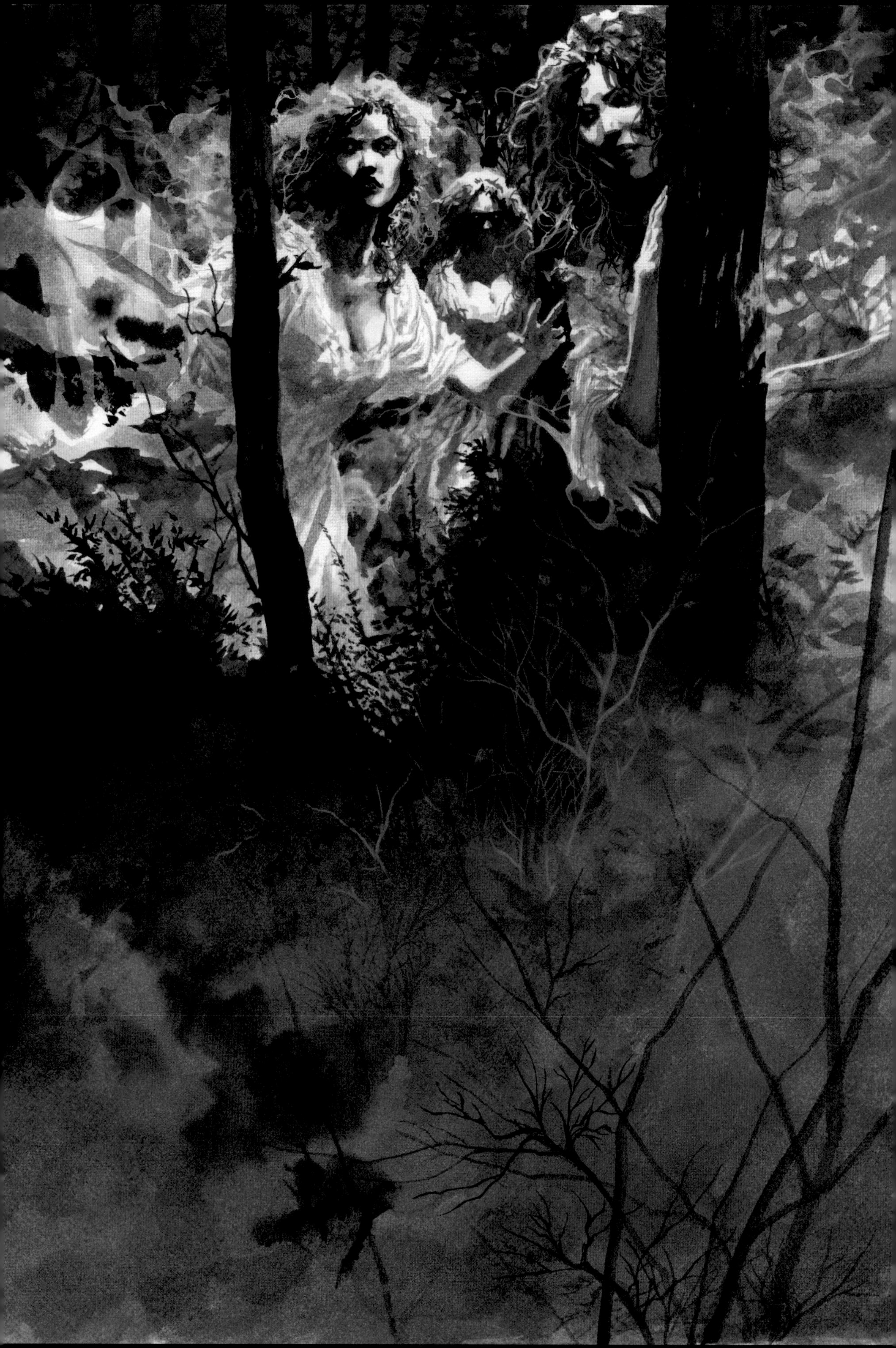

Mina and Professor Van Helsing travel by carriage.
In a forest near east of Borgo Pass they seek respite.
The Professor builds a fire and a protective circle.
He repeats the ritual of placing Holy Wafer against Mina's forehead.
The pair will not get the rest sorely needed.

From the forest edge,
the three Brides of Hell that seduced Mina's beloved Jonathan
terrorize all through this bleakest of nights.
They torturously tempt Mina,
toying with Van Helsing's steadfastness,
until the breaking dawn finally chases them away.

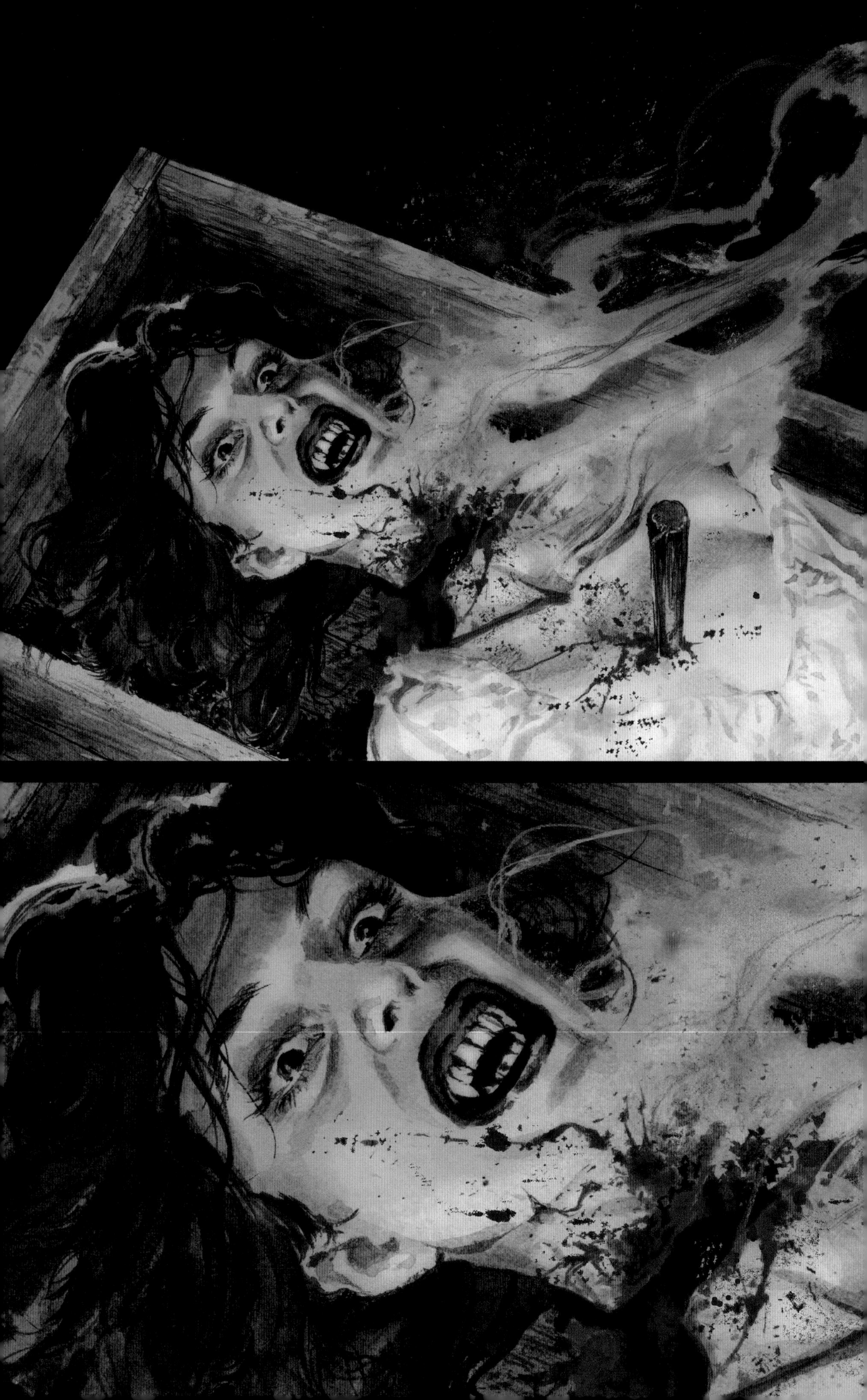

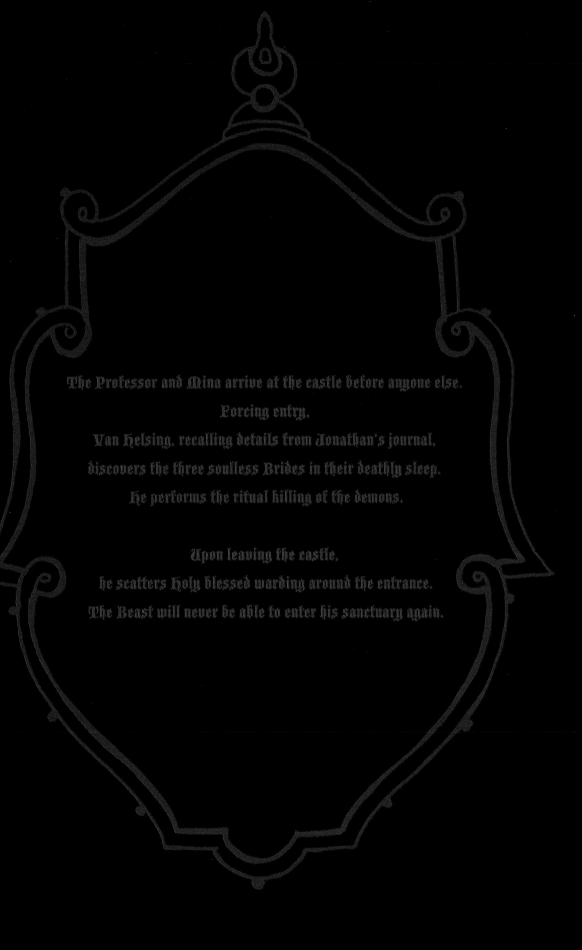

The Professor and Mina arrive at the castle before anyone else.
Forcing entry.
Van Helsing, recalling details from Jonathan's journal,
discovers the three soulless Brides in their deathly sleep.
He performs the ritual killing of the demons.

Upon leaving the castle,
he scatters Holy blessed warding around the entrance.
The Beast will never be able to enter his sanctuary again.

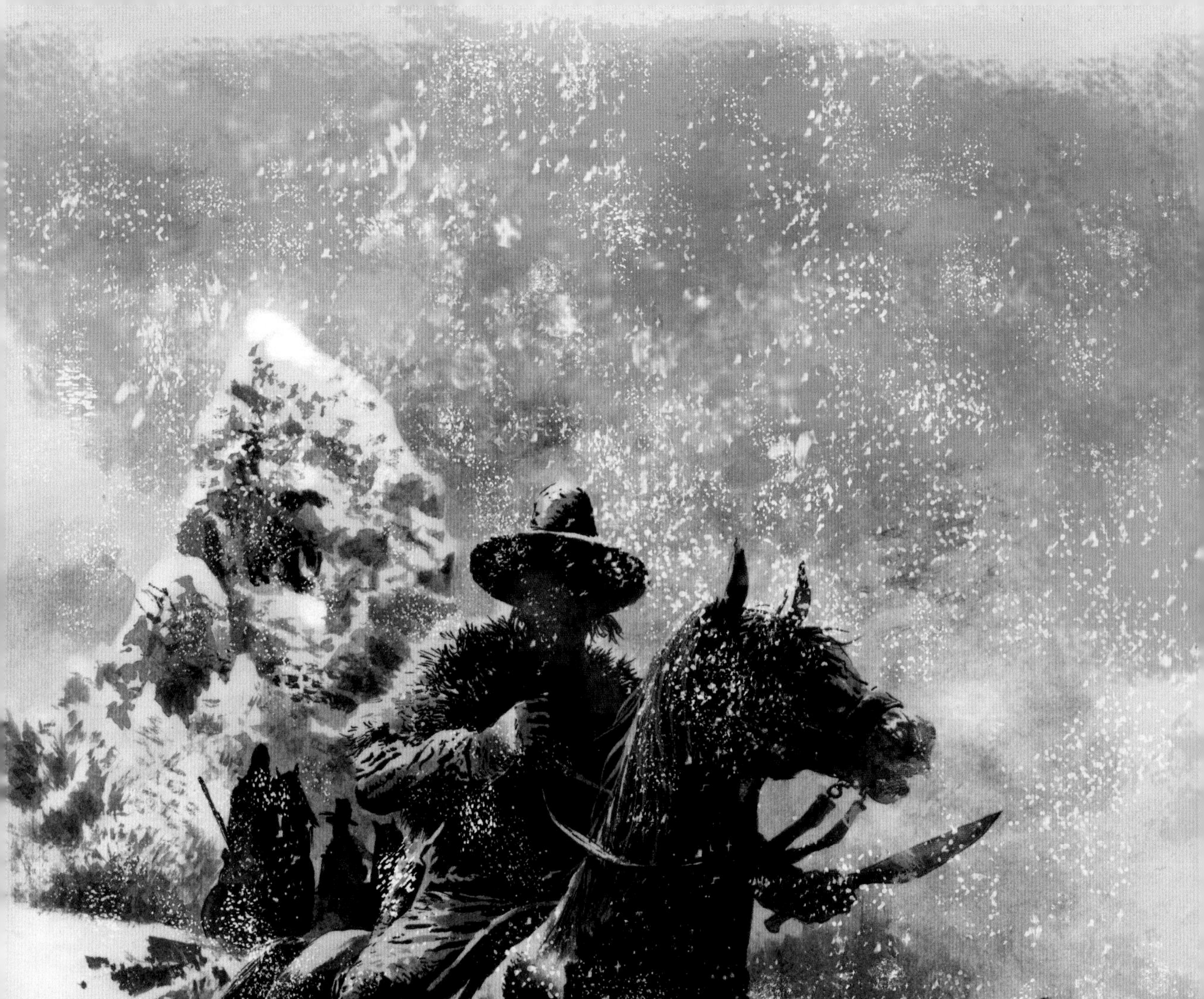

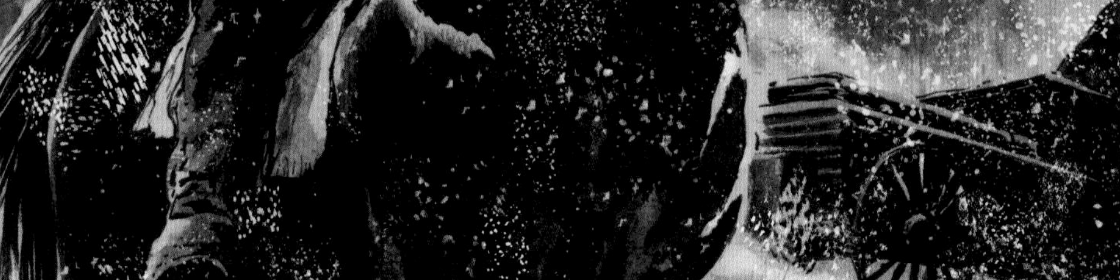

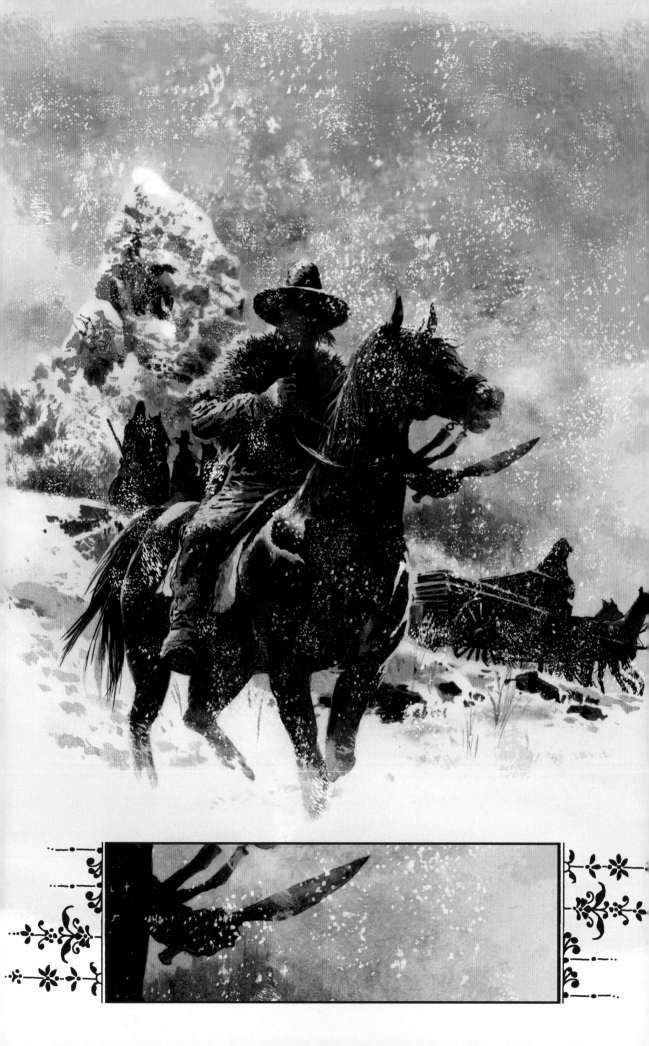

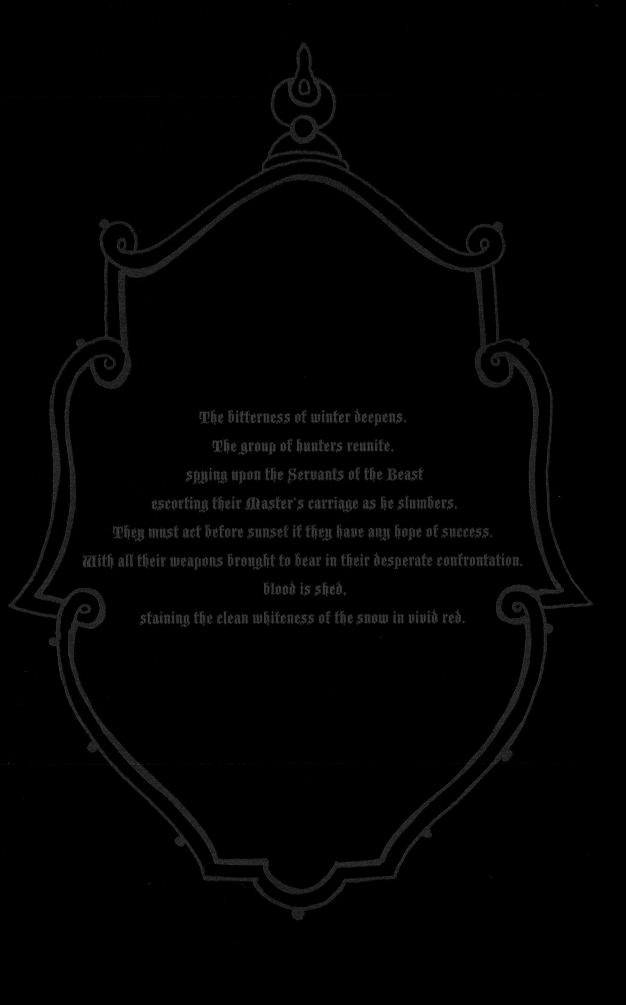

The bitterness of winter deepens.

The group of hunters reunite,

spying upon the Servants of the Beast

escorting their Master's carriage as he slumbers.

They must act before sunset if they have any hope of success.

With all their weapons brought to bear in their desperate confrontation,

blood is shed,

staining the clean whiteness of the snow in vivid red.

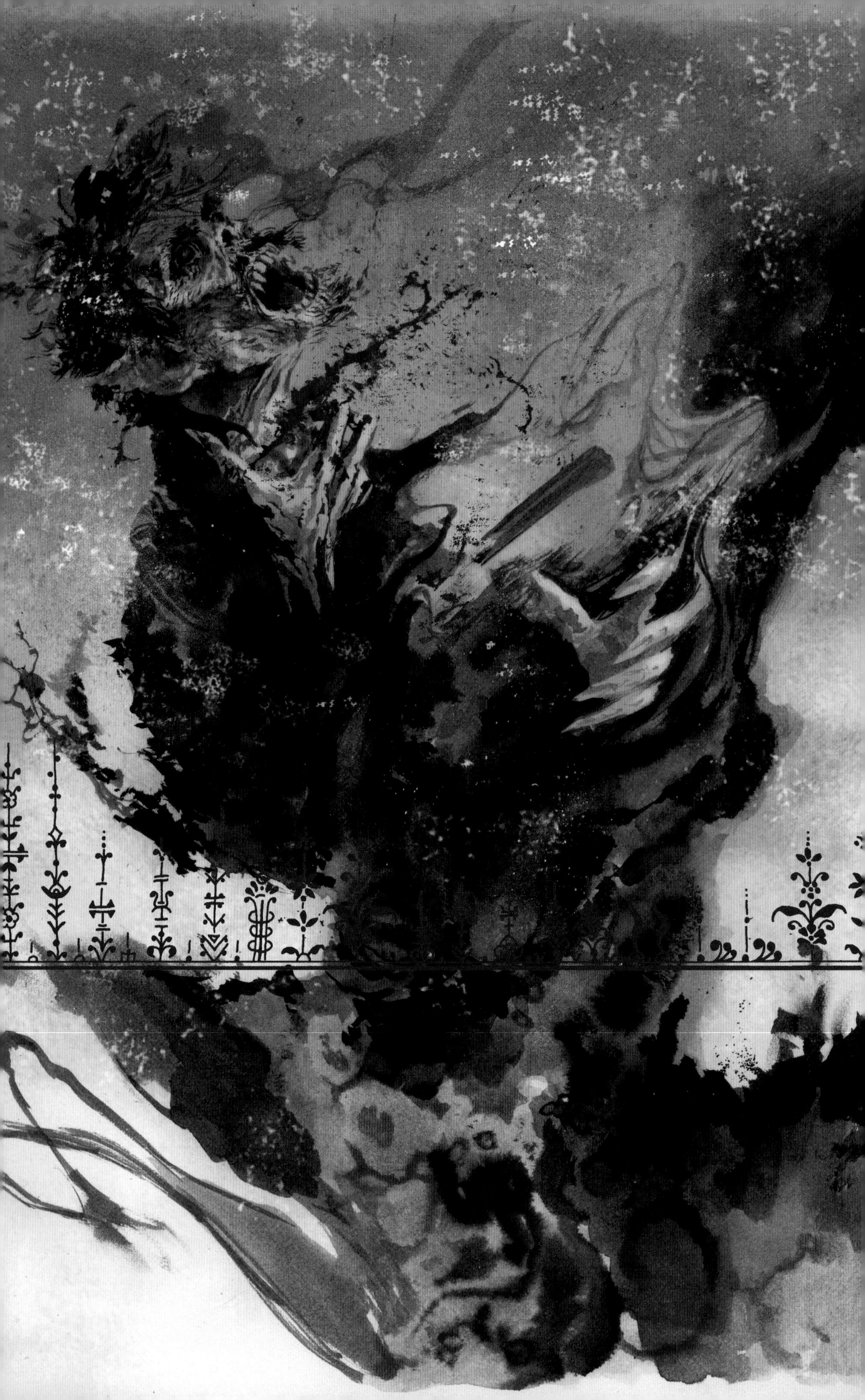

Sunset is here.

The Beast emerges in a violent burst,

hissing in defiance.

Its dark eyes full of loathing.

Quincey Morris plunges his bowie knife deep,

piercing the Demon's dead heart.

Jonathan Harker, with all his love and conviction,

hacks his blade in the thing's neck.

The Beast's blood boils forth, frothing,

then flashes into sparks of fire.

Ash disperses on the wind.

Ages of decay set upon the creature's body,

as if Time itself speeds up and only dust remains.

Its corruption has left the Earth.

The scourge of the vampire ends.

And the curse of its infection is lifted from Mina's soul.

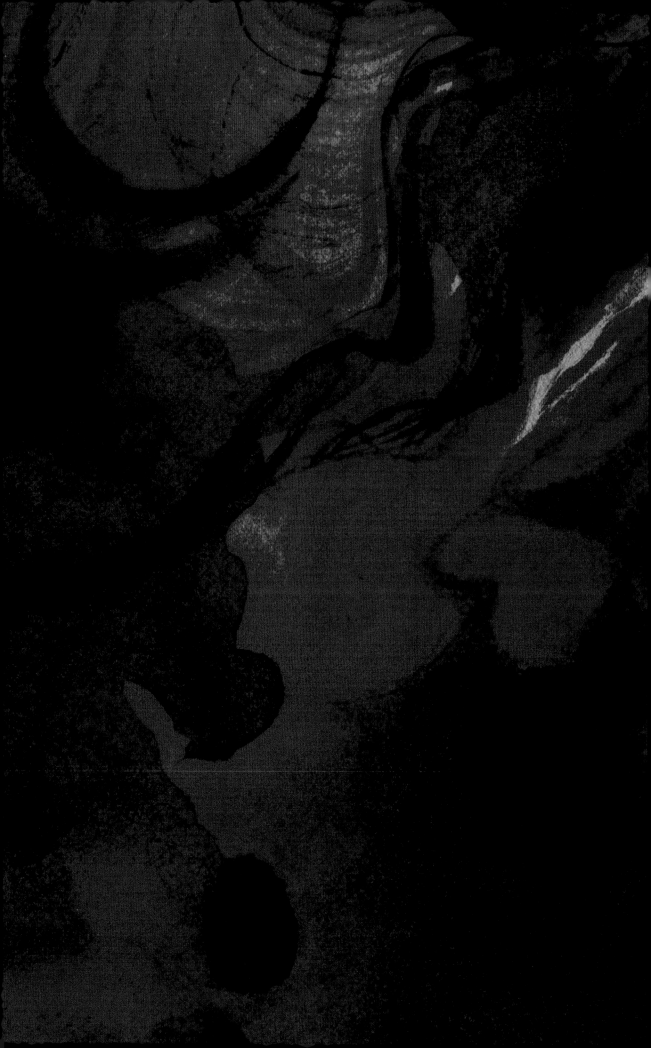

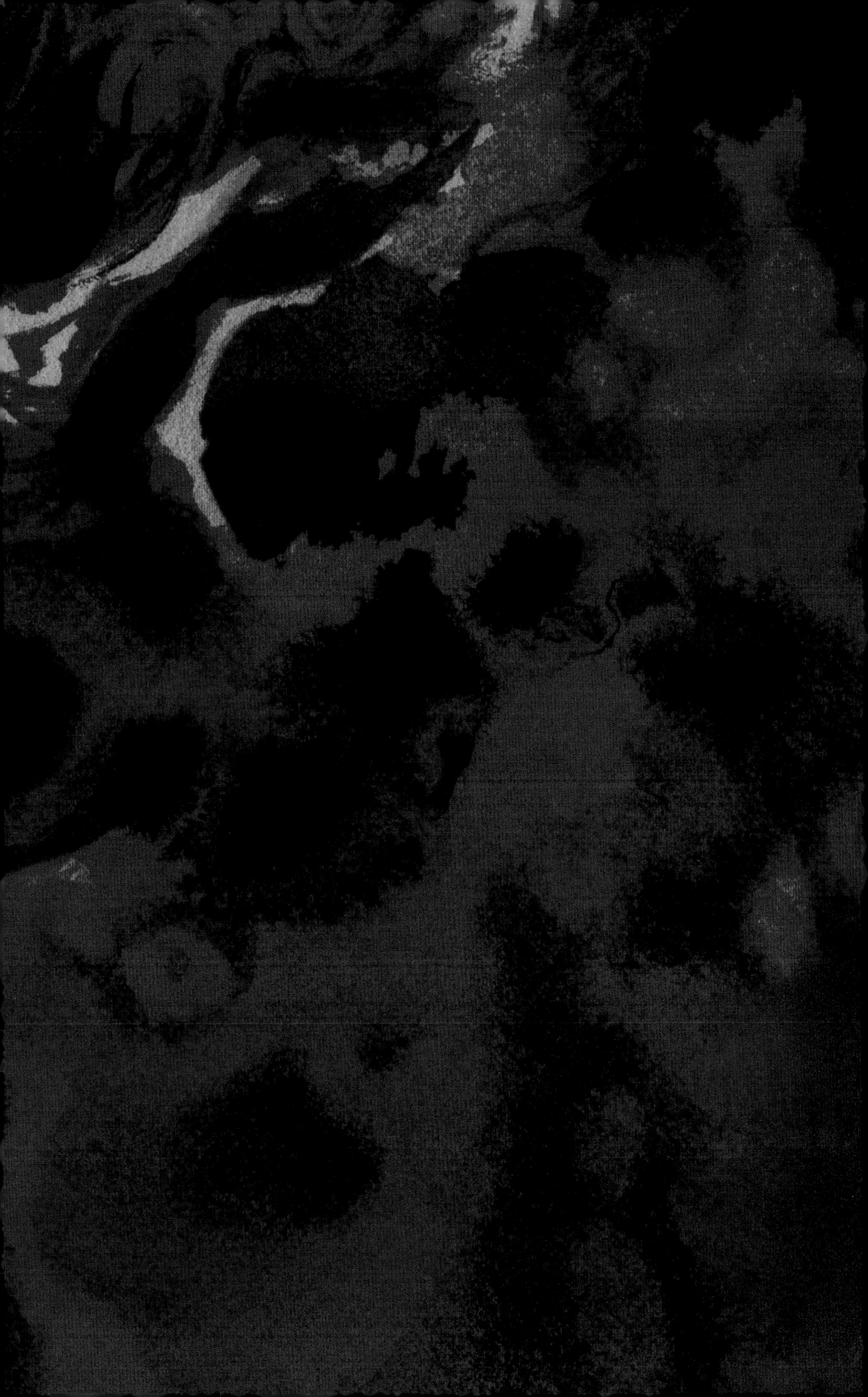

THE FOLLOWING PAGES
PRESENT THE ORIGINAL
RAW ART SCANS OF
THE 50 ILLUSTRATIONS THAT
BECAME THE FINAL PAINTED
VISUALS OF THE MAIN WORK.

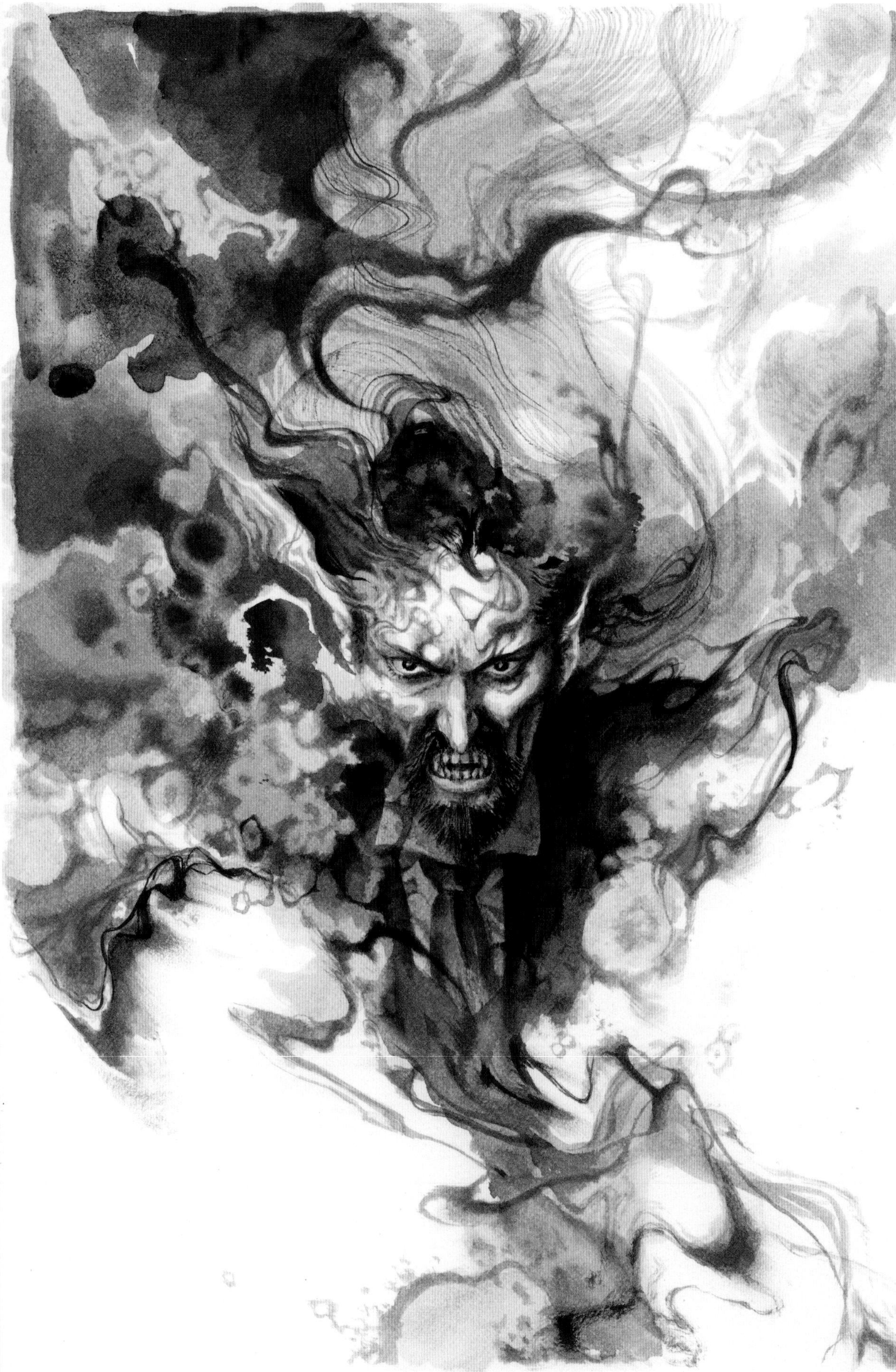

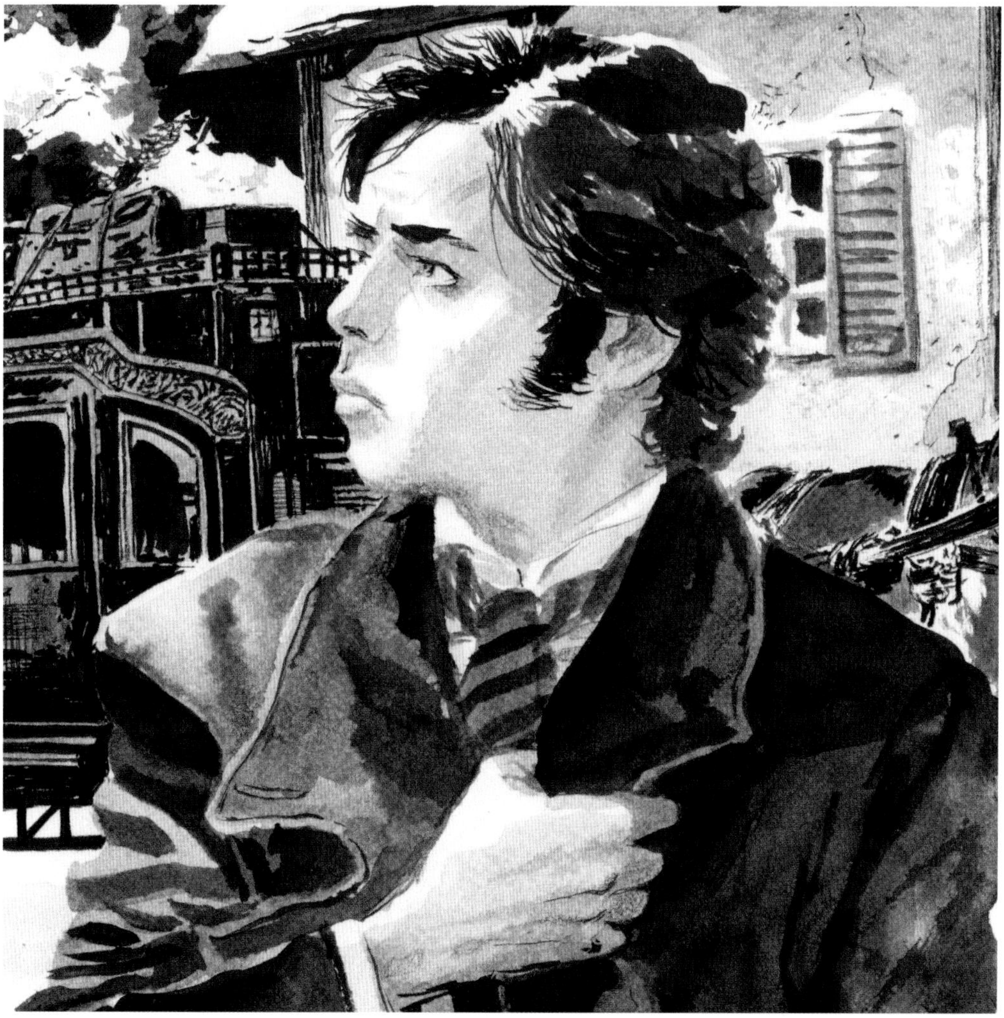

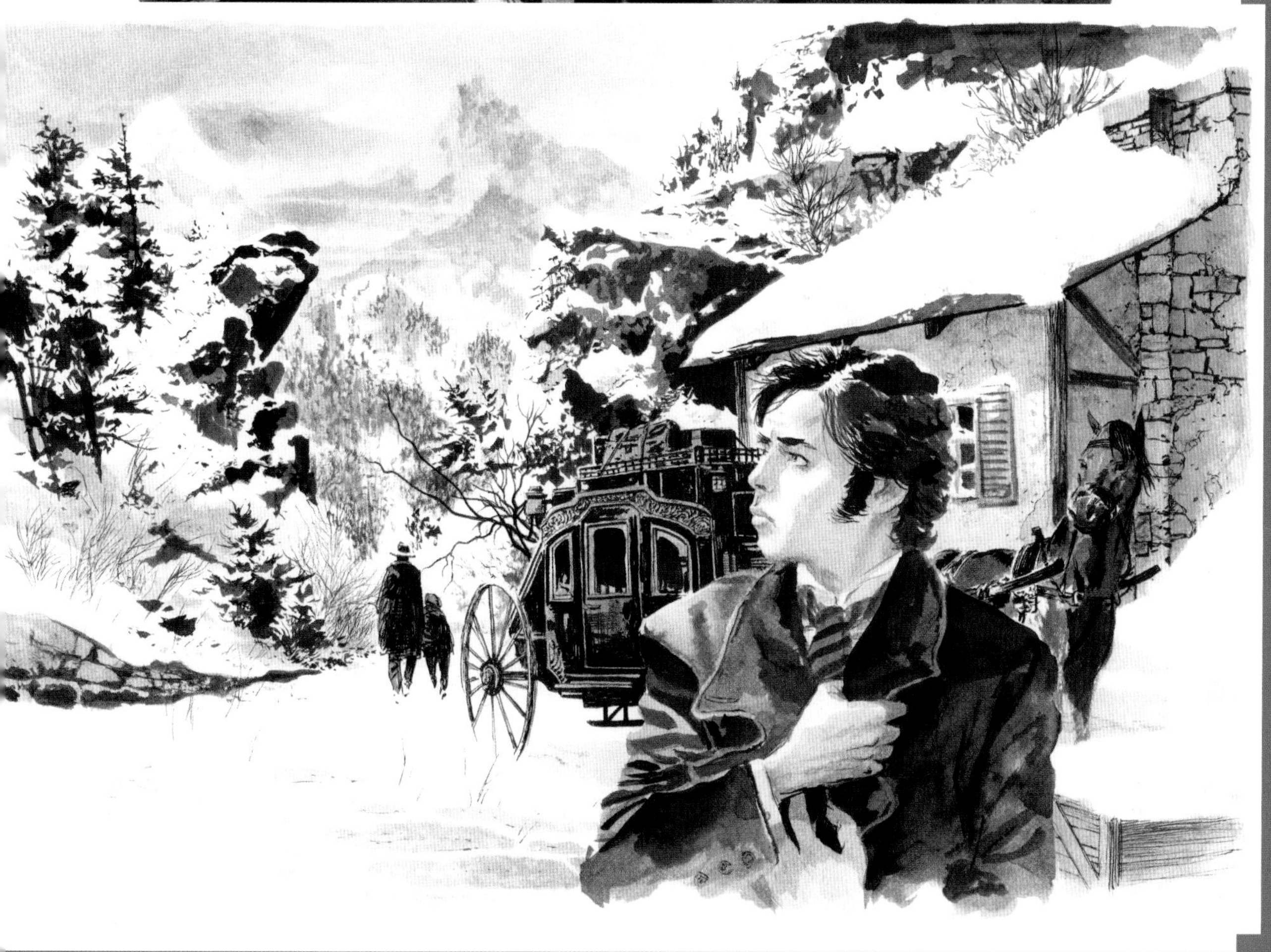

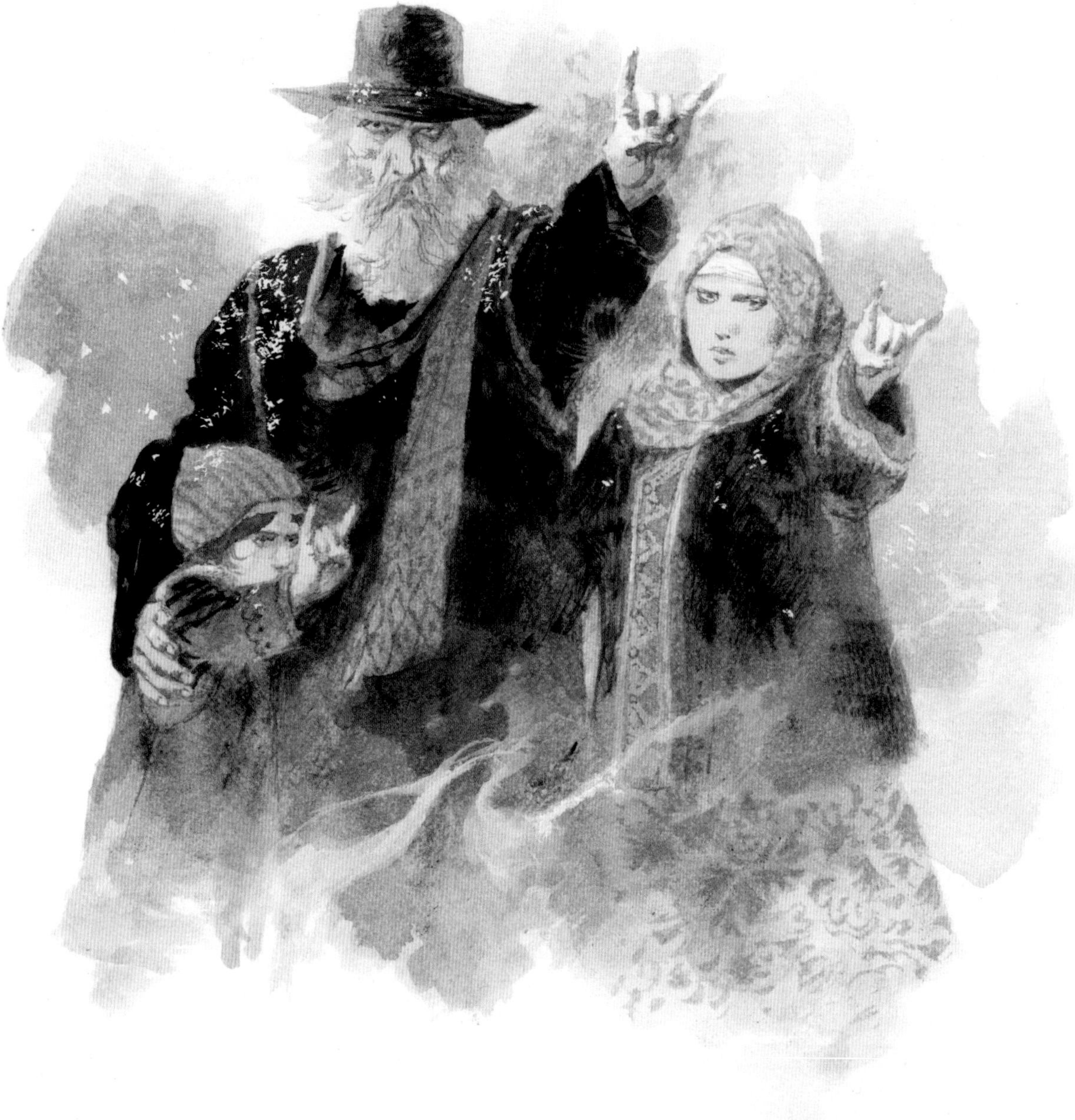

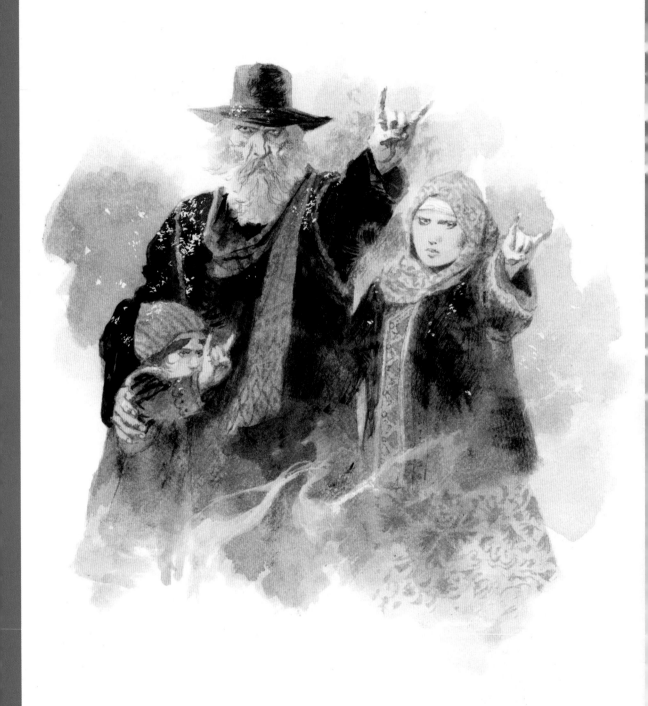

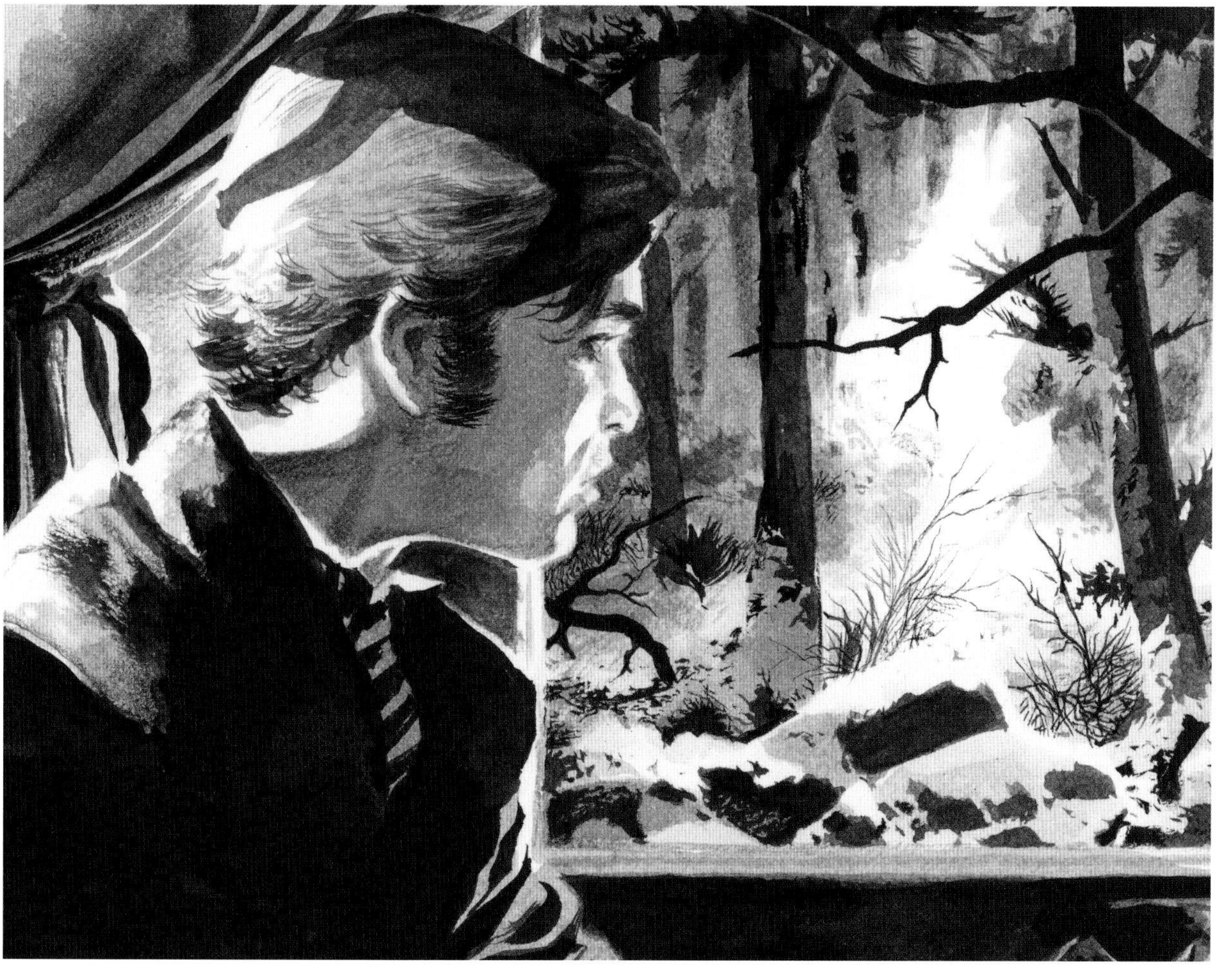

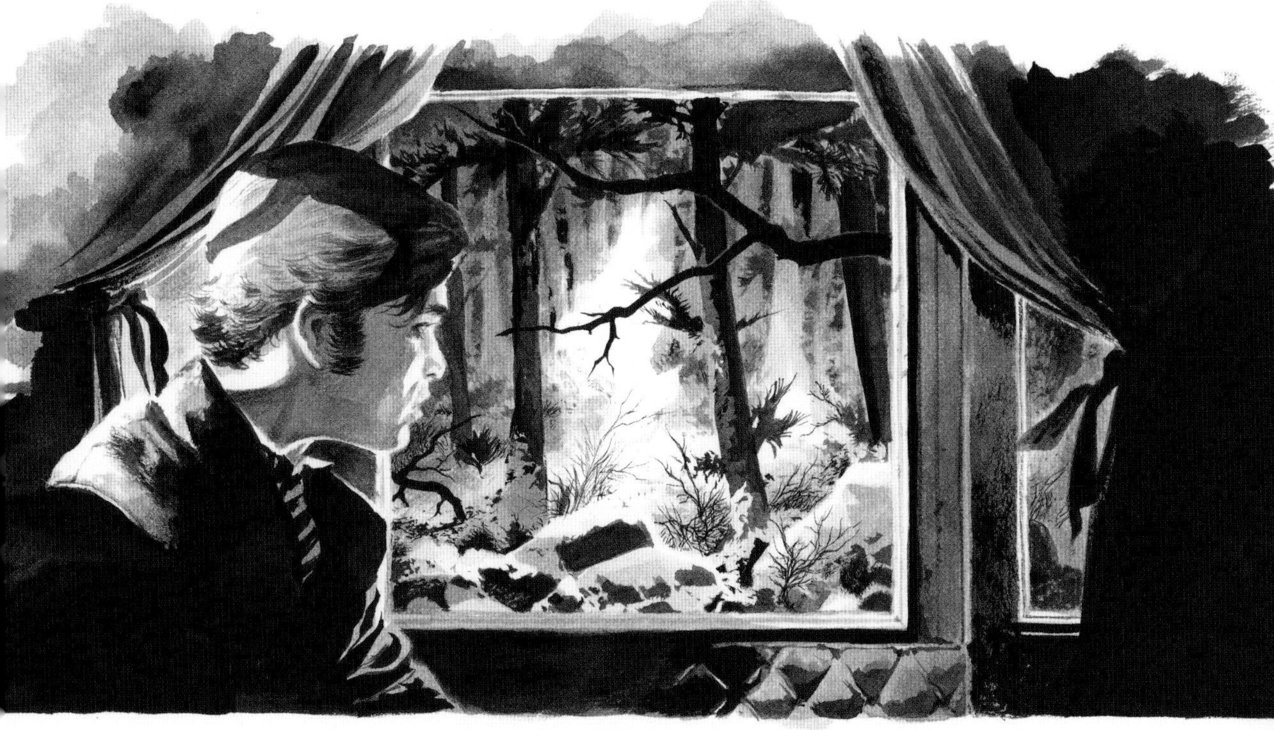

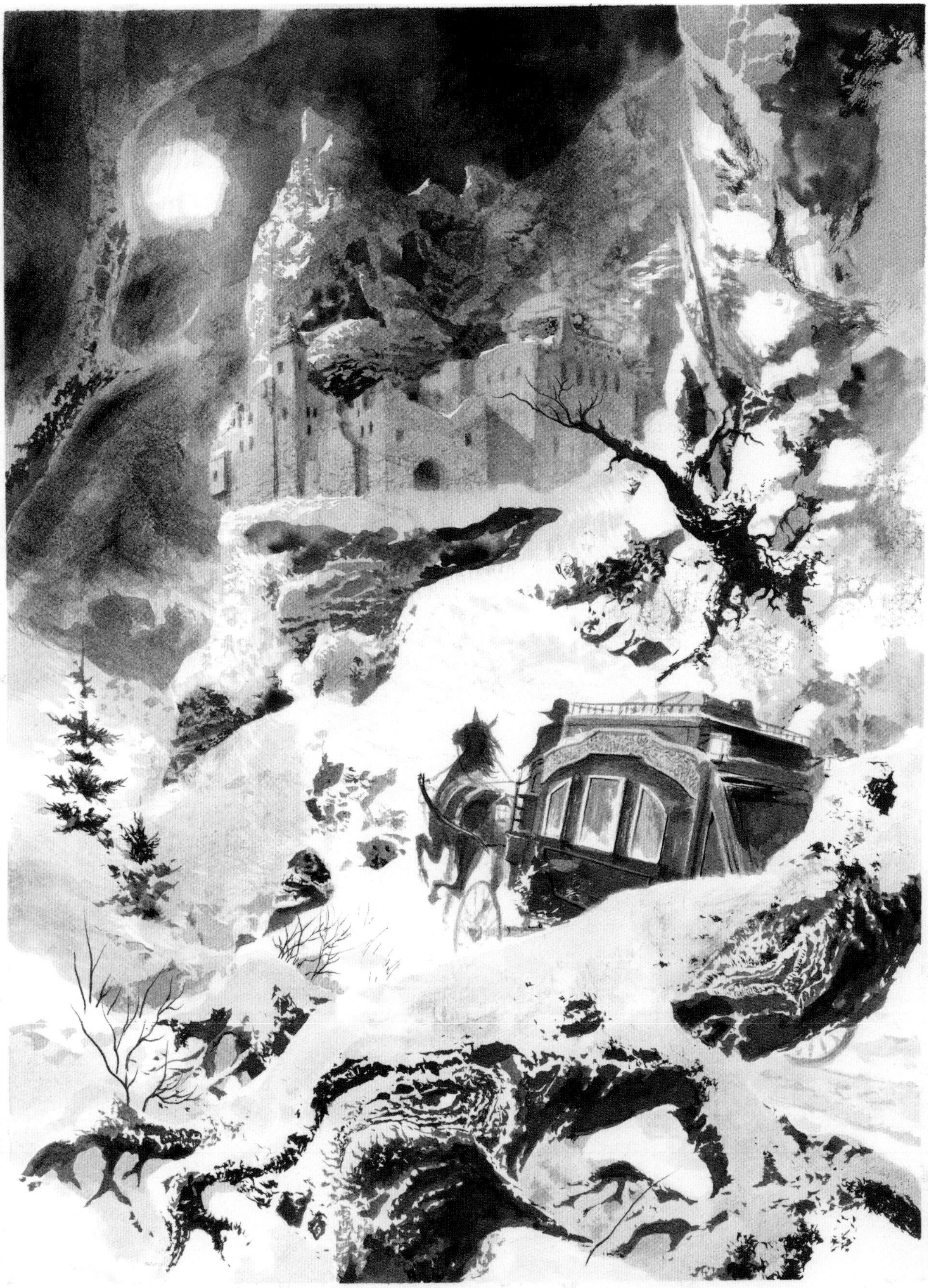

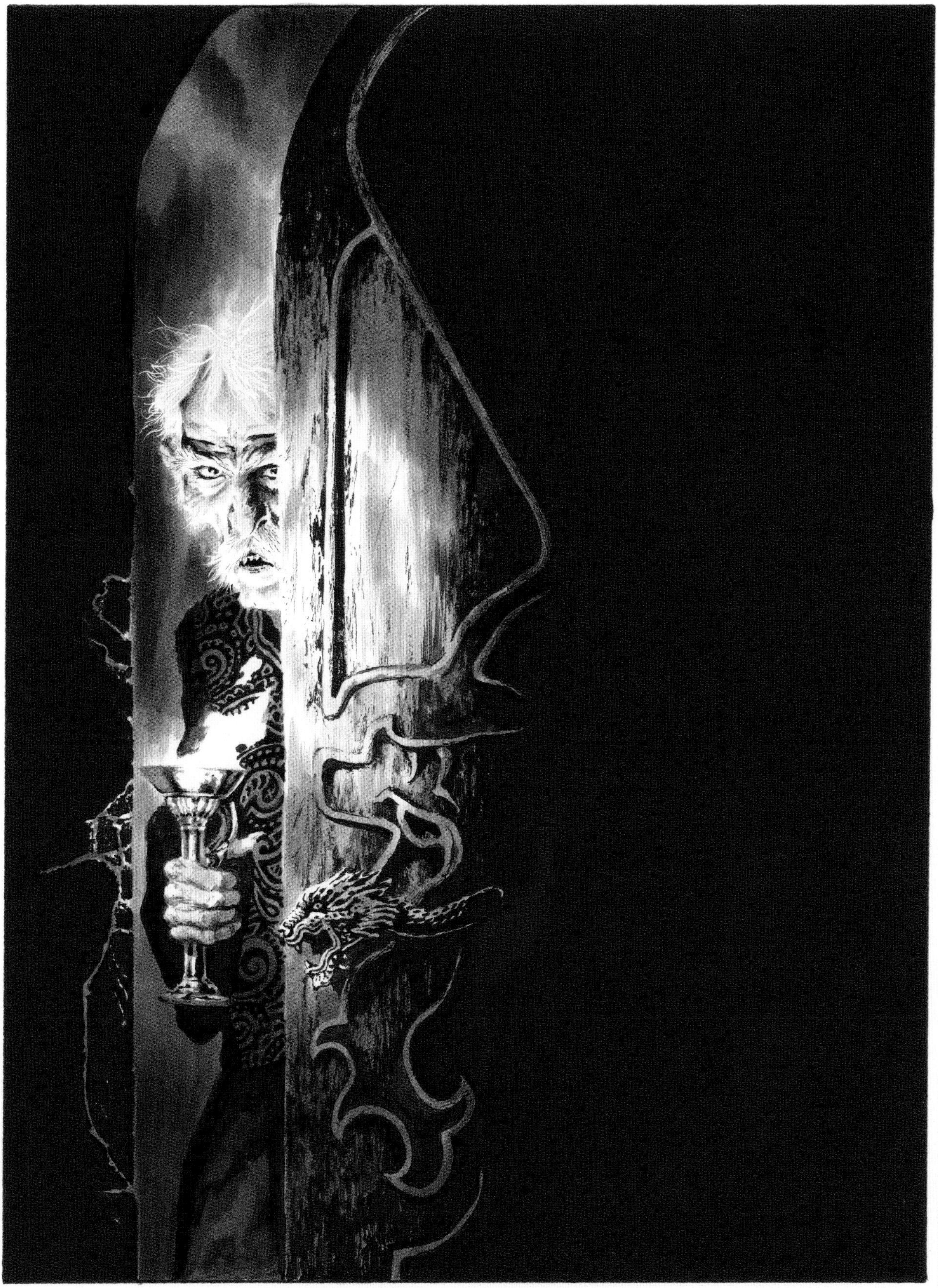

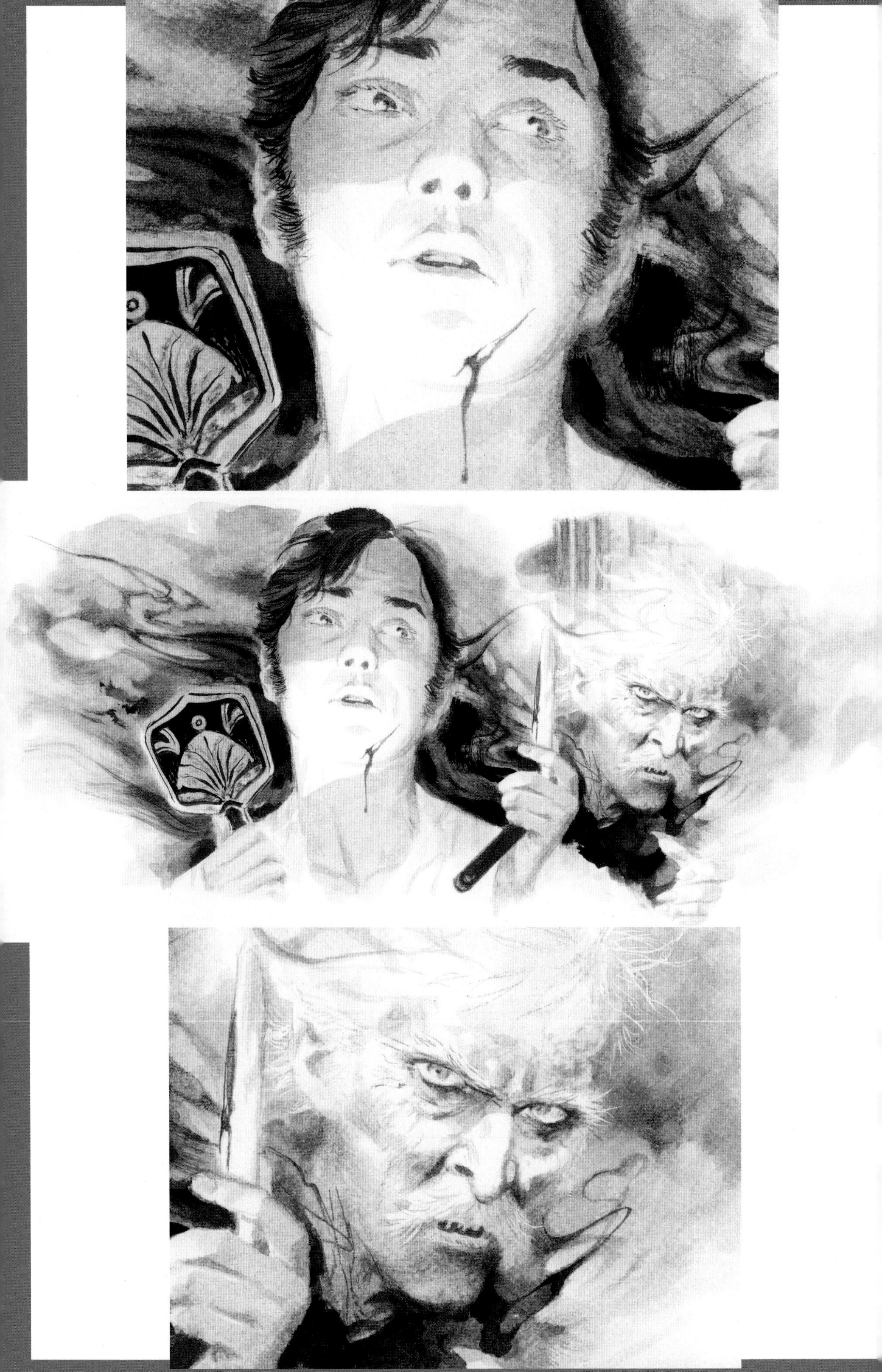

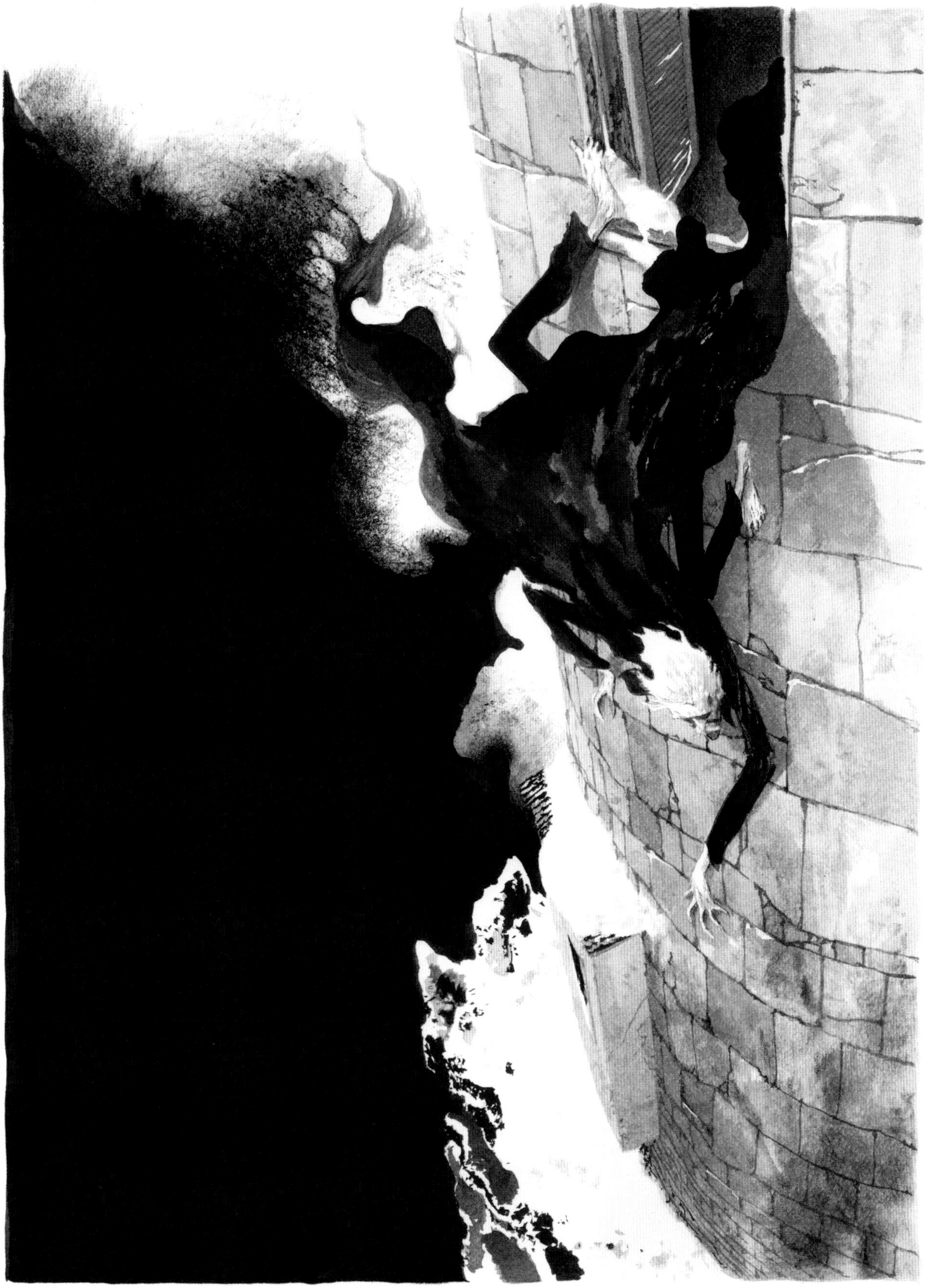

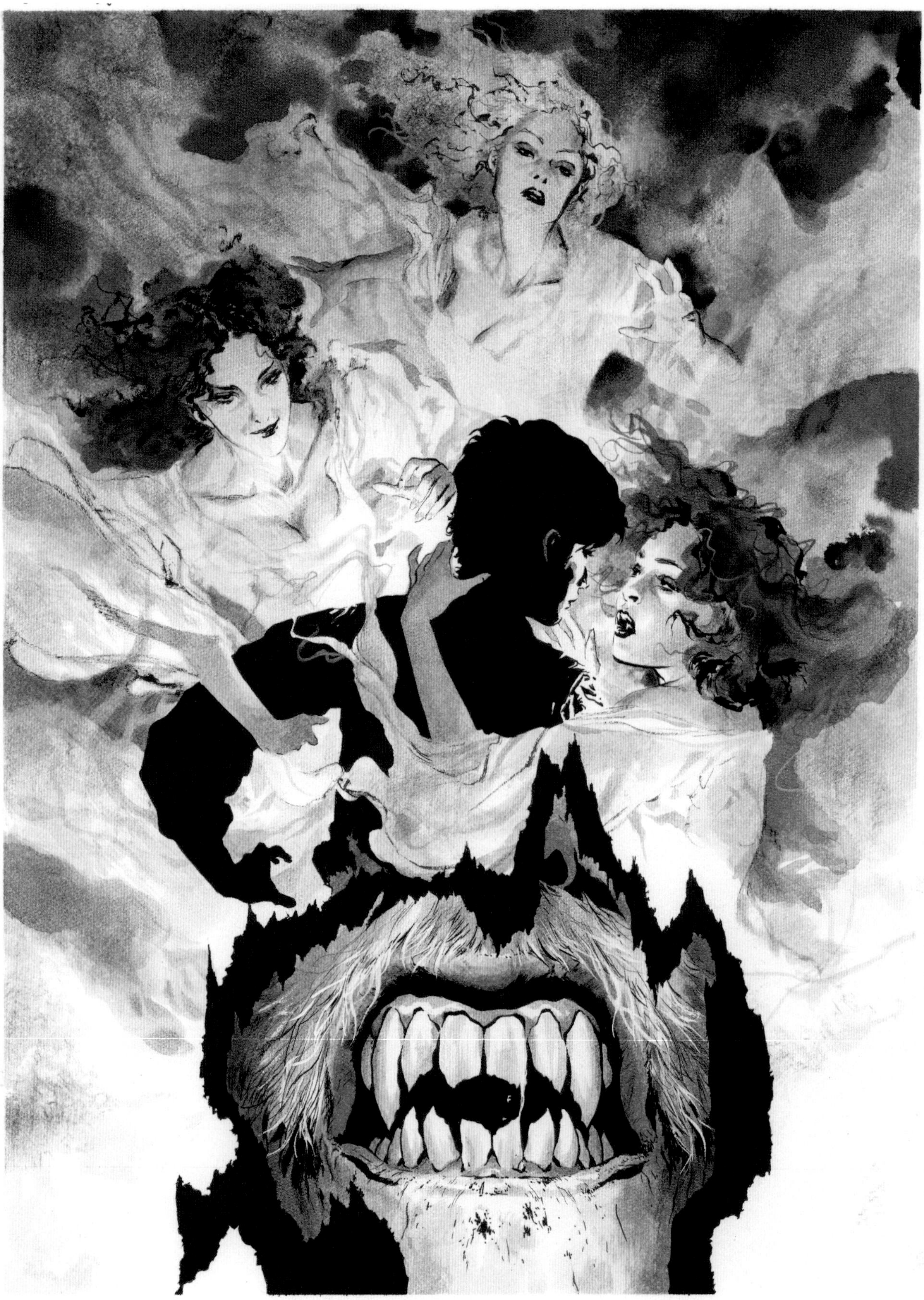

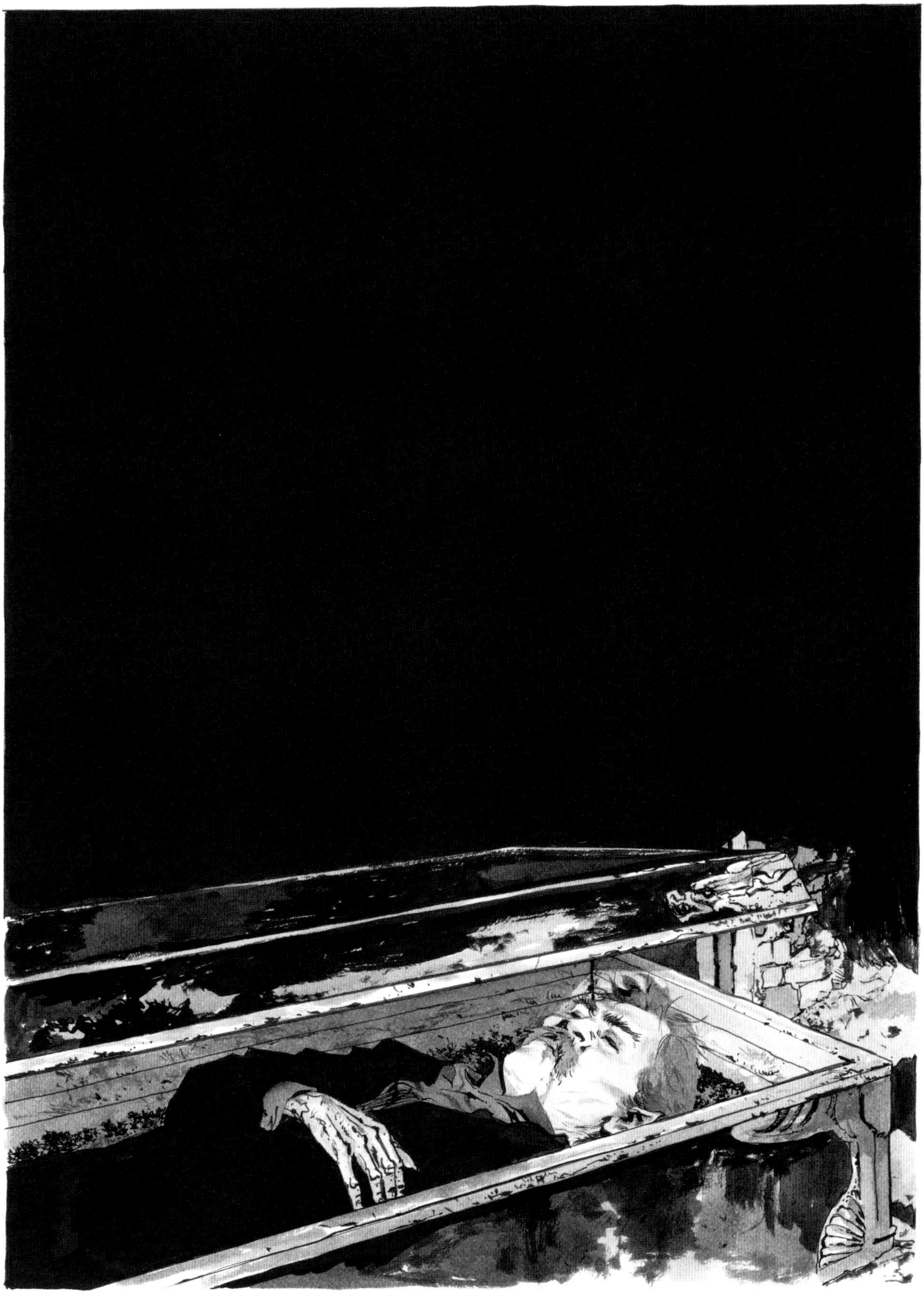

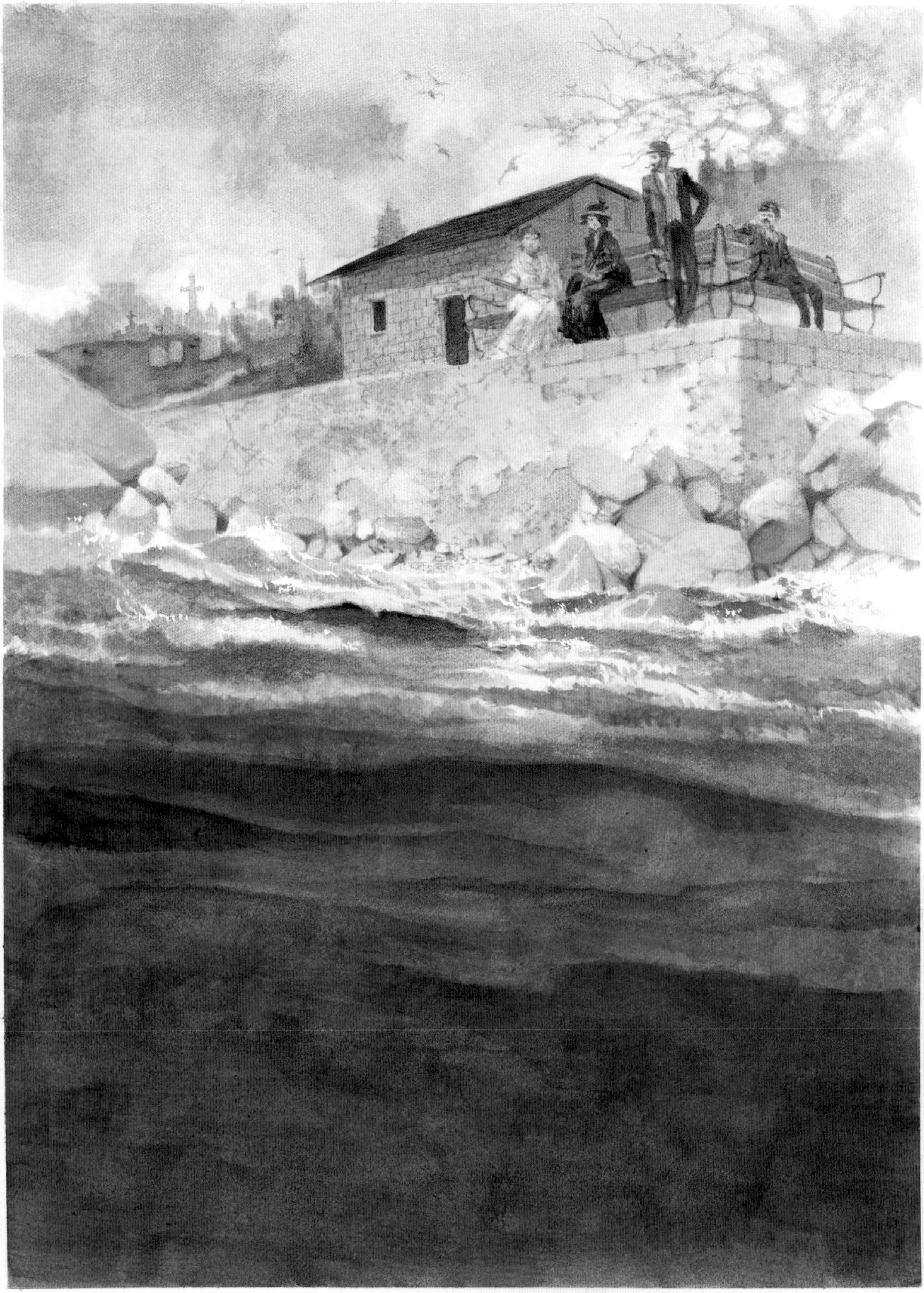

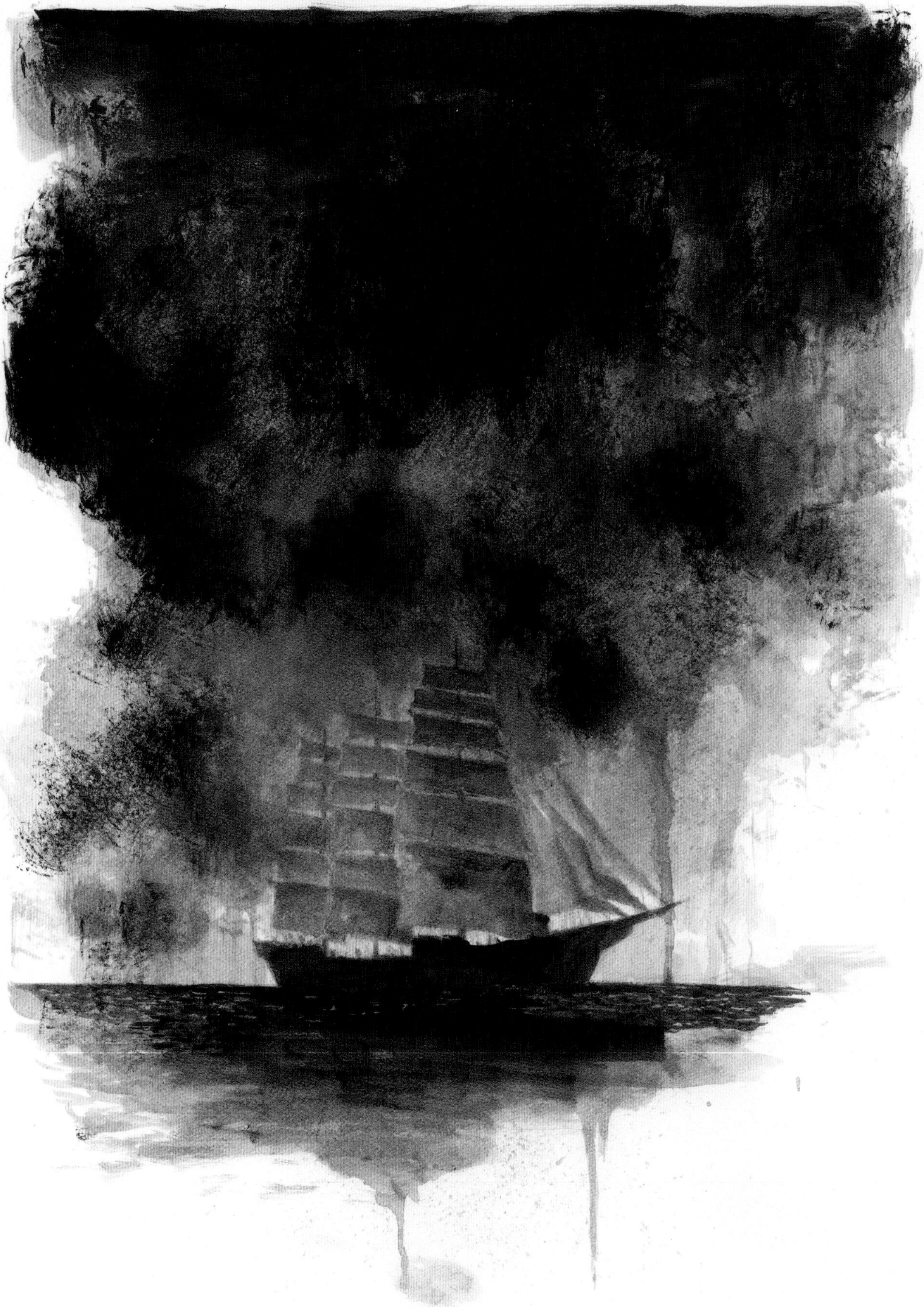

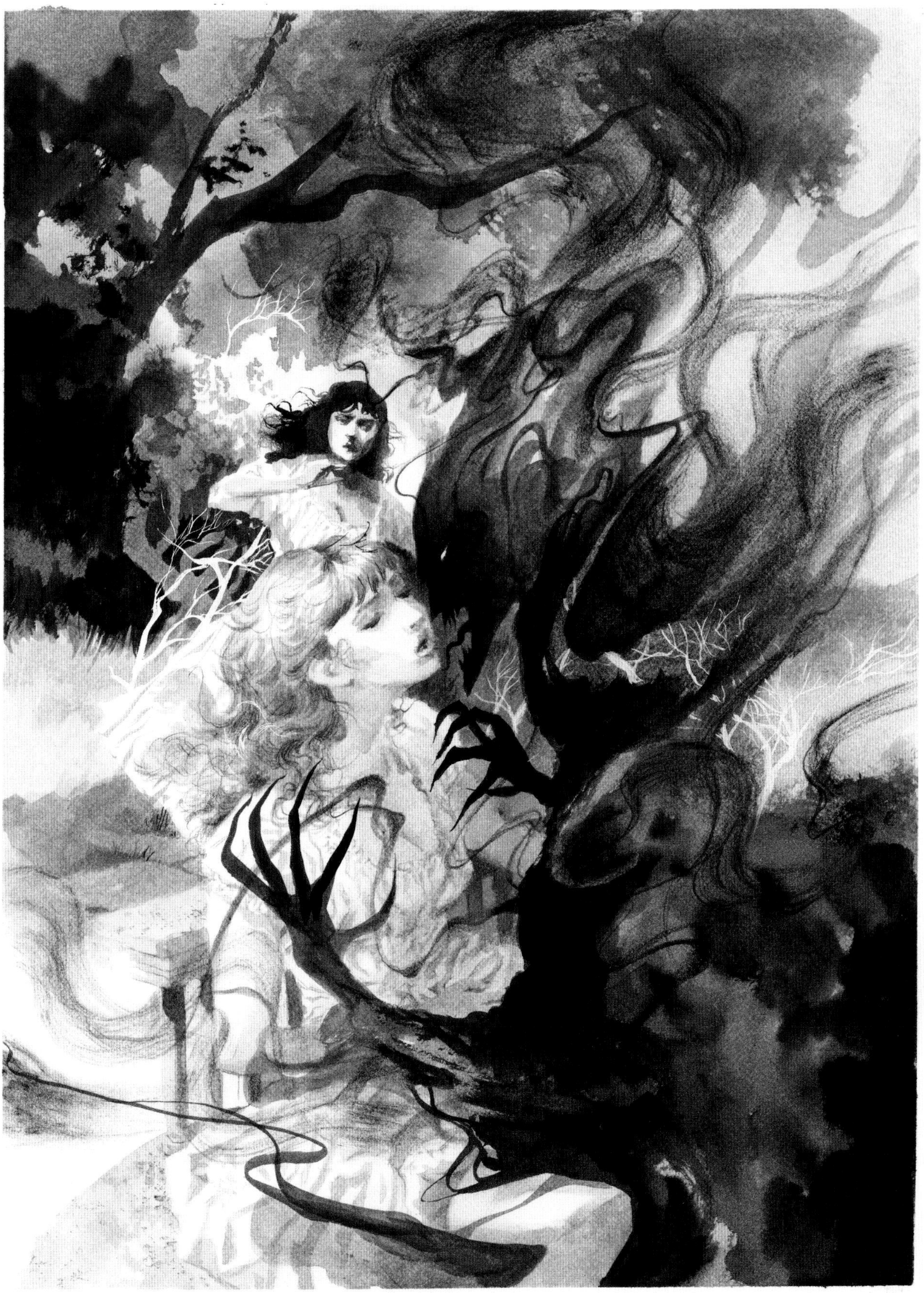

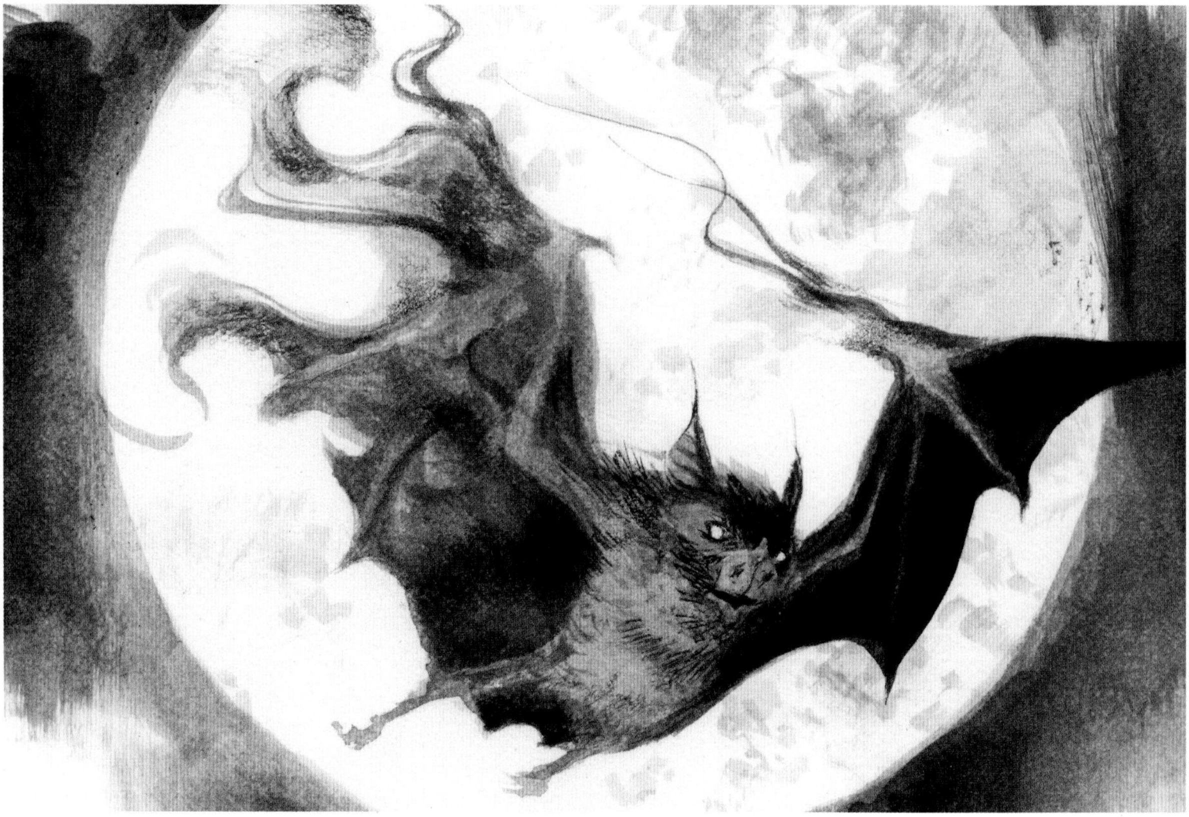

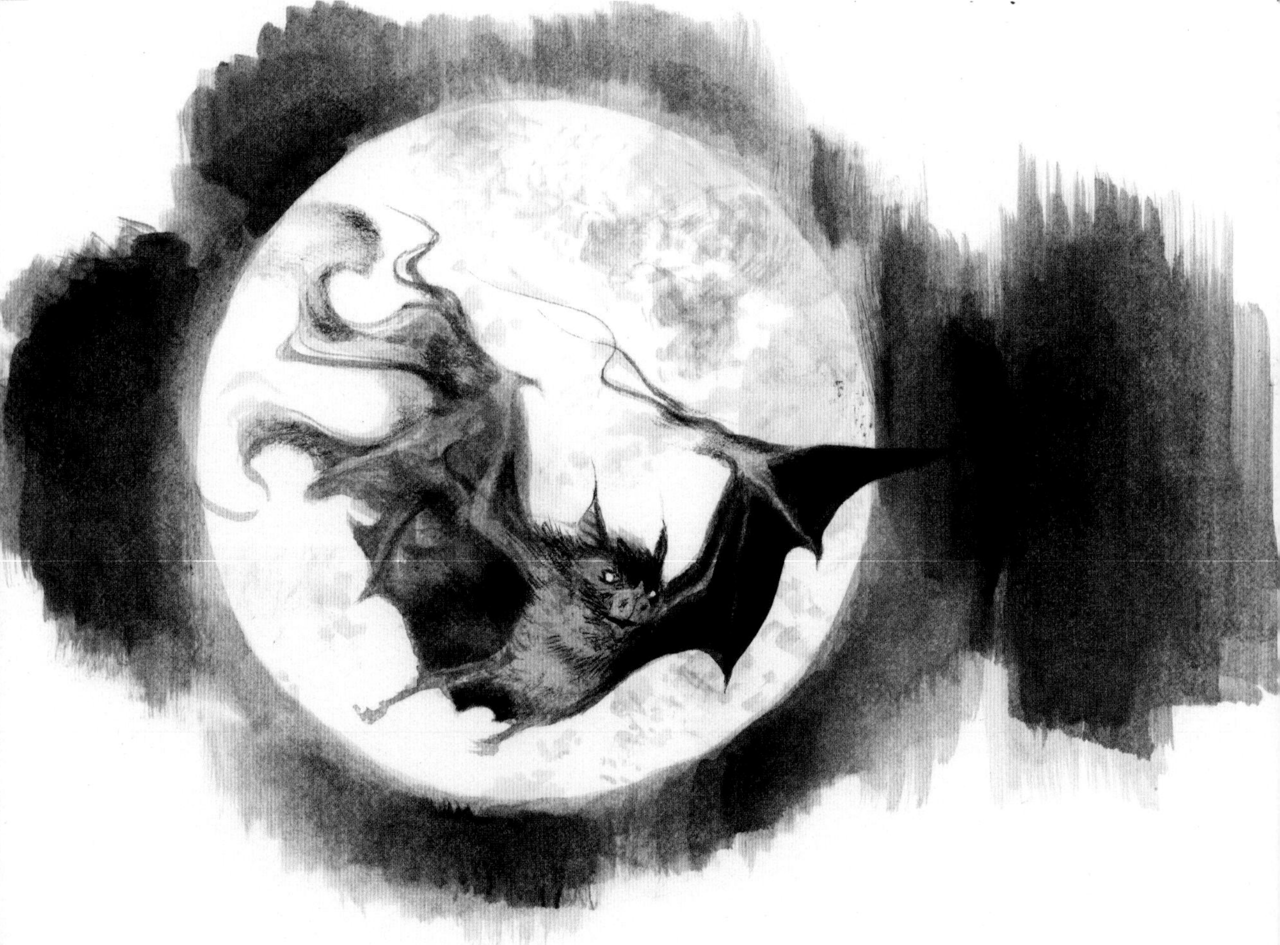

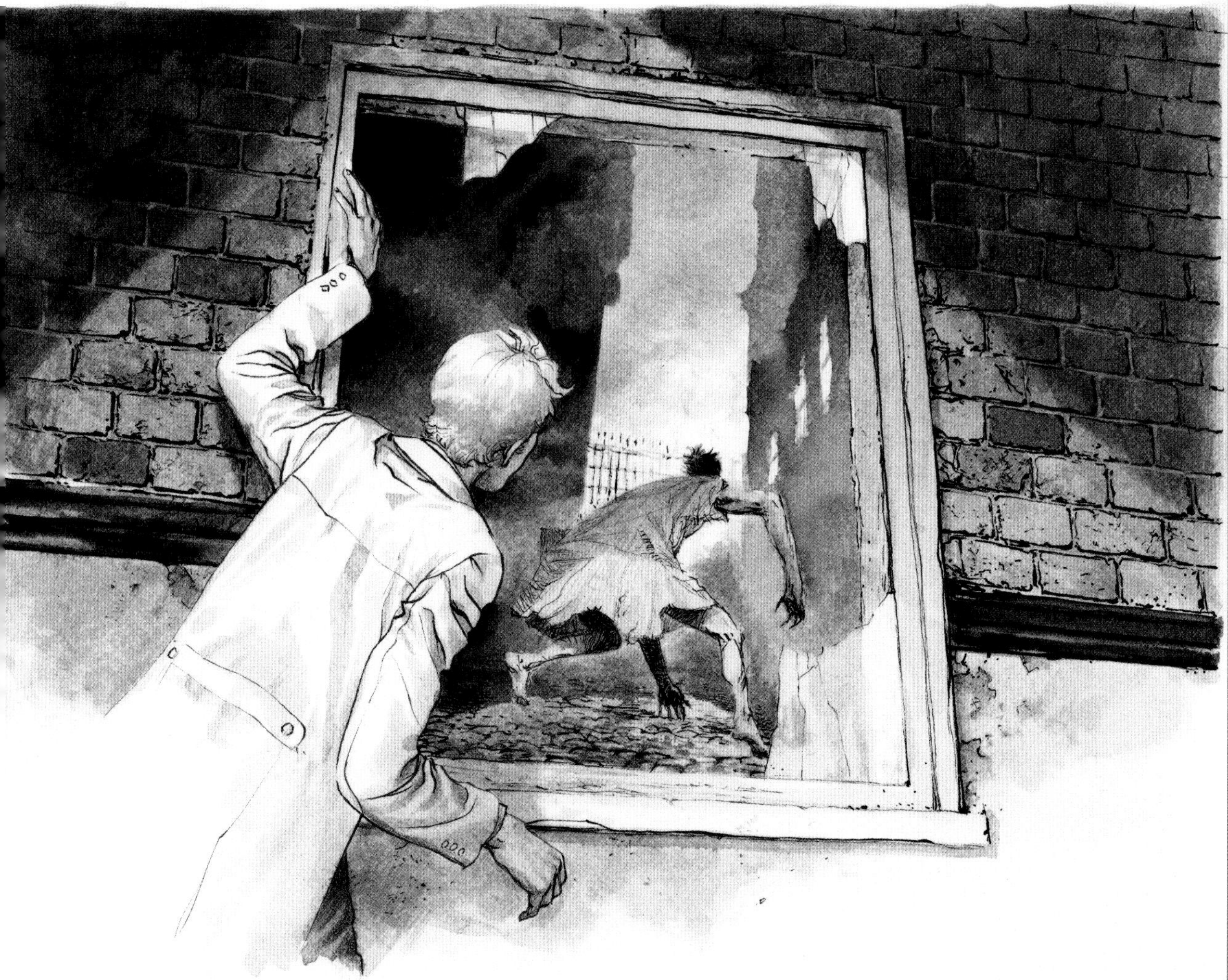
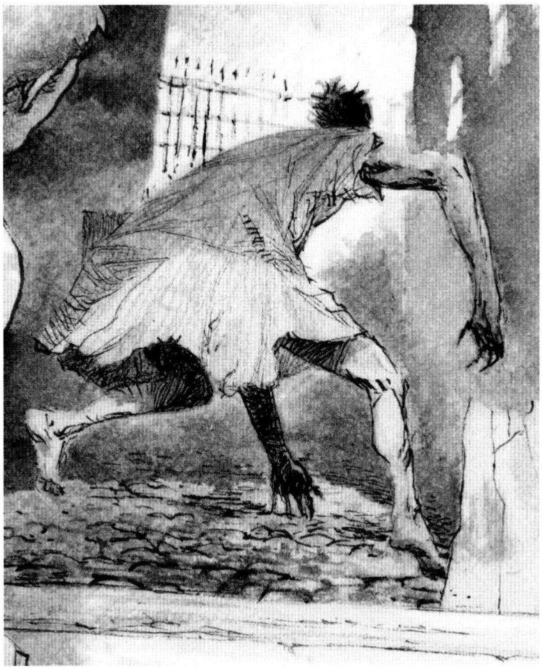

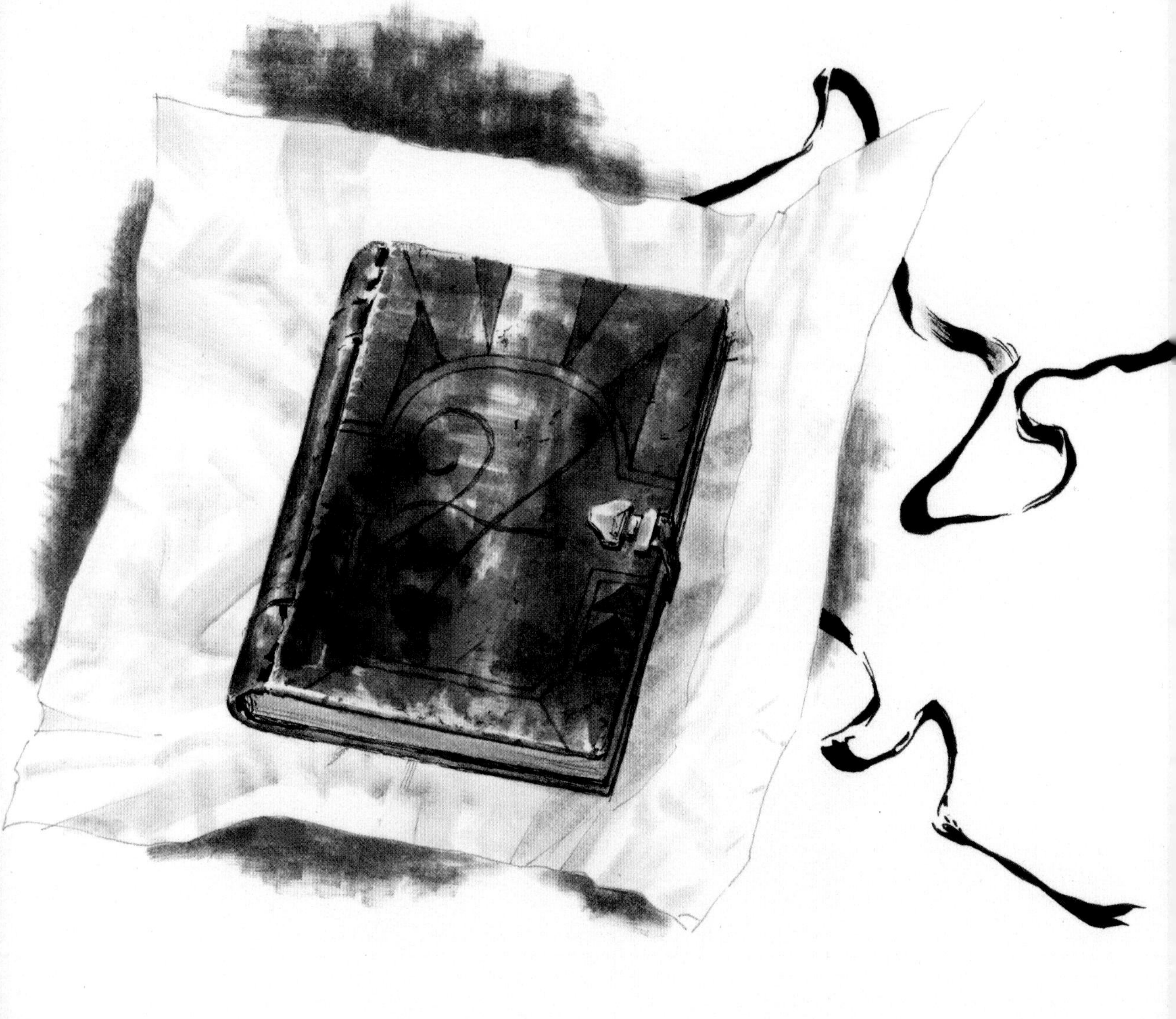

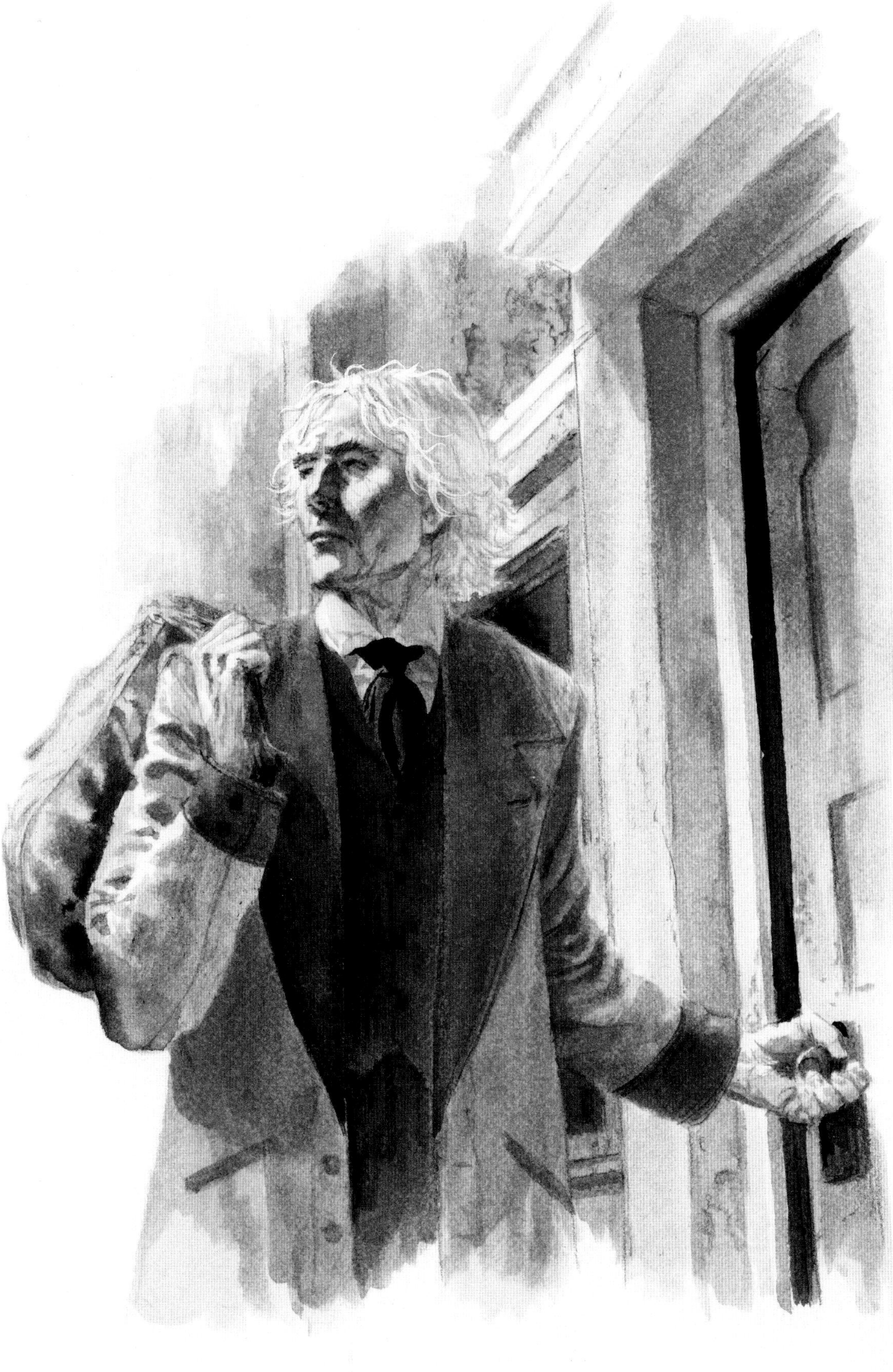

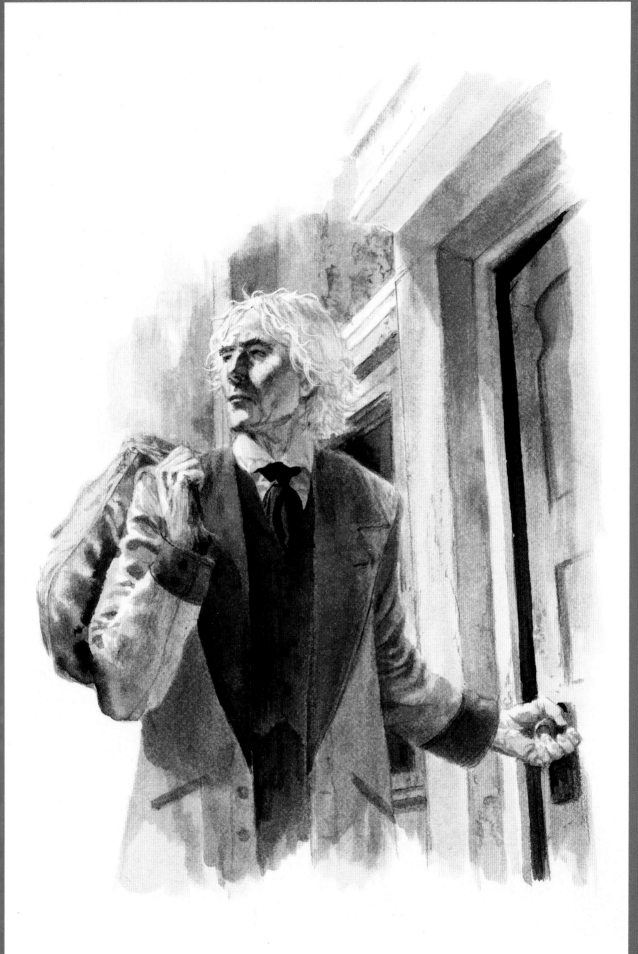

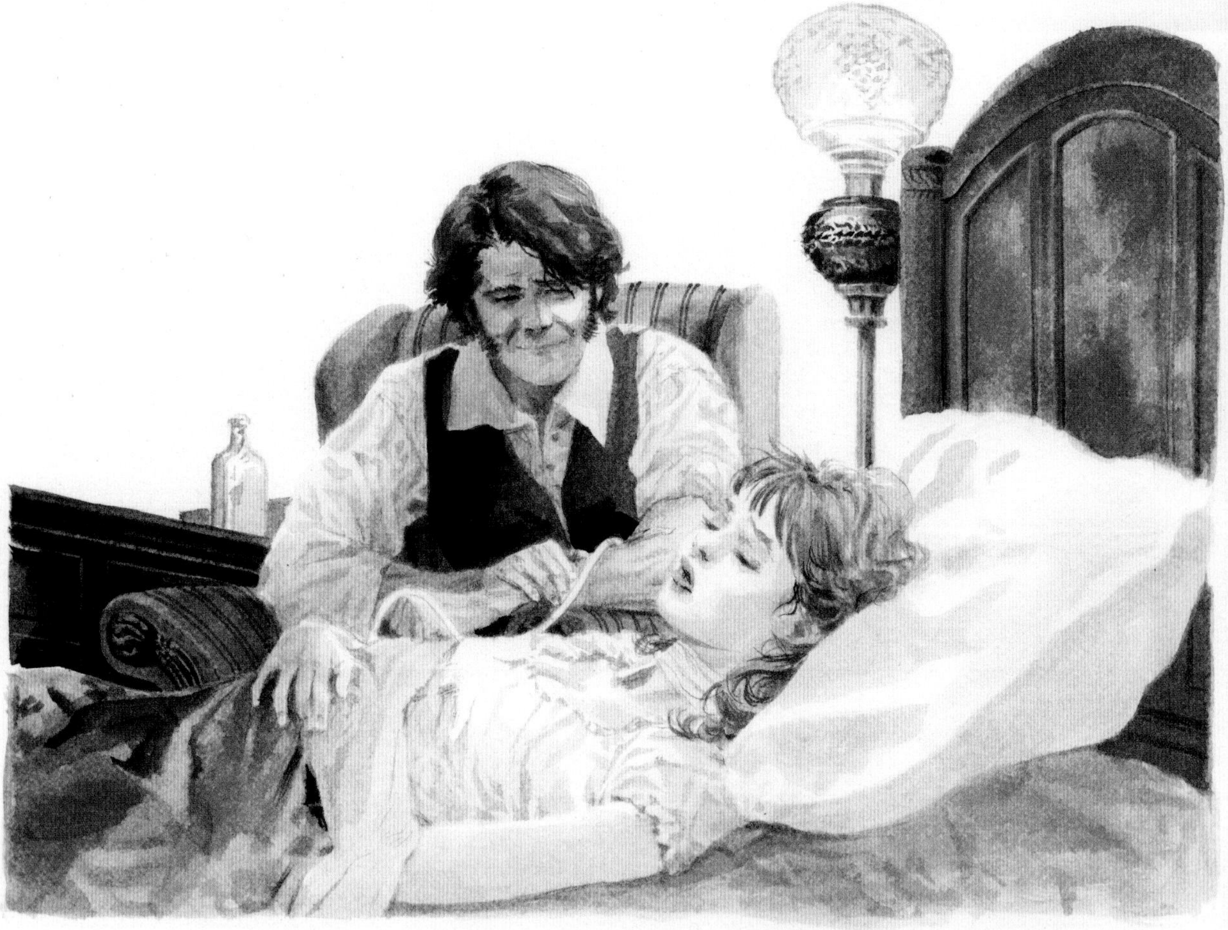

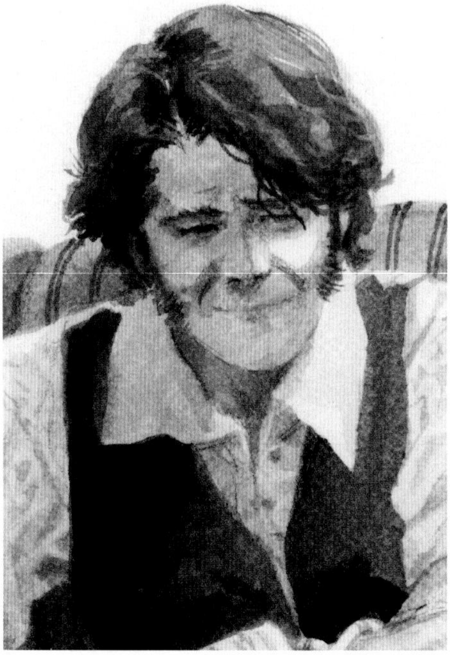

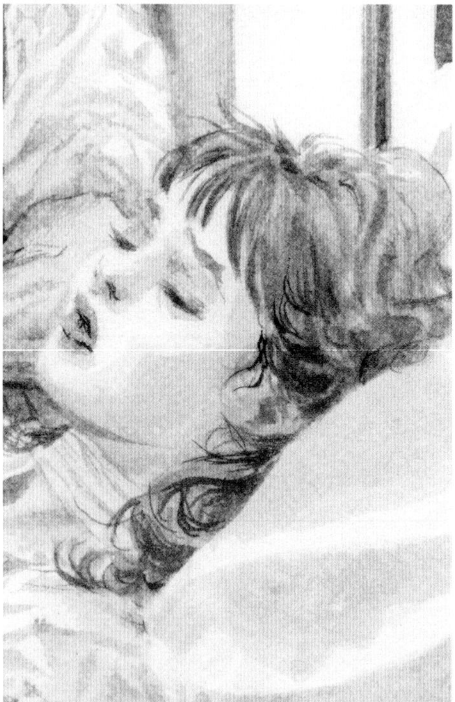

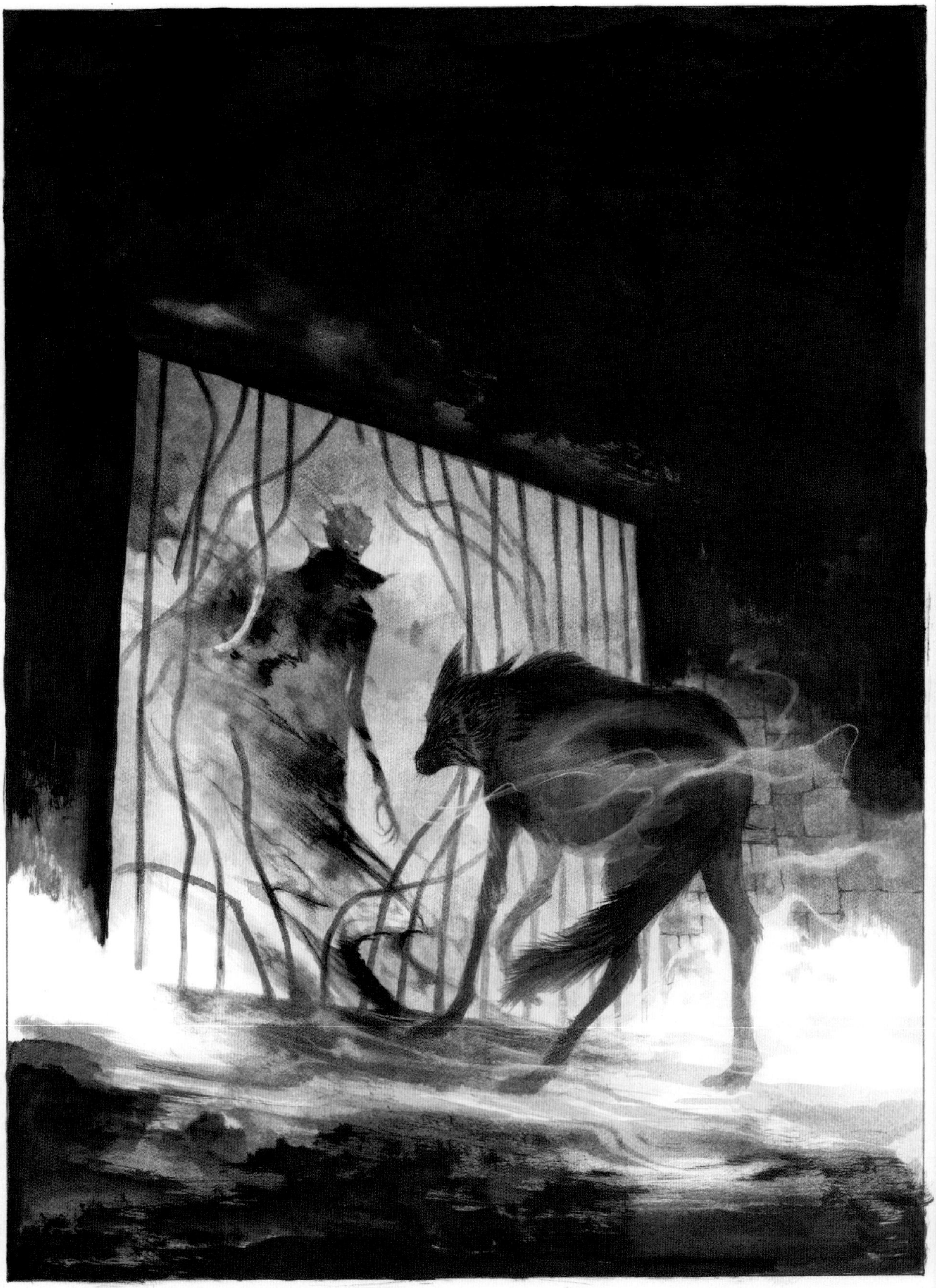

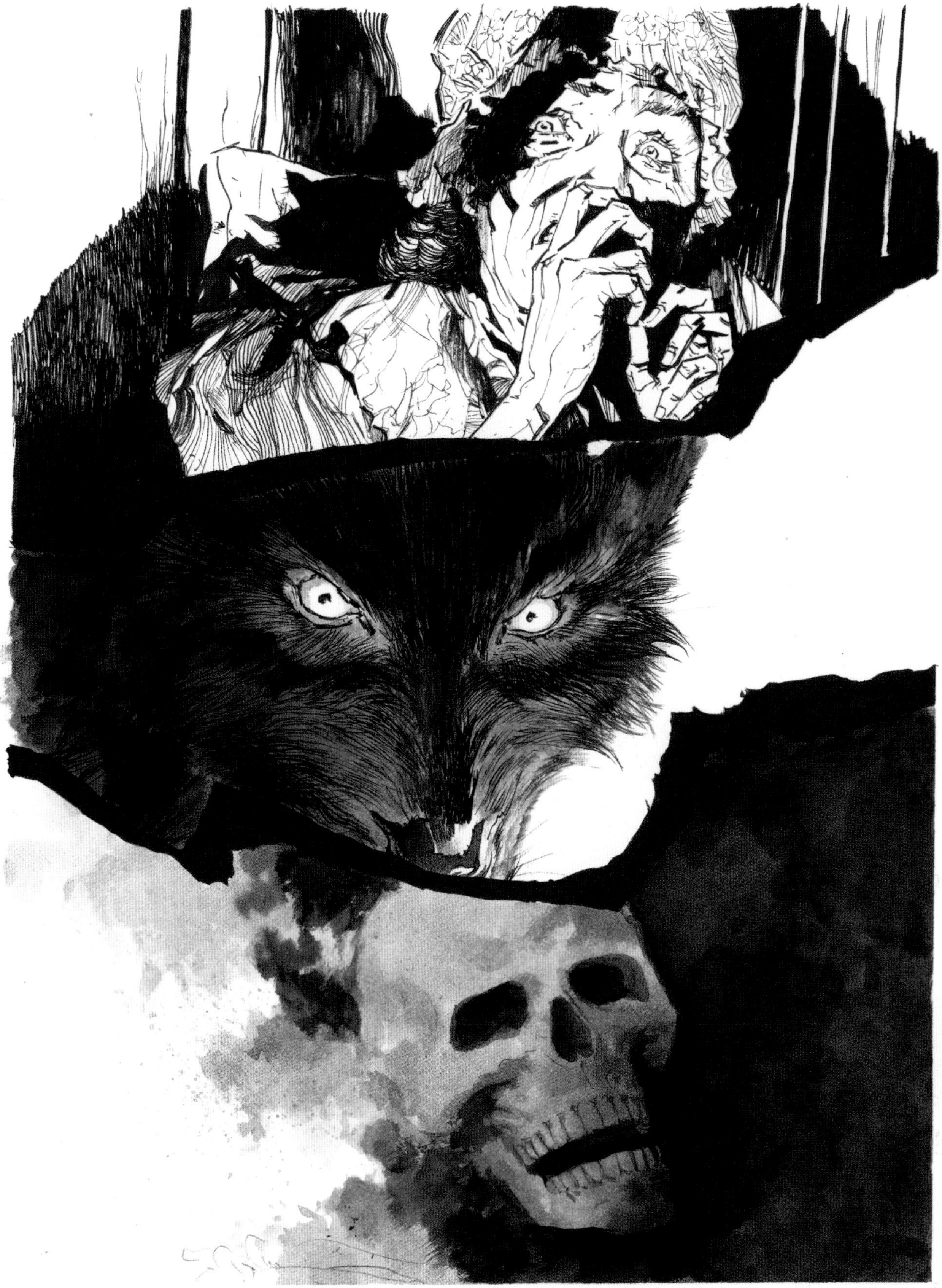

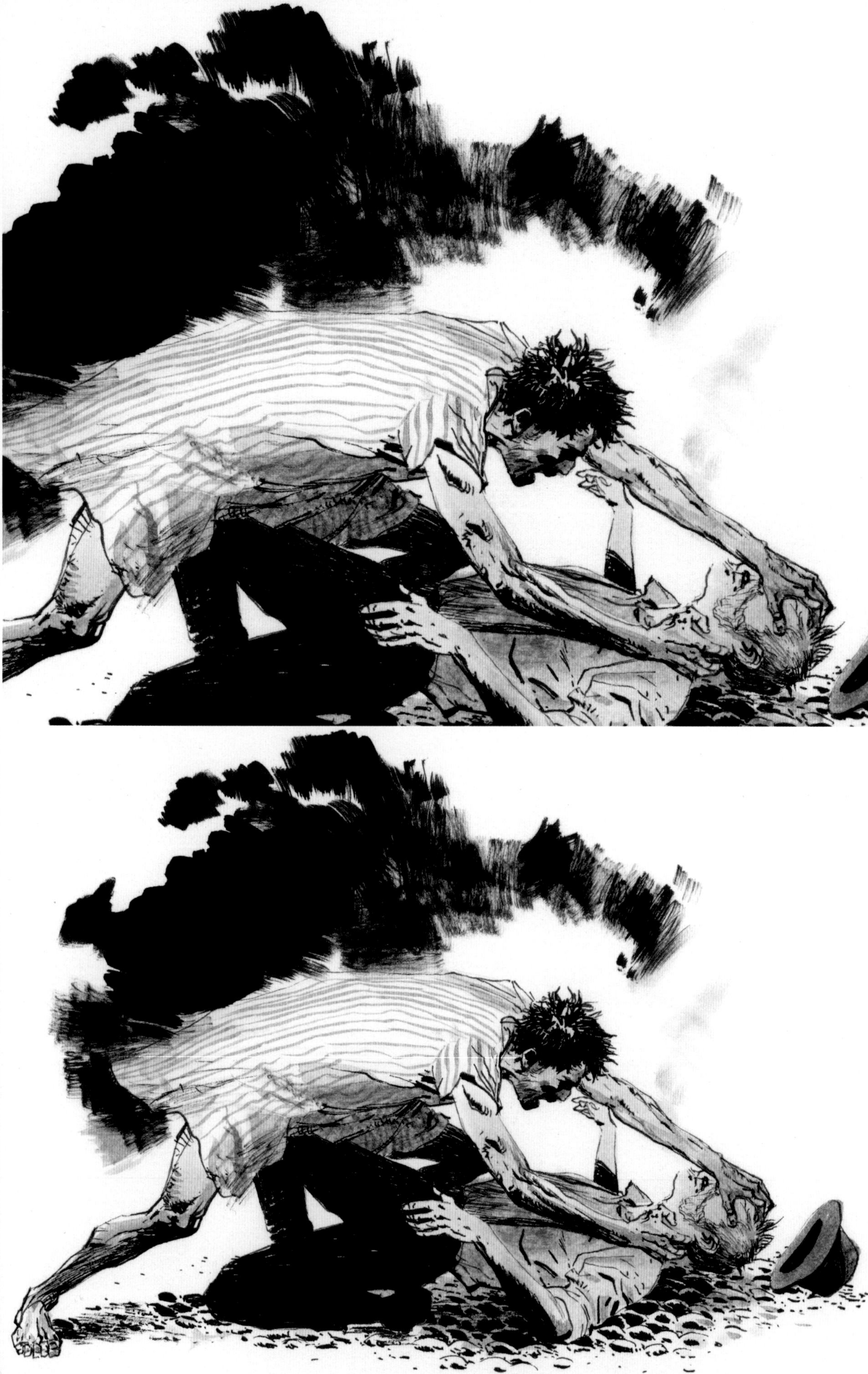

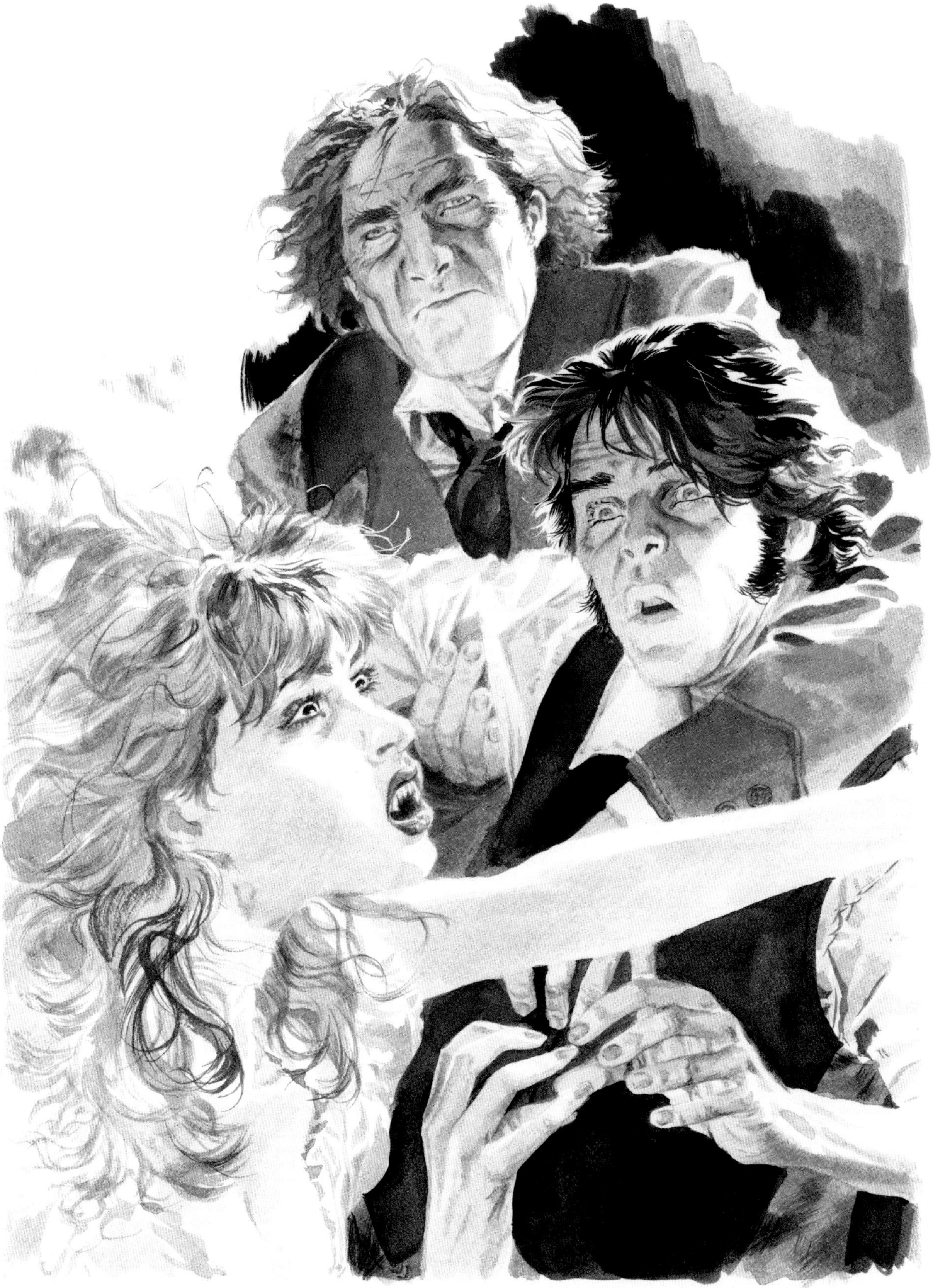

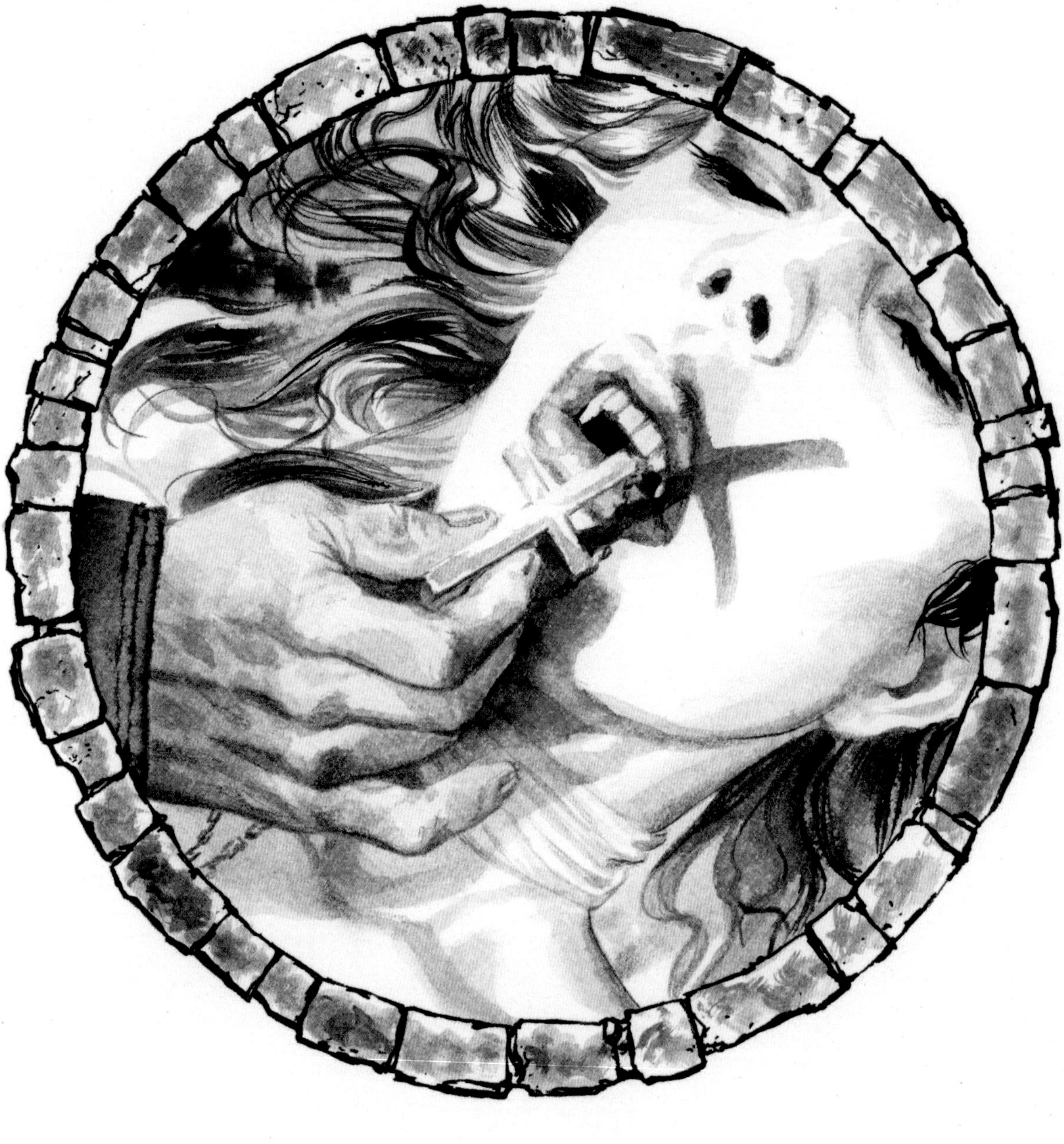

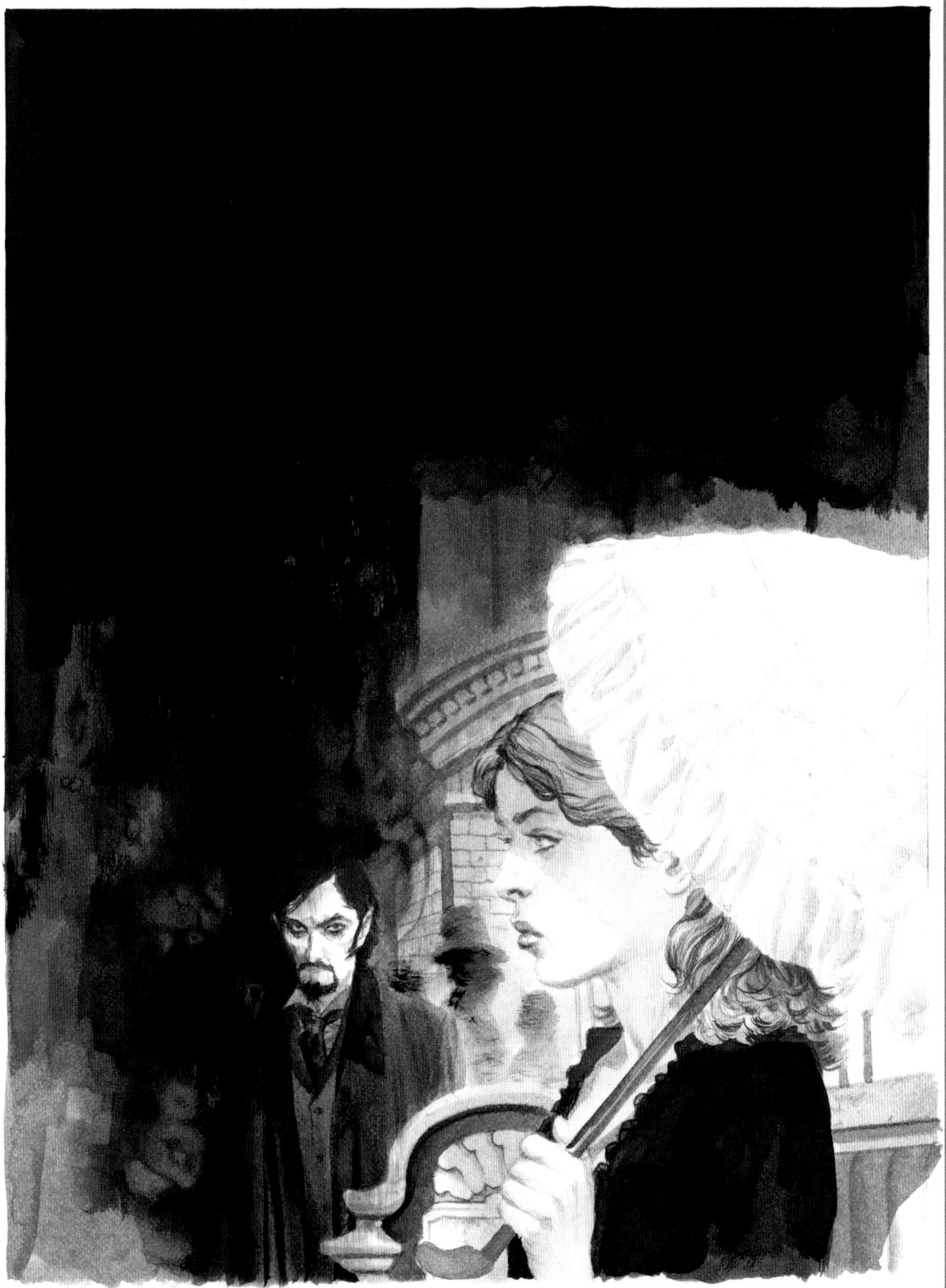

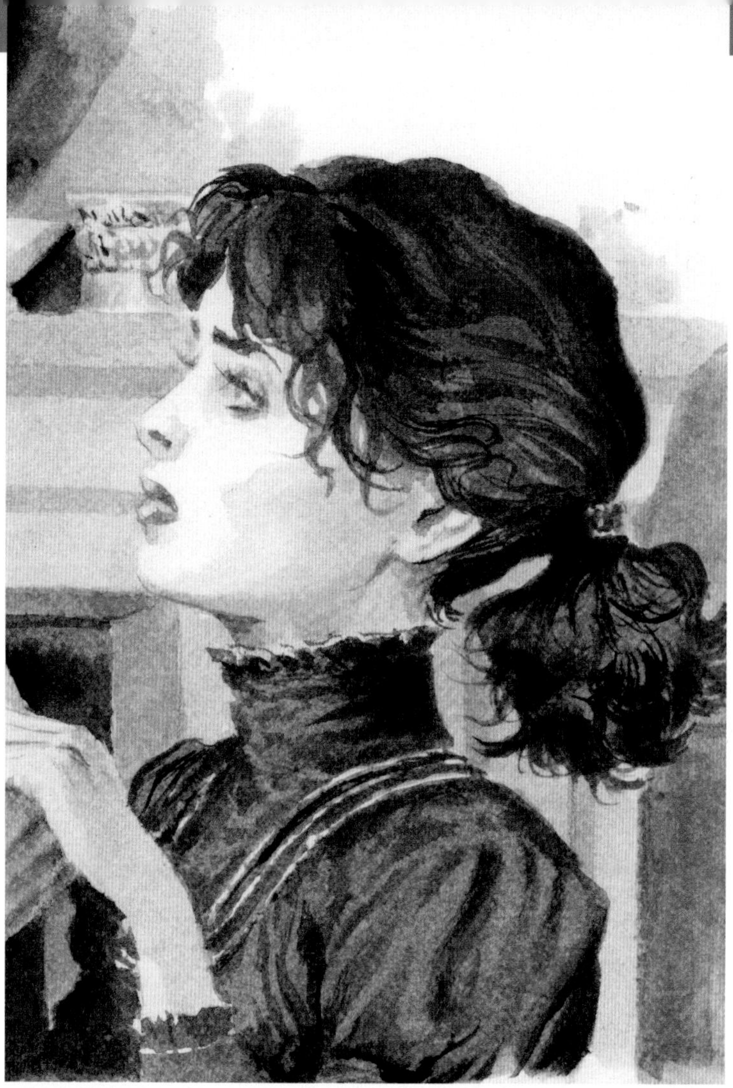

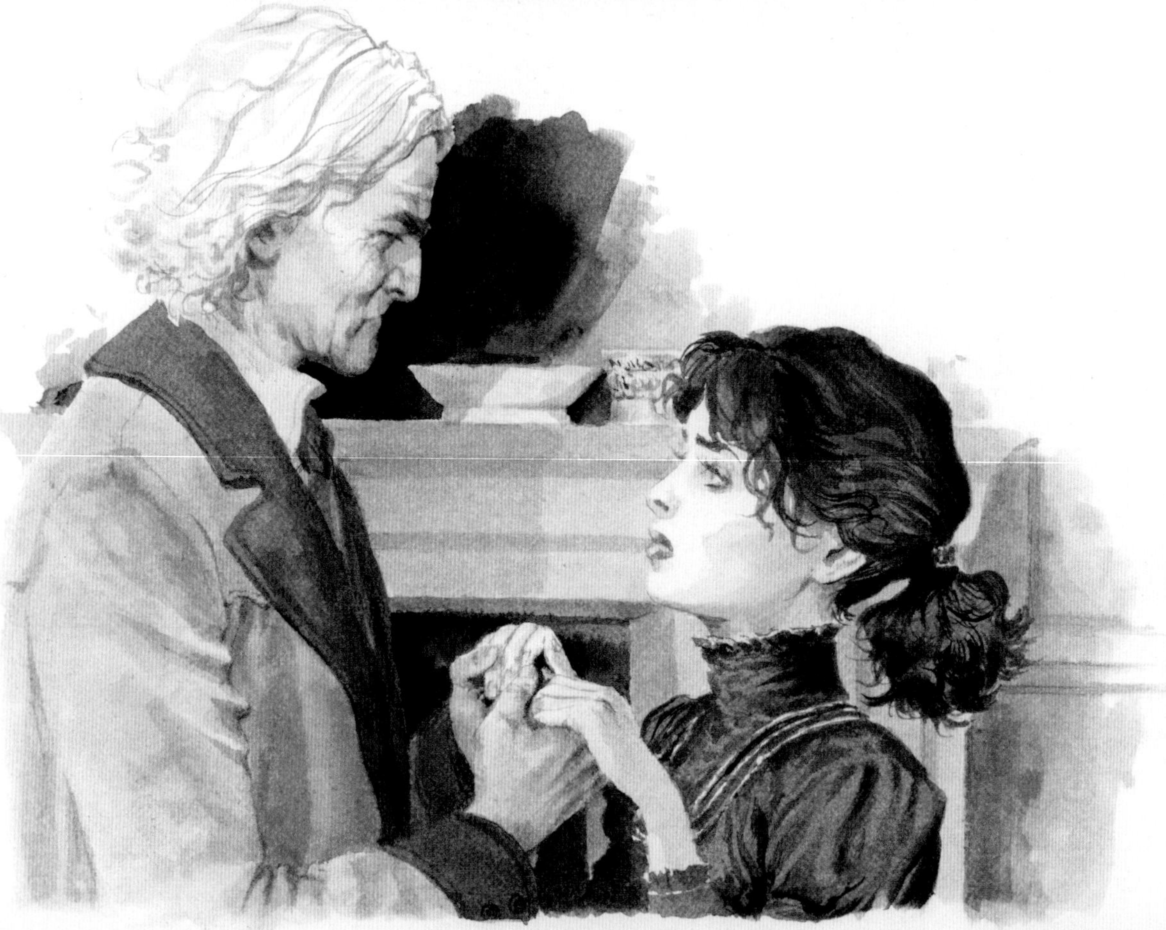

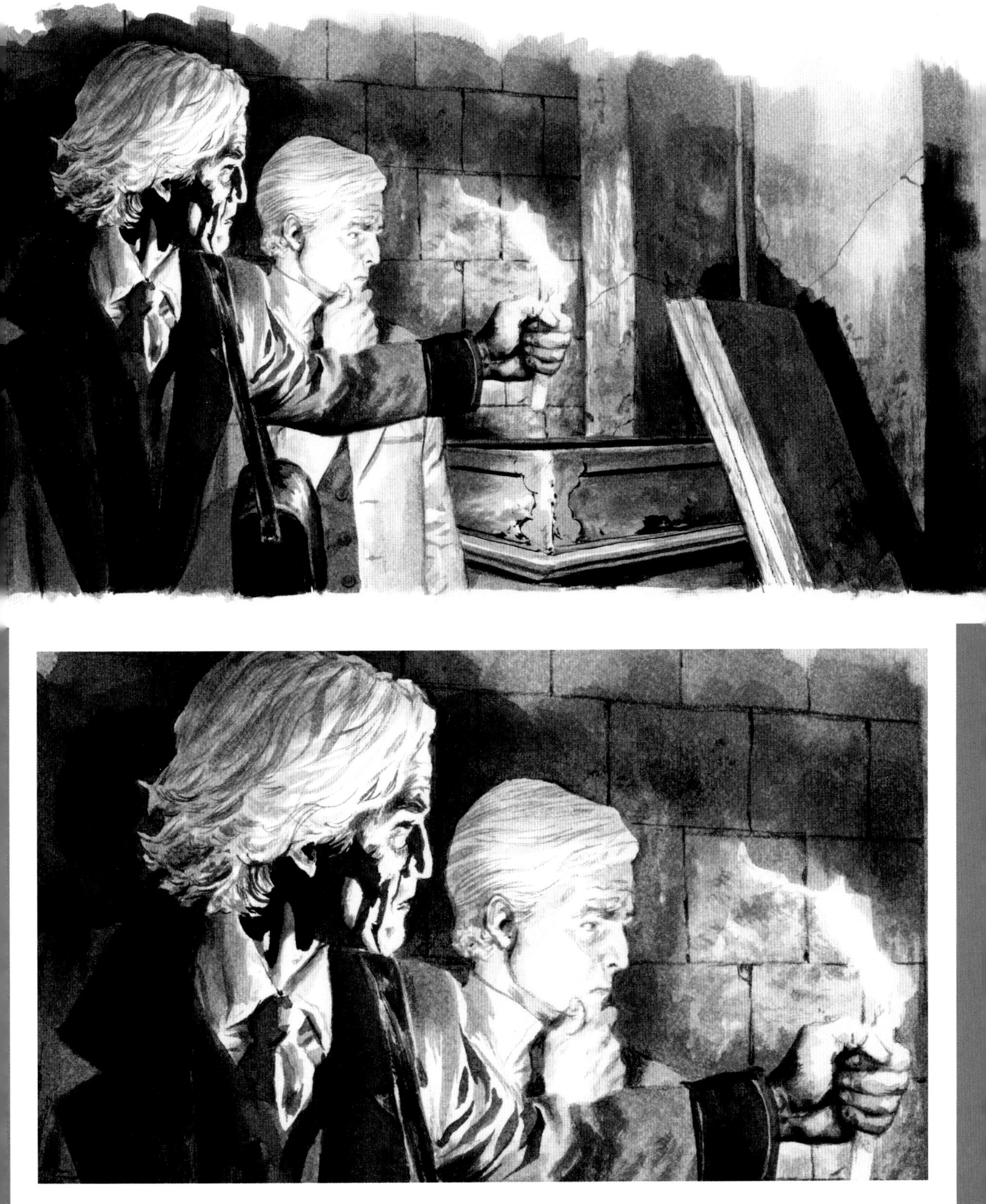

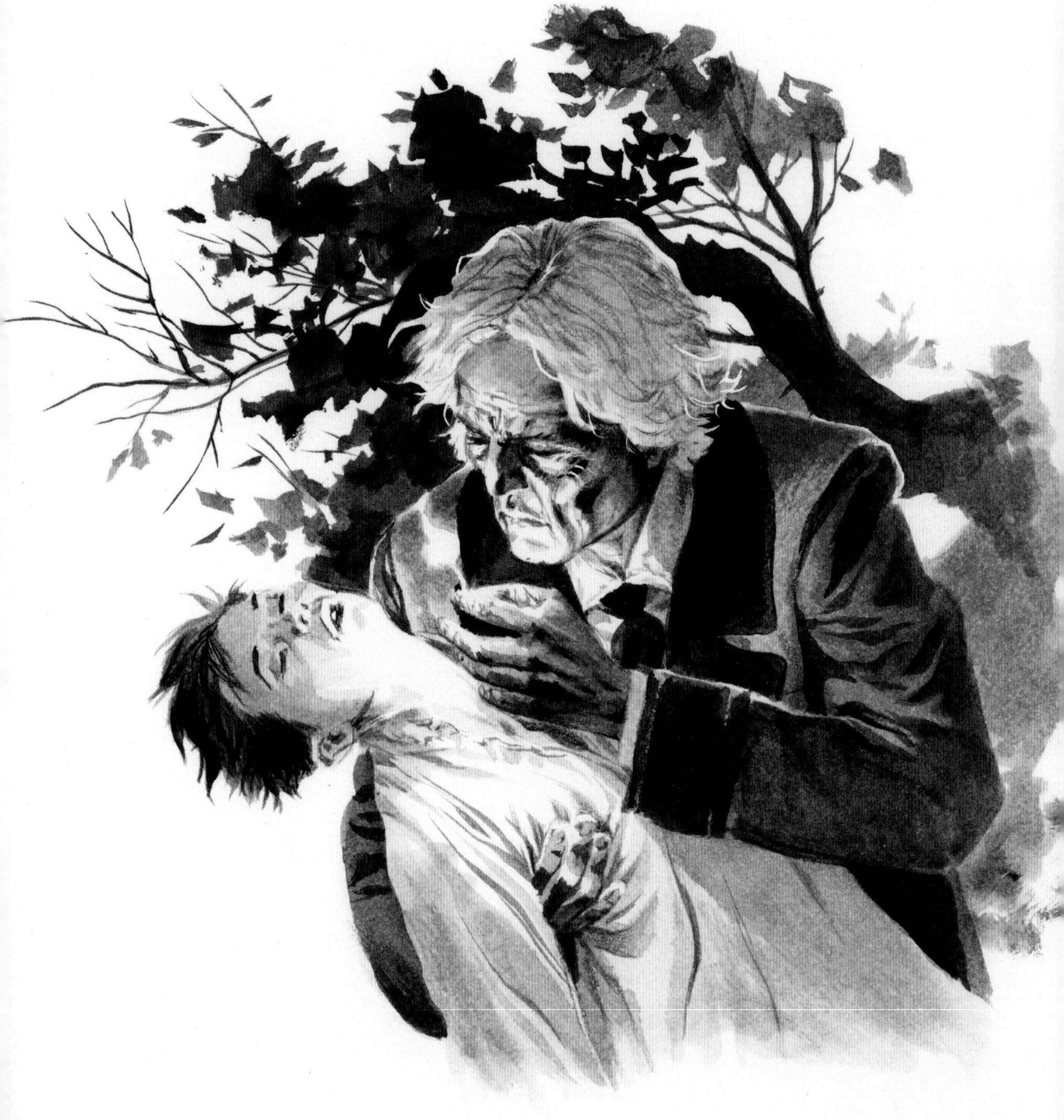

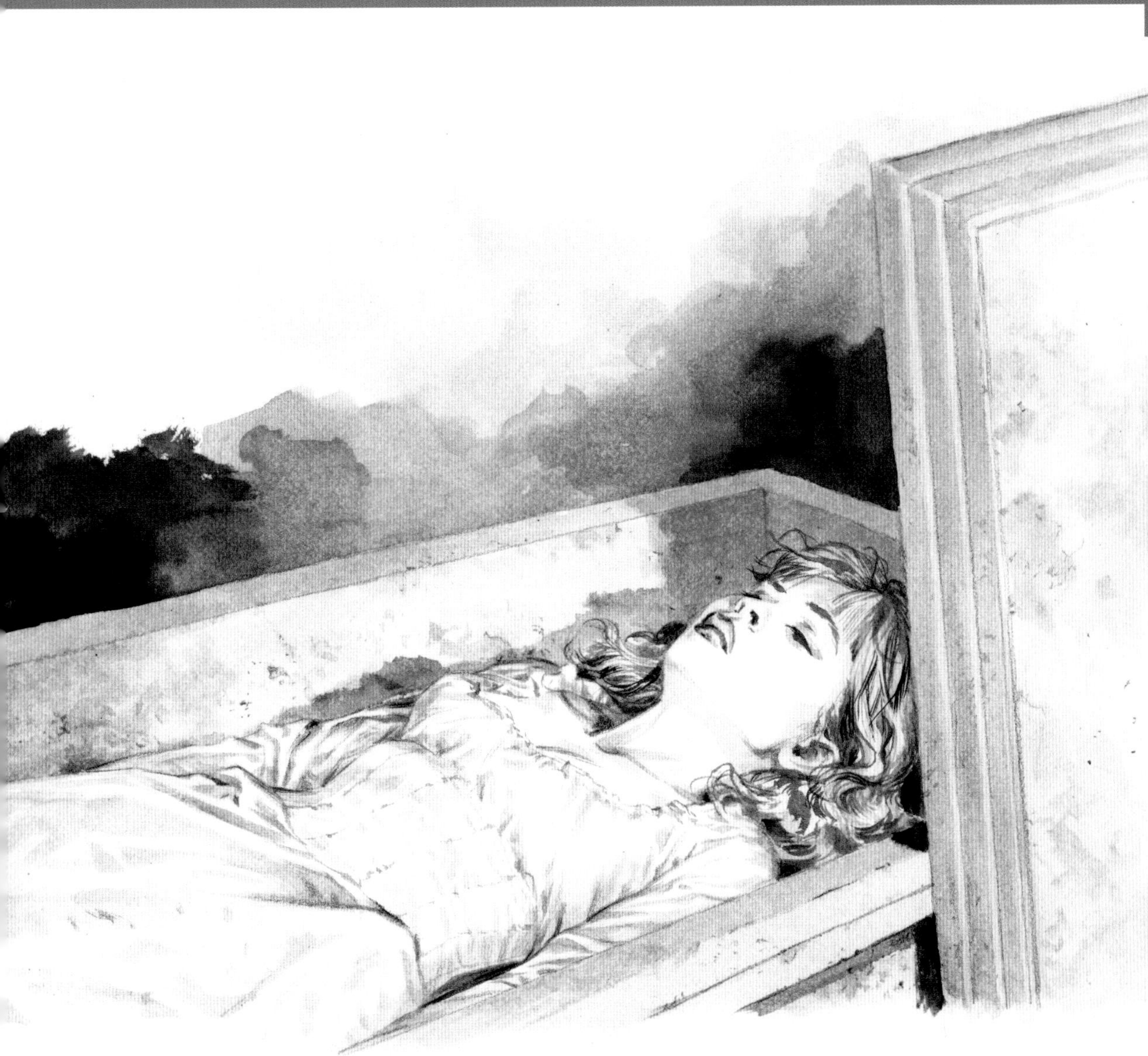

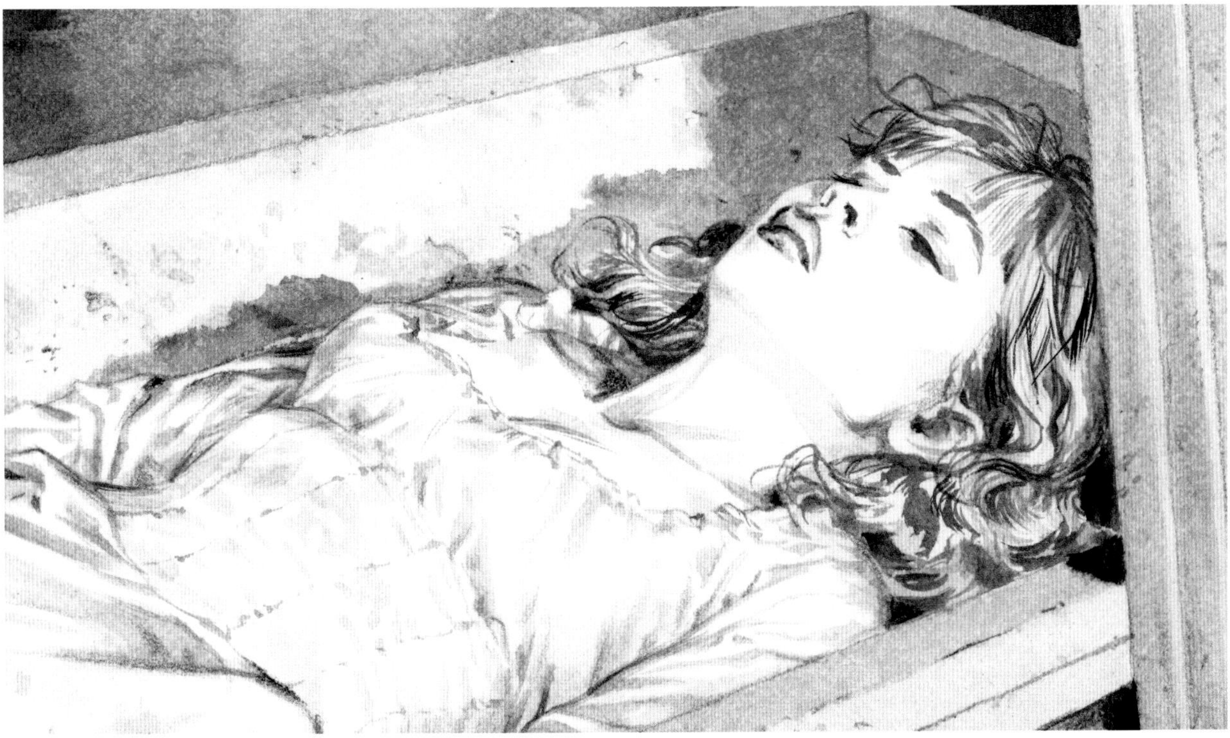

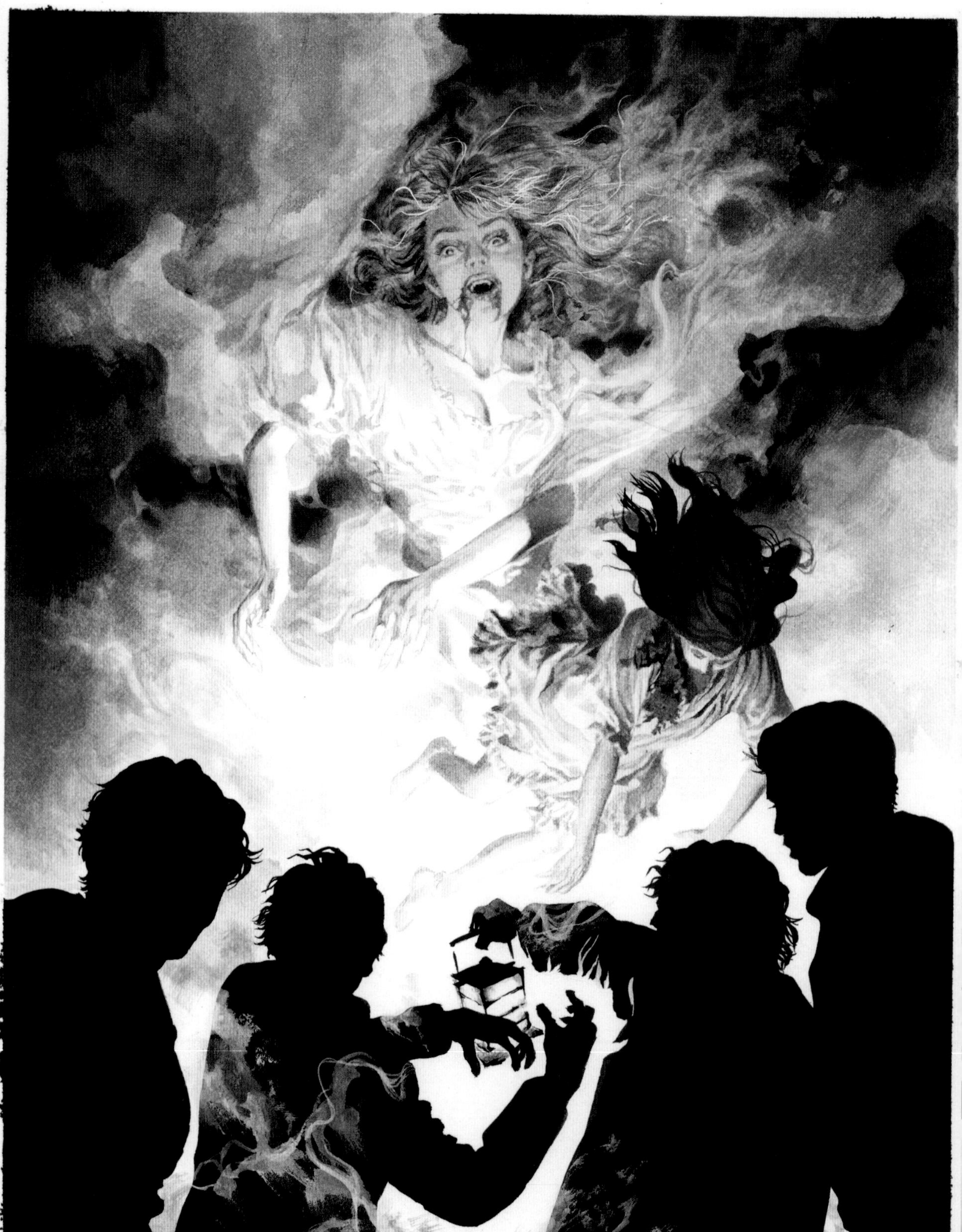

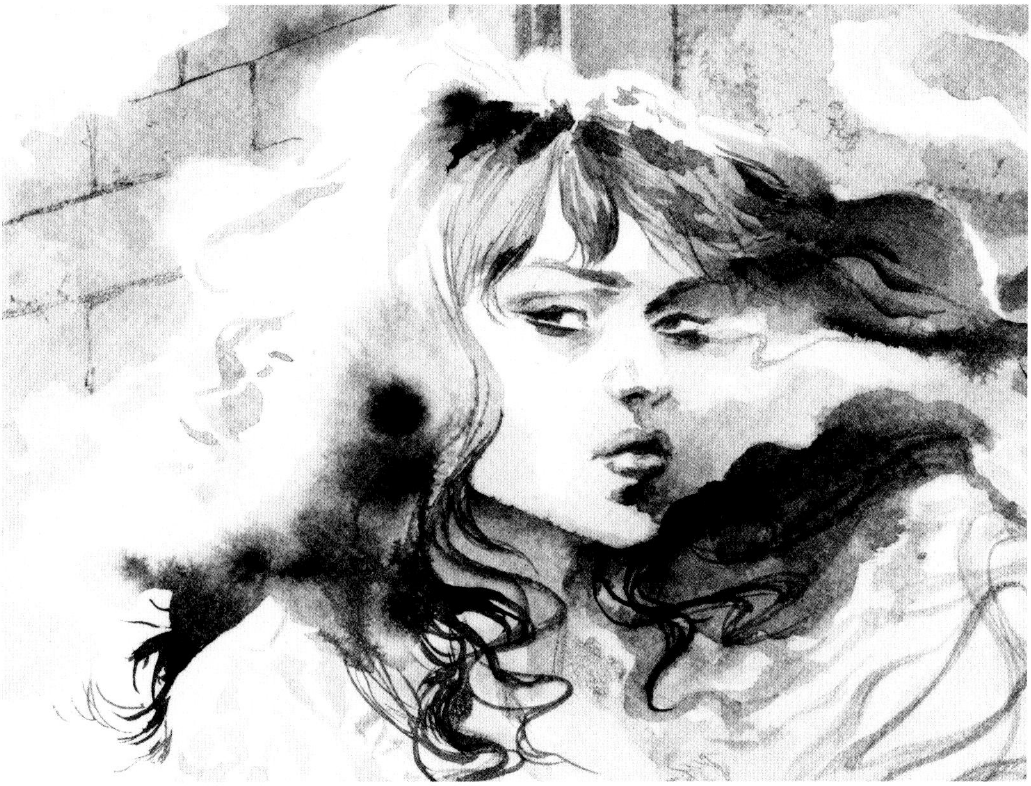

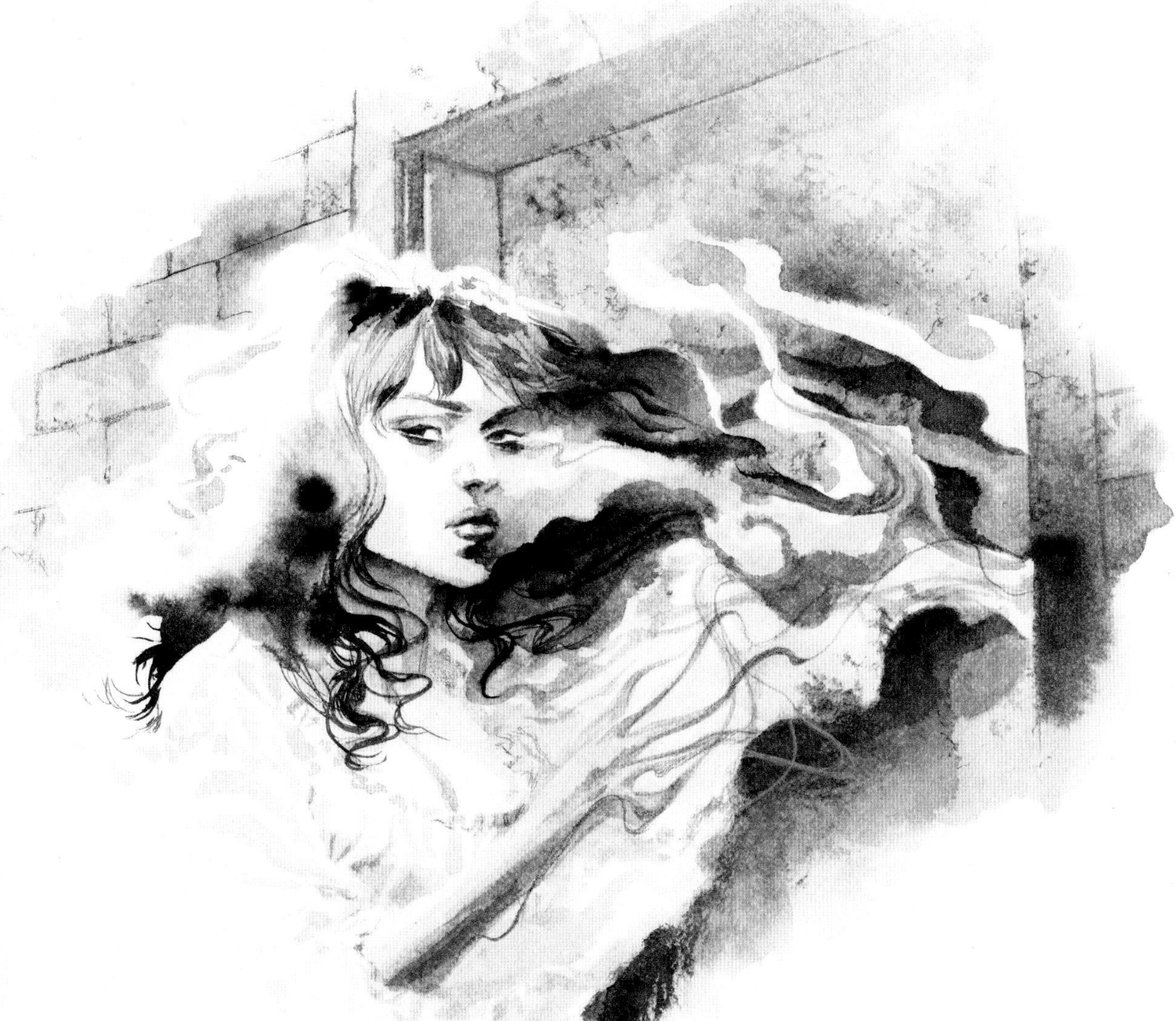

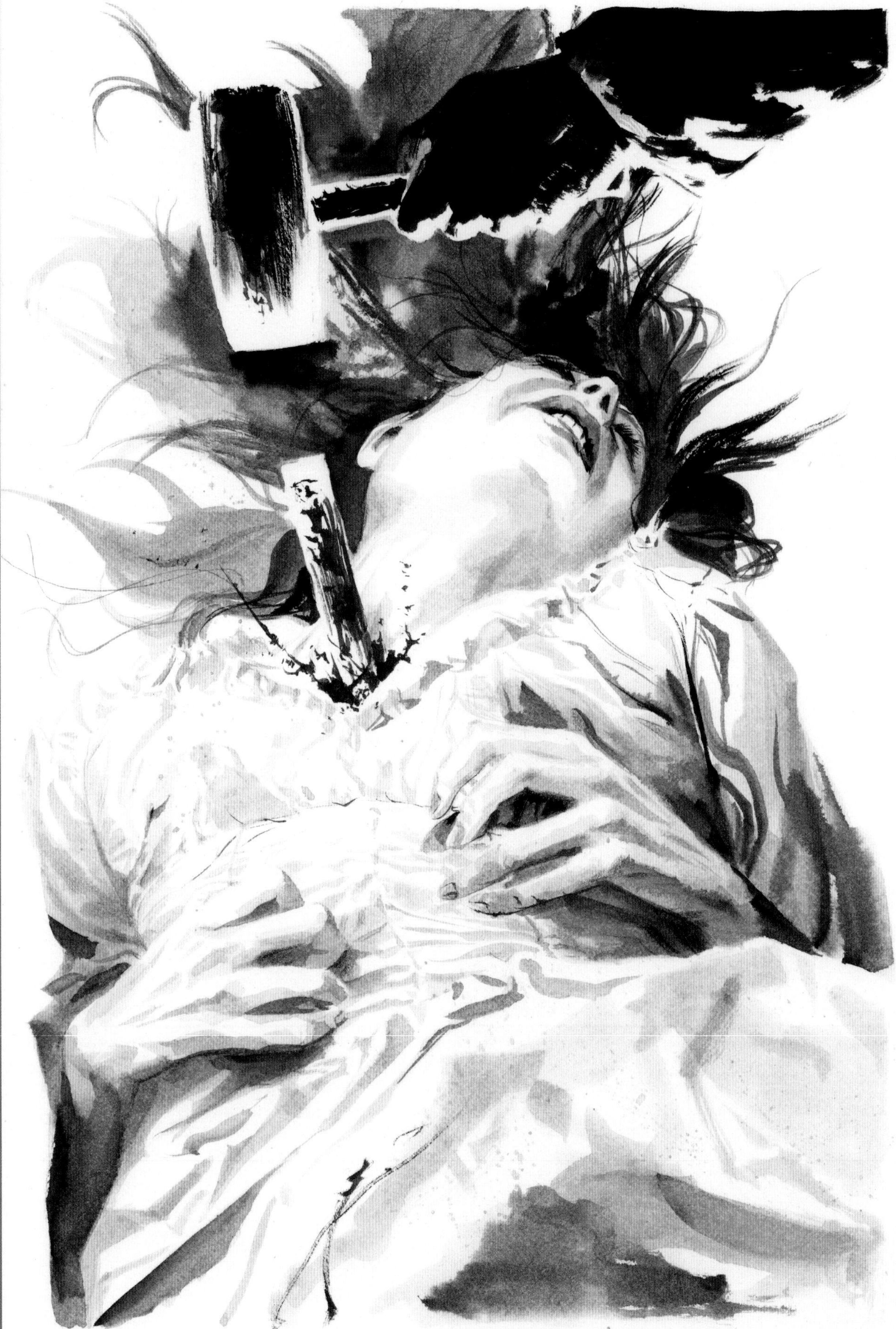

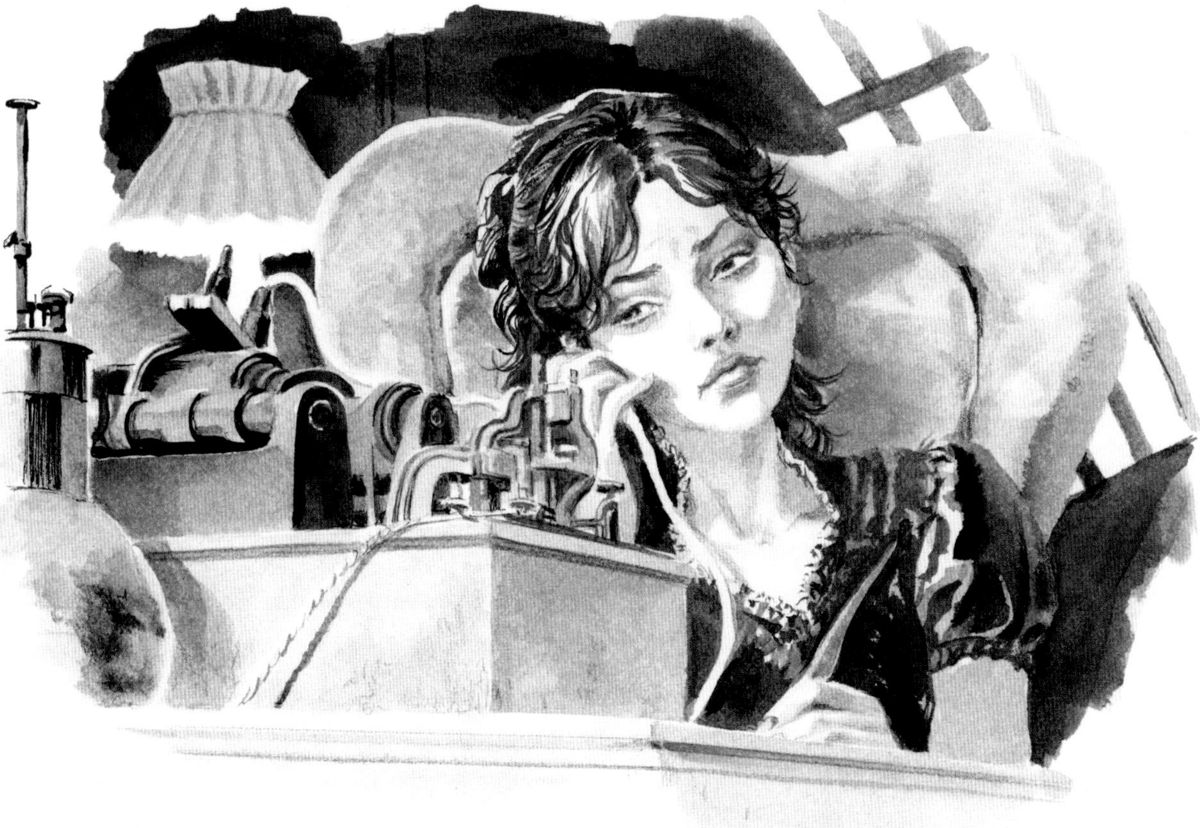

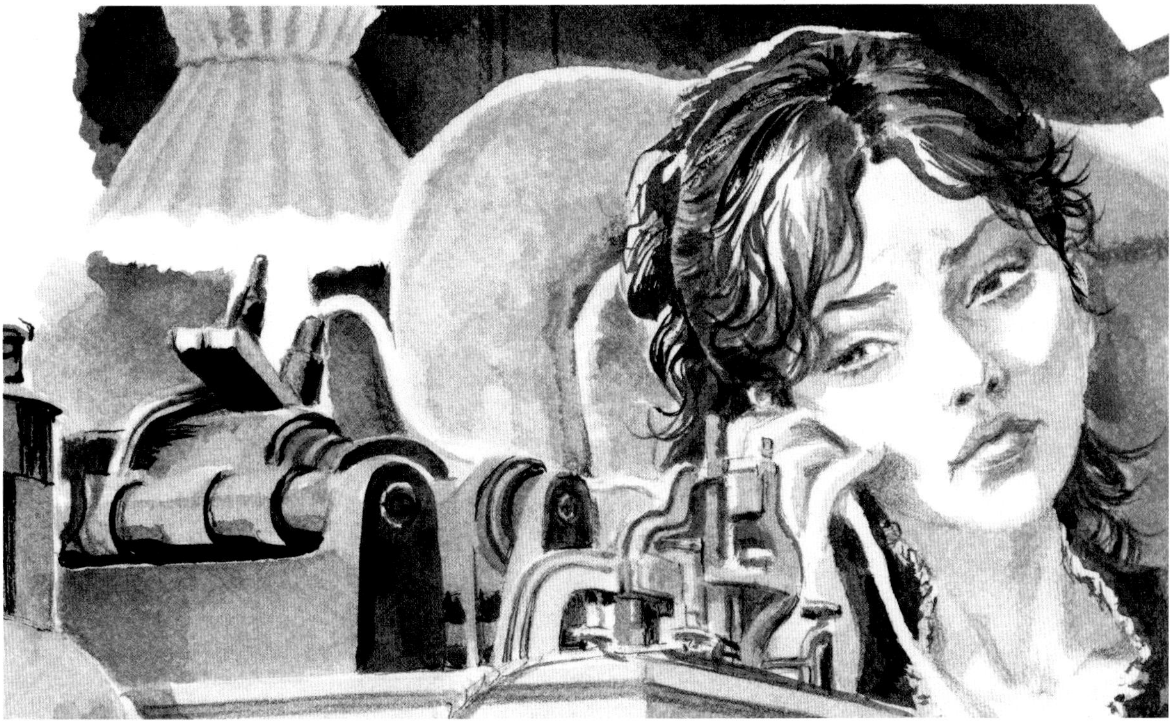

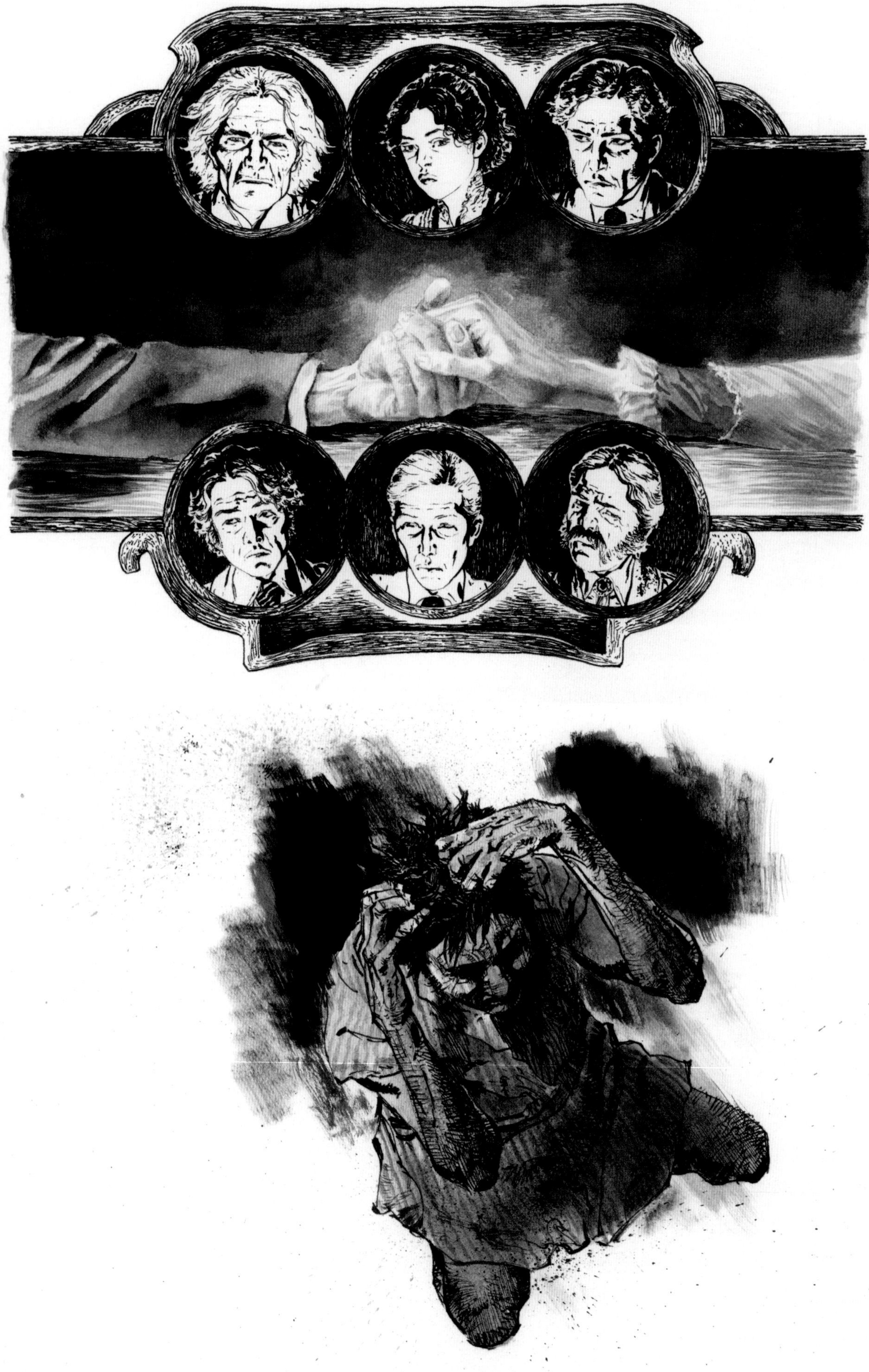

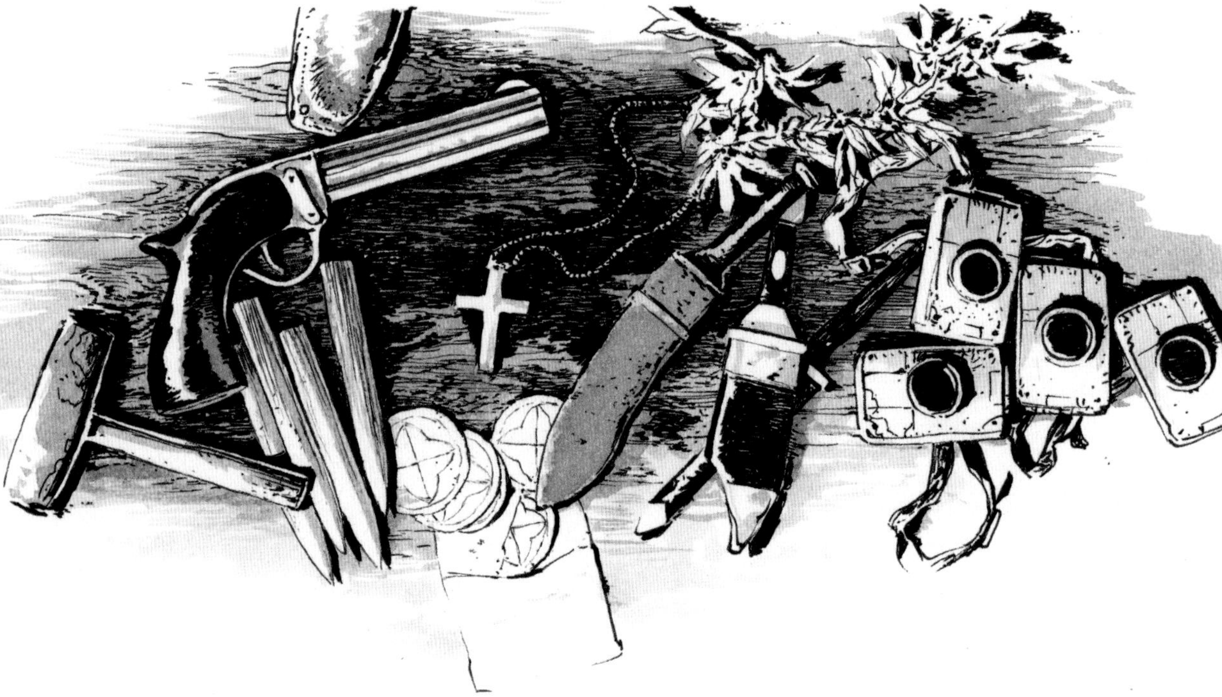

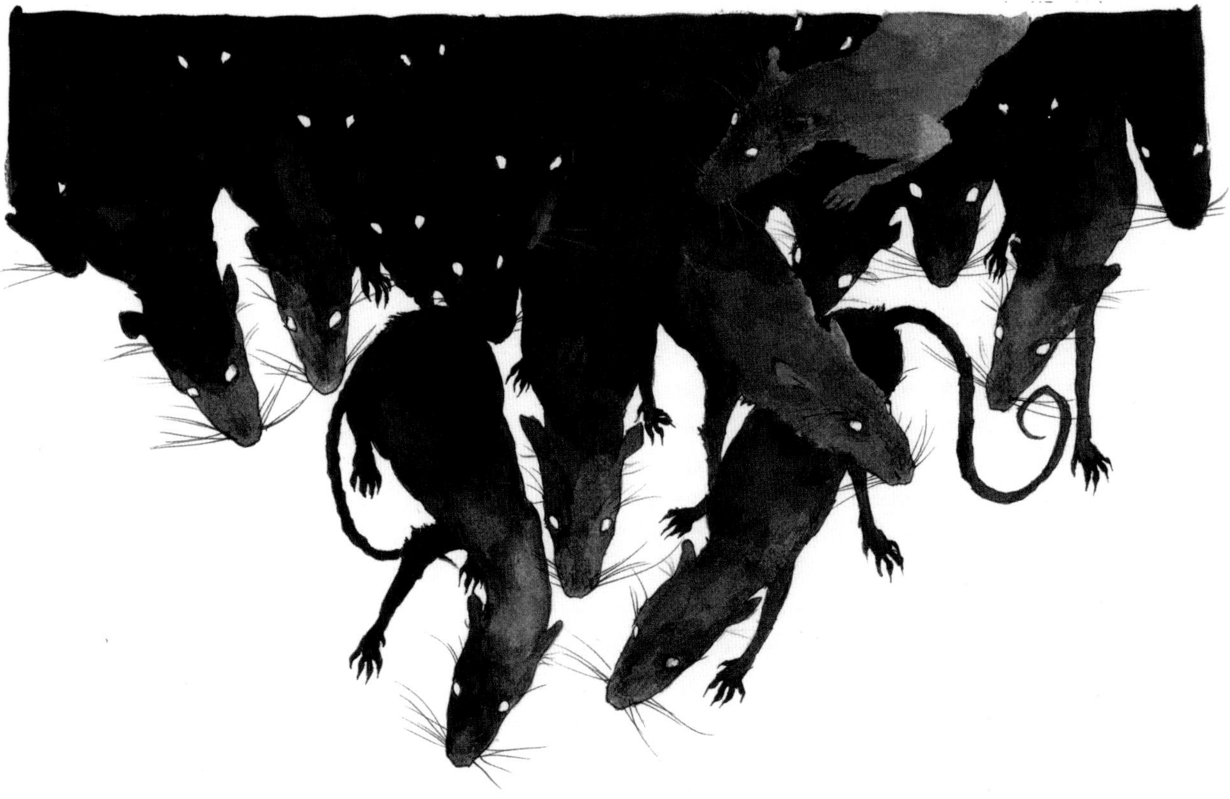

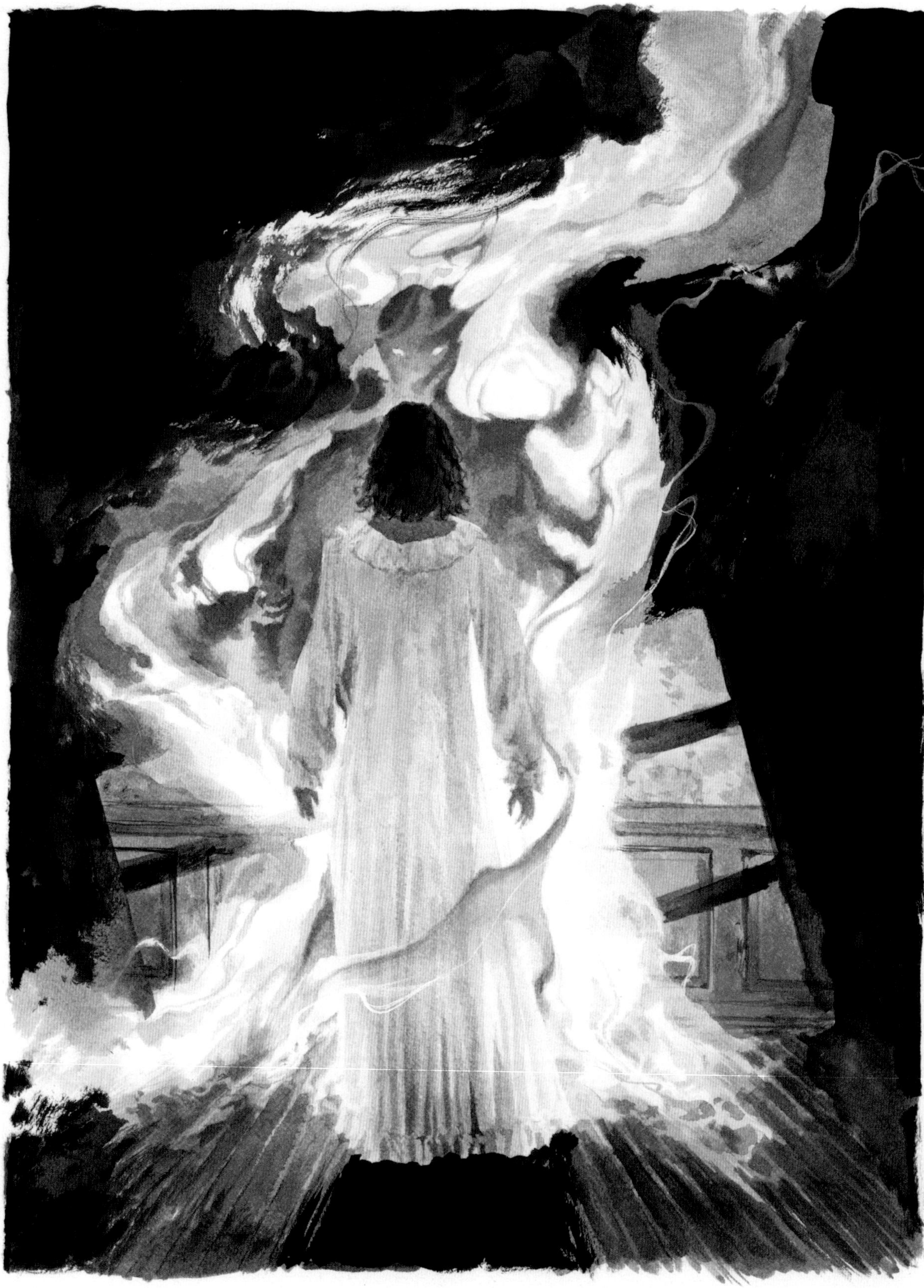

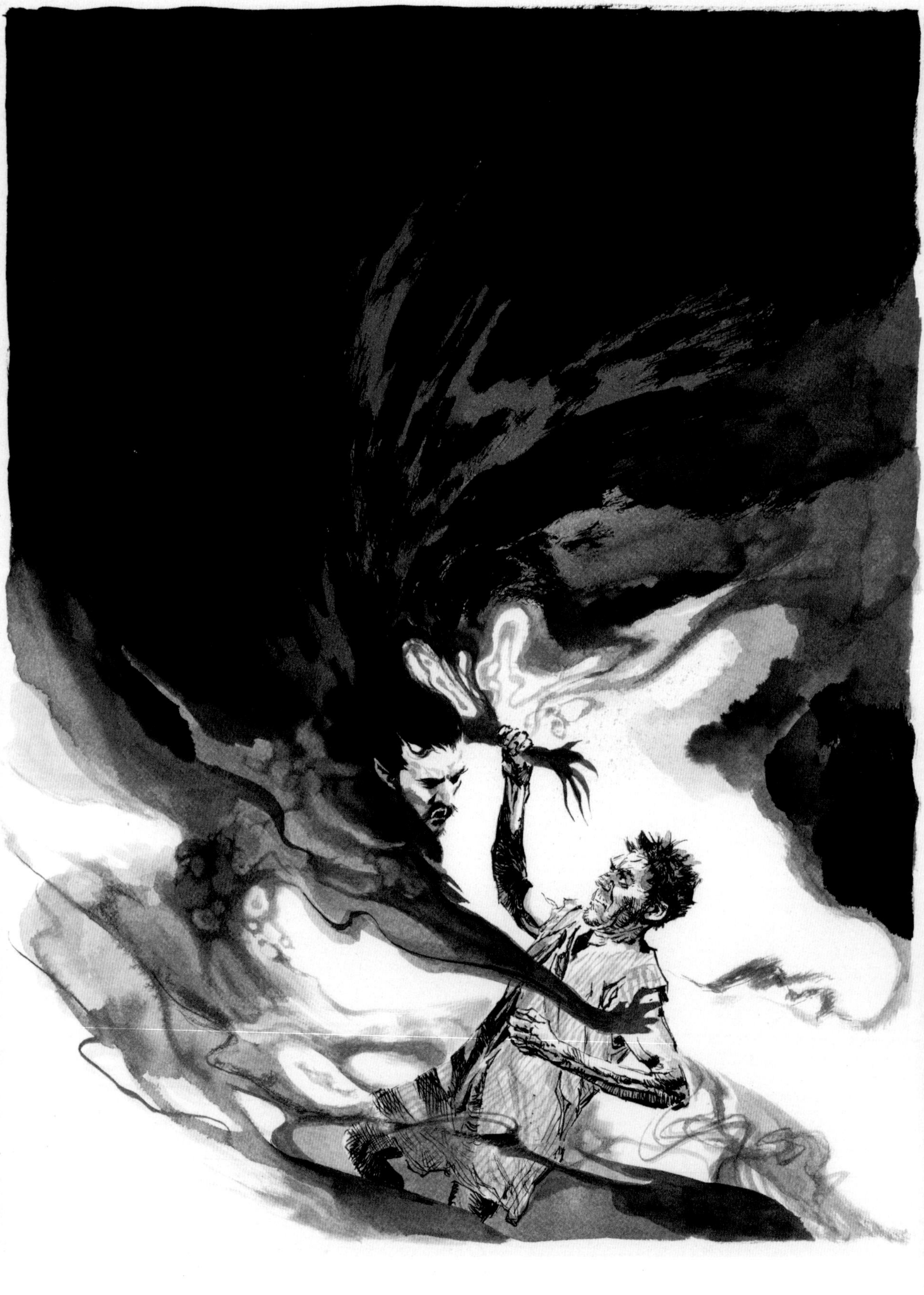

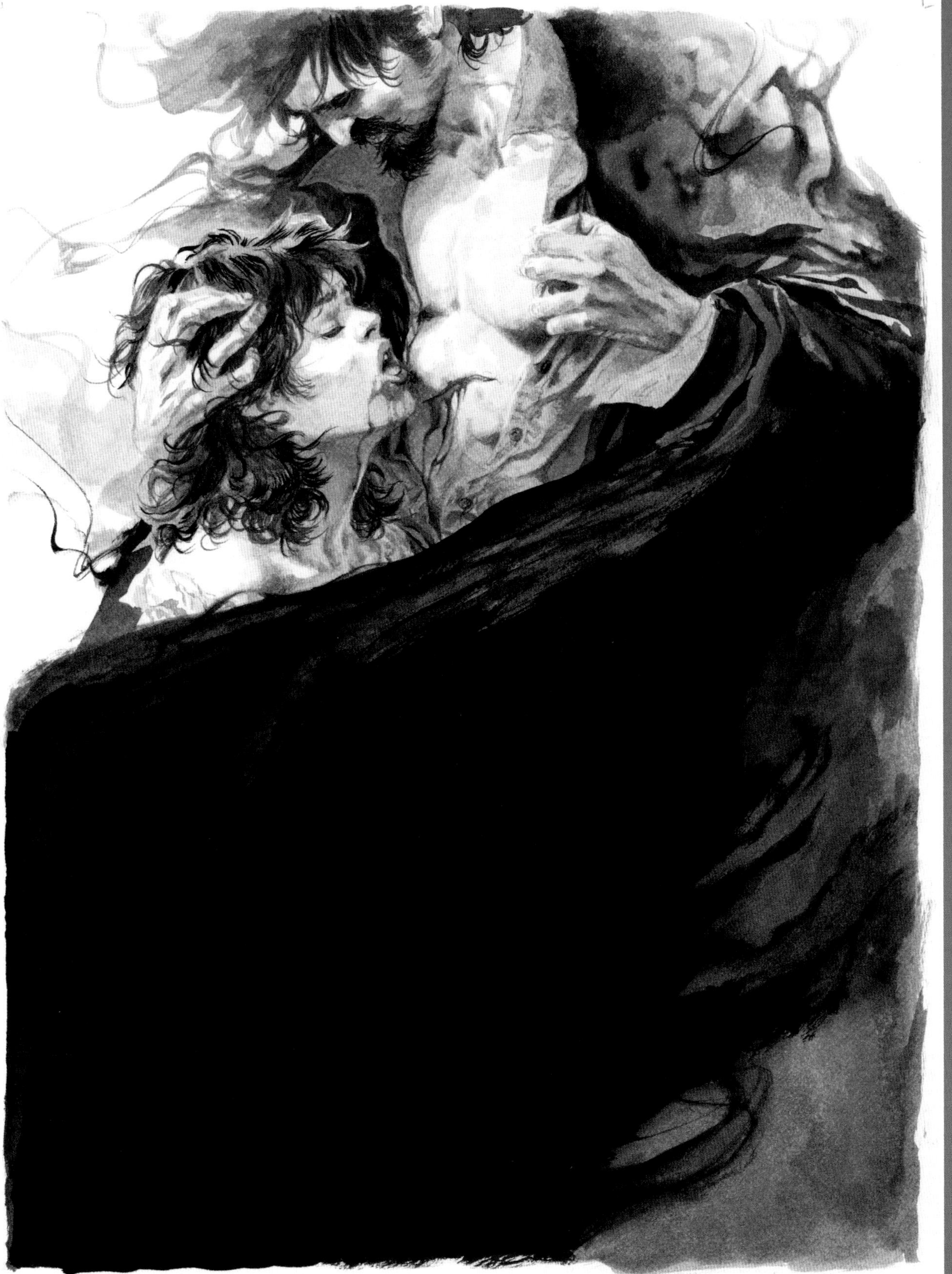

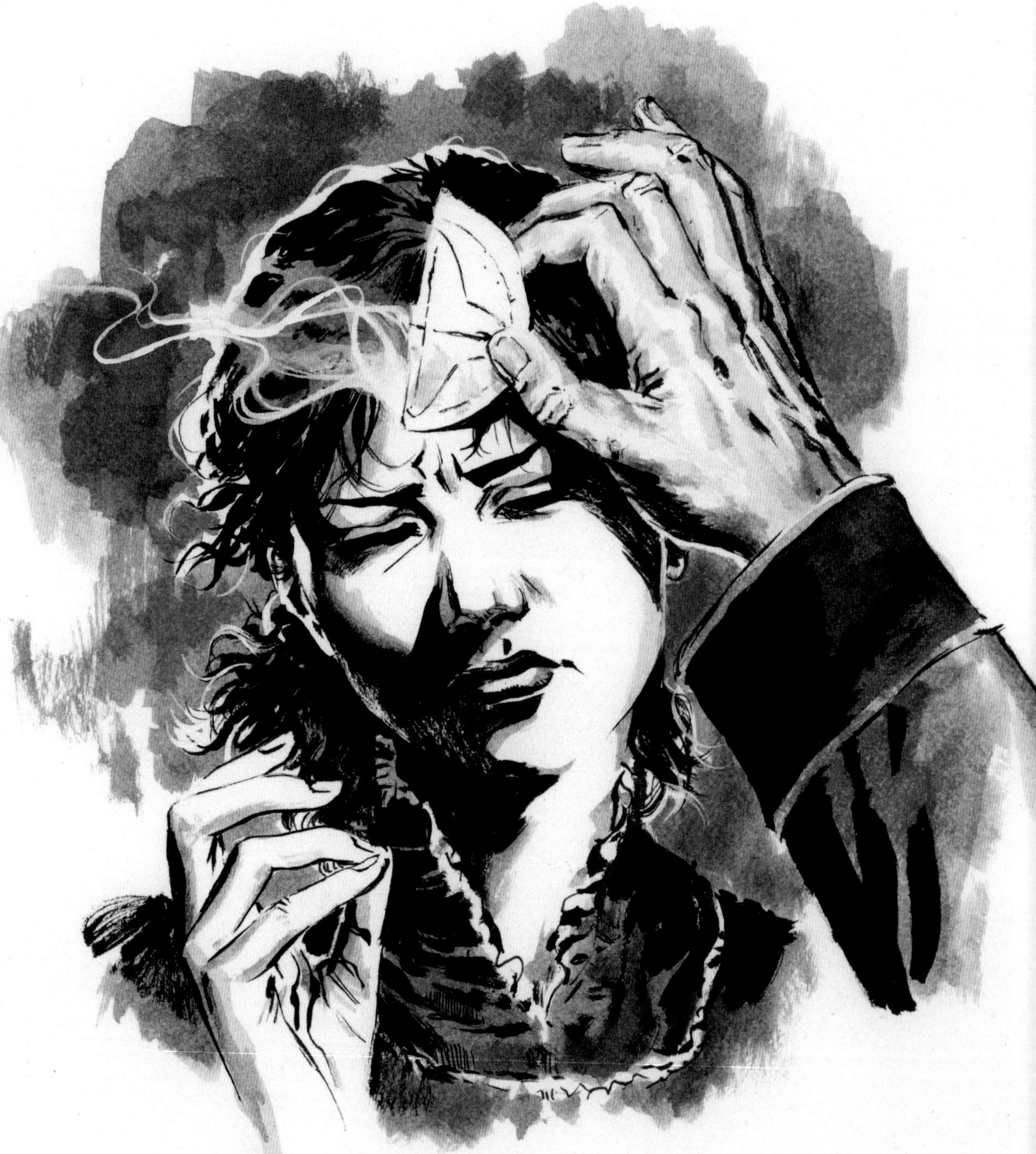

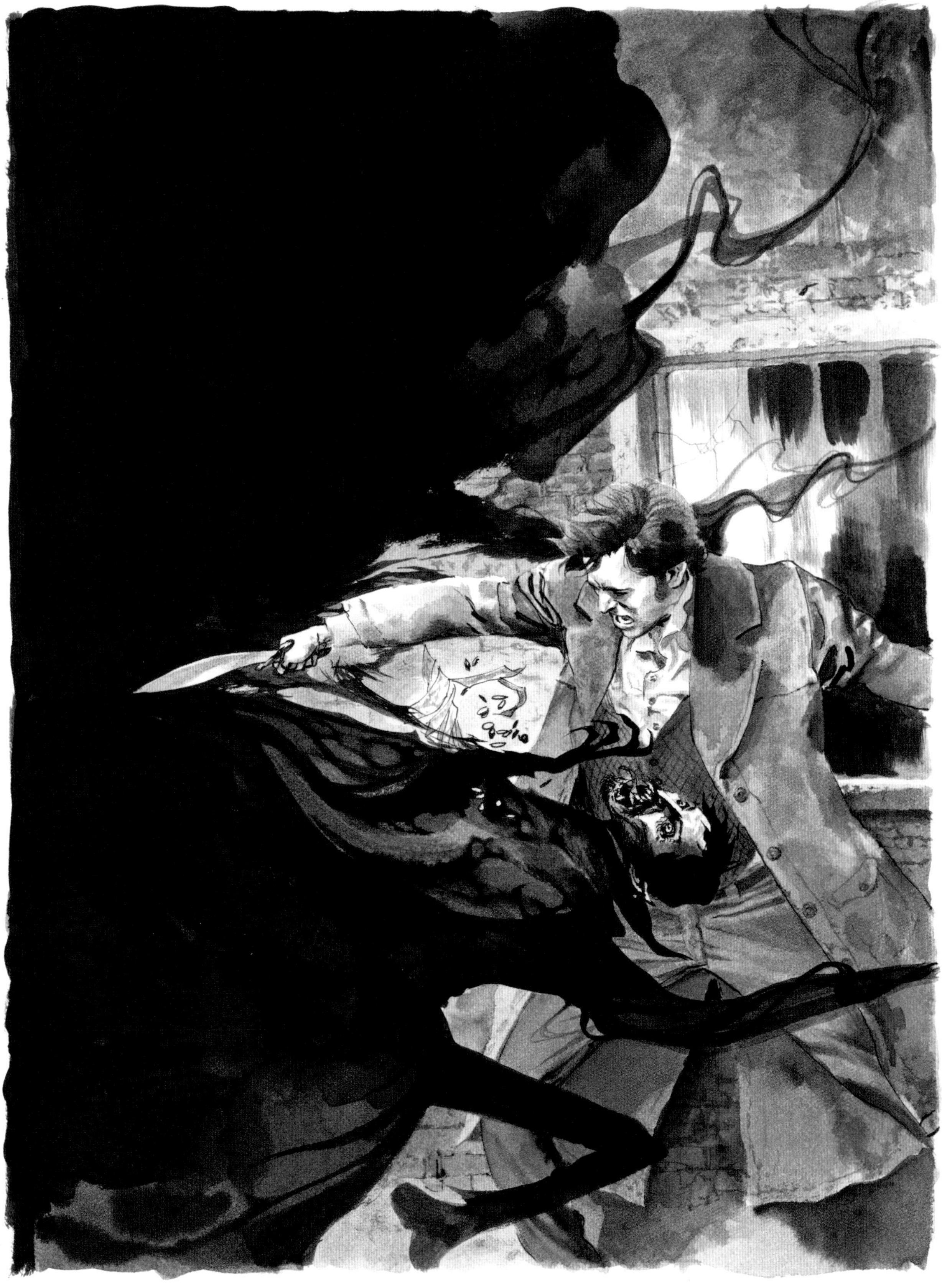

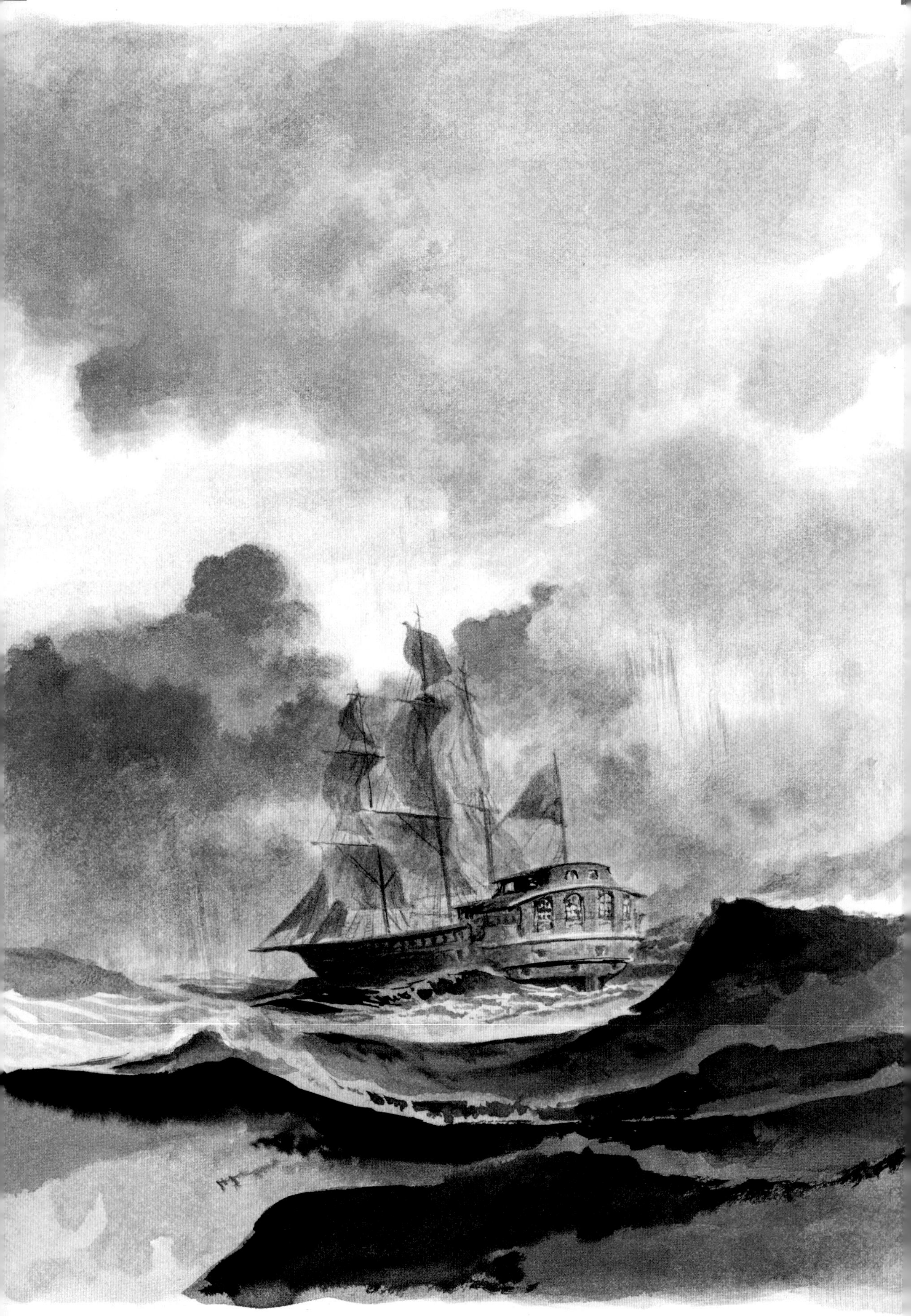

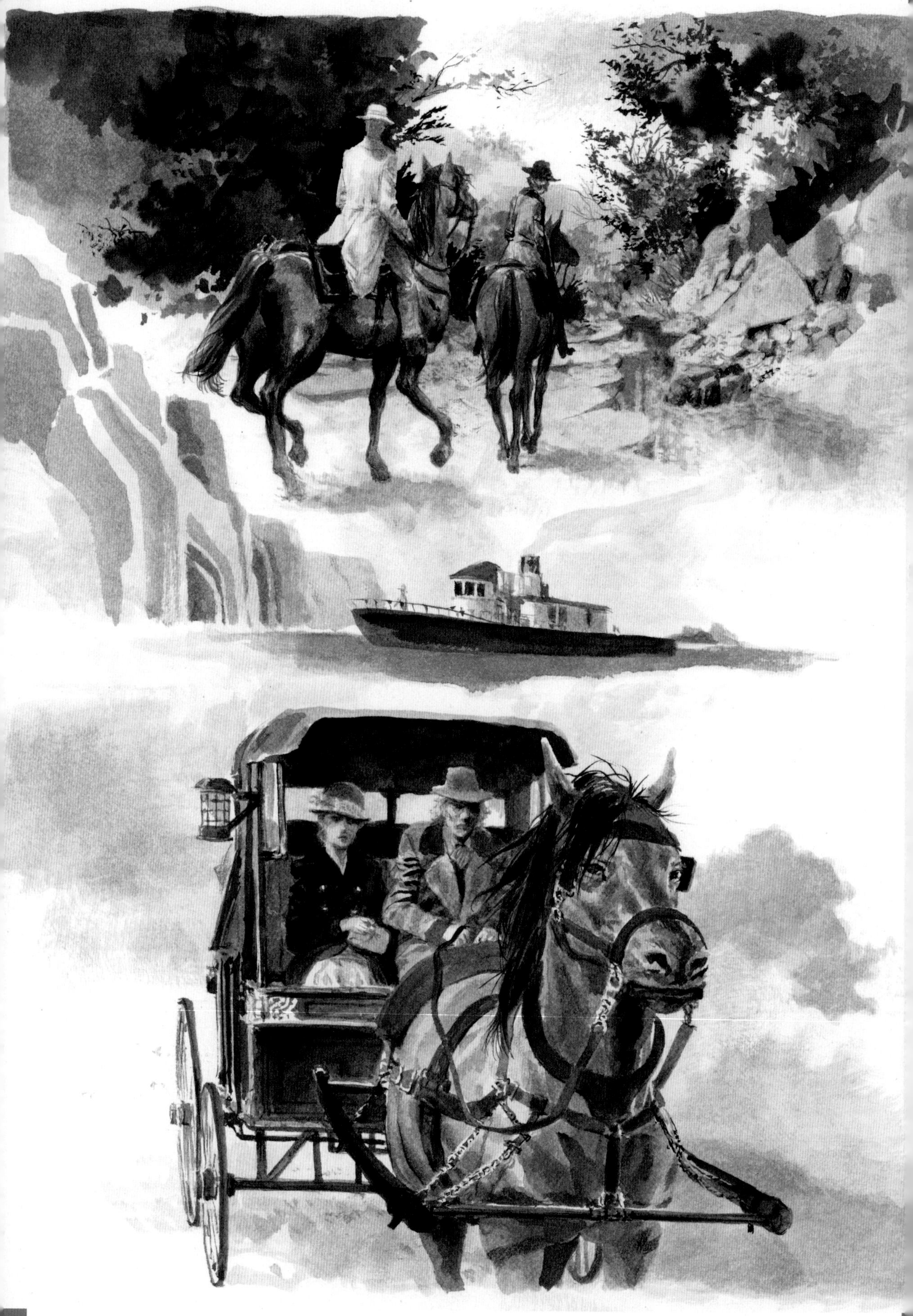

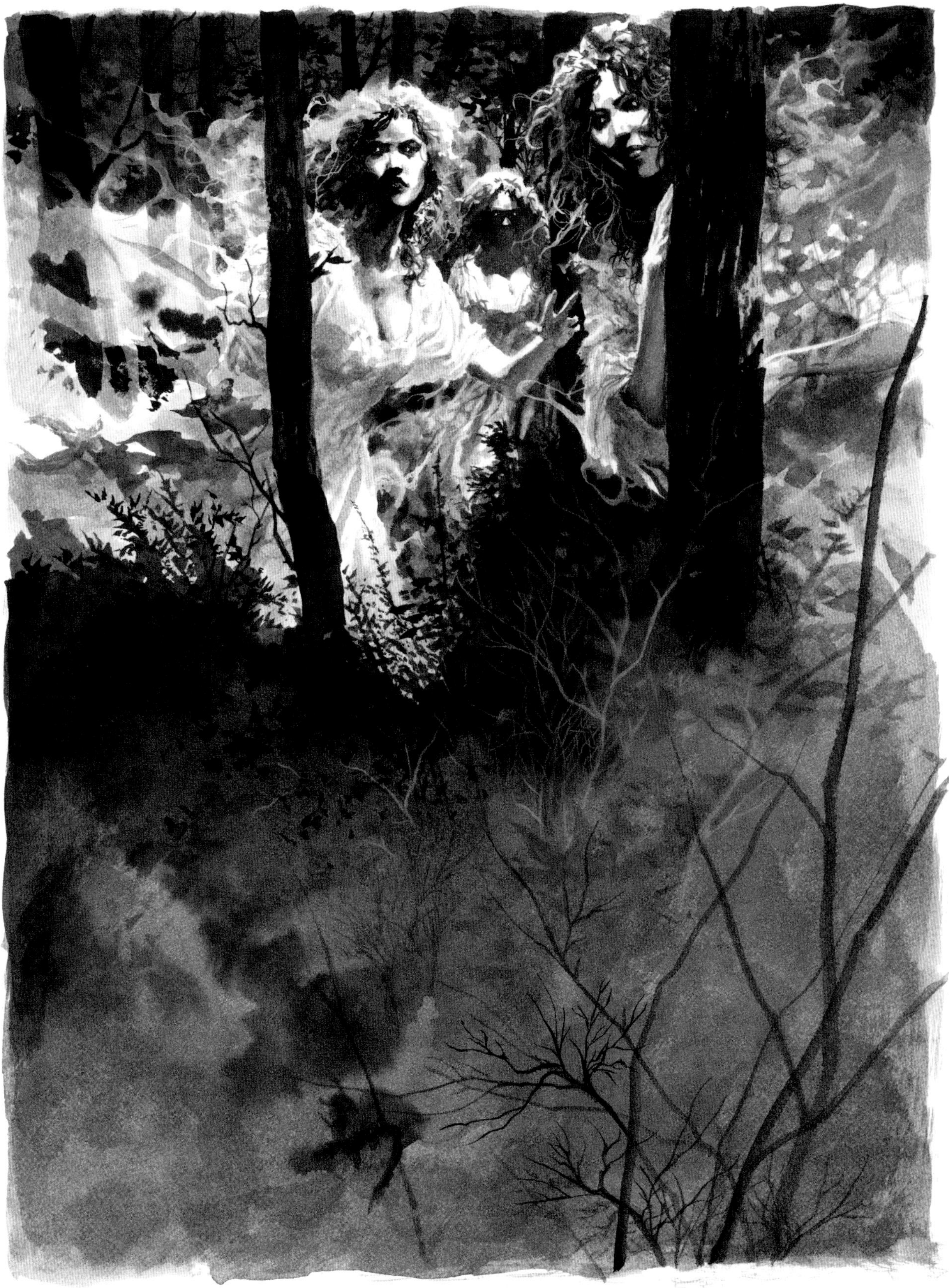

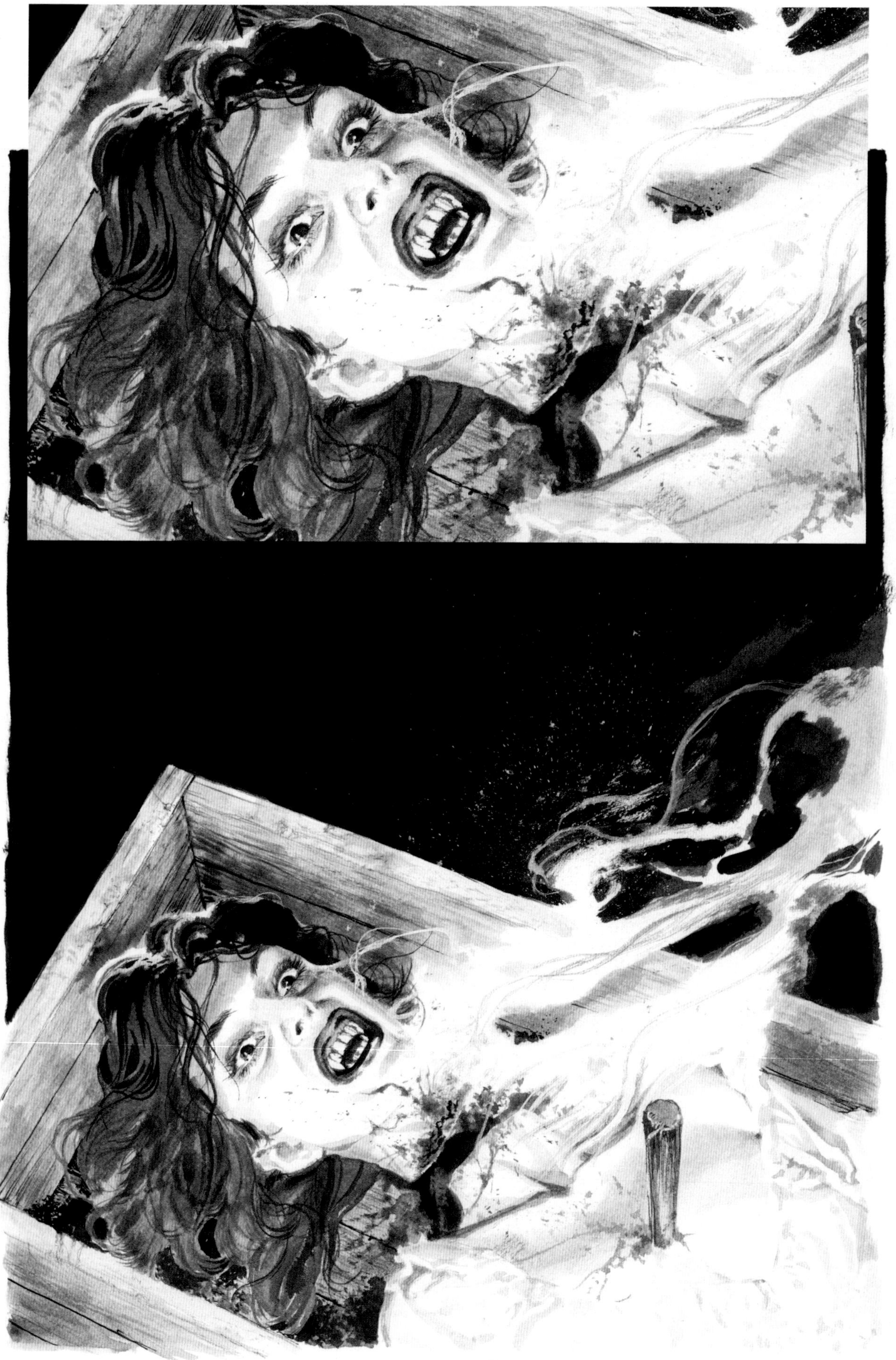

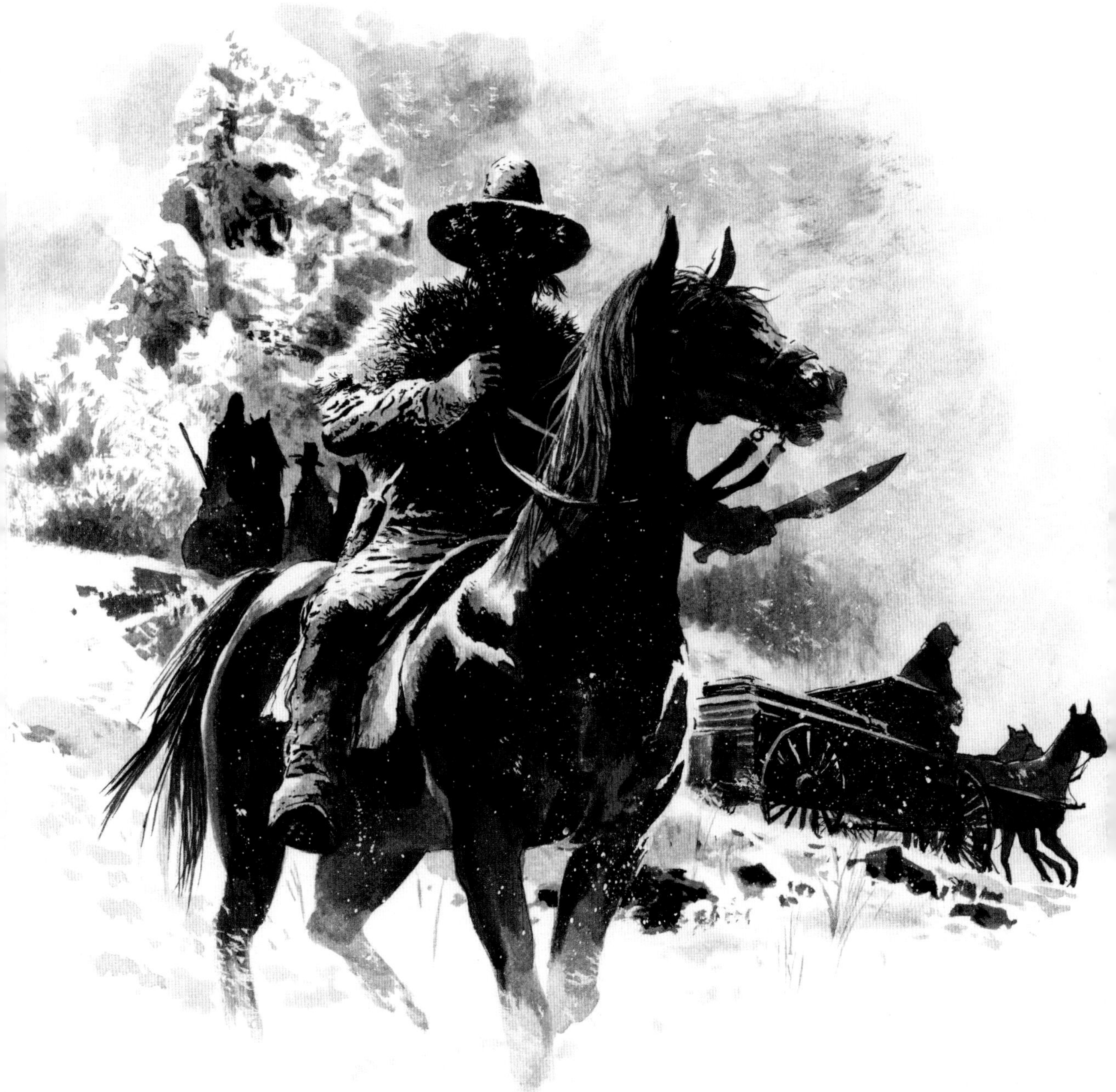

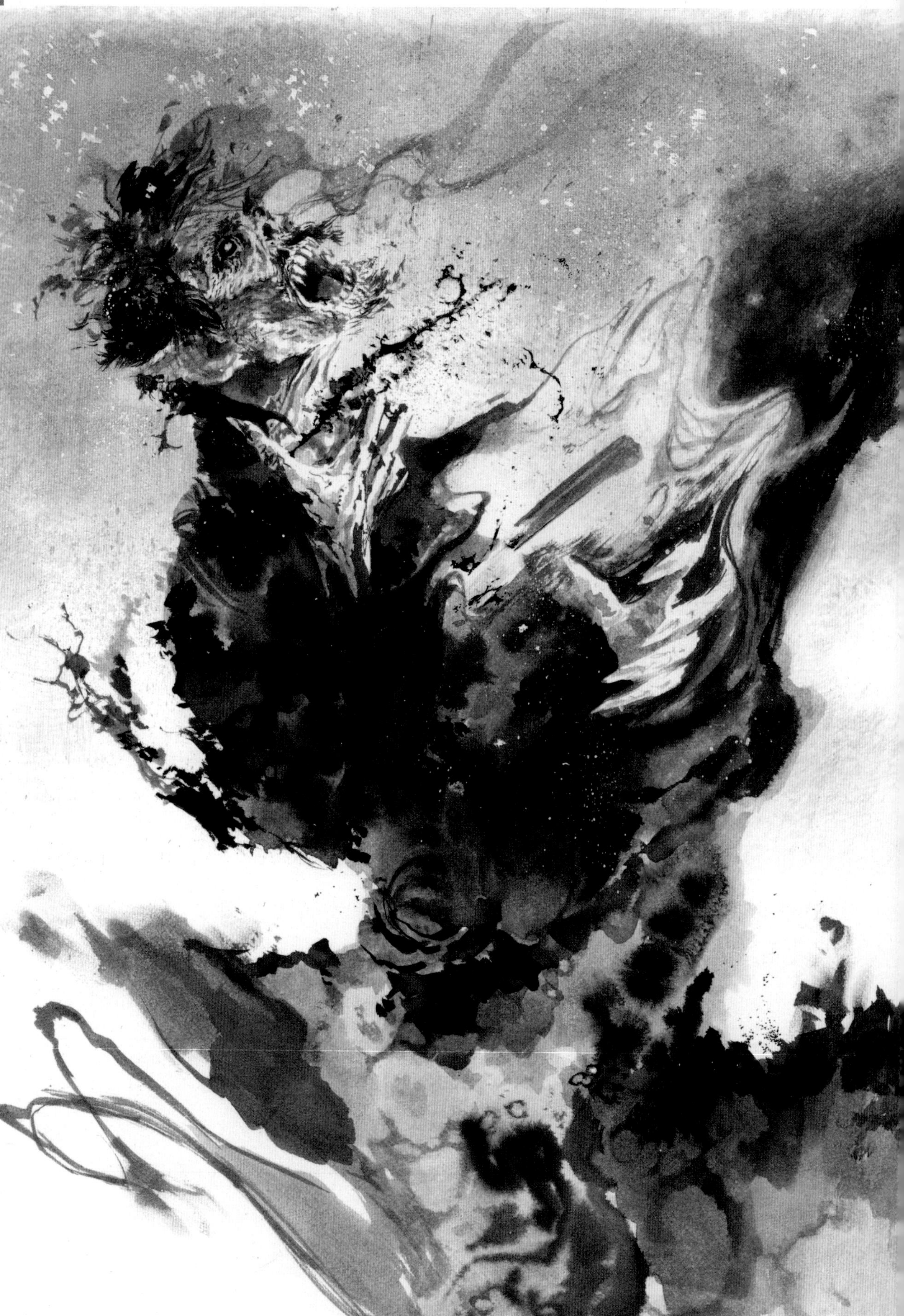

J. H. Williams III is a longtime veteran of the Arts and a New York Times bestseller. He has created significant works for Image Comics, DC Comics, Amazon, and Marvel, among others. J.H.'s current work on the ACBD award-winning Echolands from Image Comics has been met with critical acclaim. He's garnered multiple awards, including Eagles, Eisners, GLAAD, Harveys, Ringos, Inkwell, National Cartoonist Society, a coveted Nebula — all for projects such as The Sandman Overture, Promethea, Batwoman, Batman, Desolation Jones, and Where We Live. And he has happily gained an honor award from the Grey School of Wizardry. Never one to settle for a single artistic vision, Williams has also branched out into arenas beyond the comics industry, illustrating album covers for legendary rock bands Blondie and The Sword, art design for Jerry Other of the Misfits, music and art collaboration as one half of The Sound And Paint Men, illustrations for Bram Stoker's Dracula novel and The Witness novella by J.M DeMatteis, and even has briefly dabbled collaboratively in fashion. Beyond visual arts, his other creative endeavors include various writing roles, with Echolands and Batwoman being prominent examples. J. H. lives with his ever cherished wife and adorable cats in a land of desert mountains and valleys of sand, listening to music and collecting vinyl records.